AF268585

LAIRD OF STORMS

Hearts in the Highlands
Book 1

(originally published by Penguin as
Taming the Heiress)

Susan King

Copyright © Susan King 2026
Text by Susan King
Cover by Dar Albert

Dragonblade Publishing, Inc. is an imprint of Kathryn Le Veque Novels, Inc.
P.O. Box 23
Moreno Valley, CA 92556
ceo@dragonbladepublishing.com

Produced in the United States of America

First Edition May 2026
Trade Paperback Edition

Reproduction of any kind except where it pertains to short quotes in relation to advertising or promotion is strictly prohibited.

All Rights Reserved.

The characters and events portrayed in this book are fictitious. Any similarity to real persons, living or dead, is purely coincidental and not intended by the author.

AI Statement: No AI or ghostwriting was used in the creation of this story, or any story, published by Dragonblade Publishing. All text, structure, content, ideas, and concept are 100% human generated solely by the author whose name appears on the cover. It is prohibited to use this material, or any copyrighted material, for AI engine training.

ARE YOU SIGNED UP FOR DRAGONBLADE'S BLOG?

You'll get the latest news and information on exclusive giveaways, exclusive excerpts, coming releases, sales, free books, cover reveals and more.

Check out our complete list of authors, too!

No spam, no junk. That's a promise!

Sign Up Here

www.dragonbladepublishing.com

Dearest Reader;

Thank you for your support of a small press. At Dragonblade Publishing, we strive to bring you the highest quality Historical Romance from some of the best authors in the business. Without your support, there is no 'us', so we sincerely hope you adore these stories and find some new favorite authors along the way.

Happy Reading!

CEO, Dragonblade Publishing

Additional Dragonblade books by Author Susan King

Hearts in the Highlands Series
Laird of Storms (Book 1)

The Whisky Rogues Series
A Rogue in Firelight (Book 1)
A Rogue in Twilight (Book 2)
A Rogue in Moonlight (Book 3)

Highland Secrets Series
The Scottish Bride (Book 1)
The Forest Bride (Book 2)
The Guardian's Bride (Book 3)

Celtic Hearts Series
The Hawk Laird (Book 1)
The Falcon Laird (Book 2)
The Swan Laird (Book 3)

The Lyon's Den Series
Lyon of Scotland

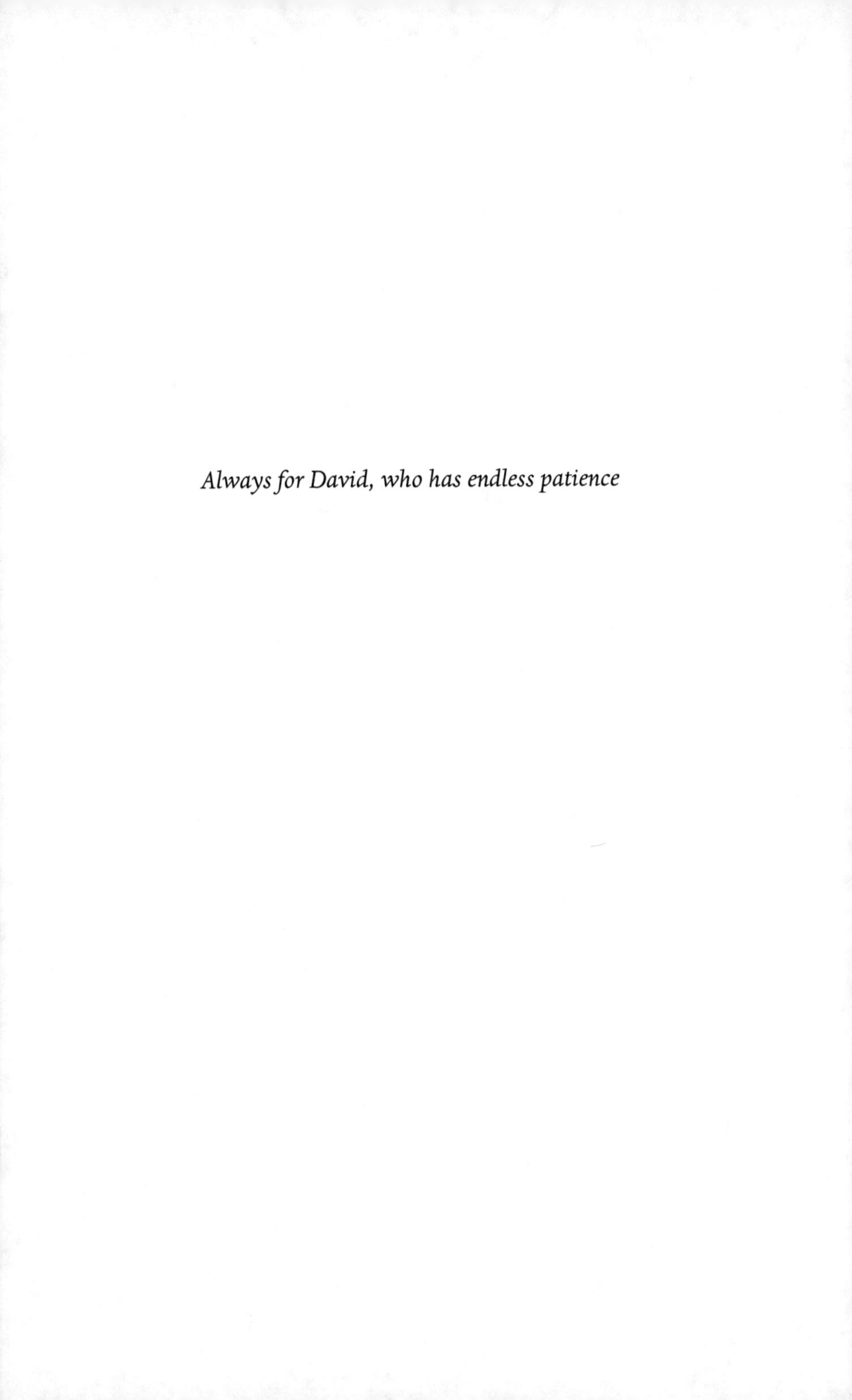

Always for David, who has endless patience

Acknowledgments

I'm grateful to so many for years of true friendship as well as plot-storming, encouragement, and commiseration, especially Mary Jo Putney, Patricia Rice, Jaclyn Reding, Julie Booth, and Joanne Zaslow. Thanks also to Meredith Bean McMath for accurately dressing my Victorian characters and suggesting that gorgeous Worth gown—and thanks to Linda Lawhorne, diving instructor, for help in sending the hero down into the deep!

PROLOGUE

Scotland, the Inner Hebrides Summer, 1850

H E WASHED OUT of a cold sea in darkness, finding a grip on a huge rock that thrust upward through crashing waves. As he lay motionless on the bulwark of rough stone, the water swept over him, withdrew, and surged high again.

Lungs burning, he crawled higher on the sloping rock and collapsed, shivering and half naked. Peering through darkness and lashing rain, he recognized the unique profile of his sanctuary: Sgeir Caran, the largest rock in the notorious Caran Reef just west of the Inner Hebridean Isles. The half-mile crescent of black basalt rocks, some entirely submerged, formed a wicked lure of eddies and whirlpools, trapping countless boats and ships over the centuries—including his own rowboat.

He had found safety in a dangerous place. For now, he was glad to lie on the solid breast of the rock; glad just to breathe. He was familiar with this reef, had studied and measured its jagged points in his capacity as a lighthouse engineer, had listed the ships wrecked upon these rocks and numbered the lives lost. Some of the names were known to him, among them his own kin.

Years ago, this reef had taken his parents, wrecking and sinking their ship as they sailed on a holiday journey, leaving their thirteen-year-old son and his sisters in the care of a relative. That devastating loss had changed the course of his life and altered him, heart and soul. Now he wondered if he was destined to join his parents here.

Perhaps he was already dead, but with his usual obstinacy had not realized it yet. He closed his eyes, clung to the rock, breathed. Pelting rain and cold shivers confirmed that he was indeed alive. The gale raged on, black clouds smothering the half-light of the Hebridean night. Sunset had been a warm glow when he'd sailed out.

Foolish to come out alone, sodden drunk, on a dare. But Dougal Robertson Stewart, heir to the estates of Kinnaird and Balmossie, never turned down a challenge or quailed at danger. He welcomed risk, but should reconsider that in future, he thought as he crawled up a slippery incline of black basalt.

Waves, high and fierce, crashed over him as he scuttled toward the upper plateau of rock. He glimpsed a tall stack rock, its upward thrust an eerie tower. Caves permeated the far end of Sgeir Caran, he knew, but he was too exhausted to look for them yet. He lay watching the writhing, turbulent sea just below the ledge, feeling the sting of rain on his back through a linen shirt.

Had he only dreamed the beautiful ones who had carried him here through the storm? Graceful, frightening, the creatures had appeared as he was drowning in the deep. They had taken him onto their backs and surged forward with the waves, their manes pale froth, their hooves whipping the sea to wildness.

Sea kelpies, the legendary water horses who raced through the foam. Though he had not believed such things were possible, tonight he had seen them, had twisted his fingers in their wet, white manes and placed his feet on their magnificent backs while they carried him forward like the steeds of Neptune.

He had been drunk indeed, he thought, and in a sorry state. Concussed too, for he had taken a blow to the head when his borrowed fishing boat had overturned in a high swell brought on by the sudden squall that became a heavy storm. Caught in the waves, he had clung to the boat's under-planking, but when his wrapped plaid had dragged him under, he had stripped free of it. Still, the sinking boat began to suck him under. Then a legion of pale horses had appeared just then, sweeping him toward the rocks, where he found a grip.

Now, he rose to his feet, maintaining his balance until an arching wave slammed over him, taking his feet from under him as he knocked his head against the rock, and sank into a black void.

Opening his eyes—how long had he been out?—he saw a pair of perfect bare feet.

Pale and delicate, mere inches from his face, the small toes and slender ankles showed beneath the hem of a white gown. Rain splashed all around her, soaking her garment.

A sea fairy, he thought dimly. Kelpies and sea fairies. He was lost in the realm of legend, the wild Otherworld itself.

She sank to her knees, a sweet blur of a face above her simple gown. Wet hair spilled down in tendrils. A plaid shawl was draped over her shoulders, and she slipped it off to wrap it around him. Its thickness, even damp, felt divine. He tried to thank her, but his hoarse voice failed.

"Ach Dhia, you are come out of the sea," she said. "I have been waiting for you."

Gaelic. He understood some, spoke only a little. Why would she wait for him?

"You are cold, shivering. Not used to human form." She tucked the shawl higher. "I came here to keep the ancient promise. Even if you are a king in your world, you need care in ours."

Ancient promise? He stared at her. "I am out of the sea," he said in awkward Gaelic, trying to explain. His mind felt muddled. Who was she, and where was he?

"Hush you." She helped him to rise on shaky legs and tucked her shoulder under his so that he could lean on her as they moved forward. She looked elfin, but had solid strength. They walked across the rock, bent against the wind, the shared plaid whipping about both of them.

Was she shipwrecked too—or was she part of some legendary sea realm? She seemed magical, a fey creature made of gossamer and seafoam, leading him over this wicked rockface.

Hebridean islanders believed the ocean was inhabited by kelpies, selkies, mermaids, sea fairies, blue men, and more. He had encountered water horses himself that night—and here was a sea fairy. He might never reach home again. His head ached and nothing seemed real.

Wind and rain whipped at them, and he gathered her close under his arm, shielding her. She slipped an arm around his waist and walked beside him.

Either he was stranded half naked with a fairy creature, or he was dreaming. He hoped it was the latter and he would soon wake up after sleeping off Mrs. MacDonald's whisky consumed during Mr. MacDonald's wake.

Vaguely he recalled a night of drinking, mourning, music, and joyful stories of the deceased. He had tossed back too many drams during that fine wake for a good man. When friends dared him and another fellow to row around the reef in the gathering dark, braving sea kelpies, Dougal had taken the challenge. When the other man had paused to retch over the side of his boat, Dougal had rowed onward, straight into the mouth of the gale that suddenly opened like a dark maw.

Beside him, the fairy lass cried out against the whipping wind and rain. Dougal held her close and walked onward through a haze of rain. He was determined to survive this night and find his way out of this strange realm, and he would make sure this lovely creature survived too.

Spying the dark crevice of a cave entrance, he tugged her that way. When she stumbled, he swept her up into his arms to carry her into the rocky niche, a narrow space just large enough to shelter them. They huddled together, silent, watching the storm's loud fury—stones breaking loose in the fierceness, skating into the wild sea, waves crashing over rocks, sliding away, arching forward. Water washed into the little cave to foam and swirl around their ankles.

Holding the girl close—she was a delicate thing, easily shoved by the wind—Dougal was increasingly aware of his half-naked state, a long, wet linen shirt and soggy stockings all he wore since he lost his plaid and shoes to the sea. She wore a thin wet gown and plaid shawl, her body curving against his, a little blessed heat generating between them. As she relaxed against him, responding to the safety he offered, their breaths fell into a rhythm, and she felt calm, lush, warm in the circle of his arms.

Desire, raw and sudden, flamed through him. The girl must have felt it too, pressing closer, her arms sliding around his neck. Soaked linen garments were no barrier, her breasts soft against his chest, her waist fitting his hand. She seemed to meld into him, and he into her.

As she tilted her face to his, as he bent to look at her, the nudge of a cheek, of a nose, then lips touched tentatively, then caressed. Her lips were tender and willing. Thunder boomed, the sea slammed against the rocks, and the kiss, echoing fear and seeking safety, grew wild, deep, almost desperate. Needful kisses followed one upon another like rushing waves. Urgency blazed through him as he slanted his mouth over hers and wove his fingers through her damp hair.

The whisky was still in his blood, he thought dimly, making him woozy with desire and a vague sense that something was happening that perhaps he should stop. The darling fairy being tipped her face toward him, pushed into his arms, her lips fervent beneath his. Her willing passion and the warmth growing between their bodies seared like whisky brose, all cream and fire.

The storm faded from his awareness, replaced by this exquisite feeling of salvation and passion at the gates of hell. He pulled her tightly into his arms, her mouth inquisitive against his, her little gasps like fuel to fire. The curve of her waist, the flare of her hips, made his heart pound. In the dreamlike haze, he felt he should stop, think, draw back.

But she took his face in her hands and flattened her belly against the hard, urgent core of him, and her hands moved over him with genuine need, her body pleading against his. Rain pummeled the cave entrance as he drew her deeper into the narrow shelter, leaning his back against slick rock, drawing her plaid shawl in a damp curtain around them. She leaned against him, her kisses feverish and consuming.

Lightning crashed, rain sheeted, stones skittered. The very rock shuddered underfoot. This delicate, alluring creature, this lithesome fairy siren, offered refuge from fear and death. The tender sanctuary of her embrace reminded him that he was alive, hearty, giving him strength. She seemed to draw strength from it too, moving and arching against him, urging him onward when snatches of logic made him want to pull back.

"Please," she whispered, "oh please, I came here for you—" she murmured.

Came here for him? What irresistible magic was this? He swept his hands down her back, snugged her hips against his, letting her know—how could she not?—that he burned for now. Desire and the storm had taken what was left of his reason. He cupped her breast, and the fey creature moaned, arched, allowed his fingers to slip beneath her damp garment to find the heat at her center as she surged, crying out, graceful as the sea.

Lightning flared, and she whimpered in his arms as he lifted her. She arched and opened for him, wild, luscious, the sweetest rescue he could imagine. As he sank into her almost without realizing it was done, she shuddered with him. His heart slammed, his breath was ragged, she held him, kissed him. He tasted the salt of the sea or the salt of tears.

An exquisite power filled him, two souls raw with fear, desperate for comfort and solace. Cradling her head, he kissed her brow, her lips. She felt fragile; he felt a wash of regret.

"I am sorry," he whispered in English. He could not find the Gaelic. "I—should not—"

"Hush." She set a finger to his lips. "I came here for this. For you. It is done. We are free." She spoke in English.

I am dreaming, he thought, *still caught in this strange realm.*

They sank to the floor of the cave, huddling together to wait out the storm.

YOU KNOW WHAT you must do.

As Margaret MacNeill recalled her great-grandmother's words, she leaned against the cave wall and watched as veils of fog obscured the sea and the long reef. A faint light hinted at approaching dawn, and greenish waves frothed over the rocks. She could barely see the Isle of Caransay, her home, about a mile east of this wicked cluster of rocks called Sgeir Caran.

She glanced at the man asleep beside her in the shallow cave, while her fingers worked the red thread she had plucked from the plaid that still covered him.

You know what you must do. With a little help from the hot potion of whisky and herbs that her great-grandmother had prepared, Meg had come here to do what was asked of her. So be it.

She wove the red thread together with long golden hairs from her head, deep brown from his. She had dreaded staying one night alone on Sgeir Caran as island tradition demanded. Wary of a fearsome night, a frightful experience—fear thankfully dulled by a potent whisky concoction—she had never imagined the legend might spring to life like this. No wonder lasses agreed if and when the need arose for a visit to the great rock.

The legend snored, swathed in her plaid, his dark head and one broad shoulder just visible. Shivering with the sweet memory of secret touches and soul-stirring kisses, Meg smiled a little.

Deftly, she plaited the threads and the hairs into a love knot, then created two tiny braids that she knotted into two circlets. Sliding one on her finger, she leaned over the sleeping man, found his hand, and slid the second circlet on his ring finger.

There. She had done what Mother Elga had instructed. The magical marriage was fixed. Smoothing a hand over his soft, damp hair, she sat back.

If the kelpie appears to you while you wait on the great rock, her great-grandmother had said, *you must offer to ease his loneliness and love him. Such is the ancient agreement. Every hundred years, the lord of the deep must claim a maiden from Caransay for his bride. In return, he will protect the island. If the maiden bears his child, he will bestow favor and fortune on the islanders.*

We need his help now more than ever, sweet Meg. You know what you must do.

Educated in the island village and later in a fine school on the mainland—courtesy of her maternal grandfather, the wealthy Lord Strathlin—Meg felt part of the remote little island and the modern world that existed beyond it. She tended to dismiss the old beliefs, but Elga, her great-grandmother, and Thora, her grandmother on the island, accepted the old legends as absolute truth. The Kelpie of Sgeir Caran was treasured and revered on Caransay.

She had agreed to sit one night on the rock, fearful, warmed by sweet, bitter tea that took away doubts and fears. Certain that nothing much would happen beyond a drenching in the rain, she had agreed. She knew that the islanders faced broad eviction by a new landowner who preferred sheep and money to tenants. The threat to her kin and neighbors left her little choice. One night on Sgeir Caran would do no harm.

She never counted on a gale—or the kelpie. Bursting from the sea like a muscled arrow, the man-creature had appeared on the rock as if the raging storm had birthed him. He was beautiful and strong and seemed so real. Surprised rather than frightened, she felt compassion for him. He needed her help. And then she had melted in his arms, his kisses whirled her into whatever spell he concocted. That spell lingered still.

The luscious fog of the potion Elga had given her had fired her blood. She had behaved shockingly, with abandon and passion, swept up in a powerful need to be with this man.

Willingly, madly, she had craved him, followed her body, followed his urging to fulfill an ancient bargain she did not believe in daylight. His arms, his kisses, his body, his tenderness and strength were pure magic.

She ducked her head in hot shame, her head much clearer now. What had happened? Was he a kelpie, as her grandmothers expected, or was he just a man after all?

She glanced toward him, yearning, but knowing she must leave soon. If he woke, touched her again, she might lose herself to him forever. Legend or none, she knew part of her wanted to follow him down to the deepest part of the sea if he beckoned.

He sighed, stretched, and the plaid fell away. He was a long, lean, tight-muscled, beautiful man. His face had the uncommon symmetry of classical beauty, his hair was deep glossy brown, his whiskers a dark smudge on his jaw, his taut chest and belly dusted with dark hair. She blushed to remember what she had allowed and what she had craved last night.

His eyes fluttered open. Sea green. The eyes of a legendary creature.

He sighed and slept again. Meg gazed at him—her husband now by an ancient agreement. He had roused her with magic, and she would never forget him. But she had to leave. A girl could not stay with a kelpie, but the eerie pink dawn, and the lingering effect of whisky and herbs, made her wonder.

What if he were just a man, and no legend? And if so, what had she done?

He stretched, yawned. Meg stood, unsure what to do. Hearing distant yet familiar voices, she went to the mouth of the cave, realizing she was expected to leave now.

Slipping out of the cave, she ran barefoot over the rocky plateau. At the farthest end of the rock, a boat pulled closer, oared by Norrie, her *seanair,* her grandfather on the island. Grandmother Thora sat with him. They beckoned.

"Lass, are you well, then? In quickly," Norrie said, waving her toward the boat.

"I am fine, *Seanair,*" she told her grandfather. He beckoned again for her to step down into the rocking boat, but she hesitated. A pull, tangible and strong, kept her there. She could not simply strand him on this wicked rock. She had to know if he was real or magical, needed to understand if she should go or stay; had to know the truth and the risk.

She looked back. The man stood in the cave entrance now, tall and golden in the dawn light, her plaid draped around him. He gazed toward the open sea, yet away from the corner of the rock where the water lapped at her grandfather's boat.

"Oh! Look there," Thora gasped. "What a beautiful creature!"

"Huh," Norrie grunted, picking up the oars. "Margaret, hurry."

"He found you, then?" Thora asked.

Meg stood as if caught between two worlds. She felt again that deep tug in her heart, her gut. What if he was not a kelpie, but a human. If she left him on this cold, cruel rock, his fate would be her fault.

"Margaret," her grandfather urged.

"Wait," she said, and whirled to run back.

Taking a few steps on the sloped and slippery black rock, she paused for balance and watched the man, prayed he would turn and see her, open his arms to welcome her, tell her he was legend or lover, that he wanted her, waited for her.

Then she noticed the dark blur of another boat gliding through the fog from the west. Fishermen. Would they see a man or a magical being?

She wiped a hand over her eyes. The dregs of the whisky potion were still with her. She was neither seeing nor thinking clearly, and the dawning sun had not yet topped the horizon to dissolve the sense of the Otherworld.

Then her lover walked down the slope, but not toward her. He waved, called. As the other boat approached, a man tossed a rope, which her lover caught. He climbed in.

Not a sea creature, to slip into the waves and disappear. A man, needing a ride in a boat.

Dear God, what had she done?

Meg turned away. Her grandparents had not noticed the

other boat, and waved to her again. She went to the edge, let Norrie assist her into the boat, and sat.

As her grandfather pulled away from the rock to go east, her grandmother tossed a thick, dry plaid around Meg's shoulders, and their boat plowed through restless waves toward Caransay.

She said nothing. Inside, she felt ill and ashamed. She had loved a man, not the great kelpie. Just a man. She felt a fool after all.

Had some rugged fellow heard that a maiden would go to Caransay that night to fulfill the old legend? Had he gone to the rock on a drunken bet? Would he gleefully tell all to his friends?

Gasping, she bowed her head.

Thora hugged her. "I am sure the great kelpie was tender with his magic," she whispered. "The herbal potion made you willing. If a child comes of last night, the kelpie's bairn will have a good home with us. And his father will protect Caransay and bless it with good fortune."

Oh God, Meg thought. *A child.*

CHAPTER ONE

Scotland, Edinburgh
Summer, 1857

"A HOME," SAID Sir John Shaw, peering down his bulbous nose, "for young women of questionable morals? Lady Strathlin, I must advise against this investment, both as a member of the board of Matheson Bank, and as a friend of your late grandfather. Lord Strathlin would never have allowed it."

Meg folded her hands and faced her banker across her grandfather's oak desk in Strathlin Castle's study. Her wealthy grandfather's name—Frank Matheson, Lord Strathlin—was attached to the bank as well as nearly all else she usually discussed with advisors like Sir John Shaw. She had inherited Lord Strathlin's castle, his accounts, his treasures, his properties, and the very bank itself. His will had been a shock, a surprise, a gift, a burden, and a lifetime of responsibility.

"Matheson House is hardly a home for women of ill repute, Sir John," she said calmly. "Rather, it is intended to be a haven for unmarried young mothers in need of some help and a place to stay until their circumstances improve. I want to see it opened for those in need."

Sir John's frown deepened. Meg held his gaze.

In the silence, morning sunlight streamed through tall windows to highlight the blue-and-gold Oriental carpet underfoot, colors that reminded her of a Hebridean beach. That, and the painting of a seascape over the mantelpiece, helped ease bouts of homesickness for Caransay.

In the last few years, she had returned as often as she could, though not as often as she wanted. But she would go there soon to enjoy a rare holiday visit to the island. She drew a hopeful breath at the thought.

"A home for unmarried young mothers!" Sir John regarded her with bleary eyes through a monocle lens. "My lady, do not forget that they must have poor morals to be in such straits to begin with. You should not associate yourself with them."

She had nearly been one of them, she thought, but for the compassion of her family. She shook her head. "I sympathize with them, sir. Girls of good moral fiber sometimes find themselves in difficult circumstances. I just want to help."

"But as Baroness of Strathlin, and no longer a—" He sniffed, leaving the rest unsaid.

"A simple island girl?" She smiled tightly. "I am not ashamed of my origins and would not lose sight of them. I know that my inheritance of my grandfather's estate and title shocked some peers, but when an older grandson died young, I was the only heir. It is as perfectly proper in Scotland for the title to come to a female, and I am doing my best to honor the old estate."

He cleared his throat. "Some did think Lord Strathlin was mad to leave his fortune not just to a female, but a Hebridean girl. You scarcely spoke English when you first arrived here."

"And had no shoes." She smiled. "But my mother, who came to the Hebrides to marry for love despite her wealthy upbringing, made sure I had a good education and knew my manners. But proper behavior for baroness is proper behavior for anyone, sir. And my mother also taught me that if we are blessed with good fortune in life, it behooves us to show compassion for others regardless of rank."

She hoped her mother would be proud of her, for she was truly doing her utmost to balance a life of wealth and privilege with the Hebridean simplicity she preferred.

Glancing at the unopened letters piled on a silver tray on her desk, she sighed. There was work to be done, gifts to consider, charities in need of fostering. Most mornings, she usually read mail and discussed various business and social matters with her secretary, Mr. Hamilton. But dear Guy Hamilton had not yet arrived; Sir John the banker had come early and stayed overlong.

"Madam, your fortune approaches that of the very queen." Sir John sat forward, wrapping his hands over the head of his cane.

"Oh, sir, that cannot be."

"I will show you the figures again, but rest assured it is considerable, which gives you a level of responsibility that others may never face."

"I appreciate your advice, sir." She folded her hands. He could be a crabbit, but he had been invaluable to her.

"You can easily afford to support all the charitable efforts you wish. But I urge you to step away from this particular one, or at least fund it anonymously. Sir Roderick would give you the same advice, as he expressed to me just yesterday."

"Sir Roderick should keep his opinions to himself."

"He is a board member of the Bank of Scotland, as well as your cousin. And I understand he is your fiancé as well. Let me offer my congratulations. It is a suitable match and an advantageous union. And the familial relationship is distant enough that no one will be bothered by it."

Meg frowned. She was very much bothered by it. "Roderick told you we were engaged?"

"Oh, yes. He is beside himself with happiness and blurted it to me in his exuberance. But I understand it is a secret for now and I will honor that."

"He did ask me to marry him," she said slowly, thinking back on a conversation after he had downed a good deal of wine at a supper party. "But I have not accepted. His remarks were hasty."

"But it will come about, surely! It is a sensible arrangement. The matter of your marriage is of great interest to the bank's board, of course, considering your wealth. I am sure you would never become engaged without discussing it at length. So much at stake, you see."

"True. When or if I decide to marry, it would be a decision from my heart with the advice of my future husband. I would expect the board to accept that decision. But there is no such news to report. Indeed, I may never wed," she added. "I am grateful for my good fortune, but this inheritance only makes marriage complicated. It would be difficult to believe the sincerity of any man who declared his affection. Sir John, please do not discuss this with others. I value privacy."

He cleared his throat. "Of course, madam."

"And before it slips my mind, please instruct the bank to disperse funds to the new housekeeper at Matheson House as I require."

"Very well." He stood. "A cheque will be sent." He bid her farewell and crossed the room to a set of double doors with etched-glass panes.

Meg sighed. Inheriting great wealth had certainly eased some paths, but had created thorny thickets elsewhere. She had been able to help many, such as the Caransay islanders when she had purchased the island's lease, and she was grateful and determined to continue using her good fortune to help as many as she could.

But she had a deep secret that she must protect at all costs. The gift of the kelpie, as her grandmothers called it, had brought Meg not only tremendous good fortune, but a beautiful son and a heartfelt hurt that she carefully guarded.

If not for the love of close kin and a windfall inheritance, she might have been in straits similar to the young women she intended to help through her charitable institution.

Never married, mother to a little son, Meg had been surprised to be named Lord Strathlin's heir after his sudden death. Gradually adjusting to those changes with the help of her family, she found that wealth could grant true protection. She could keep her secret safe and protect her child, allowing him to grow and thrive on Caransay in a loving family. When he was a few years older, it would be time to introduce him to life as a wealthy heir.

The deepest part of her secret was that she had met the boy's nameless, beautiful, unforgettable, despicable father on a rocky, storm-swept isle late one night. No one should ever know that. The man had vanished, and she was doing what she felt was right for her son.

Now, speculating on marriage to Sir Roderick, she gave a bitter laugh. According to ancient tradition and an old Scots law, she was already married.

She touched the little golden locket tucked beneath the neck of her blue brocade day gown. Inside its spring catch cover was a tiny portrait of her blond-haired son and a small ring woven of red thread and strands of hair. The locket was always around her neck; she would never forget the passion of that night, its reward, or its betrayal.

As for the child who had resulted from that encounter, she saw her son as often as possible, though the weeks and months apart were hard to bear. Strathlin Castle was a magnificent old ruin renovated in grand style, yet despite its luxuries, it never felt entirely like home to her. The responsibilities of her inheritance, with its business ventures and wealth to manage, could not be done from a remote island. She wanted her little son to live with her, but even more, she wanted him to experience the freedom, tradition, challenges, and joys of life in the Isles, with kin to nurture him. Later, she would ensure that he had the finest education, but Nature's power and beauty was education in itself. Caransay was a part of her, bone and blood and soul, and she wanted her son to feel that way too.

She glanced at the far corner of the library, where her friend and companion sat reading. Mrs. Elspeth Berry's black skirts, a reminder of her widowhood of many years, billowed out of the leather wing chair. Looking around, Meg did not see her other faithful companion, Mrs. Angela Shaw, Sir John's young widowed daughter-in-law. Then she remembered that quiet, capable Angela would be discussing menus with the housekeeper that morning as part of her duties.

Both ladies had been a great help to her since she had inherited Strathlin, and they even made sure to be nearby as unobtrusive chaperones when Meg met with male advisers and business acquaintances, as Mrs. Berry had done this morning. Years ago, they had warned Meg that her fortune would attract all sorts of men interested in marrying her; the ladies were sweet and determined about protecting her.

A knock at the door preceded a young maid, small and brown haired, dressed in dark gray with a white apron and cap; she looked into the room. "Ma leddy, Mr. Hamilton is here."

"Thank you, Hester. Send him in, please."

A tall, lean, dark-haired man entered the room to cross with a brisk step, his handsome face familiar and welcome, his brown eyes twinkling. Meg smiled up at her secretary.

"Good morning! Do sit," she said. Guy Hamilton took a leather chair opposite her desk. His long body was relaxed and agile, and his natural verve made her feel more energetic.

"I apologize for being late, madam."

"Not at all! Sir John was here and all in knots over my proposed home for young ladies."

"He can be a sour old screw, but he has your best interests at heart. I stopped by Uncle Edward's law office on my way here, or could have helped you fend off Sir John. Hello, Mrs. Berry! On duty again, I see," he called pleasantly. Mrs. Berry waved and returned to her reading.

"Please look through these." Meg pushed several letters toward him. "I've added a list of the replies I think necessary."

"Very good. Where is Mrs. Shaw this morning?" As he glanced around the library, Meg saw a slight flush spill through his cheeks.

"Downstairs with Mrs. Louden making up menus. They are all in a kerfuffle over the soiree, though it's two months away."

"I am sure they enjoy helping to plan your event." He smiled as he studied the letters.

Meg nodded, noticing an etching of sadness in his fine brown eyes. Widowed a few years earlier, Hamilton kept his grief private and his mood calm and uplifting. He efficiently attended to his secretarial duties, from correspondence to travel plans and even her social schedule. Guy Hamilton had been a new lawyer and recent widower when he had inquired about the position as her secretary. Since then, his humor and graciousness had made him a true friend.

"Sir John said Sir Roderick also disapproves of Matheson House for Young Ladies. He does not want the name associated with him or his family. Your family," he clarified. "Frank Matheson made you his direct heir."

"Perhaps Sir Roderick has forgotten that he is a third cousin, though he carries the name. At any rate, Roderick told him that we are engaged to marry."

"He seems to have misinterpreted your relationship, perhaps due to your kind nature."

"Whatever the cause, it is a true misunderstanding." She tipped her head, considering. In the first years of her inheritance, she had relied on Sir Roderick's counsel as her cousin and as a banker. Later, when he struggled after his wife's death and she learned that his bills were mounting, she had helped him out of a financial deal that had gone sour. "It was important to me to show loyalty. I meant nothing more by it. He has the wrong impression." She scowled.

"You are generous, as I myself can attest. Not just lovely and kindhearted, but also one of the richest women in Scotland. May I say, it is a perfectly lethal combination."

"Is it?" Meg felt her cheeks heat.

"It is. Any man could fall in love with you, and some might scheme to marry you just because of your fortune." He smiled. "As for me, I adore you, but I have no illusions. I keep you firmly on a pedestal where you belong."

"I shall only topple." Meg laughed a little. "Guy, thank you, but you are wrong. Sir Roderick has asked for my hand, but no other." A little quiver went through her—long ago, she dreamed another might ask for her hand. But he was long gone, never to be seen again.

"And I am sure many others have considered it. Should anyone make unwanted advances, I want to know about it." He frowned. "I shall speak to Matheson if you like."

"I should do that myself, after I return from the Isles."

"Very well. We have quite a few letters to look through this morning, I see."

"A good number of these are acceptances for the soiree for Miss Jenny Lind in September. And there is much to do if we are to be ready. How did Angela Shaw ever convince me to host an event for the celebrated Swedish Nightingale?"

"Mrs. Shaw had an excellent idea, and you saw the worth of it. I believe all the invitations have gone out by now."

"Do you recall if you sent one to Mr. Dougal Stewart?"

"The engineer? It was delivered to his address here in Edinburgh last week. The man was deuced difficult to find, so the invitation could not be sent by daily post. Apparently, he is often in some remote place putting up a lighthouse, and his family seat is far off in Strathclyde. Fortunately, I discovered that he keeps rooms in town near the Canongate."

"I have second thoughts about inviting him, but I suppose it is too late."

"Let it be a gesture of truce."

"No doubt he will see it as a gesture of surrender."

"When you finally meet, we will hope it does not come to blows," Guy drawled.

"His letters over the past several months have been insistent, and his latest action is practically a declaration of war. Obtaining parliamentary permission to construct barracks on my island, when we had denied him the right, took me by surprise!"

"He had the right, apparently. Parliament overrides such things."

"This Mr. Stewart does what he wants, it seems. He can be

impatient and demanding." She sighed. "In his letters he shows great concern for the welfare of his men. I respect that. Otherwise, he can be obstinate, according to my solicitors."

"I hear that in person, he is the very devil for charm. Perhaps that helps him get his way."

"His actions do not reflect charm," she snapped.

"My sister-in-law knows him, and says Mr. Stewart is seldom seen at parties, rather like his nemesis, Lady Strathlin." Guy smiled. "When he does appear, she says young ladies act faint and overcome."

"I suppose he is simply terrifying."

"A very handsome fellow, says my sister-in-law, and his daring heroics give him a romantic aura. He saved several workmen who fell into the sea in the bridge disaster in Fife last year in frigid waters. Remarkable. I admire any man who risks his life for others like that."

"I remember hearing about that. *The Edinburgh Review* reported that Mr. Stewart dove into a frozen sea to pull each man out of the water before assistance could arrive. True, it is admirable. Mr. Stewart has his good qualities—if we should fall into the sea. But other matters speak differently of him."

"You and Mr. Stewart have something in common, then."

She lifted a brow. An odd ripple went through her, a memory just out of reach. More likely a warning to stay away from the man. "What could that possibly be?"

"You both saved lives in the Fife bridge disaster. Your generosity in paying medical costs and lost wages for the injured men, and donating funds toward repairing the collapsed bridge were admirable deeds as well."

"If Mr. Stewart knows that, it did not melt his heart toward me," she said wryly.

"I wonder. Oh, I am reminded. You asked my uncle to send over Stewart's latest letter." Guy removed an envelope from a pocket. "He included a copy of the order signed by Queen Victoria."

"Along with more plans?" She skimmed the pages he handed her. "He is persistent as well as infuriating. He sends letters and plans every month, and ignores our refusals. Odious man," she muttered, studying the royal permission for Stewart's project and the meticulous line drawings included on another page. "Here he has drawn the coast of Caransay, and here he sketched a lighthouse on Sgeir Caran. It is rather elegant," she admitted.

"It is a grand design," Guy agreed.

"It is. And I hope the thing never goes up on that rock."

"Uncle Edward asked me to tell you there may be a way to halt the government funding Stewart's funding to delay or even prevent construction. Stewart requires thirty thousand pounds to complete the work, funded from the government and private sponsors."

"But nothing from me." Meg frowned, reading Stewart's letter. His neat script gave her the sense of a strong, confident man with a bit of edge to his character. "His pleas on behalf of his men are stirring, but he would force the issue."

"Those rocks are dangerous. Perhaps there should be a lighthouse there to protect ships."

"Guy, do not be a traitor," Meg said. Again, a strange, hot current surged through her. Memories of Sgeir Caran stirred emotions that she must ignore, but for the moment could not, until she noticed something in the letter.

"The arrogance of the man!" She shook the page. "He means to start work on Caransay!"

"So it seems. My uncle wanted you to know. Since you will be there on holiday soon, you could finally meet with the man and explain yourself clearly."

"That would ruin my holiday."

"You can hardly avoid him on an island just a few miles long."

"I can and will," she said. "And somehow I will end this project on my island. When I purchased the island's lease, I promised my kin and tenants that Caransay would remain free from threats and outsiders. I must keep my word. The thought of a lighthouse on that ancient rock is unbearable." She glanced away. "Please tell Sir Edward that his law firm may deal with Mr. Stewart as seems fit. I will include a personal note in the next letter they send him. It is time I voiced my opinion directly to him."

"Excellent thought. When you are on Caransay you can at least see what Mr. Stewart is like from a distance. Be a spy. See what you want to do from there."

"If he looks thoroughly wicked, I shall withdraw his invitation to the soiree."

Guy chuckled. "While you are away, I will assist Mrs. Shaw with arrangements for the event."

"Thank you." Still holding Dougal Stewart's letter, Meg considered it again. Plain stationery and unadorned black script gave the impression of a practical, wholly masculine man who preferred simplicity and directness. Apparently, Stewart was handsome, well-educated, and courageous. Those were attractive qualities in a man. She wished suddenly she could like him.

But he was the most stubborn man she could imagine, and currently he threatened the island she wanted desperately to protect. His lighthouse could change the peace and safety she had ensured for the residents of Caransay. Its presence could destroy the island's privacy and erode the mystery and traditions of Sgeir Caran.

"Mr. Stewart will just have to build his lighthouse somewhere else," she said. "And he can go to Hades for all I care, so long as he leaves Sgeir Caran and Caransay alone."

"Strong words, Lady Strathlin."

"Strongly felt." She raised her chin.

Sgeir Caran. A sudden vivid memory came to her—that dark, glossy rock lashed by a wild sea, and a strong, beautiful man standing in the eerie light of a storm. As a hot blush infused her cheeks, she crammed Stewart's letter back into its envelope. The man on that rock had left her, betrayed her. That dream was empty.

"Mr. Stewart cannot be allowed to destroy the sanctity of the great rock," she said.

CHAPTER TWO

T HE GOLDEN-HAIRED GIRL caught Dougal Stewart's attention, distracting him as he stood on a Hebridean beach talking with his first foreman. Pausing midsentence, he glanced at her. Among the other islanders walking over the sands, she shone like a candle flame.

"Ah, er, the Ordnance Survey map," he resumed, looking at Alan Clarke. "Have you gone over it yet?"

"I did," Clarke replied. "And last evening I walked over the hills at the center of the island. There is good granite to be quarried there. Mackenzie will know best when he has a chance to examine it."

Dougal nodded, watching the blond woman crossing the beach. The amber sunset light diffused over her as if she were made of magic dust. For a moment he thought of the girl who still haunted his dreams—he would never know if she had been human, a dream, or a sea fairy, if such creatures existed. But he had not forgotten her.

Simply, the young woman he watched was fetching, and his proximity to that rocky islet reminded him of the past. Nothing more than that.

"Who's that, then?" Alan asked, looking in the same direction. "A bonny sight."

"Aye." Dougal agreed.

Golden-haired and reed slim, she stopped to shade her brow

with a hand, then turned toward the women and children helping the fishermen who were coming in from a day's work. Laughing, calling out to each other, they worked together to pull the boats onto the sand and then drag nets bulging with fish and creels full of lobsters out of reach of the waves. A few children stopped to speak with the girl; she nodded, smiled, waved as they ran past.

An elderly man, white haired and holding a pipe, strolled over to join her. Dougal recognized Norrie MacNeill, a crofter fisherman who regularly sailed to the Isle of Mull to fetch mail and supplies for the people of Caransay. The girl wrapped her arm in Norrie's, and he patted her hand as they chatted.

She must be Norrie's kinswoman, Dougal thought. Other islanders seemed to know her, waving and calling out. She was dressed like the other women, her clothing plain and practical; a brisk sea breeze whipped at her dark skirt, hinting at her slender form and revealing bare feet and shapely calves. Her thick, curly honey-gold hair was partly tamed by a black ribbon, and draped over her shoulders was the long plaid arisaid shawl common to Highland women. A lovely young woman with a simplicity that was beauty in itself.

As she spoke with Norrie, she glanced in Dougal's direction, raising a hand to shield her eyes from the sunset light. Her gaze met his across the beach, and he felt a tug within like the turn of a key. Again, he thought of the exquisite sea fairy he had dreamed about one wild black night when he had been in a bad way.

He shook his head, looked away. He needed some sleep. The exhausting pace of the work lately had made him imaginative and maudlin.

At the water's edge, members of his crew hauled up another boat, the vessel they used daily to cross back and forth to Sgeir Caran. Today, they had drilled and hacked into black basalt, cutting more of the foundation cavity for the lighthouse. As resident engineer, Dougal supervised every aspect of the work and often lent a hand with the actual physical labor. He had come ashore in another boat just minutes earlier, tired and gritty from the day's work.

He tensed and relaxed his shoulders to lose some stiffness, and craved a wash, fresh clothing, a hot supper, and time alone in his hut to study plans by lamplight. The engineering log needed to be filled out each day with a report of progress, and he needed to check and recheck facts and measurements against the plan before the next phase of work began.

He glanced up and down the crescent of white sand that defined Caransay's small natural harbor. Fishing boats were tied along the single-stone quay, and more boats tilted on the sand. Two headlands, tall and dark, framed the beach like enormous sentinels. The black rock that composed them matched the basalt of the reef within view of the beach.

Overhead, seagulls called and reeled, and waves swept over the pale, soft sand. Dougal savored the salty breeze that fingered through his wavy brown hair and fluttered his vest and collarless shirt; he did not wear stiff collars or neckcloths out here, and only sometimes grabbed a coat, for he needed to move freely for the work he did. Children raced past him, laughing, and a few scrambled up the nearest headland, calling out as they followed a path there.

The beauty still stood with Norrie. "Who is the lass?" Dougal asked Alan Clarke.

"Norrie MacNeill's granddaughter. She is visiting. Lives off Caransay somewhere."

"Ah." That explained why he had not seen her here before.

"I hope she will be at the Friday ceilidh," Alan mused. "Last time, I sat beside Norrie's auld mum all night. Mother Elga tells a good tale and sings a fine song, but with the fiddles and drums going strong, I wanted to dance." He chuckled. "The lads and I notice that Caransay does not boast many unmarried lassies. And you arranged for us to stay here for months, even a year." Alan laughed. "Some of us are looking for wives. Some of us just want to dance and court."

"You will all work harder without a bonny distraction."

Dougal grinned.

"So will you, clever lad, wi' nae fine lassies to flock after you as they do in Edinburgh and Glasgow, I have seen that. Och, and look! There goes my heart." Alan set a hand on his chest with flair as Norrie's granddaughter walked toward the headland with long-legged grace, skirt swinging neatly over bare feet. She waved toward the children climbing the rock, calling up to them. "What a pity if she's a married lady." Alan sighed dramatically.

"If not, perhaps you will have a chance."

"I doubt it. See that tall fellow coming toward her now? Oh, see the smile she gives him. It breaks my heart to think that bonny thing is married or claimed."

"Aye, well," Dougal commiserated. A tousle-haired man wearing the baggy jacket, trousers, and boots of a fisherman joined the young woman. She smiled up at him, then stepped forward to snatch the shirttails of a small but bold child and pluck the blond boy before he could climb the headland slope with the others. She took his hand.

"Must be her bairn, the wee blond lad," Alan said.

Nodding, Dougal felt an unexpected stab of disappointment, as if he had found his wee sea fairy at last, but she was married and beyond his reach. As Alan asked about the next day's plans, Dougal replied, forcing himself to look away from the bonny lass and her family.

Turning, he narrowed his eyes against the sunset glare on the ocean waves and looked toward Sgeir Caran. Less than a mile from the island, the massive black rock thrust up through the waves, silhouetted against the bright sunset. Sgeir Caran was the largest formation in the archipelago of the Caran Reef, a wicked cluster of rocks that littered the sea like great thorn, many of the treacherous points hidden below the constant sweep of the Atlantic.

Most of the time Dougal only thought of Sgeir Caran in terms of the challenges it presented to the work, or thought of its geology, the weather, the physics of wind and wave force and so on. But in some moments, when the light was extraordinary or the mist dense and deep, the rock appeared otherworldly, an ancient portal for legends and magic. One night, years back, he had nearly drowned out there, saved by what seemed to be kelpies and a fairy creature. He would never forget it or understand it, and it came into his mind more often than he wanted.

Do not be a fool, he told himself. He must fasten his attention to the here and now. Hard enough to work out on Sgeir Caran every day without the distracting dreams of what was past.

"She will find you," Alan said.

Dougal turned, startled. "What?"

"The Baroness of Strathlin. When she hears we're about to quarry stone from her island, she'll come after you."

"There's not much Lady Strathlin can do now but accept it. I hear she keeps a manor house on this island and comes here now and then. When she comes next, I intend to win her over to see the value in the work that must be done here. The lighthouse will benefit her island."

"She might whaup yer for causing her grief. Old hag," Alan muttered. "Though I have nae met the lady, we can be sure she is a nasty old thing."

"I will find out soon enough. I am invited to a soiree at her home in a few weeks."

"She fights you every step of the way, she does." Alan Clarke shook his head.

"Her solicitors have done most of the fighting for her."

"The lady has nearly two million pounds to her name, they say. A staggering amount. Your fine inheritance is a wee sum compared to that. If she knows your project needs money, she will pull hard on the purse strings."

"To her credit, she gives to charities and contributed to the cost of the Fife bridge collapse."

"Yet she cannae find it in her cold heart to be generous about the Caran light. We need funds. The Fresnel lenses we need for the tower are devilish expensive. The whole cost of this could be near fifty thousand pounds by the time we are done."

"We have interested investors in Edinburgh. When I attend Lady Strathlin's soiree, I can ask for their commitment. As for the lady, it seems she will never invest in a light for her island. She simply hates the idea."

"Hell's own gale, that woman is. But you cannot run from a storm."

Dougal huffed a laugh. "I try not to. We just need good weather to finish this job. Whether she wants it or not, we will see it done with the support of the government." Dougal turned to see Norrie MacNeill walking toward him. The girl had joined him again, though without the little boy.

Graceful, lovely, he saw only her. The rush of the sea was loud in his ears, and his heart beat quickened. He thought of the sea fairy and felt a deep and sudden longing.

Whoever this girl was, he told himself, she was real, and he needed to collect his wits.

HE LOOKED LIKE a pirate, dark and wild, in shirtsleeves and vest and open collar, hands at his waist, a booted foot propped on the edge of a log on the beach. He was all restrained power and assurance as he watched her walk down the beach beside her grandfather. She felt his gaze bore into her and almost through her.

She had expected Dougal Stewart to be handsome and charming, as others said, but she was not prepared for the impact of his steady gaze or his compelling presence, even at a distance.

Now she only wanted to turn and run, not ready to face him. Better they should meet when she could be proper Lady Strathlin, holding her own against the persistent engineer.

But when her grandfather waved at him and took her arm, Meg walked forward.

Crossing the beach, she heard her name and saw her cousin, Fergus MacNeill, walking with her son, Sean along the upper beach. She was glad Sean had obeyed when she told him to climb down from the headland. Though she was his mother, there was a bit of distance there, for she did not see him often enough. He knew she lived far away from the island and when he was older, he would go to live with her. When she had inherited the title and fortune, a single mother of an infant, she had agreed with her island kinfolk's opinion that it was best for Sean to spend his early years on Caransay.

Before Sean's birth, her family had put it about that Meg had married a man from another island, a man of the sea who had vanished, and made it known that she did not discuss it. Only Meg's grandparents and great-grandmother knew the truth of Sean's existence. The story was easy enough for the isle's community of fishermen and wives to understand.

Her inheritance was harder to hide, but she had the support of kin and friends in her good fortune. Once she purchased the Caransay lease and brought benefit to her tenants and life on the isle, they recognized the importance of her new role, and knew she was doing the best she could for her son, the islanders, and others. She was deeply grateful for the warm homecoming she felt each time she returned to Caransay.

And so her cousin Fergus and his wife Anna took the boy into their household. But just a year ago, Anna had died with the birth of a daughter. Left with two bairns to raise, Fergus moved in with his grandparents, also Norrie and Thora, so the children could have a family circle.

Now, watching her bonny golden-haired son run happily across the beach, Meg reminded herself that she could not follow, but must go meet the obstinate engineer, Dougal Stewart.

Sighing, she pushed back her hair, knowing she did not look her best, her hair wild and loose, her feet bare, her skirt above her ankles. On Caransay, she stayed in the Great House—a grand residence on the other side of the island. But in other ways, she reverted to the lifestyle she had always known, spent as much time as she could with her family and her son.

She loved the freedom here, loved dispensing with crinolines,

stays, stockings, wide skirts, and snug shoes in favor of comfortable, practical clothing and simple shoes or bare feet. Caransay was
the only place she could do that now.

"So will you tell the man you are the lady herself?" Norrie
asked.

"That odious engineer? I will tell him nothing just now. He
hates me," she answered in the Gaelic she usually spoke while
here. "I can hardly tell him I am Lady Strathlin when I look like
this. I suppose I should invite him to tea at the Great House and
tell him then."

"Ha! The surprise will do him good. He is too serious, that
lad."

"I hoped my solicitors would find a way to stop his work
project before I arrived on holiday. But they have not been able
to do that."

"*Ach,* solicitors, useless fellows. Look there." Norrie gestured
with his clay pipe. "See those huts they put up. Those Lowland
structures will not stand against a good rain. That is not the sort
of house we need here. But we told them they were very good
houses!" He chuckled. "May their huts blow out to sea and carry
the engineers with them!"

"*Ach, Seanair.* That is wicked!" But she laughed with him. A
glance toward a cluster of thatched-roof little cottages told her
that they were hastily erected, not as solid as Hebridean stone
houses with thick thatched roofs weighted with rope nets and
stones. "I never agreed to putting up a lighthouse out there, you
know that, *Seanair.*"

"I know." Norrie clamped his teeth over the pipe stem. "And
the people wonder what you will do about it now that you are
here."

"I have already tried everything. He is a stubborn man."

"Stubborn, wants his lighthouse, but he is not a bad fellow. I
have spoken with him myself many times while you have been
gone. I like the man, I do. It is the construction I do not like, for
the harm it causes Sgeir Caran and the colonies of seabirds that

settle on the rock each year."

"The birds, the rock, the harm to our privacy, the threat to our legends—oh!" She stopped walking. Norrie frowned.

She stared at Dougal Stewart, who calmly waited for them. And she saw his face clearly for the first time.

"Oh!" she said again, as the beach seemed to tilt under her feet.

"What is it?" Norrie asked.

"I—nearly tripped. That's all."

She had expected to see a handsome man, a devilish, infuriating, obstinate man, the heir to a fortune, a builder of lighthouses. A persistent man whose work took real courage and daring.

She never expected to see the cad who had fathered her child and had broken her heart forever.

Stewart frowned at her, his gaze intense and penetrating. Did he recognize her? Oh God, she thought. Please, no.

Drawing closer, she was convinced this was the man she had met on that rock years ago. She would never mistake that face or the lean, stern toughness of him, a rugged, masculine beauty. The man she dreamed of—in dreams where she told him frankly what she thought about what he had done that night. Yet a man she loved and could not forget.

Dark-brown hair fell in sun-streaked waves, framing a face with rounded cheekbones, a firm jaw, a dusting of dark beard; his brows were straight, his smooth skin tanned from sun and wind. He wore a brown vest, dusty black trousers, and no coat; his shirt sleeves were rolled, and his open collar showed a strong, tanned throat. He stared as she approached.

Dear God, this was him, and no mistake. Meg touched the locket at her throat, and drew her plaid shawl over her hair to shadow her face as she approached him beside her grandfather.

He could not be allowed to recognize her. She could not bear it. Her legs quivered. She would be very foolish now to reveal that she was Lady Strathlin. She felt desperate to run away.

"Grandfather," she said urgently. "Please do not tell him who

I am. Not yet. We must all keep that secret until I decide what to do."

"We can let it wait," he replied.

Dougal Stewart stepped forward and held out his hand. "Mr. MacNeill! Good to see you, sir." He smiled at Meg and nodded, his eyes inquisitive, narrowed, so keen on her.

She prayed he would not know her. In seven years she had changed, matured. And he was still the most beautiful man she had ever seen. Sun and years had etched intelligence and wisdom around his eyes and in the slight creases beside his mouth. He had filled out, was larger, even more powerful. His eyes, edged in sooty black lashes, were the muted gray-green of a stormy sea.

He waited for an introduction, smiling politely. Meg lifted her chin, feeling defensive. He had hurt her deeply once, and she must tread carefully, not let him know just yet.

But the urge to tell him, corner him, find out why he had done what he had done, filled her, pushed at her. She flared her nostrils, tightened her lips. He sent her a puzzled glance.

"Good day, Dougal Stewart." Norrie spoke in English. "And Alan Clarke. This is my granddaughter, Margaret Fiona MacNeill. Lass, this is Mr. Stewart and Mr. Clarke."

She offered a hand in silence as Stewart took her fingers. "Miss MacNeill, good to meet you."

Touching him was a dreadful mistake. That ordinary contact shocked through her. Catching her breath, she met his penetrating gaze. He frowned. Did he recognize her?

She snatched her hand away, nodded to Clarke, and stepped back. Dougal Stewart turned to Norrie with a question about the mail runs to the Isle of Mull.

"Miss MacNeill, are you from Caransay?" Alan Clarke asked politely. He was a pleasant fellow, blond and blue-eyed, stockier and shorter than Stewart.

"Originally, aye, but I live elsewhere now. I come back to visit when I can."

"It is a beautiful place," Stewart said, having heard their exchange. She felt caught once more in his piercing gaze. Earlier she had wanted to flee—but now she wished for the courage to confront him. Slap him, give him her fierce thoughts on being betrayed. Not now, not here.

But suddenly, fiercely, she wanted him to know that she had felt betrayed, had felt angry toward him ever since that night, not knowing who he was or if she would ever see him again. Now, certain of his identity, she was stunned. How could he return to Caransay in this capacity, an engineer planning to destroy a legend by building on the very rock where he had once betrayed an island girl he did not even know?

Yet her heart conflicted with her sense of indignation. Sometimes she dreamed of him and yearned for him, wished for the return of that love, that bond. He had been protective and tender that stormy night, had wooed, won, loved her—and tricked her. He was only ordinary after all.

Temper rising fresh, she urgently wanted to tell him exactly who she was, and what had become of her after he left. But she had to wait, had to keep her identity secret from the engineer.

She must summon dignity and bide her time. The baroness would invite the engineer to the Great House to reveal the truth when the time was right.

"Mr. Stewart," Norrie said then, "I heard you hired the Mac-Leod lad to take you over to the Isle of Mull in his wee boat. Just so you know, I sail to Tobermory on Mull once or twice a week when the weather allows. Next time you wish to go, I will take you and bring you back. No need to ask the lad, though he was glad to do it."

"Thank you. I shall remember." Stewart nodded.

Meg stood silent, quelling rising emotion. Sea foam lapped at her feet, cooling her body, cooling her ire. She had to think of her child and find the right moment.

Then she caught her breath. Would Dougal Stewart want to take his son away from the island, away from her and her kin, board him in a school as was common for young lads? She wanted him to stay on the island where he was safe, away from her other life. She could never allow him to be put in a school until he was ready—and she was ready.

Thinking that, she glared at Stewart. He returned a quizzical glance.

"Miss MacNeill, I must ask. Have we met before?"

CHAPTER THREE

"I DO NOT think we have met, Mr. Stewart," replied Margaret MacNeill. Her voice was soft and melodic, her English perfect, with the soft, precise lilt of the native Gaelic speaker rather than broad Scots English. She seemed wary or troubled. Perhaps she was shy.

"Ah. I thought I had seen you somewhere before." He smiled a little.

"I cannot think where," she said primly, glancing away.

Dougal nodded, studying her. She was slim and neatly made beneath her plain garments, her feet sand-dusted, her clasped hands smooth and lovely. If she gutted fish and worked with nets, like many Hebridean women, her hands did not show it. Her thick golden curls were loosely pulled back with a leather tie, and her features were delicate, though he saw definite stubbornness in the set of her chin and her lush mouth.

But fair coloring and elegant bones were common in Hebrideans due to Viking ancestry, so it was said. Her grandfather had similar fair coloring with high cheekbones and vivid blue eyes.

In the late daylight, Margaret MacNeill's eyes were a luminous aqua. Dougal was reminded of a girl he had met and loved years ago whose eyes were the same extraordinary color, a sea-washed blue-green—he had glimpsed her at dawn just before he left the cave. The eyes of a sea fairy, he thought whimsically. He had never discovered who she was.

But Miss MacNeill had the same eyes, and she otherwise resembled that gorgeous creature, the sea fairy he had dreamed was a girl. A shock of recognition ran through him—a prickling on the skin, a clutch of certainty in the gut. He had been muddled that long-ago night, thinking the girl he met was a magical being. In the years since, he felt she must have been real, and he feared he would never see her again.

He had tried to find her, searching on every isle in the vicinity of Sgeir Caran. But he had never found a girl like the ethereal, lovely lass he had met on the rock.

Could she be the one? His heart thumped. Could she?

She gave no sign of recognition, a calm, cool, natural beauty who all but ignored him. Yet he noticed nervousness in the tight clasp of her hands, the tucked frown, the clench of her narrow toes in the sand.

Not sure, he turned to smile as Norrie MacNeill addressed his granddaughter. "Mr. Stewart is the chief of the lighthouse on the rock."

"Resident engineer," Dougal amended. "Assigned by the Northern Lighthouse Commission. We have permission to build on Sgeir Caran and to set up buildings for our needs on Caransay."

"I see," the girl said crisply.

She was not pleased to meet him, that was clear. He was aware that the islanders did not approve of the lighthouse plan, nor did the island's owner, Lady Strathlin. Miss MacNeill echoed the sentiment of her kin and friends; surely that explained her scowling glances.

But—what if she was the girl from years back? That girl would be unhappy to see him too, nor could he blame her. She had left first, but as he sailed away with the men who'd come to get him, he'd noticed a boat pulling away—had it been Norrie's boat, even back then? Dougal had been in a haze still, thoughts blurry from a knock to the head, his comprehension of things not quite fixed.

Keeping his outward calm, he promised himself to speak with her alone soon. What would he do if he discovered she was indeed that girl? Beyond apology and explanation, what more could he do? He had been a fool then. He had wanted to return immediately, but work duties had called back to the mainland for months. Later, he could not trace the lass.

Heart beating fast, thoughts distracting, he lost the thread of the conversation. Norrie cleared his throat.

"Mr. Stewart! I saw you and your men cutting into the hard place today," Norrie said. "I heard the noise of your sledges and chisels when I went over the waves to draw in my nets."

"The hard place?" Dougal asked.

"Sgeir Caran," Margaret MacNeill explained. "My *seanair,* my grandfather, will not say the rock's name aloud."

"It is not good to speak it," Norrie admitted. "No one should say it when directly on the sea. The hard place has a power that can pull you in so you would be lost."

"Ah." Dougal understood that more than Norrie could guess. "I will try to respect the local traditions."

"If so, why would you build on the great rock," the girl asked tartly, "when it is a place of legend and significance to the people of Caransay?"

"I am not aware of a legend about Sg—the hard place."

"The hard place belongs to the *each-uisge,*" Norrie said. "The lord of the deep."

"The ech-ooshka?" Dougal asked.

"Sea kelpie," Margaret MacNeill explained. "A horse-like sea creature of great magical power who can take the form of a white horse in the waves and sometimes takes form of a man."

"Aye, they say he comes to our great rock now and then to find himself a bride," Norrie went on. "The black rock is his place, you see. If he claims his bride, he will be good to the island. He will quiet the storms and summon more fish into our nets. He will bestow peace and good fortune on us. If he is displeased, he will raise great storms and the fish will flee our waters. His power and his wrath could destroy our lives and even sink Caransay into the waves."

"That kelpie is no fellow to cross," Dougal said, a smile quirking his lips.

"It is nothing to laugh at," Margaret MacNeill snapped.

"Our tradition is to make sure the *each-uisge* is always pleased," Norrie said.

"Do you bring him oatcakes and whisky as well as bonny brides?" Dougal meant it lightly, but saw the girl's sudden scowl. Norrie chuckled, but stopped when she glared at him too.

"We have honored our traditions for centuries," she said.

"I understand, Miss MacNeill."

"Do you?" she asked sharply. "The kelpie will not want a lighthouse there."

Dougal inclined his head. He knew that Hebrideans relied on age-old superstitions and rituals that created a sense of security and power in what could be a harsh and unpredictable environment. He saw the girl send a stern look to her grandfather and back to him again.

"Stewart, we know you have had some trouble with the lady," Norrie MacNeill said. This remark earned him another pretty scowl from the granddaughter. Even anger could not chase the sweetness from that face, Dougal thought.

"Lady Strathlin? Aye, some trouble. I hear she has a house on Caransay. If she comes here, I definitely want to meet her."

Silence followed as the old fisherman dragged on his pipe and clicked it between his teeth, and the girl gazed out to sea. She raised her chin, a gesture of truculence.

"She may not want to meet with you, sir," she said.

"The lady who owns the isle is not here just now," Norrie said.

"Not here," the girl echoed.

"I will be on the island for a long while. When she visits again, I need to speak with her."

"A long while?" the girl asked. Her voice had an odd tremor.

Dougal sent her a sharp glance. That nagging feeling that he had seen her before grew stronger. He had been back and forth to the island for weeks and had not seen this girl until today. Yet she seemed all too familiar.

"She stays up in the Great House," Norrie said. "Sometimes no one sees her."

"The Great House?" Dougal asked. The girl stood silent, the sea breeze filtering through her wild honeyed curls.

"Clachan Mor is her home on the other side of the island," Norrie replied. "If the lady comes here, I can deliver your note to her."

"I prefer to meet with her in person."

"She does not like visitors," the girl said.

"I am thinking you need her permission to use her beach and harbor," Norrie said. He drew on his pipe. "And yet you go ahead and do it without asking."

"I have no choice, sir," Dougal said. "I work for the Lighthouse Commission, and the commission and the government have ordered this work to be done."

"The lady does not like strangers on Caransay. But if we see her, we will tell her you are here." Norrie pointed with his pipe toward the black rock out in the sea. "If you want to please the lady, find another rock for your tall light. She wants privacy for her island."

"That rock is a dangerous place," Margaret MacNeill said then. "There are wild storms and high waves out there."

"I know, Miss MacNeill. I have been out there in all sorts of weather." Dougal met her gaze. "So I know that a light is needed there to protect the ships that pass."

Her aqua-blue gaze caught his, and he saw a flash of awareness. Then she looked away again, hastily, nervously. Those luscious lips trembled. She glanced back at him, then away.

Certainty slammed through him, clarifying the elusive feeling of familiarity.

Oh aye, he thought. *You are the one. Now what do we do, my lass?*

RESTLESS, UNABLE TO sleep, Dougal left his small hut in the darkness to walk over the machair, the wildflower meadow that stretched over part of the island to the dunes. Overhead, the sky had finally gone indigo—Hebridean summer skies could hold a lavender light nearly through the night. The moon, high and pale, reflected in ripples on the sea as he strolled.

Deep in thought, he considered a stubborn problem. Rectangular stone blocks, each weighing several tons, had to be precisely trimmed to fit the circular foundation cavity of the lighthouse. He had drawn diagrams and devised measurements, but knew each block must be hand-shaped in situ to ensure a tight fit. The figures he gave his masons had to be accurate. Long walks often helped him think such things through.

Pausing to gaze out over the dark sea, his mind was as restless as the waves, not because he puzzled over granite blocks, but because Margaret MacNeill had invaded his dreams. He had startled awake from a dream of the girl in his arms, her embrace comforting, luscious, then passionate.

He had awoken in warm sweat with a wrench of longing, half aroused and needing to shake off the dream's haunting power.

The wind picked up as he stood there, and waves poured to the shore, rolling, plunging, in seductive rhythm. Moonlight gleamed pale through watery arches, their high lacy curls like the proud heads and breasts of white stallions.

There are the water horses of Sgeir Caran, he thought. *There is your kelpie.*

Seven years ago, washed onto that black rock, he had been drunk, concussed, and half drowned, imagining that the water creatures took him there. A man might see anything under such circumstances, imagine anything.

So he had been saved by waves pushing against the rock, not pale, proud water horses, and the sylph he had encountered had been a lass of Caransay. And he had been daft and lost that night, and yet found in his soul somehow. That night had changed him, bound him to her.

Now that he had found her, he had to make amends. He could not bear knowing that he had so wronged an innocent girl. Her glaring look, hours ago, had been angry, accusing—and deserved.

Girl or none, he had work to do here, and a private mission that drove him to complete it.

Far out, Sgeir Caran was a dark, commanding silhouette. Lesser rocks jutted through swirling water, part of the long reef where ships had sunk and lives had been forfeited over time.

His parents had drowned out there, lost in a storm along that wicked reef, their ship wrecked along its lethal points. Had a lighthouse been in place out there, his parents might still be alive, and he would not have been orphaned so young. The light would have guided their ship and others through the treacherous archipelago and safely to port.

He shoved fingers through his hair, sighed. He was determined to fight for the lighthouse on Sgeir Caran to prevent tragedies and save lives. Lady Strathlin and her lawyers had to accept that. For Dougal, that light would be a monument to those who had died among those rocks. Publicly, its beacon would serve well. Nothing must prevent it from going up on the great rock.

He hardened his mouth, fighting a flash of memory—his parents' faces, their smiles, their voices. He could not think too long about them, or feel the loss dreadfully, keenly, once more.

Growing up, he had honed self-control and daring as a way to fight those feelings. Death was no matter to him—he faced it often and no longer feared it. Death was an element of the work he did, and so far he had escaped. He had been shipwrecked, had endured outrageous storms, dived deep, climbed high on scaffolds, and had risked his life too many times to count in the work of making lighthouses. There was a thrill in the dare, a thrill in the courage. And there was a sense of rightness in what he did. No matter the risk to those who built them, lighthouses were needed.

Of all the lights he had constructed, this one was far and away the most important for him.

He was known for daring and stubbornness, and he would never give up this fight, despite resistance from the island's owner. The physics and logic of the matter dictated that Sgeir Caran was the best site. And he had the support of the Northern Lighthouse Commission and the Stevenson firm; they had entrusted him to build it in this godforsaken place.

Somehow, he would do this. He owed it to all the souls lost under those waves, owed it to his father, strong and kind, his mother, bookish and lovely.

He sucked in the salty air as if it were a remedy for old pain.

"Mr. Stewart." The girl's voice was sweet and soft.

He whirled. She stood a few feet behind him, surrounded by moonlit flowers and grass. Wind rippled through her hair, shifted her skirt. She was magic after all, appearing just when he needed her in a lonely, dark moment. He felt a strong urge to take her into his arms, make his apology, ask forgiveness. Instead he tilted his head in question.

"Miss MacNeill." He watched her walk toward him, skirt hem swinging through the flowers. She seemed vulnerable, brittle with tension. "I am surprised you are out here at such an hour."

"I like to come out before dawn on Caransay," she said. "The chance of seeing the northern lights is worth losing a bit of sleep. Did you hope to see them, too?"

"I came out to walk and puzzle out an engineering problem." And to shake free of a dream, but now the dream stood beside him. He looked up at the sky to keep from staring at her like a cow-eyed fool. She was beautiful. He felt smitten, awed, awkward suddenly.

"Dawn is near," she said, searching the sky as he did. "We will not see the northern lights now. Well, good night, Mr.

Stewart, or is it good morning?"

"Let me see you safe home." He turned with her.

"I am perfectly safe on my island. Good luck with your puzzle." She stepped ahead.

He caught up with a long step and walked beside her through the long grass thick with blooms. The early light rose quickly, illuminating the wild colors and dancing shapes of the flowers. "The machair is a beautiful thing."

"It is," she agreed.

"Do you know these flowers?" He did not care, just wanted something to say. "Buttercups, just there? And bluebells."

"Buttercups, bluebells, daisies," she answered. "Over there is yarrow and wild oat grass, and meadowsweet too. Underfoot, those tiny purple flowers are small irises past their bloom. Over there, you can find wild strawberries and brambles and clusters of wild roses growing thick over the stones in the turf."

"Lovely." He watched her.

"Over there, the heather blooms are so thick that the hills look purple from out at sea."

"I noticed that the other day."

"No one planted these flowers, no one tends them, but they flourish. It has always been thus. In summer, the daisies turn the machair to white and gold and the bees tumble over them, drunk with nectar as they head home to the hive."

He chuckled. "You love this place. You know it well."

"I do, Mr. Stewart." Behind them, the sea shushed endlessly to shore. "It is paradise."

"I suppose the baroness agrees."

She stopped. "You can go back now. I will head home from here."

"I would rather escort you. It is still rather dark."

"There are no strange men about," she said. "Just you, I suppose."

He drew a breath. "I have the sense you do not like me much, Miss MacNeill."

"I like you fine. Go back to your hut, Mr. Stewart. I do not need you here now. None of us need you here."

"I suspect you refer to lighthouses now. Are you acquainted with Lady Strathlin?"

Her steps faltered, then she walked on. "Why?"

"She shares your poor opinion of me. So do her passel of lawyers."

"We cannot all be wrong."

"Ouch," he said. She chuckled, walking beside him, and he took her elbow to guide her around a rock at their feet, half submerged under the flowery blanket of the machair.

That quick and simple touch went through him with crackling awareness. He let go, a bit stunned, telling himself it was only the dim light, the lush sound of waves, the strange magic of the hour before dawn. In daylight, he would hardly have noticed. Or would he?

Ahead, he saw a croft house tucked against a hill, whitewashed with a thatched roof and darkened windows. The house faced a small bay, sparkling and peaceful.

"Yours?" he asked.

"My grandparents live here. You can leave now, sir."

"No need to bristle so, Miss MacNeill. I am no harm to you."

She stopped, staring up at him, seemed to bite off a reply. A sea breeze fluttered her skirt and plaid shawl, and loose strands of golden hair wafted away from a thick, messy braid. "I am not bristling."

"You," he murmured, "are like a porcupine when I am near." He reached out to brush wayward tendrils away from her brow and eyes. She leaned back.

"Do you know Lady Strathlin very well?" He felt compelled on the subject.

She shrugged. "Everyone here knows her. Why do you ask?"

"Just curious. I hear she inherited an enormous fortune from a grandfather from Edinburgh or the Lowlands."

She shrugged. "So they say."

They stood on a rise above the croft house and its little bay, where the machair dropped away into a sandy bank that led to the shore. Dougal saw that the house had two wings added to the main house, its thatch roof held down by ropes and stones. It was a pretty picture with the sparkling bay and pink dawn billowing up from the far horizon of the sea.

"Is that what they call the Great House?"

She laughed. "That is my grandparents' croft. We call it Camus nan Fraoch—Heather Bay."

"Though you do not live on Caransay now, but elsewhere with your husband?"

"Husband? I am not married. I have a house on Mull and another on the mainland."

"Is it so? Some prosperity in hard times, then?"

"Just—an inheritance."

"Like Lady Strathlin?"

She laughed. "No one has a fortune like Lady Strathlin, so I am told."

"Aye. Well, forgive me. I saw you earlier with a man and a boy and assumed they were your family."

"That was my cousin Fergus and…small Sean."

Not married. He felt relieved. "I see. Where is Clachan Mor, the baroness's great house?"

"That way." She pointed. "At the foot of those hills."

Narrowing his eyes, he could just see a stone manor house in the distance, a boxy shape with a flat facade and several windows nestled in the protection of a dark hill. Fronting the house, a grassy sward and a sandy peninsula stretched in a crescent to form another quiet bay.

"Do you know when the baroness might come here again? Are you privy to her plans?"

She tilted her head. "You ask a great many questions."

"For good reason." He sensed she knew more than she would say.

"The lady values her privacy and avoids conducting business

when she is here. Caransay is a place of rest and joy for her. She does not want that spoiled."

"I understand. But I have been unable to see her to explain myself and my goals. She refuses all meetings."

"That may come from her lawyers."

"Possibly. Well, if she will not see me here, perhaps you will convey a message to her. Though I wager Lady Strathlin is tired of messages from me," he drawled.

She was looking up. The soft light caught the curve of her cheek, and her eyes grew wide. "Look!" she cried, pointing out to sea. Dougal turned.

A pale-green arc bloomed on the horizon and expanded, exploding in sudden swaths of light and color. Pink and green swirled overhead like silken veils. Dougal watched, entranced. Without thinking, he took her elbow again, a gentlemanly gesture to lead her closer to the beach. He wanted to be closer to her as they watched the dancing flares in the sky.

"So beautiful," she breathed.

"Aye. The aurora borealis—it is always a thrill to see them."

"The Merry Men, we call the northern lights here."

He smiled. "In the old days, I hear, the lights were believed to be gigantic supernatural warriors—especially when the sky flowed red as if from blood." He had read it somewhere.

"When I was a child, I thought they were angels dancing in heaven."

"They do look like that. I have seen them before, but never as lovely as this."

She smiled up at him for an instant. The sky's lambent colors gave her a graceful glow. Dougal felt an urge to touch her creamy skin, her silken curls. She was a stranger, cool and distant, and yet to him she seemed familiar and dear.

"The colors are pale this time," she said. "Sometimes they are quite brilliant when the Merry Men go dancing."

"The sky is not dark enough. In fall or winter they would be brighter."

"True. Will you still be on Caransay then?" She looked up.

"I hope the building will be done by then, but we will see. If so, we should walk out in the early hours to look for the lights again. If you like," he added.

She did not answer, staring up at the magical glow. Dougal thought suddenly of the rainy shadows in a cave and the pink light of dawn glowing over this very girl's face. He recalled how she had felt, drenched and shivering, in his arms as they comforted each other. His body pulsed.

"Tell me," he said gruffly. "Are you sure we have never met before?"

She shook her head, and would not meet his eyes, though he watched her.

"Tell me," he repeated. "Was it you that night, out on the rock? Or was it a dream?"

He noticed her gasp, saw the flash of understanding in her eyes. Though she continued to watch the sky, her silence seemed a clear admission. Then he saw tears glint in her eyes.

"My God," he breathed. "It *was* you."

For a long moment, she stood in silence, arms crossed, shoulders rising in tension. Wishing he could ease her anxiousness, he fisted a hand against it and waited, heart thumping hard.

"Was that you, then?" she asked quietly. "Out on the great rock in a wild storm?"

"If we both remember that night, then aye. That was me. And that was you."

"What were you doing out there?"

"I should ask the same of you. An accident brought me there. Capsized."

"An accident," she repeated. "Not—a prank?"

"Good lord!" he burst out, surprised. "Is that what you think? What were you doing out there, for all the world like Andromeda tied to the rock?"

"Oh, and you were Perseus protecting Andromeda from the sea monster?" she snapped.

A barefoot island girl who likely spoke better Gaelic than English, versed in Greek mythology? That intrigued him. "Something like that," he said, huffing a little laugh.

She whirled. "Hardly amusing, sir."

"You vanished. I could not find you."

"You vanished first," she said. "Gone off with your mates."

He frowned, then dimly recalled the fishermen who happened by and took him off the rock. He had left her alone there, still in such a haze that he did not realize it until later. That had haunted him.

"I looked for you. I missed you," he said.

"Missed me!" She tilted her face to him, arms crossed, cheeks flushed, eyes snapping bright. As he regarded her, all the years of wondering, wanting, dreaming, filled him and pushed him.

"Truly, I did." He took her by the shoulders and leaned down, sliding his hands down her arms, drawing her closer. "Now here you are at last. Finally, I know your name."

"Do you?" It sounded like a dare.

"Margaret," he breathed. She leaned forward, not away. He lowered his head, close enough to nuzzle her brow, close enough to kiss, overwhelmed by the desire to pull her to him.

She stiffened in his arms, yet even so leaned her head back, closed her eyes. Silent, still, she seemed to wait. Tipping his head, Dougal touched her lips with his and gently kissed her.

Her lips softened beneath his, and she clutched at his shirt-sleeves. He felt her body sway against his, sensed a moment of surrender and allowance there. Sliding his hand to the back of her waist, he pulled her close and deepened the kiss. She accepted it, gave a little moan of need. Perhaps she had missed him as much as he had missed her.

A force poured through him, relief, joy, shaking free the years of searching for her, hoping for something more with her. Now she was here, and she was real, no dream, no magic. One of the great losses of his life had been restored. It felt like a miracle.

"Margaret," he whispered, the name a caress on his lips.

Her hand rose to cup his jaw, her breath warmed his mouth. He sensed a hunger in her that matched his own, and he sensed her need was as sincere as his. He wanted just to hold her, cherish her, heal her reluctance, ease the hurt he had caused her years back. He truly regretted it. At last he could try to make it up to her.

She gave a breathy little moan, as if caught in the same heated fog that held him captive. Then, pushing at his chest, she stepped back, and lashed her hand upward to crack across his cheek, whip sharp.

"What the devil!" he burst out.

She whirled and was hurrying away over the sandy slope, breaking into a run as she neared the croft house.

With his palm nursing his stinging cheek, he stared after her. Overhead, the kaleidoscope sky was fading into gray dawn, and a cool, damp breeze cleared his thoughts.

She was no illusion, and he was a fool. He had ruined her that long-ago night, shamed her. No matter that she had gone willingly, wildly, into his arms then. Small wonder she hated him.

But why had she been out there on that wicked night? He wanted to know. And he wanted to explain himself further and apologize.

He owed her more than an apology. He should have married her years ago, and it had been on his mind—but he had not been entirely certain she was real, nor could he locate her. Now, short of marrying the girl far after the fact, he was not sure how he could best make it up to her. After that crack across his cheek, he doubted she would consider a marriage proposal.

He shook his head, called himself every sort of bastard and fool. Margaret MacNeill deserved more than an apology. He had been a heartless cad, a concussed idiot, far enough gone that night to think himself enchanted. Morally, socially, deep in his heart, he knew he should marry the girl. He wanted to. Now that he had found her, he could not live with himself otherwise.

Yet suddenly the prospect seemed a greater challenge than any risk he had ever faced.

CHAPTER FOUR

"H E IS STILL there." Thora opened the door to peer out.
"Grandmother, please, he will see you!" Meg
hissed, trying to close the door.

"He will just think I am feeding the chickens," Thora said,
and stepped outside.

Hearing a chuckle behind her, Meg turned to see Mother
Elga, her great-grandmother, laughing. Seated at the table, she
was feeding porridge to Fergus's daughter, Anna, perched on her
lap. "The kelpie came back for you," Elga said. "I told you he
would!"

Casting a sour glance at her great-grandmother, Meg went to
the window, seeing Thora heading toward the chickens under a
dawn sky shining pink and blue-gray. Beyond the small kailyard,
Meg saw Dougal Stewart standing on a hillock above Camus nan
Fraoch, facing out to sea.

If he stood there waiting for her, he could wait all day. She
would not go out to him.

Yet her mind went back to another dawn when that same
man—no kelpie, not a bit of it—had waited on a black rock for a
boat to fetch him. She could never forget watching him sailing
away. At the time, angry and hurt, she hoped he had fallen
overboard.

Now, her mind was spinning from discovering that Stewart
was that same man—and her heart still thumped with the

memory of new kisses and powerful urges awakening in his arms.

She leaned her forehead against the window frame. That night had been wild, desperate, joyful, full of passion and promise—and betrayal. But she had burned for him, body and soul, had loved him, could never forget him. Now she was pressed to either forgive him—or stir up all the hurt and regret again. The only thing she could not regret was wee Sean, born of that night.

Yet she had been foolish. Too trusting. And today, with the dawn, she had succumbed to his same irresistible magic. Well, it would not happen again. She was not the same foolish girl as before, and she would do her best to avoid him.

"Margaret, the bannocks!" Mother Elga reminded her.

"Oh!" She whirled to see smoke rising from the iron griddle over the fire and hastened to the hearth. Grabbing a wooden spatula, she moved the burned cakes to a wooden platter.

"Your mind is elsewhere." Elga bounced the towheaded baby in her lap. Tiny, bent as a blackthorn stick, the old woman pointed a finger at Meg. "You are thinking of the kelpie-man. He has come here disguised as the lighthouse-man."

"He was always the lighthouse man, Mother Elga. He was never the *each-uisge*. We were all fooled." With silver tongs, she flipped the bacon slices already cooking in an iron pan suspended over the fire. She had purchased an iron stove for her grandparents' cottage, but they continued to cook in traditional ways, while the gleaming black oven and cookstove in the corner provided a shelf for stacks of dishes.

Elga snorted. "That kelpie is very clever."

Cheeks hot, mouth pinched, Meg flipped the bacon too quickly and it spattered.

"*Tcha,*" Elga said disdainfully. "You have forgotten how to cook, now that you are a fine spoiled lady in a great castle!"

"I know how to cook and do chores, but I do not need to do those in my house near Edinburgh." She smiled at her great-grandmother. "This is supposed to be my holiday, and I enjoy doing things the old way. Though I do wish you would use the cookstove."

"Hah, that beast! Now listen, lass. The *each-uisge* is real. Even if you do not believe, he can still be real. You met him and felt his enchantment."

"There was no enchantment." But her knees felt curiously weak as she recalled those recent kisses. He had some kind of magic—and she would firmly resist it.

Thora breezed inside again, skirts swishing over wide hips, plaid shawl fluttering as she closed the door. "He is still out there, watching the sea."

"He longs to return to his home under the waves," Elga said.

Meg took up the steaming iron kettle suspended over the fire, and poured hot water into a teapot. "He can jump in the sea for all I care."

"A kelpie cannot wear his human guise for very long." Elga looked hard at Meg. "He must return to the water, and he wants you to go with him."

"Ridiculous! He is just a man, can you not see it? A stubborn, infuriating man who intends to build a lighthouse on our rock whether or not we want one. He is no kelpie!" She transferred the bacon to pewter plates, scraped the charred bannocks, and spread them with butter.

"Then why did you kiss him up on the hill, if he did not cast his spell over you? We saw you. We saw magic. The love of a human and a kelpie," Thora said, smiling.

"We did see that! The kelpie's kiss means he will bless our isle again," Elga said.

"Oh, my dearie dears," Meg sighed. She knew very well Elga's vision was especially weak for detail now, but her belief in the old ways was strong; Thora, as her daughter, shared that belief.

"He may look human to a young lass, but we elders know better," Elga continued. "The kelpie and his ilk have ruled our isle and reef since the time of the mists. The kelpie lives forever and changes into his man-form. Now and then he needs the gift of a bride. All part of the old bargain to watch over our isle. That is you. Where's my tea?" Elga demanded. "Take the bairnie."

"Here, Mother." Thora took the baby and sat down to hold her in her lap.

Meg set the breakfast plates on the table and poured tea into cups, adding cream and honey. She poured a little tea into a tiny wooden cup, adding cream to cool it, but no honey, and set it in front of the child.

"Small Anna wants to feed herself," Meg laughed as the little one grabbed a bannock, though Meg reached for the hot bacon before Anna could burn her little hand. Thora broke the meat and bannock into small pieces, while Anna picked contentedly at the food.

"That laddie should be up, it's past dawn." Elga gestured toward the little room curtained off from the main area of kitchen and parlor. "We make sure he is up with the dawnlight to feed chickens and do chores. He is a good lad and learning good habits here."

"Let him sleep this morning. A fretful dream woke him in the night," Meg answered. Sean, six years old now, still slept in his box bed in the little curtained room. She had woken too, having spent the night on a cot, for she had not gone back to the larger house last night. After whispering reassurance to Sean, who slept again, she lay awake. Finally she had gone outside to walk a bit, where she had encountered Stewart and the northern lights.

"If you say he should sleep, fine," Thora said. "You are his mama." She glanced at Elga.

Meg nodded, wishing again that she could be with her son all the time. But she had made the hard decision to leave him here for his well-being until he was a little older.

"Norrie and Fergus have gone out to start the day's fishing," Thora said then. "Fergus said he might join the lighthouse crew to earn extra money."

"He does not need to earn more," Meg said. "They do not

need to work so hard. I will see to everything, you know that."

"They will do the work they have always done here," Thora said. "And Fergus is proud. He will not let you, his cousin, provide for him and his daughter."

"He could work for me," she said. "Up at the big house. You could all live at the Great House."

"Your heart is generous, lass, but Fergus needs his pride. And we like our wee croft. Norrie says it is closer to the harbor, and he will not stop his fishing until he cannot lift his nets."

"I know," Meg said. She had managed to convince them to enlarge the croft house with sleeping quarters and a separate cow byre. She had provided new furnishings and the disdained cookstove, and made sure Norrie and Fergus had fine boats and nets. She wanted her kin, indeed all her tenants on the island, to have whatever they needed. But they did not ask very much of her.

"Did you tell Mr. Stewart to leave Caransay?" Thora asked.

"I tried, but he refused. I did not tell him who I am otherwise. None of that."

"*Ach,*" Elga said. "That Stewart. He will know soon. He is a prince of the sea. He prances about in the waves at night."

"He was not prancing when I saw him."

"Why does he want to build his high tower on the great rock? It belongs to the water horses ever since the first *each-uisge* came out of the sea and took the form of a beautiful man, and fought the great Fionn MacCumhaill. He made a bargain with Fionn to keep the rock and let the people have the island, but he must have a bride from Caransay every so often."

"Just stories," Meg said.

"Easy to say, now that you are a fine rich lady with a castle and servants," Elga said. "When your heart was pure and your life was simple, you knew the truth."

"I am learning the truth of it," Meg murmured.

"Does this Stewart know who you are?" Elga asked. "His bride?"

"He recognized her," Thora replied. "In the harbor yesterday, I saw the very moment he knew her. His eyes went wide."

Meg felt her cheeks grow hot. "Even if he suspects, he does not know about Lady Strathlin. And you two must keep quiet."

"He has come back for his son." Elga nodded.

"Hush! The very thought frightens me." Meg glanced toward the chamber where Sean dozed. "Stewart knows nothing of my son."

"You must tell him," Thora said.

"When the time is right."

"I looked into the fire and knew he was the one for you," Elga said.

"The kelpie? Or the engineer who makes my life miserable?" Meg asked bitterly.

"The one that heaven and the magical ones intend for you to have," Elga replied.

Meg took a sip of tea and did not answer. Her great-grandmother blithely mixed religion and myth, and there was no harm in it. But too much talk of the kelpie of the rock was unsettling.

"*Tcha*, Mother," Thora said, as if she knew Meg's thoughts. "It is bad luck to talk so often of the kelpie."

"Why not? He's part of our family now. Bring him to supper, Margaret dear."

"Oh, do stop," Meg said.

"A prince of the deep builds a tower on his rock for his bride, while he is disguised as a working man," Elga said, nodding.

Meg sighed and leaned her chin on her fist. Through the window, the sky was taking on the blue of morning.

She loved and respected her great-grandmother, growing up on Elga's endless stories of ancient heroes, gods, goddesses, mythic trials, and magic. As Caransay's oldest inhabitant, Elga was in a way its mystic and its bard, respected by all. Elga seemed more eccentric and stubborn with age, clinging to the old ways, the legends and superstitions, and she sometimes practiced spells and charms as she had always done.

Mother Elga lived in a medieval world in a way. The rest of the world had moved on, while she kept to her beliefs, certain they were right.

Though Meg loved Caransay and its isolated traditions, she felt removed from the world of her childhood. Living on the mainland had changed her. Wealth, education, and privilege had given her a pragmatic and modern bent, though she saw the benefits of both the mainland world and the older island ways. Time rolled slowly and reliably in the Hebrides. Here on Caransay, tradition, routine, and simplicity ruled beautifully. She would not interrupt that or expect it to change with the times, as life had forced her to do. Besides, following the old ways had caused her deep hurt.

"Mark me, that man is the one," Elga said. "You made a binding promise with the kelpie by bearing his child. Now you must honor your agreement."

"I have honored and paid more than anyone can know." Meg fought back sudden tears.

"It was our bargain as much as hers, Mother," Thora said. "Margaret did that for us, for the island. Our homes and our livelihoods are safe. We have all we could ever want, thanks to the blessings that came to her, and thanks to her generosity."

"The luck of the kelpie," Elga said stubbornly. "Good fortune, and a sweet little lad too."

"The good fortune came to me through my maternal grandfather's will," Meg said.

"And would not have come to you at all if the other heirs had lived," Elga said. "Unexpected luck, just after your marriage to the kelpie. He made that magic happen."

"No water horse could have arranged that much money," Meg said as her patience slipped. "There is no magic. And he is not my husband!"

"He is. You did not resist him that night, girl," Elga said. "Once the kelpie loves a woman, he will haunt her dreams and hold her heart forever."

Meg set down her teacup with a loud clink. "Mr. Stewart is not my husband," she insisted.

"One night with him decided that," Thora said. "The child decided that. Such marriages are still made in Scotland. Now that he is here, he should marry you for everyone to see."

"And then what, we dive into the sea?" Meg asked.

Elga huffed a laugh. "Happiness will keep him a man for you. I believe it is so. Find him and tell him who you are. Riches and happiness await. I've seen your fate in the fire and in the water."

"Enough!" Meg burst out. She would never marry the cad who tricked her that night. "He is just a man. Leave it be!" Truly, she had never told her grandmothers how he had left her there to sail off with friends. "I am going up to the Great House," she said, standing.

"No need to fret over the truth," Elga said.

"I have letters to write. Send Sean up to the house after he has had his breakfast and does his chores. He will have lessons with Mrs. Berry in reading and mathematics today. If the weather holds, we will take him to the beach to play."

"We will come too," Thora said. "We like Mrs. Berry. And small Anna loves to play in sand."

"Small Anna likes to eat sand. Come up later." Meg took up her shawl and went to the door.

"We will have a ceilidh to celebrate when that lass finally sees the truth," Elga told Thora.

"He is very handsome," Thora said. "What woman could resist a man like Stewart?"

"I can." Meg closed the door behind her. She should have resisted him before dawn.

Out on the machair, Dougal Stewart had gone, and the sun was bright over the sea.

His shelter was snug and cozy, the walls plastered thick to cut the wind and muffle the sound of rain. Barely ten paces side to side, the single room was warmed on cool nights by a coal brazier, and cozy during the days when the sun beat on the thick thatch roof. The small windows let in sea breezes, sometimes rain or blown sand if he forgot to close the shutters tight.

The best luxury of his little hut was privacy, for many of the huts were shared. He had a canvas hammock, a small cupboard, a wooden chair, and a table large enough to hold maps, charts, and a lamentable number of documents and letters. As supervising engineer, he also kept a daily progress log crammed with figures and observations. The Stevenson firm and the lighthouse commissioners expected to be informed regarding problems as well as progress.

The wind howled and the night was heavy with rain. Dougal felt weary and achy from another long, trying day out on Sgeir Caran. He and his men had drilled and hammered their way through solid rock for hours in a beating sunshine relieved only by sea spray and splashing waves.

While out there, he had paused now and then to watch seals cavorting on the rocks, and laughed with the men watching the antics of dolphins playing in the waves. Later, upon returning to Caransay, he and the crew had eaten supper in a tent and had gone off to their various huts to rest. But Dougal often stayed up late to work on notes, reports, maps, and drawings by lamplight. He knew Alan Clarke and Evan Mackenzie, another engineer, would be doing the same. Such a huge project required a great deal of detail work to ensure that the resulting structure was safe and solidly built to last the ages.

Finishing his current report for the commissioners, he wrote a note to David Stevenson, the brilliant engineer who had recommended him for the job on Sgeir Caran; Dougal had assisted him in the nearly impossible task of building a lighthouse on Muckle Flugga, a challenging and inhospitable environment.

Out on Sgeir Caran, Dougal was finding similar issues related to safety and a design that suited the location. He fully trusted his worthy and experienced crew, and knew that they could build a fine lighthouse on Sgeir Caran, one that would serve many for centuries.

Sealing the envelope, he reached into a small wooden box to retrieve a recent letter from Lady Strathlin—more correctly, from her Edinburgh solicitors, Dundas and Grant.

Be assured that you shall not build on Caransay without Lady Strathlin's permission. Despite your parliamentary order, we will stop this enterprise. Your structures will come down, if not by Nature, then by legal writ.

Dougal frowned, reading the threat again. Structures? Could they mean the huts occupied by his men? The huts the Caransay harbor were protected by a high headland and would not easily blow out to sea, though huts had done so on other sites. But these could withstand high winds and heavy storms for the most part. Some storms, he knew well, were relentlessly powerful.

Regardless of legal threats, Dougal intended to see the lighthouse completed. Somehow, he had to convince the baroness and her lawyers of the worth of this project. He not only wanted to end their protests—he wanted their full support. The project, the island, and its people would be better for cooperation when possible.

Turning the page over, he read the curious postscript that he had noticed earlier. It was the first direct contact he'd had from Lady Strathlin in this ongoing ordeal.

Mr. Stewart,

I wonder if you know that hundreds, perhaps thousands, of birds make their homes on Sgeir Caran each year. They may lose that security if a lighthouse is situated on the rock. A magnificent pair of golden eagles also nests there each year, and all year the rock hosts gannets, puffins, shearwaters, and little storm petrels that nest in small niches on the rock. Gannets are sometimes hunted cruelly elsewhere, bludgeoned in a horrid ritual called "the hunting of the Guga." But on Sgeir Caran, all the birds are safe, protected by ancient tradition and honored by local islanders.

We must protect these birds. I ask that you recommend to the commission that they find another location for the light-house. I understand the need for a light to aid seafarers, and I applaud the courage of the men who would build it. But I beg you, sir, to erect your high tower elsewhere.

Yours sincerely, Lady Strathlin

Birds! A new action in this little war of words. Dougal sighed. Each letter was like a chess move and countermove. He never knew what might come next, but he had begun to enjoy the game.

But the birds introduced an unexpected challenge. He had heard of the lady's charitable acts and knew she preferred privacy. He knew little else about her. Now he knew that she cared about the birds that lived on that rock.

To be sure, that did give him pause. But the project had to go forward.

Sometimes he imagined the baroness to be a formidable older woman; other times, he thought of her as a magnificent, mysterious, beautiful young creature. He rather hoped the latter, but respected the former as well. Whomever she was, he sensed that she liked their little game of wills. Through her lawyers, her responses could be commanding, haughty, plaintive, even witty. But this personal message about the birds tugged at his conscience.

He had a grudging respect and a sincere curiosity about the baroness. He did not care for her lawyers at all and dismissed them out of hand. She was the driving force, that was clear.

Her handwriting intrigued him too, now that he had a note from her. It was not the wobbly hand of an elderly lady, but flowing, feminine, confident, educated. It was the hand of a well-educated woman who might indeed be younger than he had initially thought.

Although she might have a younger companion who wrote her letters. That could be. His elderly Aunt Lillian rarely wrote her own notes these days, dictating letters to his sisters, who lived with her.

If the little handwritten note from the sainted baroness was meant to cajole him, he would not relent. And he told himself that birds would adapt to any changes on their rock, and likely still flourish there. He would tell the lady that.

Smoothing a fresh piece of foolscap, he dipped a pen in ink.

Madam,

I am dismayed that your solicitors did not better inform you. Even as I write this, I am installed in comfortable quarters on Caransay with a view of Sgeir Caran. This evening's sunset was most spectacular, and the northern lights graced the sky last night. The weather is glorious at the moment.

The wind howled strong enough to rattle the door, and rain gusted against the shutters. Dougal eased his back against the stiff wooden chair and squinted in the oily lamplight.

I appreciate your concern regarding the wild birds on the great rock. I assure you it is not my intention to disturb Nature or to significantly alter that rocky isle.

I have seen gannets and puffins. They seem content even with men arriving on the rock. The stormy petrels are elusive, but that is their nature. I have not yet seen the golden eagles. When I do, I will give them your regards.

He signed the note, sealed the envelope, and dropped it in the mail pouch for Norrie MacNeill to post at Tobermory. He would tell Norrie about the letter for Lady Strathlin. If the lady planned to visit Caransay, Norrie would know, and deliver it directly to her.

Another move on the chessboard. He doused the light and sought his cold cot.

CHAPTER FIVE

"MADAM," THE HOUSEKEEPER said, opening the door to the drawing room, "is something required?"

"Ah, Mrs. Hendry," Meg said, looking up from the writing table where she sat. A minute earlier, she had tugged at the bell pull, knowing the housekeeper liked her to do that. Although Meg preferred less formality, Mrs. Hendry, keen to maintain a household fit for a baroness, insisted on doing things properly. The woman seemed to enjoy it, so Meg indulged her.

"Mrs. Hendry, please inform Mrs. Berry that I will shortly be ready to go down to the beach with her and Master Sean," Meg said. Mrs. Berry had enjoyed a few schoolroom duties with Sean whenever she and Meg visited Caransay.

"Very good, madam." Mrs. Hendry was as tall as any man, wide-shouldered and formidable. Her usual scowling expression was softened by pretty brown eyes and luxurious silver hair. Meg knew Mrs. Hendry had a good heart and wanted everything to be perfect in the household and for the lady and her family when they were there. Otherwise, she spent her time caring for a sickly husband who could no longer fish to support his family. Meg's heart went out to her, and she appreciated the woman's steadfast loyalty.

As Hendry closed the door, Meg went back to her task. She wrote a quick note to Mr. Charles Worth in Paris, thanking him for his offer to send an assistant to Edinburgh to fit her gown for the September soiree. Mr. Worth was eccentric and exacting, but his creations were so elegant and lovely that Meg had traveled to Paris a few times to be fitted for her wardrobe at his shop on the Rue de la Paix. Her companion Angela Shaw, who understood such matters, had advised it. The newest Worth gown promised to be exquisite as the others, judging from the sketches and fabric swatches he had sent.

The next note was from Guy Hamilton, who reported that the Northern Lighthouse Commission had notified the law firm of Dundas and Grant that Mr. Dougal Stewart did indeed have governmental authority to proceed with the lighthouse on Sgeir Caran. Stewart had the right to do the work. Guy assured Meg that they were still looking for a way to stop it, and he reminded her that the engineer was on Caransay and to avoid him.

Too late, she thought. The damage was done.

She answered Guy and sealed it, adding it to the envelopes for Norrie to post when next he ran the boat to Mull.

Then she penned a quick note to her cousin, Roderick Matheson, who had written saying he planned to visit her at Caransay, since he and his mother would visit the isle of Mull nearby.

Oh, dear, she thought. She did not want to see him. *The days here are rather dull, and you would not be entertained,* she wrote, hoping to discourage him. Truly, he would not enjoy the quiet routine of life on Caransay.

Glancing through the other letters, she found nothing from Dougal Stewart, and felt strangely disappointed. He had not replied to the law firm's last letter, to which she had added a postscript pleading for the welfare of the birds on the sea rock.

No doubt he was too busy drilling holes in Sgeir Caran to write letters. Through the open window, Meg could see an angle of the sea rock where even now his crew of men were wielding sledges and drills to alter—and deface, in her opinion—that ancient rock.

For a moment, she was strongly tempted to sail out there, announce her identity, and demand a halt to the construction.

Stewart would know the truth, or at least some of it, but it might save the birds, the rock, and the island. But that would not be easy. He had permission from the government, which could prevent what she wanted and bring Stewart what he wanted. And that made her bristle with indignation.

If her past with him became known, she risked genuine ruin, with repercussions that could bring harm and dismay to her family, her island, and her son's future. She knew that some on the mainland, including bankers on the board, might relish her downfall, as they had never supported the idea of a woman controlling the wealth of her grandfather, Lord Strathlin. If there was another heir, a male, they would be far happier.

That did not bother her as much as what might happen if Dougal Stewart learned the whole truth. He would have enough fuel for real fire—he could demand his son. She could not trust him.

Her stomach twisted, for she knew that one day she might have to tell him before the truth emerged, as truths would do.

She went to the window of her study to look through the window. The Great House was set on a high rise overlooking part of the island and a beautiful, calm, private bay. The expansive view included rocky beaches nudging sandy crescents and lacy waves; in another direction lay steep heathery hills and the wildflower machair sandwiched between the endless sky and ocean. Eastward lay the coast of Scotland; westward, Sgeir Caran was a glossy black wedge on an ocean that stretched on and on.

Sighing, she leaned her head in her hands, wondering what to do. Stewart could ruin the peace of this place, her life, her son's life.

"Mama!"

She turned, smiling as the door of the drawing room burst open and Sean ran toward her, a happy, excited boy. His thick blond hair, shaped by a bowl cut that needed a trim, fell over his eyes. Meg smiled, brushing back the golden locks to see his gray-green eyes. His father's eyes.

Her heart bounded, turned deep each time she saw him. Her love for this child overtook her again. She smiled, giving no hint of an almost desperate emotion. He deserved only her best and warmest, with no hint of her own fears.

"Berry says we can go to the beach!" Sean said, speaking Gaelic.

"English, dear," Meg reminded him.

He nodded. "I did my lessons and read in English to Berry, who says I did good—well."

"That is excellent, Sean," Meg said, and looked up as Mrs. Berry, buxom and bustling, entered the room. "It is a lovely day for a walk on the beach. Grandmother Thora and Mother Elga will meet us there with small Anna, and you can play together."

"Small Anna is too small. She does not like to play with me."

"She does. She just does not know as much as you do," Meg replied. "You can teach her."

"Master Sean did very well today in his lessons," Mrs. Berry said. "He's speaking nicely and reading well. His maths need work, and his handwriting too, but that will come. He made a fine drawing of a sea monster. So fantastic, it frightened me out of me shoes!" Mrs. Berry folded her hands over her black gown, brown eyes crinkling in a fond smile. Sean giggled.

"I like sea monsters!" Sean said.

"Och, I am so scared!" Elspeth Berry laughed. As a girl, Meg had stayed in her grandfather's castle sometimes, and had spent long winter weeks there too. Mrs. Berry, part of that household, had been kind and amusing, and Meg grew to love her. Now she felt a tug of gratitude. Wealth, family, friends, motherhood, and her full life were boons. But a dark secret had bruised her heart.

"My laddie," Meg told Sean, "bring a bucket to the beach so you can collect winkles and shells. If you find some, we can make drawings of them. And I will add drawings to the little journal I like to keep. And Berry would like to splash in the water, too. The day is perfect for a bathing costume if you would like to fetch yours, Berry."

"Och, I'd like that! And you, my dear, must remember to bring a bonnet and almond cream. You canna return to Edinburgh looking like the nut-brown maiden of the song! Your soiree is only weeks away."

"Of course. Sean, will you fetch your bucket and ask Mrs. Hendry if she has packed some things for the beach? She mentioned a luncheon basket." As she spoke, he bolted for the door.

"Walk, Master Sean!" Mrs. Berry said.

He slowed. "I hope she made cheese sand-witches. Come, Berry. Hurry!"

Alone again, Meg sighed.

Years ago, Mrs. Berry and young Mrs. Shaw knew that their new mistress, Lady Strathlin, had a child on the island. But they never asked much about the father, believing him to have been lost at sea in some tragedy. Nor did they question leaving Sean on Caransay. They understood that Meg wanted her son to have that freedom. Too soon schooling and social expectations would take some of that freedom and adventure away from the boy. Meg trusted them completely as part of her small circle of kin and friends.

But she felt her world crumbling around her. What if Dougal Robertson Stewart realized he was the lad's father? He might claim his child and expose their night on the rock. Few would doubt his paternity. Meg had been startled to see the strong resemblance between the man and his son.

One day the each-uisge *will return to Caransay for his bride and his son,* Elga had told her, *and take them to live with him deep in the sea.*

The sea kelpie, Meg thought, was less a threat than the lighthouse engineer just now.

DOUGAL LEFT SGEIR Caran to sail back to the island at midmorning, while Alan Clarke and two others laid a black powder charge in preparation for clearing the foundation pit. Intending to fetch some plans from his hut, Dougal intended to return before the fuses were lit.

He had promised the baroness and her lawyers in writing that the construction would not significantly alter the landscape, and he meant to keep his word. The beauty of the Caran Reef meant more to him than they could guess. He hoped to dedicate the lighthouse to all those whose lives had been taken by the reef, and he looked forward to the day when rays of light swept the waters to protect those who sailed past the reef.

He had one more errand on the island before he sailed back to the rock. Walking across the machair, he looked for the Great House, the baroness's home at Clachan Mor. The island was not large, seven miles long and just three wide at its broadest point. The manor house, he had discovered, was just two miles from the harbor that faced the rock. Following the previous night's rain, the sky was summer-blue and filled with puffy white clouds carried by brisk winds. As he walked, he heard the soothing rush of the waves and the constant call of seabirds.

Glancing at gulls wheeling overhead, he remembered that the baroness seemed to care very much about the island, the rock, and the birds. He could hardly blame her. Caransay had a strong, peaceful beauty, a balance of water, air, earth, rock, sunshine, and breeze. The magic of the place was also due to its earnest, handsome people and their fascinating legends. He would never deliberately disturb the beauty and serenity, no matter what the baroness thought.

Climbing a low slope, he saw a grand stone house on a heathery hill. A pathway led down to a small bay and a crescent of beach. He wished the baroness was home; he would knock on the door, preferring direct conversation to the delay of letters.

Strolling closer, he heard laughter and women's voices, and soon saw women and children. With them, hair a golden glow in the sunshine, Margaret MacNeill sat on a blanket on sand, legs curled under her skirt, a straw bonnet beside her. She held a book in her hands as she watched two other women. He recognized Norrie MacNeill's wife and elderly mother playing with a chubby baby and a young boy. A fourth woman waded in the water, her elaborate black swimming costume ballooning around her.

The little boy waved at Dougal, who lifted a hand in response, recognizing the bold wee lad who had climbed the headland the other day. The women turned, and Margaret stood quickly as Dougal crossed the beach toward them.

A breeze fluttered her hair and blew her skirt against her body, revealing long slender legs, graceful hips, taut body, firm breasts. Lust plunged through him. She was honey bright and lovely, too much so, and he wanted her with a surprising quake of spirit as well as body as he recalled powerful shared kisses—

But those were followed by a stinging slap. The awkward matter between them could not be addressed here. He paused.

She stared at him, then walked to the water's edge. Her attitude warned him to be cautious; it would need time to clear the matter between them.

The little fair-haired boy, dressed in short trousers and a linen shirt, padded barefoot over the sands toward him. "Hello! Are you Mr. Stoo-ar?" he called.

"Stewart, aye, lad. Who might you be, young sir?"

"Sean MacNeill, I am." He puffed out his chest and pointed to himself. "Norrie MacNeill is my great-grandfather, and he is a fisherman. I will be a fisherman someday too. Did you come here to catch a fish?" His English was good for such a small Hebridean. Dougal smiled. He was inexperienced with children, knowing few of them, but judged this one to be five or six years old, a fine, fair, healthy child with wide, very green eyes. A fearless creature, too, from the way he had swarmed up the rocky headland before Margaret had plucked him down.

Dougal bent to shake the boy's hand. "Pleased to meet you, Master MacNeill. I came out to find Clachan Mor, hoping to see the lady who lives there."

"I know her! She is my mother. She owns all this, every bit." He spread his arms wide.

Mother! So the baroness had a son here, perhaps a husband? He was puzzled, but it was not really his business to know. "Is she here on the island, then?" Dougal asked.

"She's here," Sean said. He gestured vaguely behind him with a closed fist, then opened his fingers to reveal a periwinkle. "I found a shell. See?"

"Very nice! The lady is here? Which one?" Dougal asked, surprised. The boy pointed toward the water, where Margaret MacNeill splashed barefoot in the surf, her back to them as she put on a straw hat against the sun. Norrie's wife and old mother were close to the water too, while the lady in the black costume walked farther out.

"The one in the water?"

"Aye," Sean answered, distracted as he poked in the sand with his fingers. "I have other winkles, too. I have a whole bucket of them. Crabs too. Some are alive," he added. "Come see."

"I would like that. Is your mother the lady with the big hat?"

Sean glanced around. "Oh, that's Berry."

Confused by that, Dougal heard Sean's name called as Thora MacNeill hurried forward to take the child by the hand. The elderly lady followed, moving fairly quickly given her age. Elga, he remembered.

"Sean, do not bother the gentleman," Thora said. "Greetings, Mr. Stewart."

"Good day, Mrs. MacNeill. And Mrs. MacNeill." He nodded to both older women. Elga, the very old one, tiny and wrinkled, stared at him intently.

"Mr. Stoo-ar," she said, her elderly voice shaking. "Left your great black rock, did you?"

"Aye. I will go back soon," he said, wondering why she ogled him so.

"And sure you will," Elga said.

"Come, Sean," Thora said. "We'll go down to the water the way you like."

"Will you carry me the way you would carry old *seanair* out to his boat when you were young?"

She laughed and bent so Sean could clamber onto her back. Then she hefted the child, grabbed his legs, and began to walk. Dougal smiled and strolled beside her.

"So that is how Hebridean women bring the fishermen out to the boats?" He had seen fishermen's wives bend to take their husbands on their backs, wading through the water to keep the men dry for the long day at sea. Thora was wide and strong, and he could well imagine her toting long, lanky Norrie out to his boat for a day's fishing.

"It is the way, aye," she said.

"Young Sean says he wants to be a fisherman someday."

"Och, the lady wants him to be educated. He already has a tutor, and he so small. He takes lessons at Clachan Mor when the lady visits."

"Is his mother the baroness?"

She set Sean down at the water's edge and tapped his bottom to send him on his way. "Did he say mother? Och, that lad! Just a kinswoman, she is." She shrugged.

Dougal glanced toward the lady in the swimming costume, who now floated in gentle waves, wide straw hat shading her face. Along the lacy edge of the surf, Margaret strolled, lifting her skirt hem to splash along. He was sure she was ignoring him in particular.

"Aye. She will hire tutors for his cousin, Baby Anna, when she is older," Thora said. Elga followed them as they walked, now carrying the plump fair-haired baby. "It is generous to educate them, but then they might want to leave the island when they are older. We have a good life on Caransay. The baroness made us safe here as her tenants, free from the land clearings that have gone on elsewhere. We make a good living from fish and lobster, and from the kelp and salt and birds' eggs we collect and trade to the mainland. We have nothing to worry about nowadays but the weather." She laughed.

"Wicked, our weather is," the old one said. "Have you been caught in a storm, Mr. Stoo-ar?"

"Sometimes," he answered.

"I knew it!" Elga said.

"It is truly a paradise, your island," he said.

"You like Caransay," Elga said. "You like the ocean."

"Oh, aye. When I was a child, I swam like a fish."

"I knew it!" Mother Elga grinned and shifted the baby on her hip.

Puzzled, Dougal held out his hands, thinking the child was a burden for so old a woman. "Shall I carry the little one for you?"

"You shall not have our babies!" Mother Elga snapped.

Startled, Dougal wondered if he had offended her by offering to take the weight of the baby off her old bones. Was there some island taboo against men holding children? Perhaps they had misunderstood his English.

The boy ran in and out of the lapping surf, going back and forth to Margaret. Out in the mild waves, the other lady's head, capped in a wide straw hat, bobbed on the surface like a buoy. "I hope the baroness will give me a little of her time," Dougal said.

"You must not disturb her!" Thora said. "She is a proper lady and does not want to be disturbed on her holiday."

"Ah," he said. "Perhaps I could call on her before she leaves the island."

Mother Elga stepped closer, studying his face, then poked at his arm with a stiff finger. "Man of the sea," she said. "Will you return?"

"She does not like visitors. Leave the lady be, sir," Thora said.

"Go back to your rock, water-man." Elga seemed to examine him, walking around him, carrying the baby. She stared at his booted feet, wet in the foamy surf. "Do you have webbed feet?"

Good lord, what a question. She was clearly eccentric in her old age. "No, madam. Perhaps you both could tell the lady that I will visit another time. Tell her I am not the ogre she believes."

Elga spoke in Gaelic, and Thora answered. Elga grinned. "Kelpie!" She pointed to him.

"I will try, sir," Thora said. Dougal wondered if she meant to help or hinder him.

He saw Margaret walking up the beach, calling to the boy. Behind her, the woman in black surged out of the water like a small glossy whale. He had not pictured Lady Strathlin to be quite so mature, Dougal thought tactfully.

"Turn away your eyes, sir," Elga said. "She is not wanting a man to see her now."

"Of course," he said, turning.

Thora snatched up a blanket from the sand and hastened to meet the woman in the bathing costume, wrapping her in the covering. They walked together, pausing to talk to Margaret, who stood watching Sean, playing in a rocky tidal pool. Margaret looked toward Dougal then.

His gaze met hers. She stilled, and he sensed a message there. Wary. Fearful. That explained her reluctance to come near him. He had to find time to speak with her before too long. Just now, he was preoccupied with Lady Strathlin's rejection—and his need to return to the rock soon.

"I had best go. Good day, madam," he told Elga. He reached out and touched touch the baby's soft pale curls. The little girl laughed, showing four tiny teeth.

Elga backed away as if he meant to snatch the baby. "Good day to you, water-man!"

He nodded and turned to go. Glancing again toward Margaret, he saw her pause to catch his gaze again. This time the look she sent was plaintive, full of longing and vulnerability. He felt the deep pull of it within.

On impulse, he whirled to walk toward her.

CHAPTER SIX

"BUT MY LADY," Mrs. Berry protested, "Thora says the man thinks I am Lady Strathlin!"

"Let it be for now, Berry, please," Meg entreated, while Thora hurried away to join Elga and the baby. "I will tell him the truth soon."

"But I canna talk to a man when I am in my swimming costume!"

"You need not speak with him. Go back into the water if you want." Meg glanced toward Dougal Stewart, crossing the sand toward them. "He will think you value your privacy."

Mrs. Berry nodded, looking relieved. Lifting her sodden bathing skirt, worn over knickerbockers and high laced slippers, she walked down to the water and stepped in again.

Meg smiled, relieved too. Let the man think the baroness was elusive. But soon she might have to reveal all to Mr. Stewart—if he revealed all to her. Nodding to herself, she waited for him.

But could she speak to him this time without feeling that deep wanting, that ache of loneliness—or without remembering betrayal?

Again she noticed how much the father resembled the son. Sean was blond like her, but his features and eye color, and his charming smile was like Stewart's. Someday Sean would have his father's build—wide shoulders, long, muscled legs, confident stride. The man had a natural physical beauty, and his son had inherited that.

She sighed. The man deserved to know his son. She must tell him the truth, and yet she feared what he might do once he knew.

Sean called out, holding up another shell for her to see. She picked up her leather-covered book and went toward him, bare heels sinking in damp sand.

"Lovely, Seanie," she said, as he dropped a conch shell into a bucket. She crouched beside him to study several tiny, nearly transparent fish in a little pool where the seawater spilled in among rocks. Sean stepped into the shallow pool, and Meg did too, laughing with him as the little fish tickled past their ankles.

"You must draw these wee fishies in your book!" Sean said.

"I will." She set the leather volume on a dry rock shelf.

"Hello, Mr. Stooar!" Sean called. Meg turned, heart slamming.

"Good day, sir," she said stiffly.

"Miss MacNeill, good day." He wore shirtsleeves and a dark brocade vest with dark trousers. He must have been working earlier, for he did not look as if he had come to visit.

"Look at my shells!" Sean set his wooden bucket on a rock as Dougal Stewart leaned forward. Sean lifted a slimy snail and plopped it into the man's palm. Stewart admired it and put it back gently. When Sean handed him a tiny crab, he laughed with the boy as it leaped to freedom and scuttled away down the beach.

"Go on, wee man, hurry back to your home and kin," Stewart said.

"Go home, all of you, back to your kinfolk!" Inspired, Sean tipped the bucket to set the rest of the tiny captured crabs free.

Dougal crouched beside the boy to watch them scurry away. "They will have tales to tell when they get home," he said, while Sean nodded wisely.

Meg watched, silent, touched more deeply than she wanted to admit. Stewart rinsed his hand in the little pool, water splashing over her bare feet where she stood ankle deep. Feeling his gaze on her toes, she stepped out quickly, dropping the hem of her skirt.

She could cover her feet now, but the man had seen all of her years ago; she wondered how much he remembered of the night she could not forget. Blushing, she caught his gray-green glance and saw awareness there. Ducking her face under the shade of her wide straw bonnet, she stepped away to sit on a rock, covering her limbs and feet with her gray skirt and petticoat.

"Did you come out here just to rescue crabs and snails, sir?"

"Not at first. But at least the wee crabs of Caransay will think kindly of me now."

She gave him a sour look from under the rim of her bonnet.

"I went for a stroll and saw you here by chance." He bent to pick up a small shell, which he offered to Sean, still splashing about in the little pool.

"Solving puzzles in your head again?" She tried to seem cool and detached, but seeing Dougal Stewart with Sean had made her catch her breath.

"There are a few puzzles I need to solve," Stewart replied quietly. He dropped another pretty shell into Sean's hand, then wiped a clump of sand from the boy's fingers.

That gesture melted her heart, but she could not surrender. She scowled instead.

"I see Lady Strathlin has arrived on Caransay," he said.

"Mmm." She tried to sound noncommittal, shading her eyes as she watched the waves.

"Now that the lady is here, perhaps I will be welcome to call on her." He looked toward Berry, paddling paddled contentedly in the gentle waves, her swimming costume ballooning around her. "I seem to have found her at a most inconvenient time."

Sean giggled. "You found Lady Strathlin! Here she is!"

"Sean," she said more sternly than she meant, "the hole you dug over there for your shells is filling with water as the tide comes in. You had better go save them."

Sean started off, then turned. "May I wade in the water, Mama?"

"Do not go in higher than your knees." She wished he had not called her that.

"Mama?" Stewart asked as the boy ran off.

She felt her cheeks burn. She had an honest nature, but life and society had forced her to keep secrets, and Dougal Stewart was putting that to the test. She hated that she must hide parts of her life, disliked feeling hollow and vulnerable when all she wanted was to tell Stewart the truth and clear the air.

But she could not trust him yet. She could not risk losing Sean.

"Anyone on Caransay will tell you that I lost my husband years back," she said.

His gaze was steady and curious and keen. The wind ruffled his rich brown-and-gilt hair. His smile was rueful. "I am sorry to hear that. Was he—ill? If I may ask."

"There was a storm. A great storm."

He hesitated at that, but then nodded, and as the moment passed, she breathed out in relief. "I am sorry. But it is good to have kin here, grandparents and parents too, I presume?"

"My parents are gone. My mother was from the mainland. She came to live here for love of my father. But she died of illness when I was eleven, just after my father died—out there." She nodded toward the sea. "I wonder if she died of a broken heart." Why had she shared so much?

"I am sorry," he murmured. "It is hard to lose parents at a young age, so close together."

She nodded, watching the waves. "A storm took him."

"Out on the reef?" he asked. "It happens a great deal here."

"Too much, aye. I thought Mother would take me back to the mainland to live with her father. He was—very well off, and was always displeased that his daughter had gone on a summer holiday to the Isles, fell in love with a fisherman, and stayed." She shrugged.

"I understand," he said.

"Do you mean falling in love out here?" Why had she said

that? She blushed furiously. Had he fallen in love out here—or had he pretended it for one night. She scowled.

"I mean losing someone on the reef. I lost my parents on the Caran reef too," he said. "Shipwreck."

"Oh!" She set a hand to her chest. "I had no idea. I am so sorry."

"A long time ago. What of Sean?" he asked.

"Sean?" she repeated, surprised. Alarmed. She had said too much, tried to cover it up, yet had opened herself to questions.

"Is he like his father?"

"Somewhat," she said, as a stiff breeze fluttered her hat brim and loosened spirals of her hair. She reached up just as Stewart grasped her hat brim. Their fingers brushed, lingered. He lowered his hand.

"Your hat was about to blow away. Golden as sunshine, your hair," he added.

Her knees went weak, and a yearning spun through her. She moved back. "That was rather too familiar, sir," she said primly.

"We were once," he murmured. "I thought—well. Forgive me."

She was not ready to forgive him and did not know if she ever would. Yet she liked the man, which she had not expected, should they ever meet again. Silent, she watched their son splash along the shore.

"Well, I must go," Stewart said then. "Please tell Lady Strathlin that I shall call on her soon."

"I will," Meg said.

He smiled, his eyes crinkling. "Tell her I look forward to meeting her."

She narrowed her eyes. Would he guess? How long before he worked it out, with his habit of walking about to think things through?

"And tell the lady she is welcome to come out to Sgeir Caran to see the work we are doing. Perhaps if she saw the site, she would understand the need for the project. And if you would care to visit the rock, as well, I would be more than glad of it."

She caught her breath at the very thought of standing on that rock with him again. "I will think about it."

"Fine. Good day, then." He smiled down at her, and that mischievous, gentle curve dissolved something deep inside her. Another barrier of resentment tested, weakened. He had a certain magic, this man, a natural ease of humor and intelligence that intrigued her. And his slightest touch, smallest smile cast a spell.

She bent to gather Sean's bucket and shells. Her notebook lay on the rock and she reached for it, but it slipped and fell at the engineer's feet. The pages fluttered open, revealing pages covered with sketches and notes.

He stooped to pick it up. "Yours?"

"Aye. Just a journal of the flora and fauna on the island."

"May I see?" He flipped through some of the pages, pausing to admire a study of a shell, a starfish, a bird.

"Fascinating," he commented. "You are a scientist and an artist, Miss MacNeill. These are very good. You like birds, I see." He glanced up at her, then back to the page. "And careful notations in English and Gaelic, too. Remarkable work."

"I have been keeping journals for years, making drawings and then looking up the names of shells, plants, birds, and such."

"You must have a fine library…where you live. The Isle of Mull, is it?"

"My grandfather collected an excellent library." She stopped, saying too much again.

He lifted a brow. "Your *seanair* has a library?"

"Not Norrie. My maternal grandfather."

"I see." He turned more pages. "Gannets, puffins, storm petrels…and eagles. I did not know there were so many birds on Sgeir Caran until I came here again."

Again. She looked out to sea. "Birds, aye. And on the island, an abundance of wildlife, plants, seaweed too. There are several varieties of kelp here."

"Kelp. Interesting." He closed the book.

"Kelp is essential to the island's wellbeing. It is gathered and dried for potash and exported to the mainland and elsewhere. It is used in manufacturing glass." She spoke too fast, wanting to rush past a mention of birds. She recalled the note she had sent him about protecting the seabirds.

"It provides a solid income on some islands, I know. I have some investments in the kelp industry, and in herring, too. Silver darlings bring a good income too," he explained. "Nicely done, Miss MacNeill." He handed the book to her.

"Every page is impressive. Will you begin another? Perhaps study birds—on the rock?"

She felt her cheeks burn. "I may do that. We—we all love the birds here. The wildlife and plant life on the island and the reef are precious, Mr. Stewart. Caransay is beautiful and idyllic. It is partly why we do not want a lighthouse so close by."

"Lady Strathlin agrees with you. No doubt she would love your wildlife journals."

"No doubt." Meg gave him a sidelong glance. He was too close to guessing. She would have to tell him, but could not bear it now. "You said you had to go. I assume you have work to do."

"I should go, aye. That lad is too far out," he said suddenly.

Looking toward Sean, still splashing and jumping in the water, she shaded her eyes with her hand. "Sean! Come back toward the shore!"

"He's an adventurous lad, that one."

"Too much so. Too likely to go swimming or climbing without a thought for safety."

He smiled. "He is young yet. But you keep close watch over him. Does he live on the island, or with you? I saw him with your grandparents—before you arrived, I think."

She felt struck to the heart. "He likes it here. I want him to have—family, at least while he is so young." Stepping away, she walked through a thin wash of water. Stewart went with her, his boots sinking hard prints beside her bare feet.

Seagulls dipped and fluttered overhead, and the long flow and pull of the waves was soothing. Even though she should be wary, she felt relaxed in his company. She could have strolled along the beach forever, surrounded by peace, with him.

"I was a daredevil child, like Sean," he mused, watching the boy splash in the shallows. "My parents did their best to keep me from getting hurt." He chuckled.

"You are still a daredevil to put up lighthouses in dangerous locations."

"There is that," he admitted. He laughed again, a deep, easy rumble.

"Your parents would have been proud of you," she ventured. "It is dangerous work."

A frown puckered his brow. "They never knew what I came to do. They would have worried about the risks, but I think they would be pleased that I do satisfying work."

"Satisfying?"

"What I do helps people. And that helps me, in its way. As for danger, that comes with it." A breeze fingered through his thick, wavy hair. "Including taking on dangerous baronesses."

"You are notorious on Caransay for that, sir."

"So I gather. I know you would like to see me leave, Miss MacNeill, for several reasons. But I will not be dissuaded from this. I have one quality that is both a virtue and a curse."

"What is that?" She stopped.

He stopped too, gazing down at her. "I never give up." His green eyes turned hard as Venetian glass. "I suggest you explain that to your baroness. And think on it yourself."

"Me?" Her voice wavered.

He leaned down. "Shall we discuss it here and now, or shall we wait for privacy?"

Heart slamming, his nearness sending a wave of longing and wariness through her, she held his gaze. "We will wait."

"Very well." He looked at the leather journal in her hands. "That is admirable work, Miss MacNeill. You could consider publishing your drawings one day. A guide to the beauty of the isles."

"I doubt anyone would be interested."

"On the contrary, Scotland is very popular with tourists. People are curious to know more about every part of it."

"This is just a hobby." She sighed, wanting to be honest with him in something. She had dreamed of publishing her journals someday, but she did not think them worthy enough. "Well," she said, "I did think they might make a handsome set of books someday." She shrugged.

"'*A Hebridean Journal,* by M. MacNeill,'" he suggested.

"A silly dream."

He touched her arm. A gentle thrill slipped through her. "Do not give up on that dream."

She took the journal, her fingers brushing his. "Thank you."

He smiled, warm with mischief and—affection, in a way. "My uncle wrote books—poetry, mostly. Romantic, lofty stuff, legends and tragedies, much beating of breasts and angst. Perhaps you have heard of him. Sir Hugh MacBride."

"I have read everything he wrote! How marvelous to have such genius in your family."

"Did your island school stretch to overblown romantic poetry?"

"We learned English and all subjects in the village school. We had math, reading, writing—including good and bad poetry."

"I stand corrected."

"And as a small girl, I spent winters on the mainland at my grandfather's house. He hired tutors for me. Literature, languages, sciences, and more mathematics than I cared to learn. I had music and drawing lessons, too."

"A mainland education as well. Impressive."

"I am not the fishwife you may think me, Mr. Stewart," she ended crisply.

He smiled, small and rueful. "I beg your pardon. I, too, had a tutor. I loved maths and sciences, and thought the rest rather deadly. I studied alongside my three sisters and our cousins."

"Three sisters!"

"My cousins and I got into some scrapes, perhaps to counter all the femininity around us." He grinned. "We made towers and fortresses out of books in the library. It did not earn approval."

A laugh bubbled up. "Now you still make towers!"

"I do." He looked chagrined. "And earn some disapproval."

"What about another island? Guga is nearby. Put your lighthouse on another sea rock."

"Sgeir Caran is the best suited for the placement as well as the construction."

"Commissioners and engineers do not consider traditions and legends or what all that means to these islanders."

"The legends are holding back progress. Should more people drown out there to save old traditions?" As he pointed toward the water, she saw the hot spark of his temper suddenly. "Tell your baroness the lighthouse will go up. If she wishes to discuss it, it must be in person. No more letters. I have had enough of her lawyers and their tricks."

"Tricks!" Meg leaned forward. "She would not trick anyone."

"Her solicitors are pulling every angle they can, but they do not seem to understand. Come here." He took her arm, firm and insistent. A fire of awareness exploded through her at his touch. He drew her toward the slope of a hill covered in purple heather. She glanced back to be sure her grandmothers were watching Sean, who skipped out of the water to kneel on the sand.

At the top of the hill, he stopped, and she looked out with him at an expansive view of the sea. Stewart pointed toward a low wedge-shaped rocky isle.

"Look there, Miss MacNeill. What do you see?"

"Another great rock, and the Isle of Guga in the distance just past it. Guga bears the scars of your quarry work still raw there. But it would be a good place for a lighthouse."

"What else?"

She looked. "Nothing else."

"Precisely. Our huts are gone."

"Ah." She remembered that one of his letters had detailed

losing those shelters to storms.

"The huts we built there were taken down by gales."

"Perhaps it was a sign for you to stop the work."

"I do not give up, Miss MacNeill," he reminded her. "Guga is an inhospitable rock amid a thorny patch of half-submerged rocks. My men took too many risks due to the weather and the treacherous seascape out there."

"Sgeir Caran is just a rock like Guga. Not—hospitable either." *Well, but for the little cave that proved a fine shelter one stormy night,* she thought wryly.

He paused, and she sensed he had the same thought. "It is— more accessible," he finally said. "We can build on it, and the visibility for passing ships is good. And though Lady Strathlin and her lawyers do not agree, the Lighthouse Commission has approved the work. This lighthouse goes up."

"Then why meet with the baroness? You no longer want her permission. You have gone past her in that."

"I want her cooperation. And we will need more stone, which can be quarried from Caransay's hills for quality and convenience."

"Quarry on Caransay? You cannot!"

"By government writ, I can. But I want Lady Strathlin's approval. Caransay stone is good granite, and it can also bring more work to the men of this island."

"They do not need the work. They have fishing and kelp industries. And the baroness helps the people of this island. She would insist that Caransay must not be ravaged or defaced. Its beauty has been undisturbed until now."

"With every project, I make certain my crews respect the integrity of the land. Modernization is not an evil force, Miss MacNeill."

"If improvement threatens to destroy eons of Nature's fine work, there is evil in it. I suggest you consider abandoning your project here."

"You are a fitting mouthpiece for the lady."

"I must get back to Sean." She whirled to walk down the slope, while he followed. The boy ran toward them.

"Did you see me in the water? I was swimming!" Sean puffed his chest proudly.

"You must never do that alone, you know that!" Meg spoke more sternly than she meant.

"Your mother is right, young sir," Stewart said. "Never go out alone. But if you like, I can teach you how to swim the foam, as they say in the old songs. You would be safer."

"No!" Meg said, alarmed suddenly. She touched Sean's hair. "No."

Stewart frowned. "He needs that skill, living on an island. I am glad to help."

Fear went through her like a warning bell. "You do not need to teach him. I will do it. We will do it. Good day, Mr. Stewart. Come, Sean. We must get back." She took the boy's hand.

"Mr. Stooar!" Sean turned as he was tugged along. "I will see you again, aye?"

"I hope so, Master Sean," he replied cordially.

Meg swept Sean along with her to join Thora and Elga, who sat with Anna a good length away. Meg glanced back to see Stewart strolling in the opposite direction.

I never give up, he had said.

Well, neither would she.

CHAPTER SEVEN

D AYS LATER, A soft, gentle rain fell on his hat and the shoulders of his dark coat as Dougal mounted the slate steps of the entrance to Clachan Mor. He lifted his hand and knocked. Though he hated wearing a hat, he had donned one out of politeness, and adjusted its brim. Damn, he had forgotten gloves. He shoved a hand in his pocket.

After a moment, the door opened to frame a tall, thin woman wearing a black dress, a white apron, and a lacy cap. She stared down her nose at him with dramatic effect, for she not only stood a step above him, she seemed as tall as he was—and he bested six feet without boots.

She was a gaunt, harsh harridan, despite the pretty silver curls beneath her little cap. Her eyes were steel as she looked him up and down. He felt like an untidy little boy. All the tutors he had ever known glared at him through this woman's cold stare.

"Good day, madam. Is Lady Strathlin at home?"

"Who is calling?" she intoned.

"Mr. Dougal Robertson Stewart, resident engineer on the Caran lighthouse, come to see Lady Strathlin."

She stared, implacable and disdainful. He did not doubt that the woman knew about his dispute with the baroness. Glimpsing movement in the shadows behind her, he saw the gleam of polished wood, brass, and crystal, rich Turkish carpets and brocaded furniture. An open doorway showed a library lined with books. Its pocket door slid shut. Was the lady home after all?

"Lady Strathlin is not home at present, sir. Your card?"

He searched his pockets. Cards were not required for setting powder charges or quarrying stone. In fact, he was lucky to have a decent coat and hat among his things. He found a crumpled card and presented it to her: *Dougal Robertson Stewart, Kinnaird Castle, Strathclyde, currently of Innish Bay, Caransay.*

She took it as if it was a rodent's tail. "Lady Strathlin will be informed that you called."

"I appreciate it. May I ask your name?"

"Mrs. Hendry, the housekeeper. I shall report that you were here."

"I am in your debt, Mrs. Hendry."

"Hmph. Good day, sir." The door closed with a solid click.

He stood on the step in the drizzling rain. Lady Strathlin would probably consider a crumpled card the height of bad manners and dismiss his visit. Looking up, he saw a curtain flutter and close in a window on the same level as the entrance.

Lady, come out, he wanted to say. *I am no threat.* Sighing in frustration, he walked away.

BIRDS FLUTTERED AWAY from the sea rock like ashes on the wind. Seated in a fishing boat watching the rock from a good distance away, Meg saw a flare of fire, a loud bellow, and a plume of smoke. Debris erupted from the massive rock, and chunks of stone flew and fell, churning the water below. Ripples spread out to bounce a dozen boats.

Cheers and applause rose from those gathered in several fishing boats. Norrie, hollering with the rest, lifted a hand in salute. In the next boat, Thora, Mother Elga, and Sean sat with Fergus at the oars; they all clapped and laughed too.

Not amused in the least, Meg sat silent in the bobbing bow. She had spent time and funds and sleepless nights hoping to prevent this very thing from happening. Sgeir Caran would never be the same. The blasts would forever alter the rock and mar its ancient soul.

She frowned, watching birds flee the rock in smoke-like spirals of dark and gray and white.

Another sky-high eruption brought more yelling and clapping from witnesses in boats scattered over the waves. Neglecting their lobster pots, nets, and chores, men, women, and children were thrilled to see the gigantic plumes of smoke and fire flaring into the bright sky.

Earlier, Dougal Stewart had come out in a rowboat with a few men, standing to shout out a request for the spectators to either leave the area or keep their boats well back for safety. The people had complied, but none had left. Most agreed the sight was a marvelous thing to behold.

Meg had witnessed pyrotechnics in Edinburgh, London, and Paris, and she had always enjoyed the sight too. But here and now, she felt only sadness. The beauty of the great rock of Sgeir Caran was a far finer sight than fireworks and explosions and falling chunks of rock.

A lull, then another flare and an enormous plume of smoke. Wild cheers rose from the audience. Meg scowled, wishing the rock could stay unchanged forever, a *sanctum sanctorum* for birds, and a monument to ancient legends. Sgeir Caran was a place of mystery and power, and she wanted it to stay that way.

But few things in life remained the same, she told herself. Wonderful dreams and ideals could flee with the dawn, that fast, and gone. She had learned that lesson too well.

LATER, WHILE OTHER boats left, Norrie rowed closer to Sgeir Caran. As they rounded the base of the rock, Meg saw a quay cut by some earlier blast to create a broad ledge of raw stone.

Looking up at the towering height, she saw that a ramp and steps had been cut into the side of a slope to form a pathway.

Alan Clarke, the foreman, waited for them on the quay. He caught the rope that Meg tossed, looped it through an iron ring, and assisted her out of the boat, his grip strong and sure. He reminded her of a golden bull, broad and heavily muscled, his blue eyes vivid under a shock of blond hair. Glancing around, she did not see Dougal Stewart among the men standing higher on the rock.

"Miss MacNeill, welcome," Alan Clarke said. "And Norrie! Stewart said if you came in closer, we should show you the progress up here." He led them toward the steps. "After the explosions, it's a bit of a mess on the roof, I'm afraid. Step carefully." Walking on the outer side of the rough steps, he ushered them carefully upward.

Reaching the high, flat plateau, Meg glanced around in dismay. Chaos had transformed the ancient sea rock. A huge crater dominated the center area, and broken rock and dressed stones were stacked around its edges while men clustered about working with hand tools and heavy equipment. Workbenches, tarpaulins, ropes, kegs, crates, and stone slabs were stacked or leaning wherever she looked. Two smiths worked at an outdoor forge, hammering iron rods bright with heat.

Crane arms attached to a steam engine projected over the edge of the rock, with ropes and a platform dangling down into the water. Workmen turned the cranks of two enormous spools, reeling heavy ropes and hoses down to men who were perched on an outcrop of rock on the cliff below, while others operated a gigantic bellows. At the edge, two men peered over the side and called back orders. The cacophony of shouts, hammering, and machinery was loud and incessant, overpowering the familiar shush and slap of waves and the cries of birds overhead.

Meg looked about, overwhelmed, not sure what to say. The wind whipped at her skirts, and she drew her plaid shawl around her shoulders. Despite the warm summer day, the damp, salty winds blowing over the top of the rock always seemed to cut cool and fast.

"We built a quay to be able to bring barges and boats close to the rock," Alan Clarke said, explaining what Meg and Norrie saw. "We can load equipment and materials more easily. The foundation pit for the structure is almost ready, and we've been transporting stones quarried on Guga, while hoping to quarry more stone from Caransay."

Meg watched masons work with sledges and chisels to refine the huge stones for a snug fit at the base of the tower to come. Several stones had been placed and were being slathered with mortar. The pit in the plateau looked huge to her. She frowned, silent.

"We use the cranes to haul stones and materials up here," Clarke said. "Most of the stones weigh a ton or more. We cannot bring oxen out here, of course, so we rely on cranes, pulleys, and roller bars. It took weeks just to get the equipment and supplies moved and secured in place. See there? We finally finished a wee shelter to house things, and for men to eat and sleep as needed."

The "wee shelter" was a tall structure set at the far end of the rock. Walls and roof of metal sheeting were set on pylons drilled into the rock.

"We built it to survive the weather," Clarke went on. "There is room for hammocks and a cookstove and such, should the weather turn bad."

"*Ach!*" Norrie said. "A good storm will sweep your wee house away just like that."

"He is right. Where is Mr. Stewart?" Meg asked.

Clarke pointed toward the crane and the huge spool. "He'll be up shortly."

"Up?" Meg asked.

"Come and see." Clarke motioned them to follow.

Hearing shouts from the cliff below, Meg assumed Dougal Stewart was down there. She knew he regularly rolled up his sleeves to work alongside his men. She had a grudging respect for that, but she still wanted the lighthouse to be built elsewhere.

But even if the crews left tomorrow, Sgeir Caran would never be the same. She clutched her plaid shawl, her body pelted and rocked by the wind at the top of the mound. From where she stood, she could see the deep crevice in the higher end of the rock that hid the shallow cave where she and Dougal had found shelter and solace on that wild and unforgettable night.

Her heartbeat quickened. She had come to Sgeir Caran often enough since then to make sketches, but each time, she felt a secret thrill and an undercurrent of regret. In that cave, her life had changed irrevocably, and her heart had been stolen—if she dared admit it.

Alan Clarke went near the cliff edge, and Meg noticed that an iron railing had been installed there. Men worked noisy cranks and pumps to guide the stout ropes and hoses that snaked over the edge. Clarke picked up a hose fitted with a funnel end and shouted into it, put it to his ear for a reply, and called out to the men on the machinery. They worked furiously to spool in the ropes and hoses.

He beckoned to Meg and Norrie, who approached the iron railing. "Careful! Dougal Stewart will be cross with me if you fall into the sea."

Leaning against the railing with a secure grip, she saw that the ropes and hoses dropped down into the sea. As the men steadily winched the ropes and hoses upward, the surface of the water began to bubble.

"Here he comes," Clarke said. A platform surged out of the sea, swaying on ropes.

A monstrous creature rode the planks, saturated, swollen, pale. The large head was a glass and metal sphere, and the creature's arms and paws were enormous. Water gushed from the beast to pour off the platform as the ropes drew it higher.

"What in the wee man is that!" Norrie exclaimed.

"A diver!" Meg gasped, astonished. She had seen them in engraved illustrations, but never in reality. "Is that Mr. Stewart?"

"Aye," Alan Clarke said. "He went doon the deep to examine the base of the rock."

"Huh!" Norrie said. "Mother Elga was right. He is a kelpie for certain."

Meg blinked at him. Norrie grinned and bent to watch the diver rise higher.

As the platform neared them, Meg glimpsed Stewart's lean, now-familiar face behind the glass porthole windows set in the brass helmet. Three valves, attached to the hoses, snaked toward the bellows. Two, she realized, pumped air into the helmet so he could breathe. The third hose ended in the funnel that Alan Clarke had used as a speaking tube.

Diving was common enough, she knew, in salvage and bridge and dock construction. The Matheson Bank had financed such ventures on Scotland's east coast, and she had contributed to the building fund. It made sense that divers would be necessary in a lighthouse project.

Necessary, she thought, and very dangerous. She pressed her lips together, concerned, suddenly wanting only to see that helmet off him, see him take a breath of fresh sea air.

"Please hurry," she murmured, while Norrie glanced at her.

The platform drew level with the cliff, and men grabbed the ropes to swing it inward to safety. Two held it steady while two others took Dougal by the arms to support him as he walked, his steps slow and cumbersome. The diving suit, helmet, boots, and weighted belt must be an enormous burden out of the water, she thought.

With help, he sat on a ledge of the rock while one man unscrewed the helmet and another man unbuckled the heavy gauntlets. When helmet and gauntlets were lifted away, Dougal emerged, reaching up to tousle his hair and rub his face. He coughed, took a drink of water from an offered ladle, and glanced up.

"Miss MacNeill! Welcome to Sgeir Caran."

Meg felt a wash of gratitude, sudden and clear, to see him

safe. "Greetings," she said.

Her cheeks heated in the cool sea breeze as she met his piercing green gaze. Seven years ago, he had risen out of the sea, and again today. Mother Elga's kelpie was real, in a sense.

"Hey there, Norrie," he was saying. "Give me a minute to get out of this gear."

"You will need more than a minute, laddie!" Norrie said with clear admiration.

Stewart looked at Alan Clarke. "Evan?"

Clarke gestured toward the edge. "They've got him now."

Then Meg saw that another platform being hoisted up with a second diver. He rose to the edge and stepped out with assistance, wearing a similar suit and gear. An array of tools lay on the platform beside him. With help, he stomped forward, dripping water, to sit near Dougal Stewart.

"Two kelpies!" Norrie said. "We need not worry about the kelpies of Sgeir Caran. They are here!" His eyes twinkled.

"Kelpies?" Stewart asked, wiping a hand over his damp brow. Meg frowned.

When the second diver's brass helmet was lifted away, he sucked in breaths, rubbing his face as Dougal had done. His hair was black and curling, his eyes a beautiful hazel, his cheeks lean and dusted with dark whiskers. He murmured to Dougal, and acknowledged Norrie and Meg with a polite nod as Stewart introduced them.

"Miss Margaret MacNeill and her grandfather, Norrie MacNeill of Caransay. This is Evan Mackenzie of Glencarron."

"Pleased leased to meet you. Welcome to the rock."

"Welcome out of the deep!" Norrie said. Meg could see her *seanair* was enjoying this.

"Mr. Mackenzie," Meg said. He looked familiar somehow. His answering smile transformed his lean and serious countenance. He looked at her so astutely that Meg wondered if he had met her as Lady Strathlin. She stepped back and turned to watch the sea and the birds flying around the rock.

When both divers were divested of their belts, heavy outer gear, and leaden boots, they stood as men, acting like they were knights in armor being assisted by their valets. Meg watched, noticing that they wore several layers of thick woolen underclothing beneath the suits, for the sea would be very cold. Evan Mackenzie was a bit taller than Dougal Stewart, slender and powerful. The two of them together were equally beautiful men. Meg caught her breath to see them.

Watching Dougal, she felt a ripple of feeling that was mysterious and exhilarating, some secret chemistry she could not deny, though she could pretend to feel nothing. Yet she thought of his appearance on the rock years ago, when he sat shivering and half nude beneath her plaid.

"Forgive me," Dougal said, nodding to her, "for being improperly dressed."

She shook her head. "Hardly improper here, where it's part of this world."

Norrie lifted a sleeve of the diving suit. "That's a heavy thing to wear! Needs a strong man to stand up in this. What keeps the water out?"

"It is made of rubber sandwiched with waxed canvas," Dougal explained. "Very heavy, aye, with lead boots and the belt and helmet and all, it is near impossible to wear on land. Underwater it's not bad at all. The boots and lead weights on the belt help sink us and keep us down, or we'd float back to the surface too fast and suffer for it."

"When a man goes doon the deep, he must come up slowly or he could die," Clarke said.

"It sounds quite dangerous," Meg said.

Dougal shrugged. "A bit."

Alan snorted. "Very dangerous, miss. That is why Dougal Stewart likes it so well. He has a reckless streak. But when he dives, he must go slow and careful. No mischief." He grinned at Dougal.

"Reckless, are you, sir?" Norrie asked.

"No more than others," Dougal answered. His gaze sought Meg's, a flash of green fire. She returned it directly, boldly.

"How deep can you go in that gear?" Norrie asked.

"A hundred eighty feet without difficulty. I've been down nearly two hundred, though it's not generally done."

"A man canna go deeper than that and live in this gear," Clarke said.

Meg looked at him. "Do you dive, too, Mr. Clarke?"

"I leave that to Stewart and Mackenzie."

She glanced at Evan Mackenzie. "You like the risk as well, then?"

He paused toweling his hair and smiled. "I suppose I do."

"Mackenzie has been doon the deep and climbs high mountains too," Clarke said.

"I prefer mountains. They tend to be drier," Mackenzie said, while Dougal laughed.

Now Norrie was examining the helmet. "The air comes in here?"

"Aye, through the hoses," Dougal said. "Clean air flows in here, and exhalations escape here." He pointed to the valves. "The other is a speaking tube."

"It takes a team for one man to go doon safely," Alan said.

"The men on the pumps are essential," Evan said. "Our lives are literally in their hands." He stood. "Dougal, I'll be in the office. I need to draw what we saw down there so we can assess the condition of the rock."

"Good. I will show our guests around the site." He took Meg's elbow to guide her with him, speaking to Norrie and Alan Clarke. The subtle thrill of his touch made her catch her breath as she went with him.

"Evan Mackenzie of Glencarron?" she asked Dougal. "Isn't that region held by the Earl of Kildonan?"

"Aye. He is the earl's heir and a viscount himself, though he does not generally use his title, not in the work he does as an engineer."

"I have heard of his father—the man is notorious. Much despised in the northern Highlands with a wretched reputation for cruelty in clearing his people from his lands to allow for more sheep."

"You are aware of that?"

"I remember my grandfather, my mother's father, speaking of it. He strongly disapproved."

Dougal nodded. "Evan wants nothing to do with his father. But lately the earl has been quite ill. When he is gone, Evan will be earl—though he does not want a single stick or a coin from his father. He feels it would be tainted. But he cares about the estate and the people of Kildonan and will do his best. Still, he prefers his work designing bridges and docks. A brilliant engineer and the last to admit it. We attended university together, along with my cousin, Aedan MacBride."

She nodded, having heard of MacBride's work in engineering along the byways of Scotland. Having financed some of that work herself, Meg knew more about bridge and road projects than Dougal Stewart could imagine.

"Mackenzie is an expert in the new science of geology. I asked him to advise on the state of the foundation rock here."

"Both of them are master divers," Alan Clarke said, walking beside them. "But there is none so skilled at Dougal Stewart. Born to the sea, he was. We can hardly keep the lad out of the water, though he has had his share of trouble in it."

"Trouble?" Meg asked.

Dougal shrugged. "Shipwrecked once or twice. If you will excuse me, Miss MacNeill, I should change into dry clothing. If you will wait, I can show you more of what we are doing here."

"Mr. Clarke showed us quite a bit. You may need to rest. Go on," she said. "We are fine. We know Sgeir Caran too."

He gave her a curious glance at that, then walked across the roof of the rock toward the strange iron barracks where Mackenzie had gone.

Shipwrecked. Meg narrowed her eyes. That was part of the

reason he was so adamant about his lighthouse. He had mentioned his parents losing their lives in the sea. Had he been involved in a shipwreck too?

He had promised they would talk, though she dreaded it. Now she was impatient for the chance to learn more about him. So far, he had surprised her at every turn.

Even so, she could not forgive him so easily for the past.

CHAPTER EIGHT

DOUGAL NOTICED THE relieved glance Meg gave him upon his return, as if she hoped for a rescue from Alan, who was going on about the mathematics of lighthouse design. Apparently, she had heard enough about the calculated strength of the tower's height and mass, factored to the pounds-per-square-inch impact of a gale-force wave.

"Here is Mr. Stewart," Clarke said. "He can answer some questions for you as well."

"I can. Alan, you are needed over by the platform." As Clarke left, Dougal stood near Margaret MacNeill. He had heard others call her Meg, which suited the honesty of her approach—and her earthy beauty—very well.

With a wry glint in her aqua-blue eyes, she regarded him. "I wonder what it is truly like on the bottom of the sea."

"Rather magical. It is a different realm—peaceful, beautiful, fantastical. When the light comes clear through the water, the coral formations and waving fields of kelp are brightly colored. And the variety of fish and sea creatures is astonishing. But it is exceedingly cold, so we must wear several layers under the suits. It's noisier than you might imagine down there," he added, smiling, "with the sound of the waves and the scrape of coral in the current and so on knocking about."

"It sounds fascinating and so challenging."

"Nearly anyone could try it with the right equipment and

instruction, and a good crew up top to see to things. It's quite enjoyable. If the Otherworld exists," he added, "it could hardly be more incredible than the depths of the sea."

"There is a legendary place called Land-Under-Waves, said to be very beautiful. *Tir fo Thuinn*," she translated. "It is said to lie somewhere in the deepest waters of the Hebrides. Its inhabitants walk among us in human form, they say, so they will not be recognized as sea fairies, selkies, kelpies, and the like."

"Interesting." He inclined his head, smiled at her.

"What were you doing down there under the waves?" Norrie asked, joining them.

"Making sure the explosions did not damage the rock bed. A crack could worsen once the weight of the lighthouse tower is in place." Norrie nodded and turned to examine more equipment.

Meg looked up at Dougal. "Did you find cracks?"

"Nothing unusual at the base of the rock," he murmured so low only she could hear, "though I found a sea fairy waiting on the rock when I came up." He smiled, seeing her blink at that. He felt a warm rush of affection for her then, grateful to know she was real after all. But it remained for him to explain and apologize. How the devil could he explain to her that he had thought her some magical creature come to take a drowned sailor to the Otherworld?

"Did you," she said sourly.

He wanted to move past that quickly. "The base of the rock is enormous, but we will take another look or two. So far, all looks stable."

"I wish I could go down there to see what it is like," she said.

"You, a wee lass!" Turning, Norrie gawked at her. "You would be drowned and swept away."

"Or crushed by the weight of the gear," Dougal drawled.

"I am a strong swimmer, and have done a fair bit of sea diving with my cousins when we were younger. We used to dive off this very rock. Surely remember, *Seanair*."

"A different thing than going far down in heavy gear,"

Dougal said. "Not easy for a lass. It takes muscle and strength."

"This lass thinks all the world is open to her," Norrie said with a wink. "And it is. If she wants it, she will get it."

Seeing Meg scowl at her grandfather, Dougal thought the exchange rather odd.

"Though it could be possible," Dougal went on. "You would need good gear and a lot of courage. But I would guess you have that."

"Ach," Norrie drawled. "That wee bit lass will do whatever she has the mind to do."

"Though there are sea creatures that could carry off a wee bit of a lass," Dougal said.

She looked at him sharply. "Kelpies?"

"Basking sharks." What was this family's fascination with kelpies?

"Ach, a basker wouldna take her," Norrie said. "A kelpie, now—she had best watch out, especially on Sgeir Caran."

"We should go, *Seanair*," she said firmly, stepping away. "Mr. Stewart is too busy to entertain visitors for long."

Without reply, Dougal held her gaze for a long moment until she looked away.

"Before we go," Norrie said, "I want to hear more about the lighthouse. I canna say we will get back here again soon, with all this going on."

Dougal nodded, and led them toward the crater. "We blasted this cavity—carefully, mind you—so that it measures eighty feet wide and three feet deep." As he spoke, men swept away debris while others wielded hammers and chisels to trim the huge blocks of granite that would become the building's foundation.

"The walls will be nearly nine feet thick at the base to hold fast against waves and storms," Dougal went on. "We calculate the force of a strong gale against the mass and tonnage of the stone blocks. The curved base will further strengthen the structure." He gestured wide. "Everything is meticulously planned, measured, and fitted so the stones create a tight drum.

The design is like a round medieval tower. Even the heaviest waves wash and bounce off curved walls, just as arrows and cannon would bounce off round towers."

"Ah. How tall will the thing be?" Norrie asked.

"One hundred eight feet to the roof, with a light beam that can be seen for nearly twenty miles on clear nights. Less so in fog and rain, but far enough to make a difference in bad weather. And we will install a bell to sound a warning in heavy fog. It should be finished by next summer."

"Best hope that dirty weather willna take down your great tower," Norrie said. "The storms on this reef are the fiercest you might see."

"I know." Dougal darted a glance toward Meg. He sensed her nearness like a flame.

She was quiet, but her cheeks burned pink, as if she had windburn or sunburn. But he knew she reacted to the remark about storms on the rock.

He had to make that night up to her somehow. This time, he wanted to woo and win her, if she would allow it. The feeling rang inside him like a deep bell. He knew, suddenly and surely, what he wanted. Gazing at Meg MacNeill, he knew that in some hidden place in his heart, he had loved this girl for years, even when he was uncertain if she were real or imagined.

And she was very real, and very attractive, and he very much owed her. An intense craving quaked through him, a mingling of remorse and guilt and a powerful desire to make this right.

He had hurt her before—he realized that now. And his lighthouse threatened what she cherished. He knew that, too. His behavior years ago was inexcusable, and was an obligation of marriage. She had mentioned a husband whom she had lost early on. If she was free to marry, Dougal had a chance to offer her the security she deserved for herself and her son. If she agreed to accept Dougal after so long, he would be glad to take in another man's son.

Then he shook his head in surprise. He had always avoided

marriage, vastly preferring the freedom and danger of his demanding work over settling into domestic quietude.

"Mr. Stewart," she said then, bringing him around. "My grandfather asked about the birds."

"Ah, the birds," he said, coming back from his thoughts. He explained that he would ensure that the birds could still lay claim to more than half the great rock.

As Norrie and Meg MacNeill walked ahead of him to look at another section of the rock, Dougal followed. He had work to do, but he did not want them to leave yet. He did not want *her* to leave.

Watching her, he had a sudden memory, a strong feeling, that years ago he had married this girl in one sense. A pledge, a promise—and a little threaded ring. He had kept it safe. Did she still have hers? Had any of that truly happened?

As he stood beside her in the damp, salty air, with the seabirds reeling and calling overhead and the blue-diamond glint of the ocean sparkling bright on the water, he knew, fiercely, keenly, that he wanted to marry Margaret MacNeill. The desire and the need had been there all along, yet he suddenly became aware of it. Perhaps that was why he had never pursued marriage to another.

Despite a calm wind and a soft-rippled sea, he felt as if a gale had knocked him to his knees.

SITTING ON A ledge of stone on the far side of the rock, Meg sketched in her leather journal and waited for Norrie. Her grandfather was so fascinated by the work of building the lighthouse as well as the diving equipment, that he continued to stroll the site asking questions of the laborers, many of whom were local men who knew the reef and understood the moods of the sea and the weather here. Dougal Stewart had gone to supervise some task, and though she was ready to return to the island, Meg was content to wait. She was glad of a little time alone, a respite of peace watching the changeable clouds, listening to the shush of the sea and the creel and call of birds.

She sketched quickly as a pair of gannets returned to a nest perched on a ledge on the tall stack rock that thrust out of the water near Sgeir Caran. Turning the page, she began another sketch, but paused as she noticed a deep crevice beyond a cluster of rocks. The little cave she and Dougal had shared was just there.

A shiver went through her, then an ache of longing so fierce that she sank her face into her hand and shook her head a little. If only she had known who he was—if only he had stayed, life would have been so different. So good, dare she imagine it.

"Miss MacNeill?" He was there beside her suddenly, though she had not heard him approach. "Meg—are you well? Is the sun too strong here?"

She looked up. "I am fine," she said tersely. "Is my grandfather ready to go?"

"Not yet. He is having a fine time. But if you want to leave, I am sure you could convince him."

"Soon. He really is interested and enjoying the visit."

"And you?" He tipped his head.

"Very interesting," she said. "I did not expect some of it. The monster from the deep, for one thing."

He chuckled softly, nodded. She wondered if he caught the reference to their own meeting. "Well then. I see you found more birds to draw in your journal. They have not all left."

"Not yet," she said, closing the journal and getting to her feet. Dougal offered his hand in assistance. Hesitating, she accepted it, feeling again that thrill of comfort in his touch. Suddenly, she withdrew her hand and quickly stood. She'd made a decision.

"Mr. Stewart, let me show you something. This way."

Runnels of water over ages had worn an inclined pathway in the stone, and Meg took the slope upward, Dougal following, both stepping carefully on the damp rock.

To one side was the entrance of their little cave. She saw him glance there, then at her. She ignored that and turned to face the sea, pointing outward.

"Look there." On innumerable ledges and protrusions in the rock, hundreds of birds clustered, most of them white with black markings. "Gannets. They come here every year to nest. Thousands of them, raising their young where they can find shelter—" *From storms,* she nearly said, too aware of how close they stood to the cave that had sheltered them.

"Shelter from storms, aye," he said quietly.

She drew a breath and went on. "Shearwaters nest on the rock too, and others. Over there, under that outcrop—do you see the little dark bird on its nest?" Its feathering gleamed in the sunlight. "A shy little petrel. They are pretty little birds that skim close to the water."

"They make their nests beneath overhanging rocks where they cannot be seen," he said.

He all but quoted from Lady Strathlin's indignant letter about the birds. "Puffins nest here too," she went on quickly. "They prefer the other end of the rock, where there is more consistent sunlight. And seals gather to sun themselves there"—she pointed downward—"where there is a stretch of pebbly sand."

"Do you see whales and the like here?" He was watching the shimmering, moving sea.

"Sometimes. We also see dolphins and occasionally sharks. The dolphins flee if the sharks come around, though they are usually basking sharks, and not harmful."

"You must have come here often to know so much about this rock." There was so much unsaid in his words that she caught her breath, looked away.

"Most of my life," she said quietly. "Now I come out here as often as I can." She lifted her face to the wind that was fresh on her cheeks and ruffled her hair. "A peaceful place in its way. And a worthy habitat for many creatures.

"I do appreciate that, though you think I do not."

She slanted a sideways glance at him. If he realized she shared Lady Strathlin's opinions, he was too close to guessing the connection.

"I promise we will not disturb the bird colonies or the seals or anything else here. We will just make room for the lighthouse and be on our way."

"How long might that take?" Still, she did not look his way.

"Longer than you'd like, I suspect. It will take time. I have supervised putting up lighthouses elsewhere, and I must say the wildlife did not seem bothered except during construction. Later they came back, even with an enormous lighthouse standing there. Does that reassure you?"

"Some," she admitted.

"Take that message to Lady Strathlin, though I suspect she will never trust me. But I tell you, Meg MacNeill—I am sincere in this. People have died on this reef. I cannot forget that."

"Nor can I, Mr. Stewart," she said stiffly. "Another thing about this place you should know. Look up there." She indicated the tall stack rock thrusting out of the water, not far from the cliff edge where they stood. "That is Creig nan Iolair."

"Craig nan *yoolur*," he repeated. "What does it mean?"

"Eagle Rock."

"Ah. I heard that eagles sometimes nest around here."

She had included that in the letter too. "They have built aeries up there for generations. Golden eagles go soaring around this rock, and sea eagles nest up there too. The white-tailed *iolair mhar*, the rarest of eagles in Scotland."

"So you worry that the lighthouse will keep the eagles away as well."

"The eagles know they are safe here."

"And I promise you they will always be safe," he said firmly.

"But all the noise and activity in this peaceful sanctuary could disturb them."

"Once the lighthouse is done, the rock will be quiet again, with just one or two keepers in residence. And boats have always gone back and forth. Peace will reign again. I promise—"

"You cannot promise!" she burst out. Thoughts of birds and lighthouses fell away as the hurt of years overtook her. "You cannot promise me anything, Dougal Stewart!"

She turned to walk away, but his hand lashed out to take her arm and pull her back. "Meg," he said gruffly. He turned her swiftly, brought her close, so that she felt his heat, felt the subtle tug between his body and hers, and the answering whirl in her belly.

She pushed at him, aware that they were out of sight of others here. "Leave me be!"

His hands closed around her wrist and he held her arm against his chest. He lowered his face toward hers as if he would kiss her. Wanting to resist, she also craved his touch, craved something different, something better and stronger between them.

He only rested his brow on hers. "Meg MacNeill, be still and hear me out."

"What," she said petulantly, not giving in, though she felt herself soften. Her knees went soft beneath her, and she closed her eyes—but she was still ready to fight in defense of all the hurt, all the years of wondering, resenting, and longing.

"Let go," she gasped. "I do not want to talk to you."

"Just listen," he growled, keeping her in place.

"You have nothing to say that I want to hear, and you cannot hold me against my will."

"I thought to prevent you from slapping me again."

"Why, are you going to kiss me?"

"If you like," he murmured, his brow pressed to hers, his breath upon her cheek. She both longed for and resisted a kiss from him. His lips brushed her cheek. Her legs felt so weak that she needed his support.

He drew back. "I just want to talk."

"We have nothing to say."

"I owe you an apology."

"Too late for that."

"Allow me to apologize for the kiss when we were on the machair. It was not the time."

"It was not." She crabbed her fingers on his shirt, grabbing, wanting to push him, run, never look back. Yet even more, she wanted to stay, listen, know more about that night. His fingers were strong on her wrist, and he slipped his free hand to the small of her back.

"Let me speak before you claw me to bits."

She tightened her fingers, pressed skin through cloth. "Seven years," she hissed. "You come back here after seven years and want to apologize!"

"Seven years, I searched for you, lass. I did not think I could find you. And now you reject me soundly. Fair enough. I understand." His tone was as wry as it was gentle.

"Did you expect a happy reunion?" She wished she had a hand free to slap him again—even though part of her wanted him to pull her into his arms, kiss away the hurt, help dissolve the bitterness. She wanted to be free of resentment. But she did not know how to express that.

"Once I saw you and realized who you were, I wanted to make up for what I had done. I thought you did not remember me. So I hoped a kiss would remind you. I suppose it was ill done."

"I suppose," she said. "Let me go. I am not going to slap you."

He dropped his hands away, though he still stood close. "As for that night, I do not know why you were there, or quite what happened. My memory of it is very dim."

"I remember it," she said frostily. Truthfully, she had felt foggy that night too, having taken the potion Mother Elga had prepared.

He pursed his mouth, nodded. "That was a fearsome storm, and in the dark and the rain, I was not sure—I thought—" He paused. "You will think me mad if I tell you."

"I thought you were a brutal cad." She stepped back. "You

should leave this rock and the island. And me."

"I will stay until the work is done. But I will leave you be, if that is what you want. First, please hear me out." He pulled her back gently but firmly. "This is not pleasant thing to revisit, I know, but best we get through it and be done. What, exactly, did I do?"

"You do not know?"

"I have an idea." He watched her steadily. "It is not clear."

Her recollection had never been all that clear either. But she knew one thing for certain. "You had your way with me and left me in a boorish manner." She leaned toward him, anger rising again, fueled by years.

"Left you! My dear lass, you are the one left me. I awoke to find you gone."

"I was still there. I saw the boat that you took. I saw men come to fetch you, no doubt the men who left you there to have your fun. You had a scheme."

His brow puckered. "Scheme! Just what have you believed all this time?"

Meg saw true bewilderment in his eyes. He held her wrist, and she did not fight that. "I know what I saw. Men came to get you. So they must have left you on the rock the night before, guessing I might be there. The storm stranded us, and we stayed. And you left at dawn. I was in the boat with *Seanair*. He had come to fetch me."

"I had no idea that I would end up on that rock. I swear to you. Those were fishermen who saw me standing there. I thought you had gone."

"I watched you and saw that I had been used. Betrayed."

He swore softly, shook his head. "Not the case. But—why were you there?"

"My grandmothers sent me there for the night. And you know exactly why. It is the reason you came there."

He shook his head. "You are wrong."

"You expect me to believe your tale of fishermen?"

"More than that. A tale of shipwreck."

She huffed in disbelief and shook her head. Hearing voices calling out, she turned to see Alan Clarke and Norrie standing on another rise in the rock.

He looked up too. "They will find us. Come here." Tugging on her wrist, he led her into the shadows and down a bit, where the sea swirled in little pools and eddies near the dark arch of the narrow cave. He ducked inside with her, though she held back at first—then went with him.

"Remember this place?" he asked.

"I do. I thought you could not recall anything."

"Some things from that night, aye. Other moments are gone." Taking her by the shoulders, he turned her swiftly, pressing her back against the rock wall, his hands resting on her shoulders.

Warily, she watched him, her heart pounding hard now that they stood inside this place. Beyond the entrance, rather than a raging storm, she heard the cadence of the waves, and heard men's voices. Then the crunch of stones as Alan and Norrie came looking for them.

"We must go," she insisted. "They will think we fell into the sea—"

"Wait a moment." He bent close, his breath touching her lips. Resistance fell away from her like a lead weight and she grabbed his hard-muscled arms, seeking support even as she tilted her head to meet him as his lips gently covered hers.

Allowing that kiss, she felt a shift, as if her innermost heart opened, wanting to let him into her life, go where this could lead. One kiss and the next, tender and slow, began to fill the well heart that had been empty for too long. She caught back a sob, desperately wishing time could slip back to change their very first meeting, remake it, redesign it for happiness. Then she thought of her son, born of passion in a wild storm. He was the joy of her life, and she would protect him.

And Dougal Stewart must not discover the truth about the boy.

In that moment, his kisses transformed, deep and urgent as he pulled her hard into his embrace. Doubt cautioned her to pull back, but she paid no heed, for as his kisses built, an intense and willing need rose in her. His touch, his very presence—he was here and words could wait. Just a man, she knew that now, but he had an irresistible magic, like a sea wave carrying her along.

CHAPTER NINE

H E HAD NOT meant to kiss her, certainly not like this, his fingers sinking into her golden thicket of curls, his heart racing, fervent need flaring in him. He wanted her, needed her, had for years, and was only realizing the strength of it. He felt her heart racing too, her breath quickening as she circled her arms around his neck, pressed against him with a little whimper of need. Now he fought an overwhelming urge—this place, this woman had a hold over him that was a form of irresistible magic. He had wanted to show her that he was not the heartless, selfish fool she thought. He was not succeeding.

Stop. He pulled back, struggled for breath, sought to find reason again. But she moaned and sank against him, pulling him toward her, seeking his lips. She fitted so perfectly to him, her mouth so willing on his, her fingers tender on his jaw now, and threading through his hair.

One kiss, just one more, yet it became another, a breathless, wild chain of kisses, though he swore to himself this would be the last, that would be the last. She was so willing, so passionate, leaning in his arms like a reeling drunk. He needed to stop this.

But he slipped his hands down her back, shaped her hips, pressed her against him. Hardening like fire and stone, he could not hide his need from her.

The first time they had met on this very rock, she had been his salvation, and he had been hers. Now he wanted to keep her safe—from him in the moment.

He pulled back. Beyond the cave, no storm whipped the sea to wildness this time. There was sunshine and heat, glittering waves, sweet breezes. And friends calling out for them.

That sound was the stinging slap he needed.

"God, Meg," he said hoarsely, taking her by the shoulders to put space between his body and hers, his breath heaving. Meg stood with eyes closed, chest rising, falling. He could feel her trembling. "You must think me a beast," he said raggedly.

Her eyes opened, and in that beautiful blue-green, he saw tears shining. She raised a shaking finger to her lips, then touched his lower lip.

"Hush. It was not only you wanting this, then or now. Not just you."

"Dougal!"

"Meg!"

Then came the crunch of boots over stone. His heart slammed. He had so much to say, wanting to erase the hurt he had done her, wanting to begin again, if such were possible.

"Listen, quickly," he whispered, framing her face in his hands. "I am so sorry." He kissed her lightly, while she gave a breathy sob against his mouth. "I never meant to hurt you. That night, I had no scheme. I just wanted to survive. If I had known who you were, where to find you, I would have come for you—"

Small kisses as he spoke, for she was magic to him, a lure for his soul, and now that he had found her, he could not risk losing her again. Their names were called again, just outside.

"We must go," she whispered.

Lifting his hands, he stepped back, more air between them. "I wanted to find you. I tried. But I did not find you, and I did not expect to, because I thought—" He shook his head. It seemed even more ridiculous now.

"What?" Her eyes were glossed in tears, her lips rouged and lush from kisses.

"I thought you were not real. That I dreamed you. My

head—I took a knock to the head when my boat went over. I was drunk, out on the water when I should not have been." The truth out, he shrugged, ashamed to admit.

She stared. Then she laughed. "Drunk! And you thought me not real?" She laughed again, soft and quiet, shaking her head, looking away.

"I thought you were magic. But why were you—" He stopped as Alan and Norrie called again. "There is no time. Can you forgive me?" He smoothed fallen curls from her brow.

"I—I do not know. And I should tell—never mind. No time." She frowned as if something troubled her. She stepped away.

"Seanair!" she called. "We are just here. Coming!"

"DIRTY WEATHER ON the way," Norrie said, glancing in the distance, pulling on the oars as he rowed toward shore. Alan Clarke, wielding a second set of oars, murmured agreement. Norrie's large fishing boat was full that afternoon, Meg thought, turning to look at Dougal Stewart, seated across from her beside Evan Mackenzie, while she sat on a short crossbench in the bow between stacked ropes, folded nets at her feet.

To the west over the water, fast-moving dark clouds swallowed the sunlight and promised wind and rain before long. The boat plowed through waters gone rough and opaque, and Meg drew her plaid shawl closer.

Dougal examined the sky too. "As soon as the weather began to turn, I told the crew to leave the rock and cross over now rather than later," he said. "We never know how large a storm will be by the time it hits that rock." He sent a grim glance toward Meg, who looked away.

"There's the crew, just leaving," Evan said, pointing.

Waves slapped the sides of the boat, and Meg brushed droplets from her skirt. Then she noticed a huge fin thrusting through the water, gliding between their boat and the harbor.

"A basking shark!" She pointed as the men turned to look. Then she noticed other sharks skimming below the surface of the water, three or four in all, their bodies easily as long as the boat.

"*Ach,* baskers are not much to worry about," Norrie said. "They have huge maws and tails as tall as my granddaughter, but no teeth to speak of. They eat fish and plankton, not people. Though they are known to carry off a wee man now and then if they're feeling testy."

"But they let them go, from what is said," Meg replied. "They do not usually come this close to the harbor. But oh, they are huge, so magnificent!"

"Ugly beasts, though," Alan said.

Reaching into the pocket of her skirt, Meg drew out her leather notebook and pencil, opened to a blank page, and began sketching, though the bouncing ride sometimes jerked the pencil's path.

"She will capture that ugly beast on paper," Dougal said.

"Look over there," Mackenzie murmured as the boat bumped over the agitated waves. "That wee lad's a bit small to be up on the headland on his own."

"Sean! What the devil is he doing there?" Dougal asked.

"Sean?" Meg whirled to see a small boy standing on the crest of the headland, waving his arms in excitement as he saw their boat sailing toward the harbor. "He loves to climb up there with the older children. But where are the others? And where is his grandmother? She would never let him go so high. Sean!" she called. "Get down from there!" But her words were lost in the wind.

"Thora's on the beach," Norrie said. "She's going up there now. No need to fret."

Meg sighed in relief. But Thora went slowly up the rock, too slowly for comfort as Meg watched. The climb was not difficult, but it was steep, and though Thora was strong, she had years on her. Sean jumped about, waving wildly at the boat, enjoying his freedom while it lasted.

Raising her arms, Meg called again. "Sean! Go back!"

He leaped, skipped, flapped his arms happily. Thora was nearer the top now, beckoning frantically. Sean did not see her, running back and forth on the crusty rock. Gasping, Meg half stood in the boat.

Dougal reached out and took her arm to steady her. "He'll be fine," he said. "Thora is nearly there."

As his grandmother reached the top and hurried toward him, Sean whirled and stumbled. Falling backwards, he plummeted over the edge and down, his small form pale against the massive dark headland.

Meg screamed, stood, and Dougal stood too, as the boat rocked beneath them. Pushing Meg to sit, he tore off his coat and kicked off his boots.

"Stay here," he growled, and slipped into the water to disappear under the dark waves.

"Dougal!" she called, leaning to the side.

Mackenzie took her arm to balance her. "Careful. He will get the boy. Do you know the lad?"

"My son," she said hoarsely. Mackenzie murmured something and sat her beside him, putting an arm around her shoulders.

Norrie gave a swift order, and Alan lunged to grab the rudder as they angled the boat toward the headland. Then Mackenzie took the rudder while Alan took up the oars again as the boat went swiftly through the rolling waves.

Ahead, Meg saw Dougal cut through the water with strong, even arm strokes. Meg leaned to the side and saw Sean's arms and head bobbing in the water. She cried out, fearing Dougal might not reach the boy in time, even as the man tore through the water. Seeing her son's head disappear under the waves, she stood to grab the boat's rim, ready to plunge in herself.

Mackenzie tugged her backward. "Stay here! Dougal will get him."

Hearing shouts, she saw that men had launched a boat into the surf from the harbor beach, while a small crowd gathered on the sand. From the direction of Sgeir Caran, the workmen sailing behind them rowed harder now that the men saw what was happening.

Then Meg saw the shark fins turning to glide toward the splashing commotion of the swimmer and the floundering boy. She screamed out, while Mackenzie kept a steadying arm around her shoulders to prevent her from jumping into the water herself.

Norrie growled a command and Evan bent to grab a coiled rope, standing to position himself to toss it toward Dougal as they drew nearer.

The boy bobbed up again, arms flailing, then went under. Dougal was nearly there now, arrowing forward relentlessly. Pressing her hands to her mouth, Meg whispered a prayer under her breath, repeating it, heart pounding.

The basking sharks were there, too, a circling menace of enormous size. Meg cried out again, even as logic told her the beasts tended to be uninterested in humans. But a fin sliced through the water between Dougal and Sean, creating a wake that took Dougal up—and took the boy up too, which gave him a chance to breathe and reach for the man swimming closer. Dougal cleared just over the animal's tail, brushed by it. Struggling, Sean thrashed, nearly within reach.

Then Mackenzie slipped out of his coat, ready to dive into the water. They were within yards of the man and the boy now as the boat rocked closer on high, sloppy waves.

Another of the huge sharks turned. Meg could see its gigantic mouth open just under the water as it streamed steadily toward the swimmers. It only scavenged for fish, Meg told herself, but she knew it could take the boy too. Then Evan Mackenzie threw the rope to Alan and dove past Meg to lunge into the water.

In that moment, Dougal rolled to shave the big basker with his foot. It flipped its tail, upended, and dove downward, raising a deep wake that sucked Dougal under.

Seconds later, he emerged beside Sean and caught the boy to his chest.

As the little arms closed around the man's neck, Meg sobbed out. Evan sliced through the water now, and turned to reach up as Alan threw the rope outward to fly snake-like until Mackenzie snatched it with one hand. He grabbed Dougal, and together they used the rope to haul toward the boat, cutting a swath between the sharks, the huge beasts simply sinking to disappear, waves surging around them.

As they treaded water, Alan hauled them closer. Hearing shouts, Meg looked around to see the boat carrying the work crew rapidly approaching. Other shouts came from a fishing boat that had rushed toward them from the small harbor. Lifting a hand, Alan signaled all was well.

As Dougal hooked his arm over the rim of the boat, he lifted the dripping child into the safety of Alan's arms. Meg rushed toward them to gather her son to her, while the boat rocked as Dougal and then Evan clambered aboard.

Saturated and smelling of brine, Sean shivered in Meg's arms as she wrapped her plaid around him. Sitting, she held him, rocking, grateful to feel his sturdy weight in her arms, grateful to kiss his soft, wet curls. She looked up as Evan and Dougal sat near, even as Norrie and Alan rowed the boat swiftly over the water to the shore.

With his coat tossed over his shoulders for warmth, he sat close enough to press against her. She leaned into him, cradling Sean in her lap as she rubbed the boy's back and limbs to bring more warmth to him, and looked at Dougal.

"Thank you," she said, voice breaking, tears stinging her eyes. He nodded, shivering a bit, and reached out to ruffle the boy's hair. Then he rested his arm around Meg's shoulders as naturally as if he had always done it. She leaned against him, warmth springing there. Then she looked at Evan Mackenzie, who sat smiling, watching them.

"And thank you, Mr. Mackenzie, for helping."

"Oh, all I did was keep you from jumping into the sea after them," he drawled, as they laughed together.

Norrie left the oars to bring a plaid blanket to wrap around the boy, then stooped to murmur to his great-grandson in Gaelic, patting the boy's cheek. He looked at the others.

"Dougal Stewart," he said, "we are in your debt forever. I have seen many brave deeds in my life, but nothing like that. Went through the very sharks, you did, to rescue our lad."

"Just baskers, Norrie," Dougal said. Chuckling, Norrie went to the oars to pull for home.

Still leaned against Dougal, Meg felt wrapped in a warm cocoon. Only she knew what that close circle meant—mother, father, child huddled together in gratitude. In love, she thought.

"Dougal," she whispered, and he bent his head to hear her. "I cannot thank you enough." Tears threatened, and she dipped her head to Sean's, throat tightening, heart too full for words.

"No need for thanks." He rubbed Sean's leg. "And you, what a brave lad you were!"

As father and son regarded each other, neither aware of the relationship, Meg saw how alike their green eyes were, how similar their profiles. The sight felt like a lightning strike through her heart, bringing joy and sadness.

Tears streamed as she lifted her head impulsively to kiss Dougal's cheek. His slight beard was raspy under her lips, his skin damp, tasting of salt. She closed her eyes, savoring his closeness.

His eyes crinkled in a smile, as he looked down at her. Secret and rare, that smile, more in his eyes than on his lips. Reaching up, he brushed a tear away.

"He's safe now," he murmured. "That's all that matters."

Nodding, meeting his eyes, she felt such a wash of love go through her, a warming, nurturing sense of home and rightness. No matter who he was, what had happened in the past, what conflict she had with him as the baroness, in that perfect moment, she loved him.

The peace of that feeling overflowed, and tears filled her eyes again.

He patted her shoulder. "You and Sean are both shivering. We must get you home."

She nodded, hugging her son to her. Glancing up, she saw Mackenzie watching them. He had draped his coat over his shoulders too, his black hair wet, eyes kind and knowing somehow.

"Thank you again, Mr. Mackenzie."

"It's Evan. Not at all." He smiled. "Dougal, yon lass was determined to rescue you herself."

"I could have used help with that shark," Dougal drawled.

Sean peeked out of his blanket nest. "Mr. Stewart punched the shark! It wanted to eat me."

"You're far too tough for a shark to bother with you," Dougal said. "I just gave it a shove with my foot and it went away."

"It listened because you are the *each-uisge,*" Sean said. "Mother Elga says so."

"Eck-oohska?" Evan repeated.

"Kelpie," Dougal said. "A fearsome creature said to rule the sea. Miss MacNeill's old grandmother is convinced I am that thing."

"I cannot argue with that," Evan drawled.

Dougal laughed, then pointed. "Sean, look. Everyone on the island wants to welcome you!"

As the boat entered the shallows, cheers rose from the fishermen and families waiting on the beach. Then Thora splashed into the surf and ran toward them, tears streaming down her cheeks.

CHAPTER TEN

D AYS LATER, SEATED on the sand, Meg laughed as Sean danced a circle around her to show how he would cavort at the ceilidh, the celebration the islanders were planning in honor of his rescue. While she laughed, Sean suddenly stopped, staring. She turned to see a man approach. Dressed for the city in dark suit and top hat, he used a cane to make his way over the sands.

"Sir Roderick!" she said, getting to her feet.

"My dear Lady Strathlin," he murmured. "How good to find you here, so clearly enjoying your holiday."

She brushed sand from her skirts, avoiding his outstretched hand. "Whatever are you doing out here? We had no word of it."

"A sudden decision." He smiled and bowed, cane in one gloved hand. Tall and solidly built, he was neatly dressed and out of place, yet hardly a speck of sand clung to him. It would not dare, Meg thought. "Mother and I were on Mull, as I informed you earlier."

She nodded, recalling that. He was striking in appearance, with a proud aristocratic air, a hawk-like nose, long-lidded eyes, oblong features. Two decades older than Meg, he was graying in his side whiskers and jowls padded his jawline.

She never felt entirely at ease when she met his gaze, for his brown eyes were so dark that they seemed oddly unreadable. His eyes were shrewd, his character sometimes cunning, though she had always believed that only reflected his pragmatic character.

As Lady Strathlin, she had learned to trust him in financial matters, and he had gained her sympathy after the unexpected death of his wife two years earlier, for she saw how genuinely he suffered and seemed to soften.

"Little man," Sir Roderick told Sean, "go and play." With a startled look at Meg, Sean ran off.

He turned back to Meg, eyes glinting. "My dear, how quaint you look today. If this is how you dress when you take a holiday here, I wish I had thought to join you before this. Playing the provincial shepherdess! I will play King Cophetua to your beggar maid."

"Not necessary." She brushed her hands self-consciously over her plain skirt and dug her bare feet a little into the sand to hide her toes. "What are you doing here, Roderick?"

"Your grandfather brought me out. I saw him in Tobermory, and since I was in the Isles for a few days with Mother, I thought to come over to Caransay at your invitation, my dear."

Puzzled, she looked down the beach to where a few fishermen worked on nets. A boat was sailing back from Sgeir Caran, she saw then, with several men inside. She wondered if Dougal Stewart might be with them. She noticed Norrie on the beach, watching the sea.

"My invitation?" She realized then he would not have received her reply to his note. Perhaps he had misunderstood silence to be agreement. "Now that you are here, I hope you will enjoy our little island for a few days."

"A pretty place." He looked around, gloved hands folded on his cane. He was stiff and proper, and wholly out of context on that beach. "I thought you might appreciate some intelligent company here, with little to do but watch the sea and…play in the sand." He glanced toward Sean, who was digging a hole with a sizeable shell. "I hope you are taking care of your skin. My mother says fine pale skin is one of a woman's best assets. You have some color from the sun, and a few freckles. She will not be pleased."

Her hat hung down her back on a ribbon. She did not put it on, and thought of the almond cream his mother—a very opinionated woman—had sent. "How kind of your mother to think of my complexion. Will you be staying long?" She hoped not. "I will have my housekeeper make up a room for you."

"I only came out for the day. Norman MacNeill will arrange for someone to take me back to the Isle of Mull. Mother and I are staying at the resort at Tighnabruaich so she could relax. But I wanted a chance to speak with you."

"How kind of you to think of me." She wished he had stayed on Mull.

"Walk with me, my dear." He offered his arm.

She did not take it, though she walked beside him. In her bare feet, she soon fell out of step with his stride. In the past several months, he had gone from helpful cousin and banker to showing an eager interest in her that she found unsettling. Wanting to bring up the subject of their supposed engagement, she wanted to go about it without hurting his feelings. He seemed sincere, she would give him that.

Glancing down the beach, she saw the boat draw in, and Dougal Stewart disembarked with the others. She knew him from a distance, recognized every nuance of the way he moved, with ease and confidence. His shoulders were broad in a linen shirt and dark vest, his hair gold-streaked in the sunlight. He shaded his eyes and looked down the beach, then lifted a hand in a brief salute.

Her heart leaped a little at that small, private gesture.

"Did that man just wave at you?" Roderick asked.

"Did he?" She shrugged.

"Forward! How long do you plan to stay on the isle this time, my dear?"

"I am not sure. A week or more. The weather has been mild, and it is so peaceful here that I am not eager to return to Edinburgh."

"You've had some excitement lately, from what Mr. MacNeill

said. A child was rescued—quite a daring feat, from what your grandfather said. His own great-grandson." He tipped a brow at her.

She said nothing. Of course Roderick did not know about Sean. Someday she would have to tell him, but so far had never found enough reason to go into detail.

"Quite a daring rescue," he went on. "This Mr. Stewart who is determined to build that dreadful lighthouse is something of a daredevil, from what I hear. He made another such rescue last year, apparently. Some men simply must act the hero." He sighed.

"Another rescue?" she asked.

"He saved some men working on a bridge that collapsed, I think. But I am sure there were plenty of others there to help. Perhaps he just likes having the credit."

"We are all grateful to Mr. Stewart. If not for his quick action, Sean might have drowned."

"That little fellow over there?" He looked back at the child playing in the sand. Sean, looking up, picked up a large shell and followed. Since his rescue, he had not wanted to be far from Meg.

"Aye," she answered. "He is…kin to us here on Caransay."

"Margaret." Roderick took her elbow in a tense grip. He stopped, turned to face her.

He was very tall, the black top hat making him tower over her. His side-whiskers were shaped in the long fashion called Dundrearies. She did not find such hairy feathering attractive, preferring Dougal Stewart's simple habit of shaving every few days, so that his dark whiskers evenly shaded the planes of his face in a very becoming way.

"Roderick," she said, "you did not come out here simply to stroll with me on a beach. What is it? Are there banking matters to discuss?" She hoped it was only that.

"The lady is clever and perceptive," he said fondly. "Lady Strathlin—Margaret. I came to speak with you about a matter of tremendous importance. It simply could not wait for your return to Edinburgh."

"I, too, have something I wish to speak to you about."

He covered her hand with both of his. "Shall I hope?" he whispered. "Shall I allow my heart to beat with the rhythm of adoration and deepest affection?"

Good lord, she nearly said. "You can hardly control the beat of your heart, sir," she said curtly. When she tried to pull her hand away, his grip tightened and he brought her hand to his lips, kissing knuckles. She wanted to pull away.

"Margaret, you know I lost my darling wife two years ago. My heart broke from loneliness. I was sure I would never find a worthy helpmate again. But there you were, my dear cousin, a lantern shining in my time of darkness, offering me generous friendship and succor. You have come to mean a great deal to me, though we were cousins and friends before."

"I have been grateful for your guidance, Roderick. When my grandfather left his estate to me, I felt lost, confused, and overwhelmed. I appreciated your advice as a member of the bank's board, and your wife was kind to bring me into social circles. That made all the difference when I first inherited. But—but it was natural between cousins to be friends, though we saw little of each other in our youth. I am—glad to call you a friend."

"More than friends now. Fair Lady Strathlin, my dear cousin and now—I can hardly express to you how happy I am that you will be my wife."

She stared up at him. "Sir, I never said so."

"Do not be coy," he said, smiling. "I am several years older than you, my dear, so allow me to guide you. I know you are enamored and do not know quite how to say you have accepted. I see it in your eyes. In your invitation here. In your offer to give me a room in your house. Near your own room. Perhaps—I should be so bold—as to take it."

"Roderick," she said firmly, pulling back, "I have not consented to marriage."

"Now we see the temper! So charming. You do enjoy a game.

Well, so do I." His smile and his obstinance gave her chills. "I asked you—twice, I believe—to marry me, and you agreed in a letter."

"Sir, if you read the letter, I refused you."

"'My dear Sir Roderick,' you wrote, 'I am honored by your affection and would be equally honored to be your wife.'"

"I said I would be honored to be your wife *but*—" she ground out. *"But,* I fear it is not possible. Did you read the entire letter?"

"Come now. You did not mean it. It was coyness. Feminine wiles and charm."

"I refused you then, and I refuse you now. I am sorry if you are a little blind to that. We are not engaged. And please do not tell others that we are. It is not true."

"Not true yet," he said blithely.

"It never will be true."

"Not yet," he said stubbornly. "Tell me, my dear. That little boy…" He turned to look back at Sean, who had stopped to pile up a little hill of sand and kick it into fine sprays. "Is he your son?"

She stared at him. The blood left her face, leaving her cold. "My… what?"

"Your son. He looks like you. I know you have a child."

"Who told you such a thing?"

"Walk with me." He tucked her hand in his elbow again. Stunned, she walked beside him, her heart slamming in fear.

"I met a man not long ago," he said. "A pleasant fellow, especially when he was in his cups. A doctor, and he told me over some fine whisky, that he had attended Lady Strathlin when she first inherited her fortune. A very nice fellow," he said, smiling. "But he ran into some problems with his finances, poor man. He said the lady fell ill, and he had attended her several times. Do you know what he told me, Margaret?" He stopped again and turned to look down at her, her hand imprisoned in his arm. She could feel the hard, stringy muscle beneath his coat.

"Wha-what?" But she knew. She remembered the doctor that her friend Angela Shaw had insisted she see when her stomach did not agree with her and she had felt faint and nauseated daily for the first few months of the pregnancy she had tried valiantly to hide.

This doctor, an older man with a mild manner, told her that she was suffering from a common female condition—she already knew she was pregnant—and that his advice was to take care of herself, and take care to hide her condition. He had warned her to avoid becoming overwrought by her new responsibilities, and told her to take a long holiday among close family for several months on the excuse of her health. He had looked at her pointedly before leaving.

You are about to have a child, madam, as an unmarried lady in a prominent position. So it is my opinion that you should retreat and keep this quiet until you are married.

Somehow, Roderick Matheson had coaxed the truth out of that doctor years later.

She faced him. "What did he say?" she repeated. She had to know.

"That Lady Strathlin would have a child by now, probably a healthy child, and would have had that child in the months following her inheritance of her grandfather's fortune. He guessed that when she became Baroness Strathlin, she was already with child. And not married." He gazed down at her.

The sudden pounding in her head was so fierce that she thought she might faint. She watched Sean play on the beach, watched, far in the distance, the harbor where a few men stood in a cluster and talked. She saw Dougal Stewart standing tall among the other men. She wanted to run to the safety of his arms.

But she stood still, frozen in place. He was too far away to hear or to help. And he must never learn about this conversation.

"Well, my dear?" Roderick murmured. "You cannot deny it."

"That doctor was a drunken fool."

"And that spring, as I recall hearing," he went on, his voice smooth and his grip tight, "a little boy was born and welcomed into the MacNeill family. The child's parentage is somewhat obscure, from what my sources say. I have asked around. I sent someone here a while ago to ask about Lady Strathlin and the family—most would not talk. But some did."

Some did. Her heart pounded.

"They say you were married to a sailor, but he drowned. They say no one knew him, so it was a mysterious wedding. If it existed," he added. "They know, of course, that you are Lady Strathlin, and they say you return often to Caransay and spend a great deal of time with one child in particular, your child from that—supposed marriage." He glanced again at Sean, his smile benign, yet flat.

She wanted to slap him, shake him until the evil in him showed. But he only smiled, smug and unbending. And she saw what he wanted—his advantage. Marriage, and his silence.

"He looks like you. So blond, with that charming smile. But I think his eyes are not yours, his chin is not yours. Those came from his…father." He glanced down at her. "This news would be of great interest in certain circles in the city, don't you agree, Margaret?"

"You would not tell—" Oh, God, she had admitted it. "Nor would I care."

"I would not tell. A man never betrays his wife. Her secrets are his."

"Wife," she repeated dully.

"Now, he may wish to betray a friend, a cousin, a woman who falsely represents herself as having good moral character and has inherited a position of some merit. It might be a service to others if her story were known to the public. A moral lesson. Something humbling. Though I wonder if investments might fail. The board members would be so disappointed. And that poor boy, growing up knowing he was born out of wedlock. A bastard. Could he even inherit, hmm?"

"What do you want, Roderick?" She yanked back, and this time, he let her hand go.

He bowed his head. "Autumn weddings are so lovely. Kiss

me, Margaret." He leaned down.

Meg tipped her face up, but as he lowered to set his mouth to hers, she turned her cheek.

"How can you deny me, sweet Margaret," he murmured against her cheek, "when my heart beats only for you?" He took her hard by the shoulders and kissed her soundly on the mouth. His lips were sticky, pressing too hard, bone to bone instead of cushioning. Meg broke free. "I need time to think."

"Of course. Until the soiree, then, in Edinburgh. You will be back by then." He caressed her cheek with a gloved finger. "That night, we will make our announcement."

Leaning away from his touch, she whirled, leaving him standing, proper and out of place, in the sand. He did not follow, and she hoped he would leave soon, smug in his cruel victory. But she would not let it be his victory. She could not.

Yet she trembled, feeling as if her whole world rocked beneath her feet, about to collapse.

She glanced back to see Dougal Stewart standing with his men. He looked in her direction. Had he watched the exchange, wondered what it was? She turned away, walking quickly back toward Sean, away from Roderick, away from Dougal.

Yet she felt Dougal's gaze on her, felt an awareness of him all through her, steady as sunshine on her shoulder, and sharp as a crack of lightning.

CHAPTER ELEVEN

"**G**OOD TO SEE you here, Mr. Stewart," Fergus said, just above the sound of Norrie MacNeill's fiddle. "The ceilidh is in honor of wee Sean's rescue and your brave deed in the waves."

Dougal smiled, nodded as the fiddle music drew to a rousing finale amid wild clapping and shouts for more. "Thank you, Fergus. And thank you for the supply of fish. Our cook is making fine meals for the workmen this week." Fergus had brought buckets of fish to the barracks after Sean's rescue to express his personal thanks.

"There's more from my catch for you and your crew anytime." Called by an acquaintance, Fergus excused himself, leaving Dougal content to stand in the midst of the crowded main room of Norrie MacNeill's house.

Anywhere he turned, he was shoulder to shoulder with the inhabitants of Caransay as well as his work crew. Standing by the hearth, Norrie guided the bow over the fiddle, filling the room with music. The songs varied from happy rhythms that set dancers spinning to evocative, poignant songs that had some wiping away tears. captured the emotions and raised more than a few tears.

Norrie was accompanied by a few kin and neighbors playing drums and even a piper, and Fergus stood up to sing a tune or two. Dougal remembered that Meg had remarked fondly that

Fergus reminded her of her deceased father.

As the hour grew later and the whisky flowed freely, Dougal was surprised to see Evan Mackenzie stand to sing a tune as well, his voice so rich and sure that the room grew quiet, and applause and cheers rang out when he finished. The crowd had sung a familiar refrain with him, and Meg joined them. Silent, Dougal closed his eyes to listen to the sweet magic of her voice.

The walls and floors fairly shook with dancing and stomping feet, and the modest house glowed with music, chatter, laughter and happiness. Content to listen and watch much of the time, Dougal leaned a shoulder to the wall as Meg swirled past him in Alan's arms, cheeks flushed and eyes sparkling.

Remembering the gentleman who had walked with her on the beach the other day, he frowned. He had asked Norrie about the man and learned he was Sir Roderick Matheson, a banker and owner of the nearby Isle of Guga, who had come out for the day to visit Meg MacNeill. A cousin on the girl's mother's side, and fair smitten by the lass; with that, Norrie had sent Dougal a sideways glance and said no more of it.

Dougal had noticed how they had strolled arm in arm on the beach, and he had certainly seen her allow Matheson to kiss her. That sight felt hard as a blow. Yet he sensed resistance and displeasure in her posture and the way she stomped away, leaving the fellow alone and looking as out of place as a penguin.

Just as well, Dougal thought, that he had not met the man himself. Best he kept distant.

As the dancers changed partners, Meg whirled through some complex steps with Sean, their effort so comical that Dougal laughed in delight. Meg looked up and smiled at him. A flood of affection tinged with longing rushed through him.

The other day, kissing her within the little cave, he felt sure she was attracted to him, that she cared. Yet Matheson might be a suitor; Dougal had not asked, and she had not said. He could hardly expect her to wait seven years, knowing naught about him. He sighed, smile fading.

As Norrie began a slow, poignant fiddle piece, Meg tapped Dougal on his shoulder.

"Grandfather Norrie asked to see you before you leave tonight."

"I will not sing a tune, unless you want to hear caterwauling," he drawled. Then he noticed Sean peeking up at him. "Laddie! Having a fine time?"

"Oh, aye! I know all the dances."

"I saw you dancing with Meg MacNeill," Dougal answered. "Very fine indeed." He smiled at her and saw a burst of pink in her cheeks.

His smile went rueful. Just standing near her, speaking with her, felt good. He only wanted to enjoy her company, but the memory of another man kissing her dropped a shadow over the ceilidh's celebration.

"It's late," she told Sean. "You should be going to bed. Where is Fergus MacNeill? He was to take you home." She turned.

"He's gone off with friends," Sean said. "Even small Anna is still awake, over there with Grandma Thora. I want to stay up late with everyone else."

"This is the lad's celebration," Dougal said in his defense.

"It is," Sean agreed.

Meg shook her head. "You will be exhausted tomorrow when it's time for lessons."

"Lessons?" Dougal asked.

"Berry is teaching me English and reading and math at the Great House," Sean said. "I'm doing very well, she says."

"The baroness is teaching him?" Dougal asked Meg, confused.

"Mrs. Berry," she said, though he felt bewildered. "Look, my grandfather is about to speak," she added. Seeing Norrie beckon to him, Dougal stepped forward hesitantly as the old man set down his fiddle and took up a glass of whisky. Then he began to speak in Gaelic.

Not sure what was being said, Dougal was grateful when Meg leaned close to explain. She translated, but soon Norrie switched to English for the benefit of Dougal and his crew.

"When Mr. Stewart came to Caransay," Norrie said, "we were not pleased with his idea of a lighthouse. Some of us have not changed our minds about that.

"But we have seen that Mr. Stewart is a good and brave man," Norrie continued. "He plucked our wee Sean safe from the sea and drove off a shark, even if it was a basker," he added. "I am thinking he is the equal of the great hero Fhionn MacCumhaill himself. And on Caransay, he is as great as any kelpie or selkie, a man of courage and magical feats!" He grinned. "To Mr. Stewart—the Great Toast!" Norrie stepped up on a stool and raised his glass.

Everyone who held a glass or cup lifted it, then lowered it, held their drink out and pulled it in, all the while chanting in unison, first in Gaelic, then in English.

Up with it, up with it,
Down with it, down with it,
Over to you, and over to you,
Over to me, and over to me.
May all your days be good, my friend!
Drink it up!

"Drink it up!" They shouted in unison, walls ringing, lifting their glasses. Norrie drained and smashed his glass on the hearthstone to rousing cheers. Dougal, accepting handshakes and claps on the back, hoisted Sean to his shoulders. The little boy raised his hands toward the roof beams, yelling happily.

"Aye, my wee friend. Celebrate! All this is for you!" Dougal grinned. As he held Sean's legs, he saw Meg's sparkling smile. But he sensed an undercurrent of sadness in her eyes.

"What is it?" he asked.

"Just thinking—thank you, Mr. Stewart," she said quietly.

"You are very welcome, my dear Miss MacNeill," he answered magnanimously, realizing that the whisky and the merriment had loosened his tongue a bit and had even set his restrained spirit free for the moment. Her answering smile was all in her eyes now, and he felt as if the room all but disappeared.

Norrie spoke again in Gaelic, and the crowd cheered loudly, clinking glasses in salute.

"What did he say?" he asked Meg.

Meg blushed. "Oh, they're drinking a toast to me now."

"'And here's to our Margaret,'" Fergus translated, standing nearby, "'the finest lady with the kindest heart in all the Western Isles. May she have all the happiness she deserves!'"

"Quite a compliment," Dougal remarked.

"Grandfather has half a keg of whisky in him by now," Meg said. Her cheeks were fiery. "When his fiddle playing goes wild and beautiful and he calls for the Great Toast, the drink has opened his soul. They say the more whisky in the fiddler, the better the fiddling."

Dougal laughed. "Whisky or not, I agree with Norrie. Our Meg MacNeill is a fine lady." He leaned toward her. "If Mackenzie had let you jump into the water, I have no doubt you would have saved the lad yourself, and kicked that shark away, as well."

Instead of laughing, her eyes were somber, so beautiful with it that he ached. "I would never let the sea have my son," she said fiercely.

"Sean should learn how to swim. I've offered to teach him. He's like me, I think. He's drawn to the sea. It's in his blood."

"In my blood!" Sean said giddily from his high perch on Dougal's shoulders. He stretched his arms high and laughed as Dougal turned around with him.

Meg stared, still serious. Then she whirled and shouldered through the crowd. Hands resting on Sean's knees, Dougal watched her go. Then he slid the boy to the ground to go enjoy a cup of the fruit brose that Thora had prepared with cream, oats, and wild strawberries.

As Meg left the room, Dougal wondered what the devil he had done to upset her.

MEG STOOD NEAR Alan Clarke, listening as Norrie ended another song and an off-tune string gave a narrow whine. She wondered when she could leave, take Sean with her, and flee to Clachan Mor.

"Miss MacNeill," Alan said. "I am curious. Is that Lady Strathlin over there?" He indicated the woman who now chatted with Thora and some of the fishermen's wives as they served food and drinks.

Seeing Mrs. Berry, Meg hesitated. She had dreaded this question ever since her grandmothers had let Dougal believe that Mrs. Berry was the baroness.

"I—ah—oh," she said, as Dougal Stewart joined them.

"I am curious too," he said, having heard the conversation.

"That lady? She is Mrs…. ah, Berry, Lady Strathlin's… companion."

"I have seen her," Dougal said, "but we have not met." He frowned, and Meg could see that he was working out the puzzle of who Berry was, which would lead him to wonder who Lady Strathlin might be.

"Everyone is here tonight but Lady Strathlin," Alan said. "Even such a high-and-mighty shrew as that one should be moved by Sean's rescue."

"I am sure she was quite moved," Meg snapped.

"I hope she is not as shrewish as she seems through her lawyers," Dougal said. He was still staring thoughtfully at Mrs. Berry. "I could swear that Mrs. Berry was Lady Strathlin."

"You were simply mistaken," Meg said.

"Apparently. And once again I have not found her even on her own island." Dougal watched her steadily. "Though they say she is here."

"Somewhere. She keeps her distance." She met his gaze. *I am your shrewish baroness, Mr. Stewart,* she thought. *And I need you very much just now, and cannot let you know.*

He narrowed his eyes, and she looked away. The risk was too great now that she wanted to reveal all to him, but feared to take that chance.

"She might be here in this room, disguised as a fishwife," Alan chuckled.

"Fishwife or baroness, I need to talk to her," Dougal said.

Silent, Meg scowled. Dougal leaned down. "If you can get a word to the lady," he said, "tell her I sincerely want to meet her." His voice was dark velvet, soft and comforting.

She pursed her mouth without answer, and he gave her the small, intimate smile she had come to cherish—an impish curve to his lips, a green dazzle in his eyes. Her anxious feeling vanished, replaced by longing.

For happiness with this man, she realized. Grateful as she was for the happiness her son and her family brought her, she yearned for more, something as intimate and kind as that smile. Love, partnership—imagining that with him took her breath away.

By comparison, Sir Roderick Matheson was even more dastardly, a true threat to happiness. But Dougal, if she could sort out her feelings, was an unexpected beacon, beginning to shine in her life.

Watching Sean jumping and laughing as others danced, she remembered Dougal's sweet playfulness with him, and his tender strength in saving a child he did not even know was his.

Sighing, she brushed her hair back, her fingers shaking. She had hardly slept the last few nights after Roderick's smooth, sly threat. He wanted an answer—and she faced inevitable surrender unless she found the courage to risk the safety of all she loved to step away from him.

Heart pounding, she clenched her fists, feeling as if her spirit beat its wings on cage bars, desperate to be free to be happy, to feel loved. But Roderick had trapped her. Whether or not she married him, she would live in fear that he could expose her youthful dilemma if she crossed him.

But with each moment, she knew with more clarity that she could not find happiness without Dougal Stewart. The other day, those mad kisses and breathless apologies had brought revelation. He had not played her falsely that night. She had been wrong about him. She could begin to trust him, day by day. She could let that old hurt go like stale water poured back into the sea, cleansed and carried off.

She had begun to hope for that until Roderick had arrived.

Meg folded her arms tightly, feeling a piercing loneliness, even standing beside Dougal, for the craving and the need weighed on her now. She yearned to tell him all the truth. She yearned to seek the wildness of her soul in his arms.

She knew what she wanted, but did not know what he wanted. Not entirely. Soon she would return to the mainland, to her other world, to Sir Roderick and a life of lies and fear and constant caution. She would have to leave Sean again, and Dougal, and her hopes and dreams.

As the dance ended, she turned to see Dougal tip his head toward her, brow puckered, as if he asked silently if all was well. She tried to smile, looked away.

Another tune began, with dancers separating into two lines, ready for the Seann Triubhas, or Chantreuse, as Lowlanders called the old dance favored in the Isles.

Dougal held out a hand. "Miss MacNeill, if you would?"

"Of course," she said, relieved, glad for the chance to be near him and feel his touch.

The dancers shifted to offer them the lead positions. Facing Dougal, Meg curtsied and he bowed, and they moved forward, folding into the center, gliding back, turning with the music. Reaching the end of the line, she lifted her hand from his arm as they separated.

When she faced him again across the gap, he smiled in the way she adored, private and quick, eyes twinkling, as if his heart were hers alone. She knew her heart was his now.

Here in this place, she was simply Meg, dancing carefree with handsome Dougal, and dreams were possible. Elsewhere, she was Lady Strathlin, with a desperate secret and a vile enemy—and she knew Dougal despised that lady.

Later, as the dancing slowed, the food was consumed, and kin and neighbors began to take their leave, Fergus walked over to Meg.

"*Ach*, look at the child," he said with a smile. "A happy lad, but he cannot keep his eyes open, and should go to his bed. I can carry him—will he sleep here in Norrie's house, or will you take him up to the Great House?"

Meg smiled too, seeing Sean half asleep on a bench beside a table loaded with empty platters and cups. "He should sleep here. I do not want to disturb him," she said. Time with Sean was precious to her, as she only saw him on Caransay. She would go back to her house, a short walk, and see Sean in the morning. Days ago, he had nearly drowned, and now another threat loomed that only she knew about.

"Aye. But I want to ask you something, cousin." His brown eyes were troubled.

Meg smiled. "What is it?"

"I hear the lad is doing well in his schooling with Mrs. Berry."

"He's a bright lad, and she is a fine tutor."

"I am thinking he needs more than Berry, unless he plans to stay on Caransay and become a fisherman like so many of us here. But I am thinking you do not want that for him."

"He should do as he likes, fishing or something else. Though I want him to have more education when he is older."

Fergus rubbed his head. "We love him here. But after we almost lost him, Norrie and I were talking. We were saying he would do well in a mainland school, living with you. Safe, away from danger."

She blinked, surprised. Fergus had no idea what danger might await both Sean and her on the mainland. "I did not think you wanted him to leave the island."

"He would visit here, with you." He kneaded his cap in his

hands. "Meg, take him back to Edinburgh to live in your castle and send him to a real school. Let him grow up to be someone important. A doctor. Or an engineer like Mr. Stewart, making lighthouses to keep the seas safe."

Startled, she reached for something to say. "You support the lighthouse, then."

"I do. The reef is powerful. It can destroy lives. And Dougal Stewart is a good man."

She caught her breath. Her cousin did not know the truth about Sean and Dougal, and yet had found the tender spot of the hurt, all unwitting.

"For now, Caransay is the best place for him, Fergus. He would be heartbroken to leave you and all his family behind."

"We nearly lost him the other day. I just want the lad to be healthy and safe. And happy. We would miss him, but he is smart and needs schooling. The other day, he read a story to small Anna. Read it aloud! She is too tiny to care, but I was proud."

She smiled, felt tears sting. "He is happy here. I am in no rush to move him."

"But you are his mother, lass," he said quietly. "You deserve more time with the lad."

"I do. But I want what is best for him. Strathlin Castle is cold and lonely, with only servants there and advisers visiting, some friends. Not all of them are fond of wee lads." She thought of Roderick and suppressed a shudder. "Besides," she added, "he would not see the water there."

"Now that would be a sad thing. It is the magic of living on an island, the sea and the wind and being so close to nature and the heavens. And for yourself?" He tipped his head. "Do you miss the sea and sky when you go east to the mainland?"

"Every day." She gazed at Sean's golden head. "And I miss my son on those days too. But he needs to be here, where he is—safe," she murmured.

Her cousin frowned. "Safe away from the hurried life in Edinburgh, I suppose. But someday you will take him. The time is coming."

"Not yet, Fergus. Not yet."

Soon, Lady Strathlin might have to marry a heartless banker to protect her beloved son, his future, and that of the island. Roderick's threats could go far enough for her to lose Caransay too, if he influenced the bank board against her based on a false picture of her morals and intentions. The more she looked for ways to avoid marrying him, the more she saw no choice.

CHAPTER TWELVE

ABOUT TO TAKE his leave, having thanked Norrie and Thora, Dougal looked around, wanting to say goodnight to Meg. Seeing her with Fergus, the two in a quiet conversation while she frowned and shook her head, he wondered again if something troubled her. Despite the evening's revelry, she had seemed preoccupied. Moments later, she stepped away to rouse a sleepy Sean, leading him through a connecting door. Rather than leave as he had planned, Dougal waited.

When she emerged, he came forward. "I did not want to leave without saying goodnight," he said. "Sean looked very tired, poor lad."

"He is already asleep, and will have good dreams after all this, I think." She smiled.

"It was a lovely ceilidh," he said.

"Lovely, aye. Thank you for coming." The fold of a frown, a depth in her blue eyes, told him she wanted to say something else. Her trembling smile confirmed it.

"What is it?" he asked quietly.

She shook her head. "Just tired. I—I need some air. It is stuffy in here with the lamps and candles, and the heat and noise of so many. But they are leaving now, and I should help Thora clear the things away."

"We could go outside for just a bit," he offered.

As he spoke, a small black dog padded toward them and

scratched at the door that Meg had just closed. Dougal recognized the little terrier that had dozed blithely by the fireside during the noisy ceilidh. Tail wagging now, she jumped up at the door as Meg opened it.

"Go on, then, Falla. You want to sleep near Seanie. You are such a good nursemaid," she said, rubbing the little head. The dog scampered into the room and Meg closed the door.

"She is older and a bit deaf," Meg said. "She can sleep through the music and dancing, but if Sean leaves the room, she knows it. Shall we go outside?"

She led him to a side door, crossing the large room away from the entrance where guests were taking their leave, while some of the women remained to help Thora. Originally, Camus nan Fraoch had been a small croft, Dougal noted, though two additions had been built to either side under one long thatched roof that covered the main area, kitchen, and sleeping rooms. With low ceiling beams and thick whitewashed walls, a stone hearth where a peat fire crackled, and fitted with sturdy, simple furnishings, the enlarged house was cozy yet roomy.

"This way." She opened the door and Dougal slipped out after her, closing the latch. Under the purple glow of a summer midnight, Meg hurried through a small kitchen garden and toward the dunes, where the sea glittered and stars sparkled overhead.

A warm blend of contentment and desire rushed through him, smooth and fiery, as reviving as a good whisky and cream. He wanted to pull her into his arms, but knew she needed time. Walking beside her, boots sinking in sand, he took her hand to pull her with him toward the shush of waves in the darkness. Silently, swiftly, she went with him. Her fingers curled, pressed, fervent in his hold. At the water's edge, he paused as the water foamed toward them in lacy ripples.

She looked up at him, silent, expectant somehow. The curve of her cheek was a cool blue crescent, her hair haloed in starlight.

A moment ago, he nearly pulled her to him. Now he sought

for something to say, to keep her near and not overwhelm her with the feelings that nearly took him down in that moment. "The, ah, ceilidh was a grand celebration," he said, feeling awkward suddenly.

"We had much to celebrate, and wanted to show our thanks."

A breath of wind sifted a few loose curls over her brow and cheek. He brushed that softness back. She watched him.

"Any man could have done what I did. And Evan Mackenzie was there too."

"What you did took strength and courage. The islanders will talk of it for a long time." She smiled. "Even now, while you stand here with me, they are spinning a legend about Dougal and the shark."

"Dougal and the fat, placid basker," he drawled.

"Still, it was brave. And—" Her eyes gleamed with quick tears that startled him. "You cannot know how much it meant to me. If you had not—we might have had a wake tonight." Her voice quavered.

"Come here," he murmured, taking her shoulders, pulling her toward him.

He felt her hesitate for a moment, then she melted against him and gave a soft little sob. He simply held her, rubbing her back, murmuring soothing sounds while she pressed her face into his shoulder in the darkness.

He felt sure she rarely leaned on anyone for support. Sighing into the fragrant cloud of her hair, he wrapped her close and felt her arms slip around his waist.

Just this embrace felt so good, as if he were needed, essential. It was new to him. He had faced danger and urgency often enough, but the other day, pulling Sean safely into his arms felt almost more important than any other danger or deed he had ever faced. And comforting Meg now—not knowing quite what troubled her—he felt that he belonged here with her. For her.

That sense of being needed had been lacking in his life. Growing up in a family devastated by tragedy, he had wanted to create safety and security for others. It was a way to counter what he had struggled with as a boy. Building lighthouses to save people sailing on treacherous waters was a way to do that. His skills were needed, but he had never felt necessary to someone for himself, not his skills or his inner mission to combat a problem common on the ocean.

Meg needed him. And he needed her. He hadn't even realized why, or how much, until now. If she had needed him like this these seven years, he hurt to think of how she had felt. But he had found her now. Hope existed, if only he could make up for the rest of it.

More than need and being needed, another emotion brimmed in him. Love. It had to be that. He gave into its quiet and undeniable power, surrendered to its sureness and comfort willingly. Somehow it was the easiest and most natural thing he had ever done, as if he stepped into a room warm with firelight and quiet, lasting joy.

"Dougal," she whispered, lifting her head. "I am sorry. Just— sorry."

"Hush, lass. Whatever it is, we can fix it."

Her eyes searched his. "Can we? I want to."

"Then tell me, and we will see it through, aye?" He soothed a hand over her hair, slid his fingers into that soft golden wealth of curls and coils. She leaned her head to gaze at him, her eyes luminous, awash in tears.

Gently he tipped her chin with a finger and bent to kiss her, a soft, sweet brush of lips to lips. She pressed into his embrace, wrapping her arms around his waist, urging the kiss into a meld of mouths, breaths. His heart thudded. Cradling her face in his hands, he kissed her more insistently, breathlessly, until she clung to him and the starry sky overhead seemed to spin.

Wavelets rinsed over their feet, and she cried out with a teary laugh, stepping back, splashing. Laughing too, he bent to work off his boots and toss them higher on the dry sand, then pulled his knitted socks off after them and tossed those too. The sea washed cool over his feet. Meg laughed again and kicked off her shoes, tossing them after his things. She stamped her feet a little, chasing wavelets as they sank into wet sand.

Turning, she walked a little ahead of him, then took his hand to pull him along the sand into the shadow of the headland that separated this small, private crescent of beach from the larger bay beyond. The moon spangled the rolling sea as he went with her.

"I thought you needed to go back to wash dishes," he said, chuckling.

"I will. I need to be out here for a while. Free," she said. "I need to feel free."

She walked backwards as she spoke, tugging on his hand, and he went with her, the sand soft and damp beneath his feet. Then he tugged her toward him, pulling her into his arms. Under starlight and the indigo sky, he kissed her as she curved her body against his, arms sliding around his waist.

A keen burning slipped through him, and he kissed her in full freedom now, deep and wild and thoroughly, sliding a hand up her back, the other pulling her to him at hip and waist until her abdomen pressed hard against his rigidness. He groaned low and let his hands move upward.

She turned slightly, allowing his fingers to trace over the swell of her left breast, where she tightened like a pearl for him. He felt her small gasp in his mouth, and he touched her other breast, ruching that willing nipple, feeling her sag in his arms a little. She opened her mouth to him, teasing him with her tongue as he teased her breasts, her hands easing over his waist, moving down, then behind him, pulling him against her.

He could not get enough of her. She was like fire to him, like the burn of the whisky in his blood. He wanted her intensely, could not think past that urgency. His pounding heart and throbbing blood dimmed all reason.

Part of him, blood and soul, remembered the night they had shared, and he wanted that back again, not for its incredible physical satisfaction, but for the depth of the passion he had known only in her arms.

He proceeded with care, partaking slowly of the luxury of her, of this, though his heart slammed and his body urged him onward. He framed the deep curves at her waist, and he felt her hands move up his back, shaping, clutching at his shoulders. She gave a breathy moan and curved herself against him.

When he felt that hot, irresistible pulsing of spirit begin between them, when his body throbbed and demanded, he could no longer hold back, and he pulled her tightly against him.

Sinking with her in the sand, he dropped to his knees to face her as she kneeled also, and he pressed her to him in a deep kiss. Then she sank, and he went with her, stretching out with her on a soft cushion of white sand, rolling slightly, so that he lay beside her.

Gathering her to him, he traced his hands over her. Keenly aware of what he wanted, he hoped she wanted it, too. But he could not go on until he knew that she would be his entirely, without hesitation.

Cupping her face in his hand, he pulled his lips from hers and drew her into his embrace, touched his lips to her ear. She gasped, a breathy thrill.

"Lass, tell me," he whispered, kissing her earlobe, "if you understand what we are about here, if you feel this between us too."

"I know what we are about," she said, her lips brushing his neck, his jaw. "You are here now. That is all I need to know." She stretched for his kiss.

"God, Meg," he said, dragging his lips from hers, determined to make certain all was clear between them, "wait."

"Dougal, what," she said, cupping his jaw, her face close to his.

"I must ask. The fellow on the beach the other day. Norrie told me his name. A fellow from Edinburgh, he said. Tell me—if he means something to you." Voice low and ragged, he hated himself for asking. But he had to know. "Because if he does—we need to stop, aye."

"He is no one," she murmured, her mouth tracing over his. "No one at all to me."

He lay back, gathered her into his arms, held her. "You kissed him."

He felt a little jealous of that, but more, a strange sense that she was his and he was hers, and no one could come between them now. But he had to know that was true.

"He kissed *me*. I did not want it. Nor do I want to talk about it just now."

"Then just now, my lass," he whispered, "tell me what you want of me, of us, just now." He knew what he wanted—her, with him, forever. He kept still, heart driving hard in his chest.

With her arms looped about his neck, she went still and quiet. He thought she might pull away and end this. Fair enough, if that was what she needed.

Then she sighed. "I want the dream. Just once, I want the dream."

"What dream?" he whispered.

"The dream that I am with you and we are so happy together. The dream where I have all I need, and I—I am who I am. Where one man has my heart in his keeping, and always will."

He could not speak for a moment. "I have had a similar dream. And you were part of it."

"Was I," she said, breath upon his cheek. "Then just for tonight, the dream could be true."

He felt her thumping heartbeat through her slim rib cage under his hands. "And after that?" he eased his lips over her cheek, her earlobe, teasing, tugging.

She moaned on a breath. "After that, we return to the world just as it is."

He wanted to take her with him into his world, where he moved from one beautiful, remote place to another, if only she could be with him. She had always been the dream for him. And now he dared hope that he was hers as well.

Rolling her to her back, he rose over her, propped on his hands as she lay in the sand. The water swept cool over his feet. Far beyond, he could hear the faint strain of a fiddle in the night.

"Would you go with me into this other world?" he asked.

"That is not easy, I think." She pulled him down toward her. "I have often thought about that night we spent together. Strangers, and yet we seemed to know each other perfectly, as if we were always meant—well. I often wished we had never separated. But that was not real," she whispered.

"It could be real now, lass." His feelings for her had waited, dormant, until he found her. Now, as he came to know her kind heart, her sweet honesty, he was more and more sure of love.

"It is not so easy, truly." Her answer surprised him. "Let us have the dream tonight," she said, sliding her fingers into his hair. "Please," she whispered, the plaintive sound striking through him, where longing and desire ran hot and deep. "Please—"

He took her mouth with his, took the word from her, and turned it into a kiss. He traced his tongue over her lips and shifted lower, drifting kisses along her jaw, her long and beautiful throat, until he found the swell of her breast. He fingered gently at the buttons of her plain woolen gown and opened the bodice, slipping his hand inside the warmth there, sliding beneath layered cotton and cambric. Touching the incredible softness of her skin, he heard her breathy cry, and his body tightened like a fist with burgeoning need.

Dipping his head, he touched her nipple with his tongue, coaxed it to stiffen, heard her whimper as she slid her fingers through his hair, over his ear, and down, until she was tugging at his shirt, and he in turn slipped her blouse from her and fingered the delicate laces of her camisole.

Gasping, moaning softly, she undressed him quickly, and he drew off her garments, one after the other, until they lay nude on a scattering of dark clothing and pale sand, hidden in the black shadow of the headland where no one could see them, where they had found a small private space to relish each other.

Feeling the gentle, cool evening wind on his skin, he drew her into his arms, her skin warm and delicious against his, and he traced his lips over her breasts, teasing her nipples to pearls, while she arched and breathed out in a cry. He traced his tongue over her breasts, between them, and downward over her abdomen, to where she was sweet, tender, and secret.

As she shivered under him, he teased her, stroked her, until she clutched at him and whimpered out her release. When she subsided, sighing like a wave, he could not control the powerful need much longer, heart slamming, body and soul near to bursting.

But he must not give her a child tonight, not yet, though he wanted that desperately with her—that awareness flowed through him even in that moment. Through a haze, he wanted to be cautious, even as she pleaded with her writhing body and a low, throaty moan that pulsed hot and demanding through him. She moved in the soft sand beneath him, pulling him over her, and he gave a low groan, all fire and blaze and no longer himself. When she arched and urged him into her, as his body slipped into the glove of hers, she became his crucible and he hers, all fire and passion, all wind and sea and pounding hearts. The storm of it tore through him.

But he found the strength to pull back, to spill himself into the warm sea that teased around them. Breathless, he gathered her into his arms and rolled to his side to hold her, trembling. Then he realized she wept silently, her cheek wet against his shoulder.

CHAPTER THIRTEEN

STARLIGHT AND THE moon's profile on the whispering sea, the surf rinsing her feet, and Dougal's arms around her. She would carry this night through the rest of her life, Meg thought, to treasure this peaceful night with a stormy one. Her kelpie, strong and beautiful, tender and kind.

Soon she might never see him again, once she went back to her life as a baroness. He would not be her husband, and no matter what she wanted, what her fortune could create for her, she would have to live without him. Drawing in a breath against the pain of that, she ducked her head against his chest.

"My lass, what is it?" Dougal traced his fingers over her hair. They were dressed now, seated on the sand, arms around each other, her head on his shoulder. The sea shushed and the moon sparkled, and the distant joy of Norrie's fiddle sounded in the distance. Even after the guests had gone, he played into the night.

"Just thoughts," she said, evading the truth. "Dougal, what did you want to say the other day, when we were in the cave, about how you came to be there?"

"I wonder if we have time for that now. They will look for you."

"They will not. If they know we left together, my grand-mothers will not bother us."

"Why is that?" He kissed her hair.

She shrugged. "Thora and Elga have wanted to bring us together ever since they met you. They—they think you are the kelpie come to save this island."

He huffed. "Mother Elga said so, but surely that is a joke on the island."

"Not a joke, but a superstition."

"What do you mean?".

"Tell me your story, Mr. Stewart, and I will tell you some of mine so you will understand."

He looked askance at her. "Very well. Seven years ago, one evening, I was with friends. We were fair drunk, all of us, after a wake for a fine man whose wife made very good whisky. A man from Tobermory."

"George MacDonald? We knew him. A good man, and good whisky. Why were you there?"

"I was studying the Caran Reef even back then, measuring the rocks, judging the wave force, and so on. We knew a lighthouse was needed along the reef somewhere, and we were exploring the possibility. We were staying on Mull. That night we were young fools, too much whisky, too much youth, boasting of our courage, challenging each other, taking boats out to race. My opponent fell back, but I kept going, wanting to win. Foolish, as I said, for poor weather rose up. A bad squall came over the reef as I approached, and instead of turning back, I went into the throat of it, hoping to come out the other side. But a wave flipped my boat. I took a blow to the head and nearly drowned. Then I was saved—" He stopped. "It is almost too wild to believe."

"What happened?"

"I suppose a high wave washed me onto Sgeir Caran. But in my poor state, I thought a beautiful white horse carried me over the water."

"*Each-uisge*," she said. "The sea kelpie. A legend. But you saw it?"

"I imagined it. Then I found myself safe on the rock, and I saw you. My mind was all turned about. The hit to the head, the drink, nearly drowning. The fear of being taken by the sea."

"Then you were shipwrecked on Sgeir Caran," she breathed.

"Aye. So you see, no scheme to have some fun with a girl who waited on the rock. That is what you told me. I remember that. 'I waited for you.'"

"Did I say that? I am sorry that I thought you came there deliberately because I was there. But I saw men fetch you in the morning. They seemed to know where you were."

"They were fishermen. Evan Mackenze hired them to help search for me after the storm. So he knew a little of what happened that night. No one knows the whole of it but we two." He pulled her closer. "Besides, I thought—" He paused, half-laughed.

"You thought I was not real," she said quietly.

"Mad as it sounds, it is the truth. I thought you were a sea fairy or the like. A mermaid in human form. Something other-worldly. Otherwise, how could a beautiful lass be there on that rock in a storm? It was a miracle to find you there in that wild storm. I survived because of you, I am sure of it. What is it?"

Meg laughed from sheer relief and joy. "You thought I was a sea fairy—and I thought you were the *each-uisge* of Sgeir Caran."

He blinked. "You thought that, not just your grandmothers?"

"I was not sure. But they were convinced that the kelpie came to Sgeir Caran that night."

Dougal tipped his head in bewilderment. "Truly?"

"You have more than proven it lately."

"How so?"

"You rose out of the sea the day we visited the rock. You were only diving, but Elga was certain. And she was alarmed one day on the beach when you wanted to take the children from her. You only wanted to help, but she thought you would steal them away. Stop laughing," she said, smacking his arm lightly. "And then you rescued Sean and the shark did your bidding and went away."

"My bidding! I wish I had that power." He chuckled.

"And my grandmothers think—" She paused.

"Tell me. It could not be any less ridiculous than I have told you."

"Because we spent the night on that rock…they think you are the kelpie and you became my husband," she blurted.

He stilled. "Best explain that, my lass."

"Mother Elga and Grandmother Thora sent me out to the rock that night," she explained. "Norrie rowed me over at their insistence, though he was not keen on it. An old tradition says a maiden of Caransay must spend a night on the rock every hundred years, and wait for the great kelpie to arrive. If he is pleased, he will make her his bride. They told me to submit to his will, and gave me a potion to ease my fears. I said he would not appear. But he did."

"Good lord," he said.

"If the kelpie claims his bride, he will bestow good fortune on her and the people of Caransay. We needed good fortune then. We were growing desperate. The island leaseholder was planning to evict most everyone and bring in sheep farmers and English flocks. So I agreed to go out to the rock. I never thought anything would happen. But there you were," she added simply.

"No kelpie, but a fortunate man to survive drowning—and lucky to be mistaken for a kelpie," he drawled. She shoved at him, and he captured her hand and kissed it.

"I was fortunate too, in a way." She spoke too soon, not ready to tell him about the child.

"Why was that?"

"I—I was in a haze from the herbal potion I took. I thought you were magical. You did not look like a shipwrecked sailor—you had almost no clothing. You were—magnificent, like a kelpie turned to a man. It was easy to believe." She laid a hand on his chest.

"I wore a shirt, I think. My clothing was wet and heavy, pulling me down in the water, so I shook some things off. I'd rather wash up naked on a beach than die clothed and decent."

"And I was glad to meet a half-naked man than a slimy,

wretched sea monster."

He chuckled. "We helped each other survive that night," he said, and kissed her brow. "So, did the kelpie keep his word and bestow good fortune on you afterward?"

She grew quiet, trembling inside. The truth hovered on her lips, but there was too much to say, here and now. Wanting desperately to tell him, she chose to wait, and not spoil the magic that surrounded them now, and had surrounded them then.

She shrugged. "We were not evicted, as it turned out."

"Lady Strathlin bought the island's lease, I think. That was luck indeed. You had the blessing of the kelpie after all."

Gulping, she could only nod.

He sighed. "My girl," he murmured, "you are so good, so pure and honest in your character. I am very sorry you believed I was a wretched monster, whether it was to scheme you or frighten you. I would never do that." He kissed the top of her head. "You are strong and beautiful. And I have been very lucky too."

She felt torn by guilt. "I am not what you think."

"Do not feel ashamed of what happened that night, or what happened just now, aye? Promise me."

She nodded, unable to meet his eyes just then.

"Listen to me. We saved each other that night. And I take full responsibility for what happened between us. You were an innocent, and I—should have better judgment, then and perhaps now too."

"I wanted it too, Dougal Stewart," she said in a small voice. "It was not just you. Something came over me. It just seemed— right. And seemed right again, now."

"Look at me." He tilted her chin up to kiss her gently. "Meg, I am asking you to marry me."

She gasped, felt tears gather in her eyes. "You do not have an obligation to me."

"I do. But that is not why I asked you. I want to marry you, if you will have me. There is something between us, I agree. I want to be with you, and help take care of you and your family."

She sat away from him, heart pounding. "I cannot. We cannot. You do not need to do this."

"Let me in, lass. You are—so guarded. I do not know why, but I hope you will tell me." He sat straighter, his hand splayed warm on her back. "Life is hard in the Hebrides. I can help you and your family. I have a respectable income."

"That is not it!" She got to her feet. "I appreciate it, I do. But I cannot marry you."

He stood, rubbed a hand over his face as if to summon patience. "I wronged you. I have a conscience, woman. I can make it up to you."

"I beg you, do not pity me or do this out of a sense of duty. I cannot bear it." She whirled to walk away, down the beach, back home.

"Darling wee fool," he said, catching her arm, turning her toward him. "I did not ask out of obligation. I am in love with you, Meg MacNeill."

She stared at him, wordless, filled with anguish and yearning together. He offered what she wanted and needed, and what she wished she could give him—love, desire, forgiveness, and a clear path to a happy life. But she could not accept him now, nor could she explain.

"I love you," he repeated. "I want to be with you. I have loved you these seven years and did not know it until now. You were my salvation that night, though I hurt you without realizing it."

"You saved me, too. I can forgive you the rest of it. But we cannot marry."

"We can." His grip was warm, firm. She felt caught by the spell of his presence, easily cast in the starlight and the sweep of the sea. But she could not give in, with so much at stake. "Meg, remember the dream, yours and mine, too."

"My dreams cannot come true." The awful finality of that twisted inside her.

"Then neither can mine." He let go. "Aye, then. We have time to think about this. My offer stands, lass. I do not give up easily, and I am a patient man."

Again words failed her as she watched him. She felt blessed and cursed, for he was all she wanted and more; yet she could not accept, not now, perhaps never.

Spinning on her heel, she ran, her heart sinking with each step in the sand that took her away from him. Her heart and soul beat against the cage of wealth and secrets that trapped her.

What hurt, suddenly, was that he let her go, gave her the very freedom she wanted. What hurt was that she chose to run, afraid of the truth—who she was, and how much she loved him.

DOUGAL LOOKED UP through the crystal depth of the water to see a blur of blue sky and clouds far above, and golden shadows rippling in currents over the enormous base of the great rock. A pair of dolphins swam overhead.

If dolphins swam freely here, then sharks were not in the area. Good; he did not relish meeting those beasts again. Awkward in his gear and suit, he moved closer to his companion diver. Evan Mackenzie, looking like another sea beast, his tentacle-like hoses undulating as he tapped a hammer on the side of the rock, testing for cracks or weakness.

Doing the same, Dougal moved with slow, clumsy grace, hearing constant noise through the brass-and-copper helmet. The air he breathed, pumped through the long hose attached to the helmet, whooshed in and out, smelling sharply of stale rubber, valves clicking. Overhead, waves shushed, and the wooden platform suspended nearby knocked against the great rock with the current. The sea surrounding the reef was never still, never quiet, too powerful to be tranquil.

Dougal shoved the hammer in his belt and traced his gauntlets over recesses and protrusions, searching for cracks or any sign of damage from blasts. Below the surface, Sgeir Caran was so broad and massive that he and Evan needed multiple dives to check for damage as construction continued.

"Dougal." Alan Clarke's voice was surprisingly clear through the speaking tube.

"Aye," Dougal responded. "All is well."

"Good. You two have been down long enough. Time to come up."

Dougal signaled Evan, who stepped onto the wooden platform and tugged on the ropes, alerting the men above to haul the platform upward. Dougal watched the platform rise in slow increments that would allow Evan's body to adapt to the changing depth.

Waiting his turn, Dougal brushed a hand over the rock to examine a horizontal niche, loosening a cloud of sand and debris. Something glinted in a soft spill of daylight and floated out. He captured it in clumsy fingers, finding a bit of gold coin encrusted with coral. He slipped it into the canvas bag attached to his belt.

When the platform descended again, he climbed on and pulled on the ropes. Going up, he took deep, even breaths to acclimate himself. Overhead, the water swirled blue, and finally he surged through its mass, dripping. Once in the air, he felt the crushing burden of the suit, boots, and gear. Men assisted him to the bench, where he broke out in a hot sweat inside the oppressive suit, still breathing the stale, rubbery air through the hose until the helmet was lifted away.

Cool air burst over him and he sucked it in gratefully while two men removed his cumbersome gear. Thanking them, he stood, clad only in long, damp woolen undergarments, and went to the metal-sided hut to change. Once dressed in dry trousers, shirt, and vest, he walked out again, remembered the little gold piece, and fetched it quickly from the canvas bag.

Examining it in sunlight, he flecked the coral crust away to expose a pretty blue-green pendant, an aquamarine stone framed in filigreed gold. The delicate chain attached to its loop was broken and hopelessly encrusted, but the bijou would be lovely once it was cleaned.

The luminous color reminded him of Meg's sea-colored eyes. It would be lovely on a new gold chain around her slender neck. But he hesitated, remembering her rejection the other night. Though he felt hurt and disappointed, he was not ready to give up on the dream so quickly. A few days had passed when he had been busy on the rock, hoping she might visit him. But she had not.

Opening his heart had not been easy, but he had managed to crack through old layers for her, only for her. If she did not want him in her life—she had good reasons for that—he would accept it. But he could not rest until he knew what troubled her and if he could help. He owed her. And some inner instinct told him to wait and see.

Pocketing the little bijou, he decided to give it to her as a gesture of friendship—or a gesture of love if she wanted it. Once found, love was not something to let go of easily. He would give it time. Besides, he would be here for months with the work to be done on this infernal rock.

Remembering the tasks needing attention, he broke out of his reverie to attend to them.

CHAPTER FOURTEEN

"I APOLOGIZE FOR the late hour," Dougal said.

Meg, holding the door of Norrie's house open, smiled faintly, heart pounding. A fine rain sparkled on his bowler hat and broad shoulders as he stood in the doorway. He was so handsome, so strong and earnest and dear to her, she only blinked.

"I came for my mail, just briefly. I heard Norrie brought it in from Tobermory today."

"He did," she said. A strong gust of wind blew past, nearly tearing the door from her hold. The sky was blustery, with great gray clouds hovering over the sea. "Come in."

"Dougal Stewart!" Norrie came toward the door. "I would have brought the letters to you. Come out of the rain. We will have a gale before long, with the look of that dark sky!"

Removing his hat, Dougal stepped past Meg without glancing at her. She stepped back.

"Sit you down, Mr. Stooar." Thora indicated a bench by the table. "It is a dirty night."

"It is indeed," Dougal agreed, still standing. "Thank you, but I do not want to disturb your evening. I was out walking and thought to save Mr. MacNeill the trouble of bringing the mail."

"Sit you down," Mother Elga repeated, gesturing.

"I should be on my way," he answered. Meg, silent, felt he avoided looking her way. Sensing his cool, shuttered mood, she wondered if he kept his distance from her just as she had done after the night of the ceilidh that had led to deep kisses, love, a marriage offer—and yet she had fled.

Now, standing close beside him, she felt the pull of him like a lodestone. The regret she felt at turning him down still twisted in her like a knife.

"Ach, Mr. Stooar, it is not good for a body to work all the time," Thora said. "We see you out there on the great rock day and night it seems."

"Day and night," Elga echoed, nodding.

"Sit you down and have a dram. The children are to bed, and we are just sitting here in the nice quiet, the four of us. And you make five," Thora said.

Dougal acquiesced with a polite murmur and sat on the bench. He thanked Thora for the cup of whisky she handed him. He cleared his throat, looking awkward enough that Meg wanted to reach out to him.

Elga, seated in a wooden chair by the warm hearth, smiled at him. "Mr. Stooar! Do you love the rain?"

"Sometimes," he said. "A soft rain like this can be peaceful."

"Ah," Elga said. "Peaceful like your home in the sea?"

He glanced at Meg then, and she knew he remembered the old woman's conviction that he was a kelpie come to shore. "Mother Elga, please," she said.

"A soft rain and a peaceful sea are lovely indeed, Mother Elga," he said. "Thank you," he said then, as Meg handed him the bundle of letters that Norrie set on the table. Dougal's fingers brushed hers as he took the envelopes. Startled, feeling a tug of the heart, she stepped back.

"Sit you down, Margaret," Elga said. "Ach, not here. Over there, next to Mr. Stooar!"

"Just here," Thora insisted patting the bench beside Dougal.

Reluctantly, Meg sat. Since the bench barely held two, her skirts fell over Dougal's long, muscular thigh, and her arm brushed his. The mingled scents of rain, wind, and a hint of the flowery machair clung to him. He radiated strength, warmth, security, intimacy too; he hardly looked at her, yet she felt keenly aware of him, body and soul. Her breath came faster, though she sat still and silent beside him.

While he chatted with her grandparents, she glanced at the letters under his hand. The topmost envelope, she saw, was from her solicitors, Dundas and Grant. Dread plunged through her. The lawyers intended to find a way to stall the work on the lighthouse, just as she had requested. She had not received a new report yet, for Norrie had no mail for her on this run, but she assumed that Dundas and Grant wrote to notify Dougal of a new threat to his work.

"I am thinking we do need a lighthouse out there," Norrie was saying. "I am glad you are doing the work."

Meg roused at that. "But, *Seanair*, you have always been against the lighthouse."

"For a while, I agreed with Lady Strathlin, who wants the isle kept private and the rock kept sacred." Norrie pulled on his pipe and gave Meg a meaningful look. He pointed toward the window and the bay beyond. "Now I am thinking the lighthouse will help out there and be not much bother to us after all once it is up. That wicked reef needs a light, and no question."

"The lighthouse could be placed anywhere on that reef," Meg said.

"The light on Sgeir Caran would illuminate the whole of the reef, Miss MacNeill," Dougal said quietly. "Other locations here are partially submerged in high tides. Lighthouses can withstand such conditions, but it is not my preference to risk it."

"It is not his preference," Elga repeated precisely. "He likes Sgeir Caran."

"It is the best location," Dougal agreed.

"Besides, it is an honor to have the resident engineer staying on Caransay," Norrie said. "The one who saved our wee lad." Meg scowled at him.

"Mr. Stooar is always welcome here," Elga said. "And so we like his lighthouse."

"Many ships have gone down on that reef," Norrie said. "The tidal flow between those rocks can spin a ship around and suck it down quickly. I have seen too many wrecks there."

"We never want to see another wreck," Thora agreed.

"You have witnessed some?" Dougal asked.

"Aye, we have," Norrie said. "God save us, it is an awful thing to see. We tried to help the poor souls, but there is little that men can do against a powerful storm. We saved too few souls over the years. It breaks the heart."

"You have rescued people from shipwrecks?" Dougal sat forward.

"*Ach,* aye, me and my kinsmen, and our fathers before us. We did what we could if we saw a ship foundering out there. My grandfather and great-grandfather and some before them were wreckers, I am ashamed to say. Some of them wanted ships to break apart on the rocks."

"Wreckers still do their work in the Isles," Dougal said.

"It is not done on Caransay any longer," Meg said.

"But it was done here long ago," Norrie said. "Many relied on wreckage to bring goods into their homes and money into their pockets. Some even lured ships this way with lamps and fire signals. The wood that made this table and that cupboard came from ship timbers salvaged in my great-grandfather's time," he said. "But my father never wrecked, nor did we. The screams, the groans of the ship, the prayers shouted to God. It is an awful thing, so we must help."

"I am sure you did your best," Dougal said.

"The times it has happened, we have rowed out as far as we dare, and throw out ropes to survivors in the water, though the waves tried to take us as well. Too many ships go down there, I tell you."

"Do you recall," Dougal said slowly, "a wreck about eighteen years ago? A ship called the *Primrose* went down there."

"*Primrose.*" Norrie sent a small puff of smoke out of his pipe. "I recall that name. Many were lost that night, though we rowed out. The inspectors came to the island afterwards and said the ship was the *Primrose* out of Glasgow, sailing up to Skye with people on holiday." He sighed.

"That's the one," Dougal murmured.

Meg felt a surge of compassion, of love, and nearly reached out to touch his hand, resting on the table.

"It was a sad thing. A black storm blew out of the west suddenly and took the ship down within minutes." Norrie shook his head. "We did our best."

"Thank you, Mr. MacNeill," Dougal said.

"Have you a particular interest in that one, then?" Norrie asked.

"My parents were on that ship. I was home with my siblings. I was thirteen."

Meg saw a muscle bounce subtly in his cheek. Breaching the gap without thinking, she touched his forearm, caring only about the hurt he carried in him. He let her hand linger.

"Mr. Stooar," Thora said, "I am sorry. We did not know."

"Of course not. But thank you."

"A hard thing," Norrie said. "We all know that, here in this room. Our son, our Margaret's father, was taken on the reef too."

Though he did not look at Meg, Dougal turned his arm so that her hand fell into his, and he folded his fingers over hers for a moment. That quick gesture gave her bright hope. She desperately needed to know he cared for her.

But as Norrie had just said, it broke the heart; she could not act on the love she had begun to feel deeply, keenly, certainly.

"So that is why you are determined to build a lighthouse out there," Norrie said.

"Aye, sir. The Caran light is important to me, and to your family too."

So many revelations lately, Meg thought. Listening, she realized again how wrong she had been about him over the years. The man had true integrity and compassion, some of it simply born to him, some stemming from private suffering. Tragedy had fueled his work and his persistence.

And she had acted selfishly, making assumptions, allowing solicitors to speak for her as the baroness. From the start, she should have taken the time to learn why Dougal Stewart was so adamant about the lighthouse on Sgeir Caran.

The contents of the letter under his hand might destroy what he had dedicated himself to create. Frowning, head lowered, she felt a heavy remorse and knew she must stop her solicitors from progressing.

"Though a lighthouse would not have saved our son," Norrie was saying. "He knew that reef well. It was the strength of the storm that he could not fight. Margaret," he said, looking hard at Meg, "we will tell Lady Strathlin of the noble reasons for putting a light there and urge her to give Dougal Stewart her help and support. Urge her, do you hear?"

"I hear, *Seanair,*" she whispered.

"I doubt the lady would care, from what I have seen," Dougal said.

Tears stung her eyes. Resolve washed through her—finally she must be done with holding back, done with the hurt and the ruse. Hiding the truth had not protected her or her family, but had only caused more difficulties.

No matter what she had thought years ago, she had been wrong about the obstinate, odious Mr. Stewart. She had hurt him when he only wanted to heal the hurt he had brought her.

Simple enough to tell him who she was, she thought. Far harder to tell him about Sean. But she had to try—or even more hurt was inevitable, and all of it her doing.

"Mr. Stewart, there is something—" she began.

Norrie tapped the table. "Not now, girl," he said in rapid Gaelic. "This is not the time." He must have sensed she was tempted to draw back the curtain on her life.

"Not the time," Thora echoed in Gaelic.

"The *each-uisge* loves the girl," Elga said in the same language. "Can you not see it?"

Dougal looked from one to the other, clearly bewildered, politely waiting.

Meg subsided, knowing they were right. This was not the time. But once he knew the truth, he might despise her for it. Once he knew about his son, he might take him from her, all within his rights as the father.

But too much truth was a risk for Dougal, too. If Roderick Matheson discovered that the lighthouse engineer was the father of her child, he could take steps to ruin not just Meg, but Dougal and his career. The commission that funded the lighthouse would judge their principal engineer's morals poorly, and society would do the same. Though Meg could hide on Caransay all her life, Dougal could lose all he had worked toward.

"Miss MacNeill?" He had seen that she had nearly spoken.

She bit her lip, shook her head. First, she must resolve the problem of Roderick and his hold over her. Then she could reveal the truth. Though she feared what Dougal might think of her once he knew, she could feel free at last, and learn to move on without him.

This tangle was of her own making, and the time had come to unravel it.

"THANK YOU FOR telling me about the *Primrose,* Mr. MacNeill. I appreciate it more than I can say." Dougal set his empty glass down. "And thank you for the hospitality, Mrs. MacNeill. I must go before the weather gets worse."

He stood, refusing while the elderly MacNeills protested with genuine warmth that he should stay. Smiling, he shook his head, and Meg went forward to open the door.

Wind stirred the delicate golden strands of her hair and blew her plain dark skirt back against her lithe form. The sky had grown much darker in the time Dougal had been in the house, and the wind was cold and fast, bringing rain.

"Dirty weather indeed," Norrie said. "It will blow hard to-night. Best get home, sir."

"Good night, then." Dougal nodded toward the others, then looked at Meg. She watched him, eyes wide-eyed and haunted somehow. He could not look away.

Beyond them, the fire crackled in the hearth, the elders sat quietly, the little black terrier asleep at Norrie's feet. The shadowed room was warm, cozy, and welcoming. In the amber glow of the lamplight, Meg's golden hair and creamy skin were heavenly.

He was reluctant to leave, but not because of the storm. The lure that held him was the golden girl in the shadows, as well as the hominess of the place, the goodness of these people. This humble croft felt as much a home to him as his aunt's grand manse in Strathclyde, though he dearly loved that place and the kinfolk there who took him and his siblings in after they lost their parents. Yet he felt just as comfortable among these veritable strangers.

But he did not want Meg to be a stranger in his life. He would not give up on that.

"Good night, Mr. Stewart," she said, a hand on the door. Wind and rain whipped outside.

"Miss MacNeill, good night." He reached into his pocket. "I nearly forgot. I wanted to give you this." He handed her a small paper packet.

Looking at him in surprise, she peeled away the paper—he had wrapped it in a page torn from a notebook—and gasped to see the small aquamarine pendant, polished and glittering. Dougal had cleaned it and strung it on a black cord, with no other suitable chain.

"It's lovely! Where did you—why—"

"I found it in the sea, at the base of Sgeir Caran," he said. "Evan Mackenzie and I went down in the deep the other day, and this was caught in a crevice in the rock. We found coins, too,

Spanish doubloons. They must have been caught in there after some old shipwreck. The pendant was encrusted with coral, so it has been down there a long time. It is a bonny wee thing, and I...well, I thought of you. I apologize for the black thread. I had nothing else for it."

"It's beautiful. I shall treasure it." She glanced up at him. "The woman who owned this may have lost her life out there on the reef."

"A very long time ago. It looks to be very old, an old-fashioned thing. I thought you would appreciate its beauty and its value." He shrugged, though the dazzle of happiness in her eyes meant everything to him just then.

"Thank you, Dougal," she whispered. "I will always think of you when I wear this."

That hurt, but he did not react, setting his hand on the door close to hers. "Show it to Lady Strathlin," he said. "Remind her how many lives have been lost on the reef. Perhaps she would better understand the importance of that lighthouse."

Her eyes went wide and anxious, though she did not answer, but reached up to tie the black cord behind her neck, suspending the pendant at her throat, over the simple neckline of her blouse. A small golden oval hung there, too, just below the pulse in her throat.

"You already wear a necklace." He had noticed it the night they had loved on the beach.

"I often wear this," she said, her slim fingers graceful as they popped the tiny catch. Framed in the two halves, he saw a miniature portrait of a child with golden curls—and though she closed the locket quickly, he glimpsed what was caught under glass in the other oval: a braided circlet of red thread and looped hairs, golden and brown. The sight struck him to the core.

He carried its twin tucked in the hidden compartment of his pocket watch. Instinctively, he touched the watch pocket in his vest, tempted to show her that he had kept his braided ring too. But he would not be a maudlin fool desperate for her love.

Enough to know she had kept her ring, too.

"Well," he said, stepping back with a cool smile, "I am glad you like the jewel. Good night."

Thora came toward the door. "Best stay here, Mr. Stooar. This storm could blow up so fast that you might not be able to stand up on your way back."

"I will be fine. Good night." Dougal tapped his bowler on his head and stepped out into the battering force of the wind. Holding the brim of his hat, he fought his way across the wet sand of the yard toward the slope leading to the machair.

"Mr. Stewart!" Meg cried out. "Dougal, wait!"

He turned to see her running out of the house. He waited, while the wind pushed at him, nearly whipped the hat from his head, though he held it on. Rain slanted over his shoulders.

"Stop! Come back to the house and wait this out!" She came closer. The reedy grass blew all around them, and the surf pounded loudly on the beach. "Norrie says this is looking more fierce than he thought, and you should come back. A man could get washed out to sea just going home."

"Go back inside. You'll be soaked."

Her gown was already damp, but she shook her head. "You as well. You are so obstinate."

"As are you, lass," he said. The next gust of wind beat at her skirts and blew her hair over her eyes. She brushed all of it back and held his gaze.

"I came out to thank you for the gift."

"You thanked me inside." He wanted to pull her into his arms for wild kisses in the rain. Instead, he stood with water drizzling from the brim of his hat, heart twisting for love of her, his hands flexing as if to release the feeling.

"I want to give you something in return, to remember me by." She pulled a cloth-wrapped packet from her skirt pocket. "Do not open it out here in the wet and the wind. Wait until later."

He crammed the sturdy packet inside his coat, and tipped his hat. "Thank you. But—to remember you? Are you planning to leave?"

"Soon, aye."

"I must leave for Edinburgh soon to tend to some business. I hope to see you when I return." He would not be gone long, but he was unsure if she would be on the island when he came back. Why did this feel suddenly and dreadfully like goodbye?

"Perhaps. I must return, ah, home soon. I no longer live on the island." She clasped her hands, rain slicking down her curls, wind billowing her skirt.

"Mull, I think?" When she did not answer, just stared at him, he was overwhelmed with a renewed urge to pull her to him and claim her stubborn little heart, tell her all that was in his mind and his heart now. He sucked in a breath. "Meg, whatever troubles you, we can solve it."

She shook her head. "Not this. I do not know how to solve this. Wanting—what cannot be." She whirled and ran.

"Devil take it," he muttered, and went after her. Just a few steps and he reached out, cupping her shoulder in the rain, turning her, taking her in his arms, shielding her from the rain as he kissed her soundly. She gave a little cry and pushed her fingers through his damp hair, knocking his hat somewhere, rain falling on both their heads as she kissed him, he kissed her, not knowing where it began, where it would lead, how it might end as the rain beat on their heads and shoulders and mud collected around their feet. In the distance, thunder rumbled.

She broke away, breathless. "When you kiss me like that, I cannot think."

"Do you need to just now? There is something between us, so strong, do you not feel it?"

"I feel it—and I must think," she burst out, nearly a cry, and pushed at him.

He let go as she spun away. "Meg—"

But she was running again, splashing through rain and mud, and did not stop. This time, he could not chase her; she needed the chance to think, feel, sort this through. At first, he had been muddled too, but time with her, and kisses, had clarified his feelings. Now he had to trust that her thoughts and her heart would favor him.

"Everlasting hell," he muttered, snatching up his hat and stomping off to make his way up and over the machair toward the clustered huts where sensible men were inside, dry and warm.

Entering his small hut, he removed his wet outer things, lit the lamp, and then extracted the package from inside his vest. Unwrapping the paper that sealed it, he found a leather-covered book tied with a red ribbon. It was one of her journals.

Taking a seat at the wobbly table, he turned the pages carefully. Filled with pencil and ink studies, some washed with pale color, the pages were crammed with images of flowers, plants, shells, stones, birds, and wildlife. She had added notations in lovely handwriting, a brief commentary for most of the drawings.

Fetching a drink of whisky against the chill and the rain, and to fortify his sorry heart, rejected again—yet hopeful now, for this was a tender and meaningful gift. He pored over the pages with care, then sat back, resting his hand on the book. Something was tapping at his awareness, something he had seen before, recently. Perhaps her other journal—not that, he thought. Something else familiar.

Outside, the rain was a heavy downpour, noisy on the thin roof and walls. Taking out the letters Norrie had brought, he read them by lamplight; one contained more news from Dundas and Grant, none of it promising.

The wind shook the thin walls of the hut, and he could hear the waves crashing relentlessly onshore, reminding him of another fierce storm on the night his life changed irrevocably.

Shoving a hand through his hair, he was struck by a powerful depth of loneliness for one person. But he must give her distance to discover how she felt about this between them. Then he would take her in his arms again—or walk away.

With a sigh, he turned his attention to the latest salvo from the lady's insufferable lawyers. And he had letters to write; the Lighthouse Commission needed to be informed of delays and developments. He could trust Norrie to get the letters out as quickly as possible.

First, the island would need to outlast this storm.

20 August 1857
To the Northern Lighthouse Commission
George Street, Edinburgh

Dear Sirs,

Recently we endured a storm of considerable force on Caransay, two days of high winds, heavy rain, and breakers taller than any man. We emerged from confinement in our quarters to find a world littered with damage and debris.

On Sgeir Caran, the lighthouse worksite lost one work shed, while the smithy, once riveted to the rock, now lists to one side. Various tools are missing, as well as a workbench, all blown into the sea.

Most astonishing of all, two stone blocks, weighing one ton each, were shifted off the rock by wind and wave, and now lie at the bottom of the sea. We will need to fetch the stones and other items with the help of cranes and divers in gear.

Funds will be needed to repair things and replace equipment. This will increase my original estimate by at least five percent. However, Lady Strathlin's advocates have informed me by letter that some contributors who have offered their assistance have been told they need not extend it.

I plan to return to Edinburgh shortly and personally appeal to these contributors to reconsider. If the Commission will extend additional funds in the meantime, it is much appreciated.

I also intend to pay a call on Lady Strathlin.

Yrs. respectfully,

Dougal Robertson Stewart
Innish Bay, Caransay, Hebrides

CHAPTER FIFTEEN

"I WHOLEHEARTEDLY AGREE, you cannot abandon this project, Dougal," Sir Aedan MacBride told him. "Your lighthouse must go up. The location is ideal and the need is paramount."

"It is." Dougal leaned back in a leather-upholstered chair in his cousin's study. He had come down from Edinburgh for a few days to visit with kinfolk at Aedan's home of Dundrennan in Strathclyde. "I cannot give up this cause, despite the latest maneuvers of Lady Strathlin's mob of solicitors." Nor could he give up any chance to see Meg MacNeill while the lighthouse was being built.

"Well done. Still, it is a shame Lady Strathlin does not understand that."

"More to the point, the lawyers who speak for her misunderstand it." Dougal appreciated his cousin's calm natural reserve and his ability to listen carefully. Lingering over glasses of port after a meal together, Dougal had confided some of the troubling details of the project to Aedan, an engineer of highways and byways.

Dougal circled his glass in one hand and watched the dark liquid slosh inside. "I would build the thing myself, even fund it myself, even if it broke me. I would set every damned stone with my own hands if I had to." He sat forward and rubbed a hand over his face, weary and frustrated, yet feeling trenchant determination. "The Caran light must go up."

Aedan nodded. "A more bullheaded lad has never breathed. That persistence was a bit of a fault when you were younger. But it has helped you face impossible odds and danger in building your lighthouses. This one will be a magnificent structure. The design is spare, yet elegant and practical and will outlast the ages. I have no doubt it will go up by hook or by crook."

"Aye. Perhaps you can make the journey to see it when it does."

"I would like that. How is Evan Mackenzie, by the way? Still spitting into the wind? What a sight it must be, you two rascals besting that great rock above and below the sea."

"Besting! Hardly. We barely hang on some days," Dougal laughed. He had attended Edinburgh University with Aedan and Mackenzie both, and they knew each other well. "Evan is subdued these days. He keeps to himself since the incident last year."

"That bridge collapse was not his fault, though unfortunately not everyone agrees."

"Nor is he to blame for his father's faults. But Evan takes these things to heart."

"Lord Kildonan is a discredit to the whole of Scotland. No wonder Evan rejects him."

"A tricky path, for he remains his father's sole heir. One day he will be Earl of Kildonan, which he says is the last thing he wants or needs."

"Inheriting a black mark when his reputation has already suffered—that is not easy."

Dougal stared at the tartan carpet beneath his boots. "Aedan," he said, "what do you know of Lady Strathlin?"

"Some. Just that she inherited the biggest fortune in Scotland rather unexpectedly. The male heir and the next in line both died, and old Lord Strathlin followed shortly after. Awful business for a young woman, but I understand she has been a credit to the title and estate and is generous and charitable. So her determination to interfere with your work is surprising."

"True, it does not chime with what is said of her magnanimous nature. She bought the lease of the island years ago from the English lord who owned it, fired the factor, and secured the island in perpetuity for her tenants. They need not worry about much beyond the fickle weather, which can be a real threat. For all the trouble she has caused me, the woman is admirable otherwise."

"Aye. She has provided relief elsewhere in the Hebrides and Highlands, sending food shipments and helping them start industries to support themselves. My own father spent much of his personal fortune on shiploads of grain and goods for Highlanders and Islesmen years ago when they were in desperate need. If Lady Strathlin uses her fortune and influence to make a difference, she is to be applauded."

"You have met her, I think?"

"Just briefly about two years ago. Beautiful, as I recall, younger than I expected," Aedan continued. "She had a train of attendants and hangers-on, but was neither haughty nor vain. We did not talk for long but I found her charming and genuine."

"Huh," Dougal said. "I have thought she must be an older woman."

"Young and quite appealing. A cloud of golden hair and eyes like the sea in sunlight."

"Interesting," Dougal said, brow wrinkling. Perhaps she was close kin to Meg MacNeill.

Aedan rose to his feet. "Shall we join Aunt Lill and your sister for coffee?"

Dougal rose. "Aye. Aunt Lill brought her monkey to tea today, and I heard the wee beastie chattering somewhere while we were at dinner. Does wee Thistle still keep late hours?"

Aedan grinned. "I assure you, Miss Thistle will not be taking coffee with us tonight."

"Taking coffee, tossing cups, cracking china," Dougal drawled. "She is entertaining company."

"We are in luck. Amy is planning parlor games for tonight,

and she finds Thistle tiresome, so the beastie is banned from the drawing room. A word of warning—your sister is delighted you are here for a good game of charades."

"Please, not Amy's endless games of charades." Dougal groaned.

"We must submit," Aedan said, pinching back a smile.

"Have you not submitted to her yet? I wondered if my sister would have convinced you to marry her by now, as she would be a safe and sensible match. She is aware of your hesitations regarding marriage."

Aedan frowned, and Dougal saw the humor diminish in his cousin's vivid blue eyes. "I am very fond of Amy, and she has been a great help to me in refurbishing this house according to my father's will." He gestured around the room, with its new tartan carpeting and chintz draperies. "But she is young, and we are cousins. I love her as a sister, but that is all I can offer her."

"She is made of iron under all that charm," Dougal said. "That will not break her heart."

"Good. Still, I hesitate about marrying anyone. I want a wife and family, but I have not been fortunate in that regard."

"Surely the luck of Dundrennan will change."

"According to the black curse over my ancestors—and so myself—the lairds of Dundrennan can never risk falling in love. I tested the rule and found it too truthful."

"I am sorry. Someday," Dougal said quietly, "you will take the risk again."

"Which means I would have to break a spell that has haunted this place for centuries. I am not certain it is worth it," Aedan murmured, and opened the door.

Later, in the drawing room with their Aunt Lillian and Dougal's two sisters, he could hear his aunt's monkey chittering through the door, though Amy flatly refused to let it come inside. Dougal relaxed that evening, laughing as Amy, blonde and vivacious in yards of pink flounces, firmly shooed the tiny creature out of the room when it tried to sneak past a housemaid.

Glad to be with family, content and amused, he wondered how Meg MacNeill would suit with them. Very well indeed, he was sure. He could easily imagine her here, chatting and laughing with his sisters, laughing at Lill's monkey, and deep in intellectual conversation with Aedan, who would be interested in Meg's journals. His father, Sir Hugh MacBride, had been a famous and very prolific poet, and Sir Hugh's vast library was one of the treasures of Dundrennan House. She would fit in with his family as if she had known them forever.

But he had no guarantee that she wanted to be part of his life. And he did not know when, or if, he would see her again.

He wanted genuine love in his life, wanted it with Meg. For Aedan MacBride, love was a dark curse, something to avoid, but Dougal had hope. Loneliness had become a burden, and the risk and danger of his work was less satisfying now. Meeting a beautiful, mysterious girl on a wind-lashed rock had been the turning point. He felt there was destiny there, if only she agreed.

Soon he intended to go to Caransay to resume the work—and to woo her properly. Though she had reason to distance herself, considering their initial meeting years back, he sensed that something else, something current, troubled her more.

But before he could travel to the Isles to see Meg again, he must face Lady Strathlin.

"HERE IT IS. *Campanula rotundifolia*. The bluebell," Meg said, turning a page in the volume spread open on the library table. She had arrived at Strathlin Castle a few days earlier, entering a whirlwind of demands on her time and attention, but today she had found a little time to work on her island journal. Writing a notation beneath a sketch of the tiny blue flowers, she sanded the ink and blew gently to dry it.

In Gaelic, the brog na cubhaig, *or cuckoo's shoe, she wrote, is a blue bellflower common in Scotland and prolific on Caransay's flowery machair. Fairies are said to make hats from the flowers and also use the tiny bells to ring out a warning of danger.*

Hearing a knock on the door, she glanced up to see Angela Shaw enter and come toward her. "Working on your Caransay journal?"

"Just finishing some pages I did on holiday." She felt a tug of the heartstrings to think of the island, where her son and family remained, and where Dougal Stewart had spun her head and her life around. The day she left, she had not seen him, but heard he had gone out to Sgeir Caran to work. Sailing with Norrie on her way to Tobermory to catch a steamer to the mainland shore, she had looked up at the great sea rock, aware that Dougal was either up there, or under the sea, and she wished she had said farewell—and wished she had found the courage to tell him all the truth.

"Bluebells!" Angela looked at the open page. "What a pretty drawing."

"Thank you, I am rather pleased with it." Meg inked a few refining strokes. "Is there news about arrangements for the soiree?"

"Mr. Hamilton and I are settling some of the details. And I had a letter from Mr. Charles Worth this morning. He is sending a dressmaker from his shop in Paris to fit your gown. She will arrive next week by train to Edinburgh. The coachman can bring her here if you like."

"How nice! She should stay at Charlotte Square townhouse rather than out here at Strathlin." Meg looked up. "The soiree will be held there, and we should leave soon for the city. The fittings can be done there. Mrs. Larrimore can prepare a room for the seamstress to stay and work in comfort."

"Very well. I can hardly wait to see this gown!" She smiled. "Mr. Worth mentioned that he has outdone himself with this creation for you."

Meg smiled to see the joy in Angela's delicate face. Too often her friend, a pale blonde with light-blue eyes, wore mourning colors that drained her of color. Widowed several years ago while young, she kept to dark colors out of habit, perhaps not ready to move on. Angela was a gentle, loyal friend and an invaluable aide and companion, and Meg only wanted to see her happy again.

"The Worth gown will be lovely. And you deserve some credit for that, Angela. Mr. Worth took your suggestions to heart in designing it." Smiling, her enthusiasm felt forced, her delight in the beautiful gown and her anticipation of the soiree diminished by a dull ache of loneliness and loss. But losing Dougal Stewart this time was her own doing.

She set a hand to the snugly corseted waistline of her day dress of blue plaid satin, and wondered again if Dougal would attend her soiree. He had been invited before she had met him on Caransay, but she did not know if he had accepted.

"Have we received replies to all the invitations?" she asked. "I wonder if some have responded. For instance, Mr. Dougal Stewart, the lighthouse engineer," she added casually. "Perhaps he will be busy working in the Isles."

"Let me look." Angela Shaw went to a secretary desk in a corner and opened it to retrieve a written list. "Mr. Hamilton tucked the list here with the envelopes that are coming in by post." She turned. "His name is here, aye. And his response." Rummaging through the letters, she plucked one out of the pile to bring it to Meg.

Fingers trembling, she opened the envelope to remove a reply card. *Dear Lady Strathlin, I am pleased to accept your invitation.* He had added his name in the plain, masculine script she recognized. It brought him back to her so sharply that she sucked in a breath. His answer had been sent from Caransay.

If he attended, he would see immediately that Meg MacNeill was in fact Baroness Strathlin. *Oh, dear God.* Dread spun in her stomach. *I should have told him.*

She set the note aside as another knock came at the door, and Guy Hamilton entered. Earlier in the day, she had sat briefly with him to review preparations for the soiree. The event dominated her household, looming in the future. She wished she had never agreed to it.

"Madam, the post has arrived. Good afternoon, Mrs. Shaw," he added in a murmur.

Meg often noticed a flush on Guy Hamilton's cheeks when he was near the young widow, and now pink brightened Angela Shaw's cheeks too. Glancing from one to the other, Meg felt sure they had a strong mutual affection. But each was so reserved in character, carefully guarding feelings, that she wondered if they had acknowledged it. Perhaps falling in love herself had sharpened her sense of it in others. She wanted to push them together and leave the room. Instead, she smiled calmly, watching them.

"Good day, Mr. Hamilton," Angela said with a tiny, dimpled smile. "Lady Strathlin was asking about the final guest list for the party."

"Nearly done. Oh, I see you have it there." He reached as Angela gave him the folded sheet. "Nearly all have accepted, but for a few who are traveling or indisposed. Even Mr. Stewart of the lighthouse kerfuffle will be there."

"So I understand," Meg said. "It will be an interesting evening," she added, stomach tight.

"A private assembly hosted by Lady Strathlin, following a concert by a renowned songstress," Guy said, looking at Angela, "and she thinks it will be *interesting.*"

Angela laughed softly. "If Mr. Stewart comes, it will certainly be interesting!"

"Why do you say that?" Meg asked, her voice a bit shrill.

"Let us hope your first meeting with him will not come to fisticuffs, since the lawyers have been unable to dissuade him. Did you happen to meet him on the island?"

"I did," she said curtly, and blew on her inked drawing even though it was dry.

"And you left the poor fellow and his lighthouse still standing?"

"His lighthouse is not up yet," Meg said tightly.

"Did you have a chance to discuss the situation with him?"

She sighed. "A little. To be honest, I did not tell Mr. Stewart that I am Lady Strathlin."

"What?" Guy looked at her incredulously.

"He thinks you are just a lass from Caransay?" Angela asked, looking stunned.

She nodded. "I—never found a moment to tell him."

Guy huffed. "Well, he is about to find out. What then?"

She shrugged. "I should have said something. But he—he was out on the rock out in the sea often. Now I am not sure how to approach it," she confessed.

"Mr. Stewart will be staggered when he realizes who you are," Angela said.

"And quite possibly furious," Guy said.

Meg flinched. "He does seem stubborn and proud."

"With cast-iron integrity, I believe, so he may not take it well," Guy said. "I hear he is back in Edinburgh now. Perhaps you could see him before the party."

She gulped. "I suppose that would be best."

"We can send a note to his city residence—that is the address we used for the invitation—and ask him to call on you at Charlotte Square," Angela suggested.

Again, Meg shrugged. "Perhaps we should do that." Wanting desperately to see him, she dreaded what she must do.

"At least write to the man with an explanation so he is prepared," Guy said. "He may decide to decline the soiree. Or perhaps he will be forgiving and show some humor about it."

"Perhaps. But he should hear it from me beforehand, I know." She sighed. "Was there anything else?"

"We have tickets for Miss Lind's concert on the evening of your soiree, and we can arrange carriages for those who wish a ride to your house from there. Oh, and Mr. Worth sent a bill for the balance owed on the gown. A bit hasty, I thought. I prefer to pay once the confection is finished."

"That sounds reasonable," Meg said.

"Would you like the amount paid by bank draft or deposited

to an account? It is a considerable sum."

"Sir John deposited the first payment in Mr. Worth's London account, and that can be done again. It is a rather large sum for a gown, I know."

"That crossed my mind, but it will be unique and lovely," Guy said.

"You will be dazzled by the confection, Mr. Hamilton," Angela said. "She will look divine!"

"Milady's companion will no doubt be a dazzling sight as well." He smiled at Angela.

Seeing that, Meg's heart surged with joy as she saw them blush, their eyes sparkling. Wanting to give them the moment, she turned pages in her journal, pretending to be absorbed. Hearing them murmur, she looked up to see them gazing at her now.

"Madam," Guy said, "may I inquire if anything unusual happened in the Isles this time?"

"I had a lovely holiday, but that is not unusual."

"Mr. Hamilton and I both wondered if something occurred there," Angela said. "Ever since your return, you seem…preoccupied. You sigh often and look into the distance. And you do not seem as excited about the soiree now."

"Preoccupied?" Meg raised a brow, tempted to confide in her friends. Yet she must protect her son and Dougal too. But Sir Roderick's insistence on marriage hung over her head like a sword. "A bit. But nothing troubles me," she said defensively.

"Something does," Guy said.

"We are your dear friends. Remember that," Angela said.

"I know. Thank you." Dear friends who were too perceptive, Meg thought, and glanced away. Through the window, blue hills spread into the misty distance. Far to the west, invisible to the eye, lay the island where her heart resided, and near it the great sea rock. "I am preoccupied with so much to be done before the soiree. It will be a relief when the evening is finally over. Why would you think otherwise?"

"Mrs. Berry came to me," Angela said. "She thinks you are smitten, and could perhaps use a friend."

Meg ducked her head, turning a page. "Mrs. Berry is a romantic and wants everyone to be smitten or in love. Who does she think I have fallen for?" A dangerous question, she knew.

"Mr. Stewart," Angela said. Beside her, Hamilton lifted his brow in surprise. "Berry says he is charming and handsome, and not an ogre in the least," Angela said. "She calls him brave and kind, and says he seemed quite taken with you."

Guy folded his arms. "The odious Mr. Stewart! This is surprising."

"This is Berry's imagination," Meg said, her cheeks heating fiercely.

"Berry also said Sir Roderick came to Caransay," Angela said. "But I was sure you would not be taken with him, though he makes it rather clear that he is interested in you."

"Too interested," Meg said.

"I heard through the bank that he went out there to see you," Guy said.

"To be honest, he pressed marriage. I do not wish to discuss it now," Meg said bluntly.

"I do not trust the man," Guy said. "Mr. Stewart seems far more trustworthy by comparison. Just be cautious, dear Baroness. Remember we are here to help. Aye so, Mrs. Shaw?"

"Oh, aye," Angela said, her blue gaze caught in Hamilton's dark glance.

Tears stung then as Meg saw a glow of love there. Happy for them, she felt struck by longing and regret, too. The journal pages blurred before her eyes. "I shall keep it in mind. Do be gone, both of you. There is much to do, and I feel a headache coming on."

"I shall bring you tea," Angela said, and left the room with Guy Hamilton.

CHAPTER SIXTEEN

"THANK YOU FOR taking the time to meet with me, Mr. Logan." Seated in a wooden chair beside a wide, polished mahogany desk, Dougal reached into his pocket and pulled out a small linen-wrapped package. He laid it on the desk surface.

Samuel Logan, a heavyset gentleman with gray side-whiskers and a preference for tobacco, for the room reeked of it, nodded. "I always have time for a nephew of Sir Hugh MacBride. Chambers Street Publishers was honored to produce his poems." He gestured toward the bookcases lining his walls, where Dougal noticed his uncle's volumes of poetry and other writings prominently displayed. "We published something of yours, as well. Do you have something else?"

"Nothing at the moment. Your firm was kind to publish a series of my articles about lighthouse design that appeared in the *Edinburgh Review* a few years ago. *Principles of Pharological Design with Respect to the Forces of Nature* is hardly exciting reading."

"On the contrary, it was fascinating stuff," Logan said. "We have respectable orders every autumn for *Pharological Design* from engineering classes at universities in Scotland and England too. It provides you a wee income, eh?" He smiled. "What brings you here, sir, if not another treatise?"

"I do have something, but I am not the author. It is merely an inquiry." Dougal slid the package across the desk. "I thought you might find it interesting. A dear friend who lives on a Hebridean isle wrote this wee journal. I do not have your talent for judging the best in books, but I think it worth a look."

Logan reached over an untidy pile of papers and books to pick up Meg's journal. Setting a pair of gold-wire glasses on his nose, he flipped through the book, nodding thoughtfully. Finally, he looked up.

"Did the author appoint you as messenger, sir? There is a distinctly feminine sensibility to this wee journal." He peered over his spectacles.

"She gave me her journal as a gift, and I thought to show it to you. I do not think she would mind that. But she does not believe her work worthy of publication. As you can see, it is not a personal diary, but rather a chronicle of nature on the Isle of Caransay."

"Aye, remarkable." Logan turned pages. "Your friend is quite talented. These are skillful drawings, pleasing and precise, with poetic descriptions too. Exquisite thing. It's as if we're peeking into a lady's diary while she shares her love for her home in the Isles." He turned more pages. "She brings the place to life, yet remains anonymous. Marvelous. Quite unique."

"I hoped you might like it."

Logan paged through the rest of the book, then glanced up. "Is this all of it?"

"There are other journals, I believe, and all treat the flora and fauna, weather, the geological character of the island and so on. She manages to capture the beauty and variety of life on the island, along with the seasons and the moods of the sea, too, in these elegant drawings. I assure you the other journals would be equal in merit to this one."

"I would like to see the others, if she is agreeable."

"She made these just for the joy of the work, but I think she would be happy to share them in book form for others to enjoy."

"We may be able to arrange that. This is beautiful." Logan sat forward. "There is a great deal of interest in Highland culture just now. People are mad for Scotland, its history and culture. Mad to tour the Highlands and purchase any souvenir they can find. Some think we should not perpetuate the romance of plaids and bagpipes and heather, but honestly, it helps the Scottish economy to do so. Queen Victoria herself writes Highland journals, did you know?"

"I have heard so."

"A Hebridean journal written and illustrated by a Scotswoman would be quite popular." Logan tapped the desk with his fingers. "Do you think she would agree?"

"Perhaps. I will ask her."

"Tell her of our great interest in publishing them."

"I hope to see her when I return to the island. We are building a lighthouse out there."

"Excellent! Let me give you a letter of introduction." Logan took up a sheet of paper, dipped a pen, and began to write.

Waiting, Dougal flipped pages in the little book, skimming past delicate studies of flowers, seashells, and other delightful images. He paused to read some marginal notes in Meg's lovely handwriting beside images of Sgeir Caran, the rock, the sea, the birds.

Eagles mate for life, she had noted beside a sketch of two birds in flight. *This pair has been together many years. Their loyalty is transcendent. As they soar over the sea rock in unison, one realizes the profound poetry of their devotion, the love of two souls who will never part.*

A shiver ran through him, deep and secret, as if Meg herself had whispered in his ear. He closed the book quietly.

Logan sealed an envelope and handed it to Dougal. "I have taken the liberty of enclosing a cheque in the amount of thirty pounds. I can offer the lady a little more, but I hope this will secure her interest in giving us the privilege of publishing her journals."

"Thank you, Mr. Logan. I will convey this to her and ask her to reply."

"You may wish to act as her adviser, since you have published with us yourself."

"Small experience, but I would be glad to be of assistance." Dougal slid the envelope and the little book into his pocket. "I admit, I took a risk in showing you her wee book."

"You are a loyal friend, sir. Convince the lady that this is a golden opportunity. I hope her dreams equal your dreams for her."

"Dreams?" Dougal stood. "I hope so, too."

"CERTAINLY, MRS. LARRIMORE, if you think we need extra staff for the soiree, please hire them." Meg stood in the drawing room with Angela Shaw and the housekeeper of the Charlotte Square townhouse.

"You will find willing maids of service at Matheson House," Angela suggested. "It is newly established, and there are several young women there eager for work."

"Huh, *them* lassies," Mrs. Larrimore said dubiously.

"They are well-bred young women caught by unfortunate circumstance," Meg said. "Many of them desire honest work. Hire a few as kitchen maids and upstairs maids for the evening, at least. We will need a couple of lady's maids as well."

"I suppose I could inquire," the housekeeper said.

"Now, we shall have music and dancing that evening. I believe the drawing room will be large enough if some furniture is removed to the upstairs rooms. The carpet is large in that room and should do nicely for dancing."

"Aye, and the musicians can sit in that corner, near the garden doors." Mrs. Larrimore pointed to a roomy area beside the small conservatory. "We can set conservatory plants about in pots."

"Lovely idea," Meg said. "The roses in the conservatory are plentiful. Use some of those. Mrs. Shaw, have other flowers been ordered?"

"Yes, madam. Yellow and ivory roses and some others for variety and color. And the buffet table will have an arrangement of sugared fruits in a tower, very pretty. And I made some tiny nightingales out of silk and paper in the Japanese method to set among the flower arrangements, in honor of Miss Lind, since she is called the Swedish Nightingale."

"Splendid idea! You have a delicate hand for craftwork." Meg looked around the room. "We also need to designate two upstairs rooms as dressing rooms for the ladies and the gentlemen."

"Aye, madam," the housekeeper agreed. "The rooms will be heated and well lit, and there will be plenty of soap and water, towels, combs, pins, and so forth for the guests."

"It will be a nice touch to provide rose and lavender water, and almond cream too."

"I will see it done. The grooms will be told to reduce the hearth fires as the evening goes on. With so many guests, we do not want the place too warm!"

"Good. I will leave the details to you, Mrs. Larrimore, as you know what is needed. We will arrive in groups after the concert at the Music Hall. All must be in readiness by eight o'clock, I think. And we should designate a lady's maid for Miss Lind, who will arrive after the others."

"Katie will do. She's a good lass. Did you look at the menu, madam?"

"It is perfect. I would not change a thing," Meg said. "Mrs. Shaw?"

"Very nice. And I like the plan to provide fruit ices and lemonade early, with a light buffet supper served at midnight."

"Very good, then," Mrs. Larrimore said. "I'd best get back to work. Cook will start baking well before dawn that day, and we will be busy—meats to roast for cold slices later, dishes and punches to prepare, ice to be delivered and stored. And the entire house will be cleaned and polished beforehand. Do not fret about any of it."

"Thank you. Oh, the dressmaker from Paris will arrive afternoon," Meg said. The housekeeper bobbed her head and left the room.

"It promises to be a lovely event," Angela said.

"This is not a large house for such a party," Meg replied, glancing around. "I…I am feeling a bit nervous, Angela."

"Strathlin Castle has more room, but it is too far. Your guests can quickly return to their homes and hotels from here. And it is convenient for Miss Lind, as well, since she is traveling."

Meg nodded distractedly. "I know you and Mrs. Larrimore and the others will make this a wonderful party. It is…something else entirely."

Angela tilted her head. "Can I help?"

"I must puzzle it out on my own." She thought of Dougal walking the machair of Caransay deep in the night, puzzling out his theorems as well as his feelings for her. Seeing Angela's keen glance, Meg smiled brightly. "You are always a help. We had best hurry. We are expected at the opening of the new exhibit at the National Museum of Antiquities. They have some recently discovered Celtic treasures which I hear are quite stunning."

"I am looking forward to it. The museum directors are delighted to have you attend, madam, since you and Matheson Bank are major contributors to the museum. They may ask you to say a few words."

"I shall decline, but I will sponsor their work most generously if they allow me anonymity."

"Some members of the bank's board plan to attend the exhibit's opening, as well. I know that Sir John Shaw and Sir Roderick Matheson are both invited."

The rhythm of Meg's step faltered slightly as she walked arm in arm with Angela. "How nice it will be to escape from the concerns of the party for a little while."

"LADY STRATHLIN, WHAT a joy to see you again," Sir Roderick said as he stepped out from behind a stone column. The museum's bright, spacious foyer was crowded with ladies and gentlemen attending the opening. Sunlight beamed over golden stone, green ferns, and the cheerful colors in the ladies' dresses and bonnets.

"Sir Roderick," Meg looked up at him from under the brim of her dark-blue bonnet. "I did not expect to see you here."

He doffed his top hat politely. "I am here to represent the bank. And glad to have a moment to speak with you. Have you thought about my proposal?"

She stared up at him. In the shadow of the huge column and lost in the noise of the echoing room, their conversation was private. But she stepped away from the column, looking around for Angela Shaw or any other acquaintance nearby.

"I have given your suggestion some thought," she said carefully. "But I am not ready to talk about it. Certainly not here," she added, waving a hand toward the crowd admiring the contents of a series of glass display cases containing artifacts in stone, silver, gold, and enamel.

"Of course not, my dear," Matheson said. "I only wanted to remind you."

"How could I possibly forget? Ah, Mrs. Shaw!" she called. Angela turned to glide toward them, her black bombazine skirt and purple-and-black bonnet a somber note in the bright, sunny foyer.

"My dear Margaret, I look forward to hearing your answer." Roderick then took Angela's gloved hand cordially. "Mrs. Shaw, how delightful to see you." He turned to Meg. "I so look forward to your soiree, Lady Strathlin. We are to attend in grand full dress following Miss Lind's concert, I take it?"

"The details of dress are on your invitation card."

"Indeed. Please accept my apology, for I must run. I have an appointment with Mr. Stewart this afternoon. I believe you know him, madam."

Meg smothered a gasp. "Mr. Dougal Stewart? I do."

"He and I have some business matters to discuss, now that he finds himself in a state of near ruin. I understand that he is coming to your soiree. That should prove interesting."

"Near ruin?" Meg stared up at him.

"Thanks to you and your solicitors. I suppose your advocates work independently for your benefit, sparing you the details. He needs funds for his project."

"I hadn't been told yet." Meg felt Angela watching her with a slight frown. Meg wondered in a growing panic what her solicitors had done.

Roderick tipped the brim of his hat again. "Your lawyers have triumphed over Mr. Stewart at last. We shall talk further, dearest Margaret," he said, taking her hand and bowing. "Mrs. Shaw." He turned away to stride through the crowd.

Meg watched his tall black form as he cut a path through the bright crowd. She looked at Angela.

"I despise that oily snake," Angela murmured. Meg blinked, surprised to hear that from her demure friend. "I hope you will not consider marrying him. He tells everyone you are head over heels in love with him."

"I am not," Meg said firmly.

"I did not think so." Angela took her arm. "Have you seen the beautiful jewelry in the exhibit? You must come look. And I've found Mr. Hamilton, who is talking with the antiquarian who discovered some of the artifacts herself. She is lovely and delightful. Her name is Mrs. Christina Blackburn. Mr. Hamilton can introduce you. The Blackburns are rather famous as an artistic family, although she is not an artist."

"Ah, yes. Her father was a brilliant painter. I own a seascape by him."

"Her late husband was an artist as well. She is the lovely brunette standing over there with Mr. Hamilton and the tall blond gentleman. That is Dr. Connor MacBain."

"Oh I know the name," Meg said. "He has an excellent reputation, but we have never met." She remembered Dougal once mentioning a cousin was the wife of Dr. MacBain in Edinburgh.

Her heart beat faster. Dougal's cousin. "Is there—anyone else here whom we should see?"

"Were you thinking of Mr. Stewart?"

Always, Meg thought, but she shook her head. "Is he here?" Meg asked, glancing around. "Did he accompany his cousin to the opening?"

"No, but Mrs. MacBain—she is here somewhere—said that Mr. Stewart arrived a few days ago and is staying with them. They have a house near Calton Hill."

Relieved for now that he was not in the museum, Meg knew she could easily encounter him at any time in the city through some social connection. Roderick had said he was meeting with Dougal today. For now, she could relax.

But she had to tell him the truth before her soiree. Wondering what Roderick might tell him today, she felt fear rush through her.

"I heard that Mr. Stewart has lost funding for his lighthouse," Angela said. "There is a rumor that he could be personally ruined over this fiasco."

"Oh no! I was told that withholding the funding would discourage the work on the reef. I was never told it might damage him personally."

"Mr. Hamilton explained to me that Mr. Stewart's project cannot recover from serious financial damage, and his name might be dragged down with it. Your solicitors have more than achieved their goal. That lighthouse may never go up, and the engineer may be done as well."

Feeling sick, Meg strolled beside Angela with outward calm, though she quaked inside. The weight of her secrets could cost her everything. She had never imagined Dougal would be seriously impacted if the lighthouse did not go forward.

She had to see him, and soon.

"Angela," she said, making an impulsive decision, "there is something I must do later this evening, after supper. I will need your help."

CHAPTER SEVENTEEN

"M R. STEWART!" A tall gentleman in a black suit and wine-colored vest waved, seated alone at a table in the dim interior of Brodie's Tavern on the High Street. "Thank you for meeting me here." Rising for a moment, he extended his hand.

"Sir Roderick," Dougal said, taking his hand. He had met Matheson once, and had recognized him in the crowded public room.

"I ordered two bowls of mutton stew, if you like. Ale as well."

"Thank you." Sitting, Dougal glanced at the man across from him. A pleasant enough fellow, perhaps close to fifty, a man of obvious means by his well-cut clothing and gold watch. His graying hair was combed smooth, his sideburns and mustache stylishly clipped, and his dark-brown eyes were shrewd.

"I am glad you wrote to me via the Northern Lighthouse Commission," Dougal said. He smiled his thanks as a serving girl set down steaming bowls of stew, fresh bread rolls, and two glasses of ale.

"You are not an easy man to find." Matheson sipped ale and patted his lips with a napkin.

"I move about a bit. The work, you see. I heard you were recently on Caransay, though. Had I known sooner, I could have shown you around the site of the lighthouse."

"Next time I am there, perhaps. It was a quick visit to see someone on the island. The journey out there from Edinburgh is deuced complicated, traveling by carriage, train, and boat. I do not always have the time." He picked up his fork. "But I am curious about what you've been up to on my property, the Isle of Guga. By now you've probably dug a right-size hole in it."

"More careful than that, but we did quarry some excellent gray granite there. We transported the stones to Sgeir Caran to build the foundation for the lighthouse."

"Ah. I am interested in your progress." Matheson tasted the stew and curled his lip slightly. "Ah. Good, though the vegetables are somewhat plebeian."

Having no quarrel with the dish, Dougal ate in silence for a moment. "Thank you for your permission to work on Guga. The Commission is also grateful for your offer to donate to the lighthouse fund."

"And so we come to your reason for this meeting," Matheson said.

"For my part, though I wonder why you asked to meet," Dougal said cautiously.

"I understand you have come upon hard times, both with your project and your charming enemy."

"If you mean Lady Strathlin, I am not sure of her charm, though I can attest to her hard nature—or perhaps that of her lawyers."

"They are a tough lot, I agree. Though the lady is rather winsome."

Dougal frowned. "Is she? Her advocates are a conniving bunch. My project will be greatly delayed, even cancelled, if they have their way."

"What is the current state of things?"

"To be honest, we have lost nearly half of our contributors. Apparently the bank informed them that the Caran lighthouse is a poor investment. Something about costing twice its estimate and yet bound to fail due to impossible conditions," Dougal drawled. "None of which is true. Costs and conditions can both be managed."

"As a contributor as well as a bank associate, I can tell you the lawyers put it about that if the Lighthouse Stevensons, as they are called, had supervised the work, the result would be more promising."

"The end result remains to be seen, and it will be successful." Dougal knocked his fist on the table. "I am visiting as many donors as I can while in the city. They were previously supportive but now seem to be distrustful of me. I am baffled that they would listen entirely to the lawyers."

Sir Roderick slurped ale and set it down. "Because the lady's lawyers claim that you plan to abscond with the funds, abandon the lighthouse, and make off for the Continent."

"What!" Dougal leaned forward. "Preposterous. Did you want to meet with me just to withdraw your offer as well?"

"I am a member of the bank board, so I have heard a good deal. So I have decided to double my contribution."

Dougal lifted his brow. "That's exceedingly generous. May I ask why?"

Sir Roderick leaned forward. "Because I want you to build that lighthouse."

"Lady Strathlin wants the island to stay private. Are you willing to join the dispute?"

"I can end the dispute," Matheson answered bluntly. "The baroness will not prevail. Soon I will be making decisions about Caransay with her, or over her. It is a beautiful island that could be an excellent resort for the wealthy, which means ships need better assurance of safety on that blasted reef. Nor does Lady Strathlin need a private island." He waved a hand. "She has too much freedom there, in my opinion."

"It is her island," Dougal said reasonably. He sat back. "What about Guga? You own that isle. You could consider a small resort there."

Matheson waved a hand. "That damned rock is suitable only for birds and seals and what granite and such it can give up. I bought the lease only because it is near Caransay." Matheson sipped, then wiped his mouth again.

"Why is that significant?"

"Lady Strathlin and I now have property in common, as well as affection."

"Affection? Makes sense. You are cousins, so I have heard."

"Distant only. But aye, we have become very close. Her island is a pretty place, but it is just a fishing community. It could be a sophisticated place with the right plan. I will convince her of it."

The man's sleek confidence made Dougal wary. "I hear Lady Strathlin values the simple lifestyle on Caransay. She is such a recluse when she is there that she wants no interruption to her peace. Not even a lighthouse that would save lives and make her island safer and more peaceful."

"She is a bit of a hermit when she is there. But she prefers my company." He lifted a hand with a modesty that smacked false. "I could hardly bear to be separated from her so I made the trip out there to see her. What fools we mortals be, eh?"

"Indeed," Dougal murmured, convinced now that Matheson was ten times a fool. Lady Strathlin would not fall for this man's cunning charm—Dougal had not met her, and yet was sure of that. What did Matheson truly want of her?

For an instant, he felt a protective urge toward the lady set on making his life miserable.

"You say you have never met the lady?" Matheson asked.

"Not formally. I saw her on Caransay at a distance while she was swimming in the sea. It was not a moment to introduce myself. She proved elusive otherwise."

"A pity. You would find her delectable and charming."

"Ah." Delectable? Remembering the older woman bobbing in the water like a seal, he then remembered others hinting that Lady Strathlin was a younger woman. Confused, he told himself she might be very different in person, and he should not make assumptions based on a waterlogged bathing costume and a large hat.

"Despite her lawyers, she has a soft heart," Matheson was saying, "and a coyness that intrigues a man. No doubt you take my meaning, sir." He lifted his beer glass in salute and drank.

You are a pig, sir, and likely a fortune hunter, Dougal thought. The well-bred gentleman across from him was fast revealing himself to be smug, self-centered, perhaps even dangerous.

Instinct told him not to trust the man's generous offer regarding the lighthouse. He narrowed his eyes "No question, Lady Strathlin has wealth and status. Some men might find that very appealing."

Something flashed in Matheson's dark eyes. "I give no thought to her wealth. She is my goddess. I worship her, even when she goes around like a barefoot fishwife."

Dougal blinked. "Barefoot fishwife?"

"She adopts that quaint style when on holiday." Matheson took a drink and patted his lips. "It is surprising you did not meet her, sir. Or did you?" His tone was sly. "She moves about freely on the island, known to everyone. She is quite the little naturalist, as well."

Naturalist and barefoot fishwife, moving freely about the island? Losing any appetite, Dougal pushed his bowl of stew away. "You know her quite well, then."

"Very. I will speak to her on your behalf. As I said, I want the lighthouse to go up. Once the lady and I are married, I will have a say in these matters. She can be stubborn, but in a delightful way. She will succumb to reason."

Dougal frowned, his thoughts spinning. One word had caught his attention. "Married?"

"I should not speak of it, but a happy heart loosens the tongue. I have asked the lady to marry me, and her coquetry on the matter indicates her acceptance."

Dougal blinked. "Coquetry? Sir, forgive my confusion. We are speaking of the same woman—the formidable Lady Strathlin of Strathlin Castle and Charlotte Square in Edinburgh?" *A lady fond of swimming in large hats, fond of privacy, and very fond of sinking lighthouse engineers.*

"Yes. My dear Margaret." Matheson nodded. "Do not congratulate me now. Wait until my darling is ready to make the announcement."

A cold sensation crept through him. *Beautiful, charming, winsome. Barefoot. Stubborn.* "Margaret," he repeated.

"On the island she goes by Meg MacNeill. Perhaps you met her by that name?" The man's tone was sly, his eyes narrowed.

Dear God. All this time, he had been a supreme fool. "Ah," he said. "I may have done."

A DREARY EVENING rain and the folds of a dark-blue cloak wrapped Meg in shadows inside the carriage rolling down the sloped Edinburgh streets. Swaying on the seat, listening to the rhythmic clop of horse hooves, she glanced at Angela Shaw and Guy Hamilton, seated opposite her.

"We are nearly there," Angela said. "Are you sure of the address?"

"Aye, Dr. MacBain's house is just there," Guy said. "Madam, if you are seen entering the doctor's house, word might go round that Lady Strathlin is ill."

"I will take the chance if I can speak with Dougal in private. Mr. Stewart," she added.

"Dougal, is it? So you do know him rather well. I had a feeling it was so," Angela said. "There is something in your eyes when he is mentioned—you cannot hide it, dear. Something happened on Caransay, I vow. Something good." Her smile was soft and her eyes sparkled.

Meg looked out at the glinting rain, then nodded, ready and relieved to tell her friends more of the truth. Keeping secrets was not turning out so well after all. "Something that could have been wonderful, but I made a mess of it," she said quietly.

"All can be fixed if this is meant to be," Angela said. "Does he return your affection?"

Meant to be. Once she had hoped so, but that had dimmed. "If he did, I doubt he would return it to Lady Strathlin."

"Love finds a way," Angela said.

"Unless love's way is littered with lawyers and bankers." Guy was ever the pragmatist. "This situation is difficult for many reasons, madam. It will take more than an explanation to win his affection once he learns the truth."

"Just wish her luck, Mr. Hamilton. Perhaps we should have left you at home," Angela said.

"You cannot do without me, dear Mrs. Shaw," he murmured. She gave him an impish smile.

"I must tell him the truth. I cannot live with this any longer," Meg said. "It has become so complicated, more than I can say." She felt dizzy, staring into the darkness and rain, as if she stood poised on a cliff edge. "I fear Sir Roderick may have already told him. They were to meet today."

"Does Matheson realize Stewart thinks you are just a simple girl from the Isles?" Guy asked.

"It is possible." Meg sighed.

"She *is* a girl of the Isles," Angela pointed out. "She never truly lied to Mr. Stewart. She just omitted some details."

"A considerable detail," Guy said. "You are doing the right thing, madam."

"If Roderick discovers that Mr. Stewart did not meet Lady Strathlin on Caransay, he might tell him who I am." Frowning, she bit her lip slightly.

"Knowing Matheson, he will be too busy puffing his feathers to talk about anyone else," Guy remarked. "I wouldn't worry."

"I do worry. If he sees Mr. Stewart as a rival, he might interfere. Oh dear. I must tell you two first—I have decided…to marry Sir Roderick."

The silence, immediate and profound, did not last. "You what!" Guy burst out.

Angela gasped. "No!"

"It is best for all concerned," Meg said.

"It is plain foolish," Guy growled from the shadows.

"Why would you accept him? You do not care for him, let alone love him," Angela said.

"He is a distant cousin, and so I have known him for years. He has been a support to me with the inheritance and the business matters."

"He has an unsavory nature," Guy Hamilton said. "Madam, let me remind you of something."

"What is that, Guy?" Meg tilted her head.

"Three years ago, I believe, he asked you for a loan. Do you recall?"

She frowned. "Something about—an investment gone wrong. A temporary loan. I gave permission, aye."

"He has borrowed more since." Guy Hamilton cleared his throat. "He obtained permission from the bank, based on the strength of your previous permission. Somehow ran it through, and obtained your signature. I wondered at the time, but it was your signature. Now—I wonder if you knew about it."

"I—thought he had repaid it. I gave it no mind." She left such things to the bankers. Even Guy Hamilton would accept their approval without much question.

"I see. I do wonder now. I will look into it," Guy said.

"Oh dear! How can you even entertain the thought of marrying him?" Angela asked.

Meg sighed and looked out the window, heart sinking. "Because—he found out about Sean. And he threatens to make that public if I do not marry him."

"Dear heavens," Angela murmured.

"Who is Sean?" Guy asked.

"I am sorry, Guy. I should have told you earlier. I have so much to make up to so many people," Meg murmured. "Angela, could you explain it to Guy while I visit Dr. MacBain's house? I am sorry to rush through it, Guy, but—"

"I understand. Mrs. Shaw will make it clear. Go on and do

what you must."

Angela reached across to take her hand briefly. "All of this is understandable, Meg. Truly. I would have done the same in your position."

Meg nodded gratefully. Angela and Mrs. Berry, her closest female confidantes, knew about Sean's birth and existence on Caransay, but Meg had never told Guy, nor had he guessed. Now more than ever she wanted to be truthful. She owed that to Dougal and her closest friends as well.

As the coach slowed and stopped, Guy peered out the window. "Here it is. Victoria Street."

"I will not be long," Meg said. "Once Mr. Stewart knows the truth, he will send me packing." Drawing up the hood of her cloak, she stood. Guy stepped out first, offering his hand in assistance.

"Whatever it is, Meg," Guy said, though he rarely used her given name, "it cannot be so bad."

She leaned toward him. "It is a wonderful secret—it is time you knew. Angela will tell you."

"I see." He walked her toward a tall stone house separated from the street by an iron fence. Light warmed the wide bay window. "Let me go in with you," Guy said.

"This is something I must do. Stay with Angela. Stay with her always, Guy," she added.

"I intend to, if she will have me," he murmured.

"She will. Love finds its way always. Remember that, Guy Hamilton."

"I will. So should you." He tipped his hat and went back to the coach.

She walked up the steps to the front door, heart slamming, hands clenched. She glanced at the brass address plaque: *Doctor Connor MacBain.*

A doctor's household would be accustomed to unexpected visitors, and it was not yet late, although rain deepened the darkness. However awkward to see a gentleman alone, she owed

Dougal the truth. All of it.

Drawing a breath, she lifted the brass knocker and tapped the door.

Moments later, a woman in a gray gown and white apron appeared, then stepped back immediately to bring Meg out of the rain and into the foyer. The house was warm, softly lit, and fragrant with baking spices. Toward the back, she heard the rattle of dishes, and to one side, a harmony of male and female voices mingled in conversation and laughter.

"Are you here for the doctor, Miss? Dr. MacBain has guests and is not seeing patients at this hour, but if 'tis an emergency, he may agree. I will let him know."

"I have not come to see Dr. MacBain, but Mr. Dougal Stewart. I understand he is staying here. I have an urgent message for him."

"Mr. Stewart is a guest here, aye. Who is calling?" The housekeeper produced a silver salver to accept Meg's card Reaching into her glove where she kept a calling card or two out of habit, Meg paused, reluctant to produce one that said Lady Strathlin. "I have no card. Please tell Mr. Stewart that Miss MacNeill is here to see him."

In the hallway, panel doors slid open, and a dark-haired young woman in a brown silk dress glided toward her. "Hello, Miss. May the doctor be of assistance?" She held out her hand. "I am Mary MacBain. My husband is here—there you are, sir!"

A handsome blond man, wide shouldered and dressed in dark gray with a red plaid vest, stepped into the hall. Meg recognized the man she had seen at the museum exhibit. "Who is it, my dear?"

Seeing Meg he smiled and waited as she approached. "Miss, hello. I am Dr. MacBain. Is there something I can do for you?"

They assumed she was a patient in need, and no one questioned her right to be here or acted as if proprieties were compromised. Meg felt grateful for their friendly acceptance, but she hesitated, feeling suddenly awkward and foolish.

"Miss MacNeill is here to see Mr. Stewart," Mrs. MacBain said.

"Ah. Pleased to meet you, Miss MacNeill. I'm afraid Mr. Stewart is not here. He stepped out for a little while and did not say when he would be back. Might we give him your card and message?"

Meg stared, brow folding. "Not here?"

"Would you like to wait?" Mrs. MacBain asked. "We have some guests and were about to have coffee. You are welcome to join us."

Through the half-open pocket doors, Meg saw a few others milling about engaged in conversation. Whoever they were, some might recognize Lady Strathlin if she joined them. And her friends waited in the carriage.

She smiled at the doctor and his wife, who regarded her kindly, patiently, with mild concern. But a radiance of happiness and compassion shone in their faces. A similar quality brightened Guy Hamilton and Angela Shaw when they were together.

She might never have that now.

"Miss," Mrs. MacBain repeated, "is there something we can do?"

Suddenly she felt lost, alone, unsure of herself. Wealth and social status meant nothing now. Dougal was not here, yet she needed him badly, needed his strength and calm and comfort, his arms around her, his wisdom, and his passion. She needed to know he understood and would forgive her.

Not so long ago, he had asked her for forgiveness, saying he loved her and wanted to marry her. She should have told him then that she loved him, should have been honest then. This was all coming too late.

"I—should not have come," she blurted. "Please accept my apology. I am sorry for disturbing your evening." Turning, she reached for the door. As the housekeeper opened it, Meg ran down the steps and back to the coach.

She picked up her skirts and fled down the path, her shoes

tapping on stone. Passing through the gate, she ran toward the waiting coach. Guy Hamilton leaped out, opened the door, and swept her inside, calling to the driver. The two horses launched forward up the hill toward the New Town and Charlotte Square.

"That was very quick," Angela said.

Breathless, Meg sat and settled her skirts. She looked up to see Angela and Guy sitting close together on the opposite bench seat, watching her.

"He was not there. He is out, and they do not know when he will be back. I felt so flustered that I ran out—oh!" Pulling off her gloves, she realized then that the little cream card that identified her as Lady Strathlin was gone. She glanced around, over her wide black crinoline and down at the coach floor. *Gone.*

Peering out the coach window back toward the MacBain house, she saw Connor MacBain step outside the house, watching the coach disappear. He bent to pick up something from the front step, examined it, and tucked it into his vest pocket as he went inside.

Meg sat back with a groan. "I introduced myself as Miss MacNeill—but I dropped my Strathlin calling card when I ran out."

"Oh dear," Angela said. "Will you go back?"

"I do not know," she said, fingers trembling as she pulled her gloves on again.

"Well then, no doubt Mr. Stewart will find out on his own, and you can talk to him at the soiree." Angela's tremulous smile said she was trying to make the best of it.

"If he comes at all now," Meg said. *If I ever see him again.*

She saw by her friends' somber gazes that they were concerned for her—and could tell by the closeness as they sat together that they had been deep in conversation while she was gone. Though she trusted Guy implicitly, she felt vulnerable and exposed as little by little her secrets were unraveling.

"So you know," she said quietly.

He nodded, then leaned forward and took her hand. "My

dear baroness," he murmured. "You could have told me long ago. I could have been a help in this."

"A help," she repeated.

"You have taken a great deal onto your shoulders," he said. "But you have friends willing to share the burden. Willing to love your child, and you, without judgment."

Tears pricked her eyes. Meg nodded silently, lip wobbling. She leaned back, gazing out the window as the coach conveyed them back to Charlotte Square.

If Dougal knew, she wondered, would he feel the same way? He would be angry with her for keeping the secret, certainly, but she knew that he was very capable of love and compassion. And he had a right to know his son, to love his son.

Yet some things must remain protected secrets. A sudden instinct told her that Matheson could become a dangerous threat to Dougal if he learned the identity of Sean's father.

Her continued silence, over the years, had ensured the safety of her child and his father. What now, if the truth was all out?

She watched the glittering rain as it turned to a pelting downpour.

CHAPTER EIGHTEEN

"Now this," said the seamstress as she knelt on the floor, arranging the overskirt of Meg's gown, "is what Monsieur Worth loves best about this beautiful gown—the tulle overskirt." She inserted another straight pin and fluffed out the silken netting so that its soft veiling formed transparent clouds around the wide skirt.

"Oh, it's magical!" Angela walked around Meg in a circle.

Meg paused to study her reflection in the long, tilted mirror. The shimmering gown gracefully enveloped her in a confection of pale aqua silk, its low-cut bodice sweeping gracefully under her bare shoulders. The snug waist nipped her to an illusion of impossible slimness, and the wide skirt and long train poured fluidly over a lightweight crinoline that swayed in an airy, flexible bell. Creamy silk netting caught up in small arches, and the nearly translucent tulle overskirt fell in floating waves. Tiny silver stars embroidered in metallic thread were sprinkled over the netting, bodice, and puffed elbow sleeves. It was a gown fit for a fairy princess, Meg thought, pleased, twirling.

Her hair, dressed by a maid, was pulled back gently to spill down in rippling golden waves caught in a generous silver snood pinned with a few small pearls. Around her neck she wore only the gold-and-aquamarine pendant that Dougal had given her, threaded on a black silk cord. On her left wrist, over her white glove, she wore her golden locket as a bracelet, threaded on a black silk ribbon.

"Exquisite," Miss Worth said. "Such grace and simplicity. The gown is divine, the jewelry is understated, and your hair is simply arranged. Truly perfect."

"Thank you, it's lovely." Meg crossed the room to pick up her fan of carved ivory and cream silk, slipping its cord over her wrist. She turned to see Angela and Miss Worth smiling.

"Heavenly," Angela said. "You float like a cloud when you move. It is a most splendid effect."

"Monsieur Worth meditated over the design of this gown," Miss Worth said. "He was inspired by the color of your eyes, and wanted to create a gown that would suit your beauty and reflect your gentle nature."

"He could not have designed anything more perfect for Lady Strathlin," Angela said.

"Mrs. Shaw, with your coloring and figure, you would look quite beautiful in a gown similar to this one," Miss Worth said. "The gown you chose to wear tonight is elegant, though. I love the black watered silk with the pearl trim, highlighting your ivory complexion and pale blonde hair. Though I can tell you that Monsieur Worth would love to create something marvelous for a Nordic beauty like yourself, should you ever want that."

"Oh, I could not afford it, truly," Angela said. "And I have worn second mourning for years."

"You cannot mean to wear it always. You are too young and beautiful."

Meg nodded, catching Angela's eye in the mirror. "Whenever you like, Angela," she said, "we will ask Monsieur Worth to design for you. I would consider it a privilege to give that to you."

"My dear, thank you, but I could not—"

"You have a birthday coming and would accept a gift from a friend, aye? Monsieur Worth could design something for you in mourning colors, if you'd rather stay with those."

"He might advise some subtle color after a long mourning," Miss Worth said gently.

Angela sighed. Then she smiled, her blue eyes brightening. "Someday I will surprise you and come out of mourning. I do find it dreary to have so little color in my life. Perhaps it does not always honor those who are gone, though we think it might."

"Life goes on, Angela," Meg said. Her friend nodded.

"Very true," Miss Worth said. "Madam, allow me to lift this one section. It droops a little too low." She gathered her pincushion and knelt on the floor again.

Standing still, Meg glanced in the mirror again, hardly able to believe the transformation. The sheer delight of a beautiful gown and the joy of looking wonderful in it were diminished somewhat by heartbreak and apprehension. She would see Dougal tonight, and all her yearning and love would come to nothing if he would not forgive her. If she had lost his love and respect through foolishness, then all the splendid gowns in the world would make no difference to her.

Then she gave herself a grim reminder; even if Dougal still loved her, and though she loved him, she had to accept Roderick's proposal. It might be the only way to ensure safety for Dougal and Sean. Tonight, her highly anticipated glittering party felt more like an approaching funeral, as if her lifelong dreams for happiness had ended.

Yet she must carry on, maintain a smile and keep a proud demeanor for their sakes.

Drawing a breath as Miss Worth sat back, Meg turned, aqua skirt and its tulle cloud swinging gently. "Shall we go downstairs? Mr. Hamilton will be impatient, waiting for us so that we can all leave for the concert."

Angela took up her fan and her black lace shawl. "When Mr. Hamilton sees you coming down the stairs, he will realize that waiting for you was well worth it."

"My dearest Angela," Meg said, "I suspect Mr. Hamilton is waiting for you."

LAMPLIGHT SPILLED GOLDEN over his freshly shaved jaw and set gleaming highlights over his wavy hair. Glancing into the mirror, Dougal straightened the white silk bow wrapped beneath his collar points, smoothed the lapels of his white brocade waistcoat, gave its buttoned front a tug, and pulled at his stiff cuffs. His boots were polished, coat and trousers were immaculate. Sliding his hands into white gloves, he swatted the long tails of his black dress coat.

Girded for battle, he thought. Now to see where it led.

In the mottled sheen of the mirror, his eyes were green glass, cold and hard. His cheeks were lean and shadowed, tiny lines etched the corners of his eyes, and his lips were pressed tight and humorless. Every fiber in his being had steeled to resolve and defiance.

He would step into this elite crowd with the same grit and determination he summoned to brave a gale or dive deep into the sea—or push a monstrous shark away to rescue a small boy. No one he would see tonight could be as terrifying as the physical dangers he had encountered—or so he told himself. Yet their judgments and opinions, their haughty criticisms and assumptions, were unsettling. But he had made the commitment to attend and would not take the coward's way out. He would attend the concert with his cousin and her husband, and then he would walk into Lady Strathlin's home with all the dignity and backbone that he could muster.

The woman he loved, the woman he wanted to marry—and suddenly he did not know her at all.

But in these last few days, he had shored himself against that meeting. He would greet her, move on. He had no more heart left to hurt; anger and betrayal had rendered his heart numb.

Easy enough to survive the evening, he thought, as he headed for the door. How he was to endure the rest of his life without her remained to be seen.

MEG WATCHED THE stage, its heavy burgundy velvet curtains closed. Below her theater box, the auditorium continued to fill with attendees, some of them staring up at her and her companions in the box. She looked away, wafting her fan, watching the stage. Beside her, Mrs. Berry snapped her feathered fan to hide her face as well.

Guy Hamilton, handsome in black-and-white dinner attire, leaned forward from his upholstered chair behind her, where he sat beside Angela Shaw. "With three beautiful ladies in this box," he said, "people cannot help but stare."

"Well, true," Mrs. Berry conceded. "But this isna the beach at Caransay."

"Did someone stare on the beach there?" Guy asked, sounding amused.

"Indeed so, and my lady in a simple gown, and barefoot, too," Mrs. Berry whispered. "And I was in my *bathing costume*," she confided, looking mortified. "But it was Mr. Stewart o' the lighthouses, so he could be forgiven," she added. "He is a fine man, charming and handsome, though I havena spoken with him maself." Mrs. Berry went on, "Brave, too. He saved a small lad from drowning. And fought off a shark! It was astonishing."

"That is impressive," Guy admitted.

"Madam, you never mentioned that incident," Angela said, leaning forward.

"Mr. Stewart saved—Sean from drowning. It was very courageous," Meg said.

"Oh! I must congratulate Mr. Stewart. That is remarkable," Angela said. "I look forward to meeting him here. It is a shame what the solicitors have done lately. Nearly ruined him, they say. Surely he did not deserve that."

Meg sighed, feeling miserable at the reminder. As she looked out over the sea of heads and shoulders, colorful silks and feathered headdresses, men's wide shoulders in perfect black, she could not help but search for Dougal Stewart.

He was here somewhere—she sensed the inexorable pull of his presence so strongly that her heartbeat quickened. But it was impossible to find one man in that vast and glittering crowd, no matter how well she knew the turn of that head, the set of those shoulders.

And if he did see her, she felt sure he would turn away from her. By now, he would know the truth, either from Roderick, or because she had mistakenly dropped her card on MacBain's front step.

The orchestra tuned their instruments, the gaslights dimmed, and then the voluminous draperies separated to reveal a bare stage but for a small table holding a vase of flowers, a pitcher of water, and a single glass. The theater went silent.

Then a petite woman walked to the center of the stage. Her brown hair was pulled back, tucked with a delicate spray of pink roses. Her cream-colored gown was simple and elegant. Miss Jenny Lind looked like an innocent young girl, though Meg knew she would be in her thirties by now. Clasping her hands, Miss Lind began to sing.

Her voice flowed outward, pure as crystal, a delicate trill like a lark in the morning. Listening, Meg felt her worries and fears melt and ease under that magical sound.

Then her glance caught the glint of golden highlights over brown hair, broad shoulders in black, the turn of the head, gaslight illuminating the handsome face for a moment. Though he did not glance upward, even at that distance she knew him, and her heart pounded.

DURING THE INTERVAL, as the crowd flowed into the theater's wide foyer, Dougal noticed the crush around a woman and her small party. From his vantage point in a corner, Dougal could scarcely see her, but he heard murmurings that the Baroness Strathlin was at the heart of that cluster. Not wanting to be seen, he turned, silent and guarded, back to his companions as they chatted with acquaintances.

He had come to the theater with his cousin Mary and her husband, Dr. Connor MacBain, determined to get through the evening somehow. He stood as cold and stiff as the marble column beside him, nodding greetings as necessary, polite but distracted.

For a moment, he saw her clearly as the sea of gowned ladies and black-clad gentlemen shifted. She was turned away, draped in an opera cloak of dark-blue velvet, but he knew the shape of her head, the slender set of her shoulders; had pushed his fingers through the golden waves of her hair. Now it was caught up in a silvery net and pinned with gewgaws and silver stars.

As she tilted her head with a smile for someone, her lovely profile achingly familiar, his heart surged. She was uncommonly beautiful, and he loved her still, wanting her so intensely that it hurt to look at her.

He had once told Meg MacNeill that he would never give up on what he desired in life. But standing there, he felt uncharacteristically defeated. Betrayed. Persistence was a challenge.

Yet his nature was to persevere, and he would. That beautiful young woman was not who he had believed. Somehow, he must forget her and go on, shedding bitterness if he could. And his nature also demanded that he finish that lighthouse somehow, even if he had to build it himself, stone by stone, and fund it from his own pocket by next year.

But forgetting Meg MacNeill might take him his entire lifetime.

THE CARRIAGE SLOWLY edged forward in a long line of gigs, hansom cabs, and coaches approaching Charlotte Square. Dougal peered ahead through the side window and soon picked out the baroness's townhouse a little distance ahead. In a row of homes designed to look like a single palatial façade, the grand house on the corner seemed larger, richly lit by lanterns hung about the entrance where carriages crept forward and stopped to let passengers step out with the help of liveried footmen. The lady was sparing no expense, he thought sourly.

"The concert was marvelous," Mary MacBain said as their carriage rolled slowly along. "Miss Lind has an exquisite voice. And I am ready to move about after sitting for so long."

"We shall soon be dancing, dear," her husband said. Dougal smiled, appreciating his cousin and her husband for their hospitality, freely offered whenever he was in Edinburgh. And he was very glad they had been invited to attend the concert and Lady Strathlin's soiree. At least he could be certain of two friendly faces.

As their vehicle lurched forward, Dougal flexed his gloved hands. He had felt detached from life for a few days while he absorbed the shock of realizing Meg MacNeill's identity and betrayal. Miss Lind's singing had been soothing, but he resisted mellowing this evening. He needed a hard, brittle shield of anger around his heart.

"What a crowd at the theater, and now here on the street," Connor said.

"I think the theater was even more crowded because Lady Strathlin was there," Mary said. "There has always been an air of mystery around her. That only makes people curious to see her."

"You mentioned meeting her," Dougal said. "And so you were also invited."

"We were introduced at a concert last year," Connor answered. "But in the press of the crowd and in dim light, I could not quite see her face, and Mary said the same."

"You do not have a good memory for faces, dear, though I barely saw her either in the crowd. So when she came to the house one night last week, neither of us knew her!"

"But she arrived under another name," Dougal said. His nostrils flared.

"Aye, Meg MacNeill. But after she left, I found her card, and realized she was Lady Strathlin," Connor said.

"So you said," Dougal murmured. "I wonder what she wanted."

"Just to talk to you. It seemed important to her. A private matter," MacBain said. "To do with your lighthouse dispute, I suppose. Perhaps she has had a change of heart since her law firm is doing everything possible to prevent the light from going up."

"Perhaps," Dougal said.

"She seemed nervous and wanted to remain discreet. Yet you have not yet met?"

"I have corresponded with her, but mostly through lawyers." He twisted his mouth awry. "Essentially, I asked permission to build on her island, she refused through her soliciting firm, I asked again with the authority of the Lighthouse Commission and the government. We are not acquaintances so much as…adversaries just now." He felt the impact of his words like a blow. Why had she come to the MacBain house at all?

"She has a very generous nature," Mary said. "She is kind and without arrogance, so it is surprising to see animosity develop between you over the lighthouse."

"Surprising, aye."

"After all, she inherited only a few years ago, when she was just twenty-one, from what I have heard. The fortune came to her through her grandfather. Surely you have heard of the Matheson Bank heiress."

"I pay little attention to the doings of society."

"True, you avoid parties and gossip, commendable in its

way," Mary said. "And you are often out on some rock or another."

"One does not hear much gossip under the ocean," Dougal said with a rueful laugh.

"Well, her inheritance created quite a stir, from what I heard then. She was originally from a simple Highland family, I believe, perhaps the Isles, so when her grandfather left her the greatest fortune in Scotland, she had much to learn about society and city life."

"Ah," Dougal said. He remembered that Meg had mentioned a grandfather on the mainland who had left her his library. Quite a library, he thought. "When did this happen?"

"We were newly married," Mary said, glancing at her husband. "Six years ago. It is rather like a fairy tale," she went on. "The inheritance was something like two million pounds. The grandfather's two sons had died without issue, and his only daughter had died years before, leaving a daughter who had visited her grandfather as a child. He designated her his heir, to her surprise. She even needed tutoring to train her to the responsibilities of her new position."

"She was born in the Isles," Dougal said. "I heard on Caransay that Lady Strathlin purchased the lease to protect the inhabitants." But Meg never mentioned that she was Lady Strathlin.

"And thus began your difficulties on Caransay," Connor said.

"So it would seem."

"She learned quickly," Mary continued. "She had the formidable task of overseeing a bank, and she has done so admirably. She is also known for her generosity, particularly toward Highlanders and Islanders."

"Closer to home," Connor said, "she has lately founded a home for unmarried mothers. It is apparently a beloved cause of hers, helping young mothers in poor straits without husbands."

"She is not married herself," Mary said, "yet she is a prize of real consequence."

"I'm sure her bankers and lawyers will have a say in her marriage," Connor said.

"No doubt," Dougal said. Roderick Matheson would certainly have their approval, he thought.

All this only added to the blow of her betrayal. If it was true that she intended to marry Sir Roderick, then she was nothing like the woman he believed he loved. She was neither the passionate creature he had met on the sea rock, nor the winsome, earnest girl he loved deeply.

Who was she? What did she truly want—what was her scheme?

Then a still, quiet voice inside his mind added to the puzzle. Could he love her no matter who she was? Could he forgive and understand why she had kept so much from him? Would he trust that she cared about him? And if he loved her, did anything else truly matter?

He blew out a breath at those unanswerable questions. And the carriage came to a halt.

CHAPTER NINETEEN

A FAIRY-LIKE VISION of beauty waited in the drawing room, a girl spun of aqua silk and netted clouds, sparkling with silver and pearls, filled with the warm glow of welcome. As a steady stream of guests poured past Lady Strathlin, each one receiving her bright smile, a few words, the touch of her gloved hand, Dougal walked behind Connor and Mary, his gaze fixed on Meg.

After a while, he glanced around the large drawing room at elegant furnishings, broad pattered carpets in green and gold, crystal chandeliers shining with gaslight. The walls held oil paintings, windy landscapes and blowsy portraits, and the tables held marble busts and elegant bronzes. In a far corner, musicians played violins and flutes. Through open doors, he saw a long table draped in snowy linens, gleaming with silver and crystal, an array of rich foods illumined by candlelight.

Everywhere he saw the stamp of luxury, privilege, and graciousness. He saw no hint of the girl from the Isles who preferred simplicity—yet she stood at the center of it all, impossibly beautiful in that airy, tranquil, sparkling, priceless gown.

He wanted to seethe in fury, wanted to walk away, told himself he should not be here. And yet as soon as he drew near her, he knew why he had come.

He loved her. The strength of it, the certainty and substance of it, flowed through him like whisky and honey and dreams. He loved her, he burned for her, and he wanted the truth.

Edging closer, he saw that her gown was the color of her eyes, the delicate blue-green of sunlight through water, the white veiling like the froth of a wave. She stopped his breath, stilled his heart, whirled him on the axis of his soul.

"Dr. and Mrs. Connor MacBain," the butler announced. "Mr. Dougal Robertson Stewart."

Meg looked up quickly, eyes startled wide as she met Dougal's gaze. As she focused on Connor and Mary, she gave them a melting smile. They moved on, and Dougal stepped toward her.

She tilted her head with a tremulous smile. Her eyes were beseeching. When she offered a hand, he took it, glove to glove, cool and cordial, bowing over her hand. For a long moment, he met her gaze in silence. He knew the sweetness of those lips, the softness of her skin, her silky hair. He did not know this young beauty draped in lace and silk and sprinkled with pearls and stars. Then he noticed the simple black cord encircling her throat, holding the aquamarine-and-gold pendant he had found at the bottom of the sea. Its gold was a spark of warmth in the cool, serene perfection of her ensemble. He frowned. The pendant had little value; surely she owned prettier jewels, although the stone matched her gown and her eyes. Only they knew its significance. He had found it at the base of their rock and had given it to her. Hope soared, pushed through anger for a moment. Did she feel it too, this bond, the dream of their island paradise, all but dashed now?

"Mr. Stewart," she said, "how good to see you again."

He frowned a little, though she had greeted him like a friend. "Lady Strathlin," he murmured. "Enchanted, madam."

She turned to an elderly lady and gentleman standing beside her. "This is the Lord Provost of Edinburgh and his wife, Lady Lawrie. This is Mr. Stewart."

"Of lighthouse fame? Of course!" Lord Lawrie peered at him.

"Good evening, sir. Madam," Dougal said.

"Mr. Stewart has been working near the Isle of Caransay,

where I sometimes holiday," Meg said. "He is modest about his accomplishments, but we consider him a hero on the island."

"Really? How is that?" Lawrie peered at him.

"A few weeks ago, Mr. Stewart saved the life of a child who was drowning, and in the process, he took on a fearsome shark. It was the most courageous thing I have ever seen."

"Mr. Stewart, how amazing!" Lady Lawrie said.

"It was not so grand as Lady Strathlin implies, madam. I merely kicked the shark and grabbed the boy."

"Oh, dear!" Lady Lawrie flapped her fan.

Meg touched his arm lightly to guide him forward. "My Lord Provost, do coax Mr. Stewart to give his account of it. Please excuse me, I must greet more guests."

Then she smiled at Dougal with such brilliance that he felt dazzled, lost in her eyes, and he very nearly forgave her then and there. Nearly. "Lady Strathlin," he said stiffly, as she turned to greet the couple behind him.

Soon he was surrounded by people eager to hear the details of his encounter with the shark. Swept from one group to another, he told the story more than once, smiling until his cheeks went taut. The tale spread and became embellished, whispered from one guest to another. Dougal floated through the evening on smiles, congratulations, and expressions of admiration. His hand was clasped, his shoulder slapped, his arm hugged so often that he ached.

He had expected none of that, nor did he expect to dance with one lady after another, so many that their names and faces and flower-bright gowns blurred as he swirled and dipped and escorted them. He listened to gushing praise, and turned down three coy invitations to stroll through the conservatory into the garden.

As the night went on, some new acquaintances mentioned that Lady Strathlin seemed to admire him as a man of courage and integrity. One or two confided in him that general thought was that her solicitors had been overzealous in opposing his work. He heard apologies from businessmen and others who murmured that they had been misinformed him and would be willing in to contribute to the funds needed for the lighthouse.

"A ring of lighthouses is needed all around Scotland," said one fellow. "Out in the Western Isles as much as anywhere else. Tell me what you require." He clapped Dougal on the shoulder, gave him his card, and wandered away.

Each encounter made Dougal feel heartened, relieved, and surprised. Lady Strathlin's story of Dougal rescuing the child became a tale of rescuing the boy from a shark, though he consistently denied it. Her opinion held weight with these elite folks—though of course it was her fortune and influence that mattered to them. He was not sure how he felt about that.

After a while, he was approached by Sir Edward Dundas, gaunt and gruff, and Sir John Grant, a quiet, pleasant-looking man with thick spectacles. Earlier, Dougal had seen them in animated discussion with Lady Strathlin and her secretary, a young man called Hamilton.

"Mr. Stewart," Sir Edward said, while Sir John cleared his throat. "Might we have a word?"

Dreading even a brief conversation with Lady Strathlin's lawyers, he gave a curt nod.

"Mr. Stewart, we seem to have misjudged you," Sir John said. "The lighthouse remains a matter of debate and negotiation and should not be discussed here," Sir Edward began, as Dougal nodded vigorous agreement, "it is possible we were hasty in implying that you might be unprincipled."

"We hope for peace between our parties," Sir John said. "Lady Strathlin desires it as well." He extended his hand, and Dundas did the same.

Shaking their hands, Dougal wondered if the lady desired it for herself or for the sake of her advocates.

But throughout that long and astonishing evening, he never spoke to Lady Strathlin. Not once did he murmur in her ear or dance with her, whirling her about the floor in his arms. Not once did he approach her to thank her for what she had so subtly and successfully done for him.

Now and then, he met her gaze across the room, her luminous eyes hauntingly somber in the midst of gaiety. Once, as their glances touched, he gave her a subtle nod that he meant as an expression of gratitude, of humility—he would go that far. She paused in her conversation with Miss Lind to angle her head toward him in silent, graceful reply. A glance, the slightest motion was a signal he understood. His heart stirred, and longing seared through him like flame.

But while he appreciated the magic she had worked that evening, his pride was great too. He loved her, knew now he could not stop that. But he would keep it to himself.

VERY LATE, MOST of the guests had gone, including Miss Jenny Lind and her soft-spoken English husband. Turning away from farewells at the door, Meg noticed a few businessmen in the nearby parlor, standing with Dougal Stewart. They clustered in private conversation, holding wineglasses that had been filled and drained and filled again. Dougal held no glass, just stood listening, a hand shoved in a pocket, his coat draped back as he leaned a shoulder against a doorframe, one polished boot crossed over the other.

He looked weary, Meg thought, seeing his shoulders sag, noting the subtle pinch of his lips. Weary and wary, for he seemed cautious. He glanced up then, meeting her gaze, and she felt the magical shock of it. Then he looked away.

Sighing, she gathered her skirts like a bell and went through the parlor with a few murmured greetings, unwilling to disturb their conversation even as others left. Her heart thumped as she passed Dougal. At the back of the parlor, glass doors led to the garden, and she opened those to step out, desperate for fresh air, desperate for a few moments of quiet.

Then she saw Angela and Guy strolling in the shadows, dark-blond heads leaned together. Angela's hand was wrapped around Guy's forearm. Knowing the spellbinding effect of roses and darkness, not wanting to spoil their chance to be alone, Meg stepped back.

"My lady."

She whirled. Roderick stood behind her, blocking her return to the house.

She had managed to avoid him all evening, just a word or two and turning away on the excuse of another guest to greet, another detail needing her attention as hostess. Throughout the chatting, dancing, music, and buffet supper shared with many, Matheson had been a dark and lurking presence. She had not forgotten that he expected her answer that evening, which was in part why she had evaded him.

Now his dark eyes seemed hungry and eager. And she had no escape.

"A word in private, madam?" He came toward her, slipping a hand under her elbow. "We've had no chance to talk all evening. I wanted to tell you how ravishing you look tonight."

"Thank you," she said, noticing then that Guy and Angela had vanished in the garden shadows. Glancing into the house, she saw Dougal chatting with two elderly men; in that moment, he sent a sharp glance toward the conservatory doors, as if he saw her outside with Roderick. But he turned his attention back to his companions.

"A walk in the moonlight," Roderick said, "is the perfect ending to a pleasant evening."

"I must return to the house, as my guests are departing."

"Madam, they are all gone but for a few who cannot seem to stop talking business," he said. "No one will notice where you are. Indulge me for a few minutes, I beg you, my dear." As he leaned toward her, the smell of wine on his breath was strong.

"Perhaps we could talk tomorrow," she said, edging toward

the doors.

"Margaret, just a minute of your time. You have ignored me all evening." He took her hand and folded it over his arm.

She sighed. "Very well. A minute or two." Turning, she lifted her skirt and moved forward. The garden was dark and fragrant, the breeze soft as she walked with Roderick, his hand over hers. She felt trapped as they walked down an aisle formed by shrubs and tall ferns in pots. From the back of the garden, Angela and Guy were heading back to the house. They murmured polite greetings as Meg and Roderick walked past.

She tried to catch Angela's eye, wanting to convey her discomfort. But they were gone.

THE GARDEN WAS a quiet moonlit world hemmed in by tall, close houses, though a high fence and a screen of slender trees lent privacy. Distantly, Meg heard the rattle of wheels as vehicles carried guests over cobbled streets.

She turned. "Roderick, I must go inside to say more farewells. I know you wish to speak to me, but let it wait."

"Grant me a few moments, please, for this wee question of the heart."

"Heart! Hardly that, and you know it."

He set a hand to his chest. "Lady, you wound me! I ask again. Please do me the honor of marrying me." He captured her gloved hands, his fingers strong and overly warm on hers.

Glancing past the back wall, with its tiered flower beds and small espaliered fruit trees, toward the house, she did not answer. She loved this Edinburgh house, and could not imagine Roderick living here, could not imagine marrying him and pretending to care as his wife. And the thought of sharing a bed with him—

"No." She tried to tug her hands away, but his fingers were hot as iron on her gloves.

"Is that your answer? Consider it carefully." He drew her closer until the flexible cage of her wide skirt flattened against his legs. "You will," he muttered, bending toward her. "You have no choice, and you know it. I will tell the world. You will be *ruined*."

"Stop!" She twisted against his grip.

"I just wish I had been the one to ruin you first," he growled, and yanked her toward him so fast that her back ached with the hard tug. Planting his mouth on hers in a wet and eager kiss, he ground his lips and teeth against hers. "But I will ruin you last, if that is what you like."

Repulsed, furious, she shoved hard against his chest, then again. He flew backward, stumbling to the ground with an outraged cry.

Surely she was not that strong! Dazed, she saw Dougal standing in the shadows over Roderick. He came from nowhere—he must have seen them through the glass doors—to fling the man off and away from her.

Hauling Matheson up by the lapels of his coat, he shoved him against the nearby fence, crushing a shrubbery, pinning him there, though Matheson was easily the heavier one.

"You intend to ruin the lady?" Dougal demanded. "Is that what you said?"

"No—that's not what I meant," he protested, clawing at Dougal's wrists.

"That's what I heard," Dougal growled. He pressed the man flatter against the wall, his arms digging into the banker's chest. "I came out to say farewell to my hostess," he went on, his voice rough with rage. "I heard you threaten her, saw you grab her." He slammed Roderick tight against the wall as the man struggled to get free. "Heard you say you would ruin her."

"Mr. Stewart—Dougal—please let him go," Meg said.

"Are you harmed, madam?" He continued to glare at Roderick.

"I am fine." She glanced toward the house to see the businessmen who had been talking with Dougal now gathered with

Angela and Guy, Mrs. Larrimore, the butler, and a cluster of maids, all gaping at them. "Truly. Let him go."

"When he apologizes," Dougal growled.

"I need not apologize for proposing to the lady again," Roderick said. "She was about to accept when you interfered."

"Is that so, Lady Strathlin?" Dougal asked, barely audible.

"I—well, he asked—"

"Is it true?" he demanded.

She looked at Dougal, with his strong, fierce heart, and Roderick, whose heart was cold and vicious. She loved one and loathed the other. And she had to protect one from the other now.

"He asked," she whispered. "He did me no harm. Let him go."

The silence was tense and brittle. Dougal stared at Roderick. Then, with a low growl, he let go suddenly and stepped back.

Adjusting his coat, Roderick glared at Dougal. "You will regret this, sir."

"I regret nothing that might happen if you threaten her again." Dougal flickered a glance toward Meg, and away.

"Our business agreement," Matheson growled, "is over. I withdraw my offer."

"So be it." Dougal tugged at his shirt cuffs.

"Madam," Roderick said, "we will continue our discussion later. I am flattered that you desire to accept my—"

"I never did!" Meg gasped.

But he held up a hand. "I am sure you feel embarrassed. Ladies should not indulge in more than a glass or two of wine. It sets their heads to reeling. I may withdraw my proposal in light of such appalling misconduct."

"I have never misconducted myself," she snapped.

"No? Not even once, years ago? Seven years, is it?" He smirked.

"Get out," she said low.

As Matheson moved, Dougal stepped between them as if to

shield her. Meg breathed hard, panicked, praying Dougal had not heard the cruel reference to seven years ago, praying equally that her cousin would never learn the identity of her son's father.

"Good night. An excellent party until now." Roderick gave a curt bow and turned. The crowd by the door parted as he walked through, shouldering past Guy Hamilton, who gave him a dull blow to the stomach with his elbow.

"I beg your pardon," Guy said.

Roderick stormed past, heading for the front door. Meg heard it slam even from the garden.

Dougal waited in silence as the others drifted away. She was grateful for his guarding presence, for her limbs shook so much that she could hardly walk back to the house yet. Glad just to be in the calming moonlight, she found a bench and sat, skirts spreading.

She glanced at him. "Thank you."

He inclined his head. "Thank you, Lady Strathlin, for—a pleasant evening."

"Apart from the last few minutes?"

A smile played at his lips, the small, fond smile that she loved and missed. Her heart surged. She wanted to weep. "Dougal—"

"I must go. Madam," he said in farewell, and turned away.

She stood, picking up her skirt to follow him. "Wait, please."

He paused on the garden path, the illumination through the glass doors falling golden over him. Beyond, she heard the chink and clatter as servants gathered dishes and glasses inside.

"Lady." His tone was cool, flat.

"Please." She reached out, touched his arm. "Do not go." The air was heavy with the scent of roses, of green and earth and stone. Rich with promise, heavy with the need for forgiveness.

He looked down at her. "What would you have me do?"

"Stay," she said breathlessly. "Stay with me. I miss you so."

CHAPTER TWENTY

"GOD, MEG," HE growled low, taking her arm, pulling her away from the glow of the doors, into the darkness of the garden. He tugged her with him behind the crowding ferns in pots lining the path toward shadows and moonlight and the drowsy, drunken scent of roses.

"Can we talk—please, Dougal."

He spun her into his arms, her gown floating like clouds around her, and he kissed her, his mouth hungry and tender on hers, his hands strong yet gentle on her bare shoulders.

With a soft cry, she looped her arms around his neck, and gave herself to the power of kisses that were impulsive, desperate, insistent. She opened her lips for more, her heart beating fast, and she let his tongue dance over hers, gave him hers, slipped away to seek again. Leaning her head back, she felt his mouth trail hot along her jaw, her throat, his fingertips caressing her bare shoulders, then the upper swell of her breasts. His breath heated the space between her breasts, above the snug edge of her corset.

With one hand, he snugged her tightly against him so that her skirt floated outward, its cage tipping like a ringing bell, silken tulle crushed between them. She pressed into his arms, feeling his hard torso, his heartbeat against her, even through layers of silk and fragile netting and the smooth wool of his coat. His solid, safe nearness was blessedly familiar. She needed him, had always needed him from the moment they met in a long-ago storm.

She sighed, moaned breathily as his hand rounded over her confined breasts, teasing over the soft swell above her bodice edge. Her body pulsed for him. For a moment she wanted to tear away each exquisite layer of the gown just to feel him like steel and fire against her.

As his lips found hers again, her knees went weak beneath crinoline and petticoats, so that she clung to him, arms circling his neck, fingers threading deep into his thick brown-gilt hair. He smelled of spice and wine, of vanilla and strength and caring, and she loved him.

God, how she loved him. His hands were divine upon her, caressing, teasing her so that she shivered and craved. He framed her face in his palms to kiss her again, and she felt the change in it, the withdrawal of spirit. He tore himself away, breath rough.

"Lady Strathlin," he rasped, "This is wrong for both of us. I must leave."

She grabbed his coat lapels. "Stay," she whispered.

"If I stay, I cannot keep from kissing you—loving you. So I must go." He was stonelike.

"Stay. I must—you need to stay—" She stumbled through it, knowing the hardest part was yet to come, yet to be said, and she did not know how to tell him.

"For a night—or forever?"

"Forever," she whispered. "Surely you know that."

"Forever requires trust. Honesty. Commitment. It hardly involves you marrying another."

"I have not accepted his proposal."

"Not yet. It is advantageous and therefore inevitable. Surely your lawyers agree."

"You are so bitter. I should have told you. I know that."

"Aye so. I do not like playing the fool while you withheld from me what so many knew. I did not plan to come here to say that—but perhaps it must be said," he finished with a sigh.

"I went to your cousin's house to tell you before the soiree, but you were gone." Her voice broke, and her heart felt about to break.

"I discovered it through the card you dropped that the doctor found. But I suspected it after I met with Matheson. He did not tell me outright, but made it pretty clear."

"I am so sorry." She lowered her head. "I did not want it to be this way."

"Nor did I. Let me apologize for insulting your person and your lovely gown just now. You look like a princess. Beautiful. And I cannot be near you and stay a gentleman. Good night, my lady." He inclined his head and walked away, black-clad shoulders pushing through rosebushes.

Meg glided after him. Her sleeve snagged on a rose and she plucked it free, wincing at the sting. "Listen, do!"

He sighed, paused. "Lady Strathlin," he murmured, "you are a beautiful creature, and I will never forget the vision of you tonight. Nor will I forget the vision of you on that island. You give me a great deal to think about. Too much."

She caught his sleeve. "Will you not hear what I have to say, when I listened to you?" She tugged. "I listened, and I forgave you—all of it."

They stood on the path, hemmed between rosebushes and potted ferns. "Then tell me why you kept this from me, after all of that."

"Just—when I saw you on Caransay, and realized that we— had met before, I—I hated you for part of that," she said. "And I loved you, too, all at once. And I did not know what to do. Can you understand that?"

"More than you know," he said gruffly. "Loving the dream, unsure of the reality. Go on."

"I thought you used me on the rock, and I did not want to be used again."

"I never did." He leaned down. "*Never.*"

"I know that now. I did not know it then."

"Yet even later, you still kept the truth from me. Mrs. Berry! Come now," he reminded her.

"You despised the baroness! You made that clear. What was I to do? I thought it would end what we had on the island. I feared you would stop…loving me." A sob burst out and salt tears pooled.

"I have always loved you," he murmured without moving. "I cannot stop that."

"Even if you want to?" When he did not answer, she rushed on. "And I love you. So why are in such disagreement now?"

"Love needs truth, my dear. It thrives on truth and withers on secrets. You have too many. I have the feeling there are more things I do not know." He swept an arm out. "This incredible wealth. It would change a person."

"It is not easy. But I have tried to stay the same. As for secrets—"

"I know your secret now. I need time to think. You need it too."

She caught her breath. She had to tell him about Sean. Yet she glanced up to see a few guests lingering—lawyers, businessmen waiting for Dougal, looking into the shadowed garden.

As for the remaining secret, Roderick still loomed as a threat, limiting what she could safely say. If he decided to spread the word about her son, her lover, he could destroy all of them. He could find records that proved the birth, proved she had no previous husband, though her kin had put that about. She could not bear that—nor could she see it harm Dougal.

"There are things still to say," she whispered, feeling defeated in the moment.

"Not now. We are both overwrought. A day or two." His voice was cool, flat.

She nodded, numb, wanting to feel that all would be well, but that assurance was missing.

He strode away, leaving the garden, entering the house, pausing to speak to those still waiting. They went in a group toward the foyer. When Meg finally entered the house, she heard voices at the door and heard it close.

She thought she might never inhale the fragrance of roses again without feeling her heart break. Now she must find the courage to reveal her last, dearest secret, even if that truth pushed him further away. A day or two to think—aye, they both needed that.

PERHAPS HE WAS wrong to return to Meg's house on Charlotte Square, but he had promised he would. For good or ill, he had to see her again. Then he would know.

He stood waiting in the foyer, afternoon sun pouring golden heat through from the transom window over the door. For a moment, he nearly turned to leave, but the butler had already gone to deliver the news of his arrival to Lady Strathlin.

In the two days since the soiree, he had pondered never seeing her again. But one matter still needed attention; there was that. Truth was, he could not stay away from her.

Slipping a hand into his pocket, he felt the smooth leather of her journal, with the publisher's cheque tucked inside. A woman of such wealth might laugh at that. He had wrestled for days over the fact of her wealth and status in comparison to his humble, earnest, hardworking existence. He felt foolish by comparison despite his respectable family, excellent income, and a fine inheritance. Last night, he had hardly slept, wondering what really mattered.

He loved her. But he did not love feeling fooled or diminished. It came down to an elemental test of character and courage. But he knew what his answer was, deep inside.

He glanced up at soaring, creamy walls and the graceful curve of a staircase that disappeared beyond the upper floor. Far above, the leaded glass of a roundel window in the high ceiling shed sunlight down the stairs to the foyer. In the large parlor down the hall, polished wood-and-brocade furnishings were arranged on an expanse of patterned carpet, and a march of stately portraits lined the walls. Sunlight flowed through glass doors, setting the room aglow.

He admired elegance and simplicity, and saw it throughout here, albeit in expensive materials. And he realized he might never be able to give Meg MacNeill the sort of home to which she was accustomed. His engineer's salary would never support a place like this, nor would the respectable nest egg that he had inherited at a young age, which included his own manse. He did not visit his family home, Kinnaird House, often enough due to his wandering, hectic life, and had left its primary upkeep to his elder sister, Ellen, and her husband, Patrick Graham.

He shifted from one foot to the other, waiting, wondering at the delay. Would she refuse to see him, having had time to think it over too? Perhaps, he thought, he should leave quietly, walk down the hill and over to Prince Street. He had to catch a train in a little while, and did not have a great deal of time. He could just leave the journal—write to her—

"Mr. Stewart?"

He looked up as a lovely young woman came down the stairs, a pale blonde, her blue eyes vivid. A high-necked black gown drained her delicate summery coloring, but when she smiled, roses bloomed prettily in her cheeks. He remembered meeting her at the soiree.

"Mrs. Shaw," he said. "How nice to see you again."

She glided toward him and extended a hand. "Angela Shaw, sir, Lady Strathlin's companion. May I be of service? The butler said you had a message for her. She is just now in the middle of a discussion with her secretary, Mr. Hamilton. I did not want to disturb them, but if it is important, I certainly will."

Ah, that was an answer too. "Of course not. I only came to deliver this." He pulled the book from his pocket. "If you could give this to her, I will be on my way."

She did not take it. "It seems more than a message, sir. Then do wait. She would want that."

All he wanted, all he feared, ran through his mind at once. He had come here hoping for the whole truth, but he was not sure how she ultimately felt. In the garden the other night, he felt strongly that she kept something else from him. Did she still not trust him enough? He knew she had good reason to be cautious, considering their initial meeting. Had she indeed forgiven him?

And could he forgive this latest revelation, despite wanting to? He needed to know.

"Thank you, Mrs. Shaw. I have a little time before my train departs. I can wait a bit."

"Good." In her eyes, he saw sympathy, curiosity. "Would you like to wait in the parlor?"

He shook his head, endured an awkward silence as she smiled. Then he heard the rustle of skirts and saw Meg hurrying down the stairs, skirts sweeping. He looked up, captivated, then steeled himself. Forgiveness and caution went best together.

"Mr. Stewart," she said as she reached the foyer. Her full skirt swung, a plaid satin in blue and green with a prim white collar and white undersleeves. The effect was elegant and demure, even to her golden hair, its curls tamed and gently pulled back into a black net. She tipped her head and regarded him calmly. "I am glad you came."

"Lady Strathlin," he said. "I wanted to return something to you."

"Oh?" She tucked a brow as if puzzled, then lifted her skirt to move down the hall. "We can visit in the library."

"Would you like tea? I will inform the housekeeper," Angela Shaw said.

"Not yet. I will ring for it," Meg said, as her friend nodded and departed.

Meg ushered Dougal toward the library just off the parlor, and closed the door. Dougal glanced around at tall mesh-fronted bookshelves lining the walls from floor to ceiling. The room was bright and warm as sunshine streamed through windows draped in gold brocade. The floors were covered in thick, multicolored

Oriental rugs. Over the fireplace mantel, a large seascape, a stormy night, added a dramatic note in the serene room.

"Sgeir Caran?" he asked.

"Not precisely. But it reminds me. I—I did not want to forget," she said.

"I see. You said your grandfather left you his library. I hardly imagined the rest of this."

"If I had been more accurate about the library, you might never have spoken to me again."

"I am still speaking to you," he pointed out. He held out the journal. "I brought this."

She took the book, frowning. "You did not need to return it. I wanted you to have it."

"There is an envelope inside."

She found it, extracted the page, read it. "What is this? A note…and a cheque?"

He had been uncertain how she might react to his decision to approach a publisher, or how she might regard the modest sum. "I am acquainted with Mr. Samuel Logan at Chambers Street Publishers, so I took the liberty of showing him your journal. He was very impressed, found it remarkable and unique. He'd like to publish it, and your other works, if you are agreeable. He'd like to call it *A Hebridean Journal,* by—"

"By M. MacNeill," she breathed, reading the letter. "I do not know what to say."

"At the time, I was…unaware of your circumstances." He shrugged. "I hoped you would be pleased." He twisted his hat like an embarrassed schoolboy and straightened his shoulders.

This girl tossed his heart and his head about like no one he had ever met. But he needed that, he suddenly thought. Finding his balance with her somehow broke through his reserve, cracked the shell he had not even known he had created. She helped him find his balance altogether, though she had no idea of that.

"I am—how very nice. Thank you," she murmured, and he saw the shine of tears in her eyes and she set the book on the gleaming surface of a nearby table and placed the bank draft beside it. She sniffled, laughed a little, shrugged.

"If you are not interested, I understand. I can convey your apologies to Logan."

She gave a little watery sob. "I am! I am—thrilled." The last word wobbled. "I thought my journals were nice, and I dreamed that one day—but I did not think it was really possible."

"Very possible," he said. "It is a wonderful thing, if you want it."

"Oh, but more wonderful is that you—you did this for me. You believed in my work. In me," she added. "You cared about it."

"Of course I care about it," he said. God, he wished she would not sob—it made him want to pull her into his arms and hold her. But he could not allow himself to step outside the boundary he had set for now, to protect him, protect her. "No need to cry. I know it is a silly wee sum."

Her face crumpled at that, tears streaming fresh. She touched the cheque with slim fingers. Dougal bunched the brim of his hat in one hand and stayed still.

"It is the first silly wee sum I have ever earned myself." She gulped tears, laughed a little.

"Good Lord, all this—" he said, waving his hat.

"Was inherited," she said. "I never planned on it, or wanted it. All this was meant for my cousins, but they were gone, and I was left. I left my home and my family for this. It has hardly even felt like a home all this time."

"It must feel like a great responsibility."

"It does." She pulled a handkerchief from her sleeve, dabbed at her eyes, her nose. "But I have advisers, bankers, accountants, and a large household staff at each of my homes. I feel some responsibility—and too pampered, not sure why I should be. It is not—who I am," she finished.

Who are you, he wanted to ask. "How many homes do you have?"

"This house, as well as Strathlin Castle, the manse on Caransay, and another small castle near Inverness. My bankers urge me to buy other properties, but I see no need."

He watched her without answering. Taking it all in, deciding what best to say, to ask.

She flipped through the journal. "That silly wee sum for this wee book is most welcome. I am honored. And I thank you for it."

"Not me. Mr. Logan," he said stiffly. "Well. If there is naught else, I am on the afternoon train for Glasgow."

Her eyes went wide. "You're leaving Edinburgh?"

"I must return to Sgeir Caran. I've been gone too long. The men have continued in my absence, but some matters cannot proceed until I am there."

"There were repairs needed after the last storm. Have you heard from Mr. Clarke and Mr. Mackenzie?"

Safer ground in some ways to talk about the work— treacherous in other ways. "They are overseeing things while I've been gone. The work goes forward, despite efforts to stop it."

"The funding," she said.

"That, and the sheer persistence of Dundas and Grant." He blew out a breath. "But I must thank you."

"Thank me? I thought you took great issue with what I—may have done."

"Some of it," he replied curtly. "But I do thank you for your remarks at the soiree. As it happened, attitudes turned around regarding the project. I have new offers of support, and I even had an apology from your solicitors."

"I am glad of that. They owe you that. I want you to know I was not always party to their actions." She twisted a handkerchief in her hands.

"Some of their actions," he replied in a dry tone. "Some efforts came from you, I gather."

"Some, at first. I realize I might have been wrong."

"Well. Done is done." He bowed his head, aching inside. His

train would leave soon and he must hurry. Yet something held him back, a desire, a need he resisted. "Farewell, Lady Strathlin."

Her eyes brimmed with quick tears. "Just farewell? I thought—we would talk today."

"Now that I am here again, I wonder what more there is to say." A few remaining doubts suddenly overtook the hopes that had bloomed. "Your life has no room for such as me. I am aware of that. You have many obligations, and many with expectations of a woman of your means. So, aye, perhaps farewell is justified." He turned for the door, even as his heart fell to his feet and an inner voice urged him to stay.

"No," she said firmly.

He stopped, did not look back. "I also have obligations, and those work against what you may want. And I have a train to catch, frankly."

"Tickets can be changed. But what will change this?" Her voice broke. "What do you need?"

He drew a sharp breath. "Meg MacNeill," he said softly. "I need her."

She was quiet for a moment. "And you have no use for Lady Strathlin?"

"I expect that the baroness has no use for a lighthouse engineer." He could not look at her, though in his peripheral vision the grand library reminded him of her astonishing wealth.

"Pride?" Her voice quivered.

Hurt, he wanted to say. He did not turn, for if he saw her, he would only want to pull her hard into his arms and keep her there. All his pride, all his resistance, would vanish. And he still felt something unresolved, held back, and did not know if it came from him, or from her. It was just there, in the room, in the space between them, immovable and invisible.

"I can apologize for my wealth, but I cannot change it."

"The wealth—it is not that important," he said. "What matters here is who I am, who you are. Who *we* are. And that I cannot answer."

"I am just me, as I am. And perhaps we—we care, yet we are both so proud."

"Pride, aye," he agreed. "And we both need freedom, each in our way. I have a wanderlust, lady, and I like risk too well. I would always choose freedom over the lock that wealth and status can put on a man. Even if it means giving up what I most—cherish."

"What is that?"

"You know what that is." He reached for the door handle.

Something struck him hard between the shoulder blades. He looked down.

A narrow leather boot lay on the floor, its side buttons loosened. Before he could look up, another boot hit his arm. He whirled.

CHAPTER TWENTY-ONE

MEG SAT IN a chair, having worked off her boots to fling them at him. Now she rolled her stockings down—he glimpsed lace-edged knickers and undone garters before her skirt slid down. Balling up her hose, she tossed those to float and pool on the carpet.

"What the devil are you doing?" he asked.

Without reply, she stood, rucked up the voluminous hem of her dress, and tore at the tapes of her crinoline. As the cage dropped to her feet, she stepped out of its circle, hands under her skirt struggling with hidden drawstrings. A white flounced petticoat puddled on the floor, followed by another of linen, a third of red flannel.

"Meg, what are you doing?"

"You wanted Meg MacNeill," she muttered, ripping at her white half sleeves, tossing them away. One flapped over his face. He batted it away. "I am finding her again."

Dougal huffed, bewildered, as she tugged at the black net that bound her hair and flung it away, hairpins scattering with it. As she whipped her head side to side, her hair rippled out in a wild golden cloud.

"There!" She lifted the drooping hem of her skirt to reveal bare feet, small toes curling in the plush carpet. "Meg MacNeill."

He stared at her, heart pounding, head reeling with surprise and a new, fragile hope.

"I like my freedom, too," she said, breathless, stepping out of the chaos of her underthings. "I have all but lost it. I want it back." In her voice, he heard a faint trace of a Gaelic rhythm, as if she had tossed her perfect English aside with her fancy clothing.

God, he loved her. He stepped closer. "What else do you want?"

"You." She met his gaze. "I want you."

He smiled slowly, but kept still, arms, body, aching for her. "And I want you. So much. Do you want to shed any other burden—besides all this pretty frippery?"

"I do." She drew a deep breath. Her lip quivered. "You will not like it, though."

"More about Matheson?" He folded his arms.

"He is an odious bully. But I am not afraid of him any longer. *You* are not afraid of him."

He huffed agreement. "True."

"I can break free of him." She lifted her chin. "I owe him loyalty for helping me in the past. But lately he has proven not very pleasant."

"Indeed. Is that all, then?" He moved closer, careful not to crush silks and laces.

"There is. But it might present a—challenge."

"I love a challenge. You, my lass, are a challenge of the best sort. It is easier to sail into a storm than keep pace with all your surprises."

"You said you needed Meg MacNeill. Here she is. I know you do not care for the baroness."

"Meg." He sighed. "I care about *you*. And you are the baroness—a fascinating creature who equally has my heart. I see that now. I was wrong to doubt it."

She nodded, brows tucked over eyes that were uncertain blue pools. Something sincerely troubled her, he saw, more than castles, costly things, and a small island where she could be free.

"What is it?" He moved close, reached out to tip up her chin, dabbing a thumb over a tear. "We need to be honest with each other. We both know that now."

"True." She drew a breath. She reached for him, cupping her hands on his forearms, fingers gripping. "Dougal—" But she stopped.

"Whatever it is, I love you, aye?" He bent close, touched her cheek. Doubts and reserve and resentments dissolved in the magic of her winsomeness. No matter what she had to say, nothing was insurmountable with trust and faith returning full force. He lowered his head and kissed her, felt her curve against him, whimper, surrender to the kiss. "And I am sorry."

"You are not the one who needs to apologize." She broke away. "Dougal, that night—on Sgeir Caran, I must tell you what happened."

"I AM LISTENING." He drew her in for another kiss. Meg felt herself melting into it, felt the next one turn to flame as his fingers gentled over her jaw, her throat, down until his hand was a warm cradle for the upper swell of her breast. Her knees went buttery, and she sank against him.

He leaned back. "Will you tell me? It cannot be so bad. Say it."

Heart slamming, she did not want to be blunt, wanted to ease the news to him. But not here, where someone might interrupt. She tugged at his arm and pulled him toward a narrow door in the corner of the library. Taking up a candle burning in a glass lamp, she opened the door.

"Come in here."

They entered a narrow room shaped like a tower, wrapped in dark, gleaming wood paneling, with a spiral stair to one side that accessed a platform leading to the upper shelves of the library. It was fitted with a small but handsome desk, two leather arm-chairs, with a red patterned carpet. The candle in its glass glowed, and the room had a little warmth from its close shape. Its dark masculine elegance brought back memories. She loved this place dearly.

"A secret room?" Dougal's voice echoed gently in the tower-like space.

"This was my grandfather's private study," she said. "He would come here to read and work on journals. Seeing that, I wanted to do the same. He did not seem to mind a little girl underfoot if I was quiet. I would sit over there and draw."

She went to a small japanned cabinet of black and gold and opened a little door to take out a box of inlaid wood. The exotic smell of sandalwood and memories wafted from it as she set it on the desk and opened it to remove two bundles of letters tied with white ribbon.

"When I first inherited and came to live here," she said, "Mr. Hamilton and I came in here to search for some of Grandfather's private papers."

"If he stored them there, they must have been written by someone special."

"They are all from me," she said, "to him. I wrote to him for years. I visited him every winter for several weeks, and he even hired tutors for me—Mrs. Berry and others. He was a widower, and his sons were grown but without children. My mother, his only daughter, brought me here often."

He recalled what she had said of her parents. "Even though Lord Strathlin did not approve of her marriage to an islander, a fisherman."

"He did not, but he did not disown her and welcomed us. After both Mama and Papa were gone, I visited him until his last days. And all those years, I wrote to him. He kept them."

She lifted a packet of letters, fanning the edges. "I wrote to him about Caransay—the island, the flowers, the shells I found on the beach, the birds and the seals on the sea rocks. I told him about sailing and fishing with Grandfather Norrie and about playing on the beaches and swimming in the sea. I made drawings for him too." She touched the bundle. "It's all here."

Amazed, touched, Dougal realized the importance the letters held for her. "Your journals started with your childhood letters and drawings."

She nodded. "He would thank me for the letters, though he never wrote back. Just a yearly invitation to come to Edinburgh or Strathlin Castle, wherever he would spend the winter depending on business matters. I was tutored, and often fitted for a wardrobe as I grew. Though I always preferred plain gowns and bare feet." She laughed a little.

"He must have appreciated the letters to keep all of them. He was very fond of you, to make sure you had a good education and all your needs met."

"Gruff as he could be, unhappy as he was about my father being a fisherman, he was good to my mother and me. I loved him, and I felt sorry for him, a little. I thought he was lonely. I did not know then how busy he was, building a shipping and banking empire. I scarcely knew about Matheson Bank then."

She walked around the great mahogany desk, fingers trailing. "He did not show much affection. I thought he just tolerated me, his only grandchild. An obligation."

"But he left everything to you. That says a great deal."

"My uncles were gone, and I did not know he had designated me his heir. Then I found this box when Mr. Hamilton and I were looking for something. A deed, I think."

"He not only loved you, he had faith in your intelligence and judgment, entrusting all this to a young woman."

She put the bundled letters back in the box and shut it away in the cabinet. "Nearly two million pounds, they told me, when the will was read, along with title and properties and ownership, though not authority, over the bank."

"That is astonishing," he murmured.

"At the time, it was incomprehensible. I did not want it. I railed against it, cried, refused at first. I wanted to live on Caransay, for that was my home. But the will was ironclad—

either I accepted and took on the responsibilities, or the entire estate would go into the bank's control. This beautiful Edinburgh house, the castle, the other properties, all of it would be forever locked to Lord Strathlin's descendants. My descendants."

"Your son Sean," he said. "Your late husband's child, as you let them think. But a fisherman—did your grandfather frown on that also?"

"He never knew. Sean was born after he died. But I already knew the fortune would leave the family, so I had to agree. It is easy enough in Scotland for a female to inherit a title and an estate, no matter the scope of it. So here I am."

"And doing a remarkable job. It must be a great deal of work."

"I had much to learn those first couple of years, true. Fortunately, I had friends to help. Mrs. Shaw, whom I met in Edinburgh when we were girls, came with me. So did Mr. Hamilton, who had been Grandfather's protégé. He was familiar with matters I knew little about. And Mrs. Berry had been my governess when I visited Grandfather."

"Ah, Berry, who is so fond of swimming," he drawled.

"I am sorry about that," she said, and saw him shrug it away. "The bankers and solicitors were well-meaning, if not used to dealing with a young woman. They brought me up to task. Including," she added, glancing at him, "Sir Roderick."

Dougal frowned. "You mentioned he was helpful. A cousin?"

"Aye, distant. I wonder if he expected more from Grandfather, his elder cousin. But there was no love lost between them, I gather." She looked into the candlelight, its warm glow fading into the room around her. She stared, summoned courage. "I doubt Grandfather would have wanted me to marry Roderick, though he thinks otherwise."

"Aside from Roderick lately, luck has been with you," he said. "Well, but for the husband you lost. I have not asked, hoping you would tell me when you were ready."

There it was: the door opened wide to the past and the truth.

Meg stepped through.

"My grandmothers on Caransay are convinced the luck of the inheritance came to me through magic," she said. "Because of the night we spent together on the rock."

"It was magical," he said. "But that would hardly lead to a massive inheritance. People would spend the night on sea rocks in wild storms all the time if so."

She laughed, yet was too distracted, and plunged on. "The legend," she said. "The legend of the kelpie of Sgeir Caran that comes for his bride on the sea rock. He grants good fortune to his bride and to the islanders if...." She paused, turning to look at him, her eyes wide, beseeching.

"What is it?" He reached out to brush at her hair, loose around her shoulders, wayward curls slipping free. "If you had good luck, then there may be some truth to that legend."

"More than you know. I came by this good fortune after we spent the night on the great rock, just as the legend claims should be done," she murmured.

"But the kelpie did not really appear to you, did he," Dougal murmured.

She shook her head. "But my grandmothers believe it."

"They had no proof, but that we met. Not even that, if we were not seen together."

"They had another sort of proof." She slipped a finger under the high neck of her plaid bodice and drew out the fine gold chain and locket she so often wore. Silently, she flipped the tiny catch to open its twin oval frames. One side held the little ring made of threads and the golden and brown hairs she had woven together on the rock. The other side held a tiny portrait, a towheaded infant with a sweet face.

"I remember the ring," he said, his voice rough, low. He plucked his pocket watch from his vest and popped it open to show its hidden compartment. She gasped. Beneath a glass circlet was the ring she had woven for him.

"You kept it," she breathed.

"I carry it with me everywhere. It was all I had of you. I was not even sure you existed, but if you did, I had to find you. To me, this little ring was magical. Though sometimes I thought you were just a dream, or even a sea fairy after all. But I had this. It was real."

"I was pretty certain you were real. Too real," she said. "My grandmothers thought you were the kelpie of Sgeir Caran. They still believe…well, they think we were married that night and this wee ring proved it to them. So did—oh dear God," she half sobbed, half turning away.

He tipped his head. "So did what?"

"Legend says the kelpie of the sea rock bestows great good fortune if his bride pleases him," she said, tucking the little locket back under her collar. "If she gives him a child."

He frowned. "But you did not—"

She nodded slowly. "I did."

He gasped, leaned forward. "What are you saying? A child came of that night?"

She nodded, silent, eyes swimming in tears that began to spill.

"For the love of God, woman," he breathed, "Sean? Is it Sean?"

"Sean," she sobbed, nodding.

"My God, I thought—he was your husband's child—the husband you lost—" He stopped. Stepped back, shoved a hand through his hair, turned back. He looked stunned. "The husband you lost—that was me?"

"You," she whispered. "The father of my child, lost at sea."

"Jesus, Meg," he whispered. "Why would you keep this from me?"

"I did not know who you were, or how to find you. Or if I wanted to tell you, considering—what I thought that night." Her chin wobbled. "I kept the secret close. I had to. But when you arrived, I knew I must tell you, and I tried to, but—"

"But you waited." He frowned as if wrestling with the great truth of it. "Waited on this too."

She took his wrists. He stood frozen, did not take her hands, though skin met skin. "I had to trust you first! I had to know— that you would not take him away from me." Sobs broke the words. "My son. Your son."

He stared, still, silent. Then he exhaled hard. "I would never do that. A son! Our son. I would never take a child from its mother. But dear God, Meg—I needed to know!"

"I wanted you to know. But I feared you might take him. Seeing you was such a shock. I never thought to see you again. And I did not—really know you. I do now. I do now," she insisted.

"Fair enough." He broke her hold, rubbed his brow, still looking stunned. "God, Meg. That beautiful child. Mine." His voice broke. "Ours,"

"He is so much like you," she whispered. "Our lad."

"I am stunned," he murmured, shaking his head. "Who knows about this?"

"My grandparents know that I met a man—the kelpie, they believed—that night on the rock, and now they know you were the one. Of course, many on the island know I have a child, but they believe he is the son of a secret marriage—to a man who was not from Caransay. And Mrs. Shaw, Mrs. Berry, and Mr. Hamilton know about Sean, and that you are his father." She drew a shaky breath. "Roderick knows too."

Dougal fisted his hands. "Roderick! How?"

"I did not tell him. He met the doctor who tended me and bribed him for information. He threatened to spread the news about my illegitimate child, implying I have low morals, saying he will ruin me—and you too, for he suspects you—could be the father. So he—he—"

"Blackmailed you into marrying him. I see."

She nodded, miserable. "I was afraid to tell you, afraid you would confront Roderick, who could ruin you further and do even more damage than I have done. I am s-so sorry," she gasped.

He stood still, cool, out of reach, absorbing all this, just when she desperately needed his arms around her, needed his reassurance.

"That blasted pig," he muttered under his breath. Taking a step, he pulled her into his arms. "Hush," he murmured. "I cannot apologize enough for leaving you. All this time, you bore this alone—an unmarried mother, not even sure who the father was. I am not upset with you. I am angry at myself for letting this happen."

"But you tried to find me," She tipped her head up. "You did not just let it happen."

"I came to the island more than once, but you must have been on the mainland, and I knew nothing of the baroness then. I could hardly go about asking who that beautiful girl was out on the rock one stormy night. Then, when the chance came to build a lighthouse on Sgeir Caran, I came back. Something kept pulling me back there," he said low.

"I should have told you sooner, but at the time, I only wanted to throw something at you."

He chuckled, kissed her hair, her brow, and released her. "You were not happy with me, but now I see why."

"What should we do now? What do you want to do?"

"I would never take him away from you. Know that. And I think we can fix this easily."

"How?" She stared up at him.

"Well, I ought to marry you," he whispered, tipping her chin up with his fingers. "As soon as possible."

She laughed, a watery burble, sheer relief once the truth was out. "What about Roderick?"

He gathered her into his arms again, silent, thoughtful. Then he drew back. "Why, Mrs. Stewart," he said, "I believe we were married seven years ago."

Meg gaped at him. "Oh! The rings!"

"The rings and all the rest. There is an old tradition of self-declared marriage in Scotland."

"I know of it. A couple only needs to declare their love, exchange rings, and consummate their relationship." She felt a blush heat her cheeks. "And they are considered married without benefit of clergy or witnesses. But we did not declare our love then."

"I rather think we did." He dipped down to kiss her. "Sean is the proof."

"And we have declared it since," she pointed out.

"An old married couple already," he agreed with a soft laugh.

"Then I will tell Roderick the truth—I cannot marry him because I am already wed."

"Aye, secretly married years ago to Mr. Stewart, and so we have a son. We had a rift, you see. A separation. Very secret, and lately resolved. There." He brushed her hair back. "In fact, let me be the one to tell him."

"You would do that?"

"I would be delighted." He gathered her close.

Eyes closed, she lingered in his arms, close and warm, loved and vastly relieved. The future was good now. The future glowed with hope and resolution. With love and happiness too, all she had ever dared dream. Resting her head against his chest, listening to the steady thump of his heart, she rocked with him for a few moments.

"As for what we will do now," he whispered, his lips close to her ear, "is that door locked?"

She broke away, hurried to the narrow door to click the latch, and turned. "It is now."

"YOU DISCARDED SOME of these things in the library," he murmured, his hands sliding down her ribs to her waist. "What about the rest of it?"

Freedom. She longed for it, feeling caged as the baroness. Her fingers flew to the neck of her gown, loosening the prim collar, working the long line of buttons down the front. Dougal began to help, fingers slowly working the buttons, his knuckles grazing over her skin, now over the swell of her breast.

She tipped her had back, closed her eyes, sighed as she let him loosen the rest of the buttons to open the bodice, drawing away the separate blouse, looking for the fastening on the skirt—she helped him find the tapes so that both pieces slid away to expose the corset cover, the bothersome stays, the ruched chemise. The snug room was warm, his hands warmer as he turned her to work the laces at the small of her back, drawing away the stiff whale-boned canvas. Then he spun her to face him, and she came willingly into his arms, feeling free in chemise and knickers, feeling sensuous and secret and private in the small room, in the haven of his arms, where hope, love, and forgiveness resided.

Reaching up, she tugged at his coat and waistcoat, fingering those buttons loose. In shirtsleeves and trousers, he pushed her hands away to pull her close, kissing her so deeply that she arched back with it, felt her knees weaken, moaned breathily into his lips.

When he sank to a knee to take her down to the floor with him, he lowered her to the thick Aubusson carpet of gold, cream, and blue that made her think of the beach at Caransay. She stretched out beside him, the soft, silky carpet a cushion beneath them as he kissed her. Sighing, she opened to the tip of his tongue, gave him hers, sighed again as he moved to sweep the shell of her ear, that feeling, tender and strong, plunging through her. Tugging at his shirt, her fingers nimble at the remaining buttons, she pulled the linen away to slide her palms over the warm, hard curves of his chest. She traced her lips there, tasting salt and man, feeling his heartbeat close and fast. Now he streamed soft kisses along her jaw and down the arch of her throat until his lips touched her upper breast. With a gasp, she threaded her fingers into his thick hair and writhed under his caressing lips, his deft fingers. As the fine golden chain around her neck shifted, she felt the slight weight of the gold locket against her throat, a reminder.

What she wanted so much was here now, almost full, almost—the father of her child declared, and they would be a family. It swelled through her, the gratitude, the love, the knowledge that she could at last be free to be herself, all of herself, mother and lover and wife, island girl and baroness. What went unsaid and yet acknowledged now, accepted now, burned through her as passion and hope together. He had called her honest once—now she felt that. Honest, loved, safe, and complete.

Her thoughts fled as the touch of his hands brought her to the moment, the feeling of his lips coaxing a kiss, another, deeper, hungrier, even as his fingers slid warm, teasing, exploring. She explored him too, with more boldness than before, slipping a hand under wool and linen to find him, shape him, caress. As he groaned against her lips with the next kiss, she took him full in her hands, warm velvet over heated steel, and he sucked in a long breath.

Then she could not stop, not then, not in the next moment as he found her, too, touching the tender places only he had ever touched, that honeyed slick for him now. Tearing at his shirt and his trousers, she rolled and shifted with him on the fat silk of the carpet. She pushed hindering clothes, hers and his, aside, wanting desperately to surge over him, rise and sink down as he filled her, as she gasped with it and moved in a rhythm with it. Merging and seeking, soaring and arching, she felt him move with her like waves of the sea. Then, through some sparkling natural magic that took all thought away but one—love, love—she vanished into him as he poured into her.

Later, breathing slowed, she rested in his arms on the floor, and ran a lazy hand over his chest. Dougal gasped, swore softly, sat up. Meg pulled back to look at him.

"I must go," he said, reaching for his shirt.

"Go? Oh—the train!"

"I can still make it if I hurry." He tugged on his shirt, then stood.

"Stay. Take another train." She got to her feet, taking up her abandoned corset.

"I have a ticket." He reached for his trousers, pulling them on, buttoning.

"Let it go. You can purchase another on the Strathlin account."

"Meg, no," he said as he snatched up his waistcoat, shrugged it on, adjusted his shirt.

"Just this once. Or you could miss the train and take the next one."

"That one leaves tomorrow morning." He spun her about to help with the laces, then stood back as she dropped her skirt over her head. "Stay the night."

He paused, frowned. "I could take the morning train and still reach the Isles by evening to hire a boat over. But I will pay my way."

"We will talk about that and the rest of it. Stay here tonight, husband," she said, easing into his arms.

"Are you ready to announce our marriage?" He tipped a brow. "Or do you want a ceremony first?"

"I would tell the world if I could. We should decide, though."

"We will. For now, I will go back to my cousin's house for the night. It is best," he said as she began to protest. "You know it is. Go careful, love. One step, then another."

Meg sighed. "We did just take a big step."

"We did." He kissed her slowly. "Next step, best gather your lacy things from the library floor before Mrs. Shaw brings tea."

"Oh! I forgot about that!" She rushed to the door, unlocked it, and flew out.

IN THE MORNING, Dougal knocked on the door of the Strathlin house, shifting from foot to foot, remembering his arrival just the day before, his uncertainty, his caution. Now he felt certain yet urgent, for the news he had received early this morning required immediate action. He had to take his leave of Meg now and hurry to catch the first train heading west across Scotland.

The butler admitted him, and moments later Meg fairly flew down the stairs, hearing he was there. Seeing the butler blink, Dougal then noticed Mrs. Shaw's surprise as she came down the hallway. Though no one knew of their secret marriage yet, their devotion would be more than obvious, judging by the way Meg rushed toward him, took his hands, smiled up at him.

"Why, Mr. Stewart," Meg said, coy, blushing, beautiful.

"Madam," Dougal said. "I must go soon. Now." He took her shoulders, not caring what anyone thought. She was all that mattered to him, even as Mrs. Shaw suppressed a smile and glanced at Mr. Hamilton, who came round the corner just then.

"Why? I thought we would have time—"

"I have just heard that some members of the Lighthouse Commission are heading out to Caransay. They may be there before I can get there."

"Surely they can wait a little, look at the site, and you will be there."

He shook his head. "Sir Roderick went with them."

"Dear God! He—is not happy with either of us. And Sean is there, and my grandparents do not know what has happened. He could tell them anything!"

"Just what I was thinking," he said grimly. "So I have to go now. I just came to say farewell."

"I am going with you," she said, straightening her shoulders, her hands still in his.

"Stay here. I will see to this."

"I am going with you. Mrs. Shaw!" she said, turning. "Mr. Hamilton—I am leaving for Caransay with Dougal—Mr. Stewart."

"My lady," Angela Shaw said.

"Meg, listen," Dougal urged. "He could be dangerous this time. You cannot go, madam. I do not want you to go," he amended through clenched teeth.

Guy Hamilton stepped forward. "May I ask the problem, sir? Madam?"

"Roderick Matheson," Dougal said.

"He knows," Meg said, turning toward the others. "Dougal knows now. And Roderick knows about Sean too. We have to get out there!" Her voice went thin and desperate.

"It will be fine, dear," Dougal said.

"We need tickets for the train to Glasgow, and boat passage to the Isles," she said. "Angela, if you please, I will need a satchel of clothing, a traveling cape, a few other things."

"Right away," Angela Shaw said, grabbing her skirts to rush upstairs.

"I will go to the station with you to make arrangements." Guy hurried into the study.

"Too much fuss," Dougal grumbled. "We can buy tickets at Waverley Station. And you can wear whatever your grandmother can lend you. We have no time. We must go."

"I need a few things, sir. And I do not handle cash. Mr. Hamilton handles the cash and makes my travel arrangements. We need the carriage brought round, too." Meg called the butler's name. He appeared, nodded, disappeared.

"I hired a carriage from Glasgow to Oban already, and sent word to have a boat waiting," Dougal said. "We will have to travel as husband and wife, though. You want to avoid scrutiny."

"Thank you." She smiled.

He looked up to see Mrs. Shaw racing down the stairs with a tapestry satchel in one hand, something lacy spilling from its opening. Dougal took it, thanked her, and went to the door where Meg waited. Angela Shaw helped her shrug into a traveling coat while they spoke quietly.

The butler reappeared to open the door just as Guy came toward them with a wallet that he pressed into Meg's hands. "This should be sufficient for the trip, madam. If you need more, send word."

"I can take care of other expenses," Dougal said. "But thank you." Hamilton nodded, and Dougal sensed quick understanding there.

Mrs. Shaw helped Meg don a black beribboned bonnet. "Madam, you need an escort if you are to travel with a man. Give me a moment to gather some things and I can go with you."

"I already have an escort, dear. Mr. Stewart—Dougal is my husband."

"Your what?" Hamilton said as he and Mrs. Shaw both stared at her. "When?"

"We are married," Meg said, her cheeks flushed. "We were married years ago." She looked up at Dougal, who took her hand. "We kept it secret. It was not—we were not—certain it would last." Blushing, she glanced at him.

Hamilton lifted a bemused brow. "You two are full of surprises."

"We can take vows in a ceremony," Dougal said, "when the lady decides what she wants."

"Aye, soon! Farewell, my dears," Meg said, hugging Angela Shaw again, then kissing Hamilton's cheek. She whirled to rush out the door as Dougal waited for her to precede him, just as the carriage came around the corner from its stable behind the row of houses.

Once inside, Dougal kissed her hand. "I am glad you are going with me after all."

"I want to be there when you confront Roderick about the evil rumors he plans to spread. And to make sure he does not lay a hand on my son."

"Our son. And I mean to ensure he keeps his distance. Until then, we have hours of travel ahead of us. So you can tell me about what I have missed over the years," he said. "I want to know about Sean's birth, six years and some now. I do not even know the date. Tell me all of it, what he was like as a baby and a little one. What he said, what he did, what he learned. I missed too much. But no more."

CHAPTER TWENTY-TWO

"Oᴜᴛ ᴛᴏ ᴛʜᴇ hard place, you say," Norrie said, "and you just coming in from Tobermory now? Not but a few minutes on the island, and out we must go, hey." He worked the rudder as he spoke, with full sail unfurled on his fishing boat. A fast wind moved them toward the Caran Reef under a wide sky dotted with soft gray clouds.

"Aye, Norrie MacNeill, straightaway to the hard place," Dougal answered. "But our Meg should go back to Caransay with you."

"Our Meg?" Norrie raised a brow, curious.

"We two are…in agreement now," Meg said with a little smile, reaching to cover Dougal's hand with her gloved one.

"So I was thinking when you two came together from Tobermory on the hired boat. Your grandmothers will be pleased." Norrie grinned. "We will all want to know about it."

"Aye so, and Meg can tell you when she goes back with you."

"I am going with you to the great rock," Meg insisted. She leaned toward him, clutching her half cape at its buttoned collar.

"Go back to the island, please, Meg," Dougal murmured.

She shook her head. She had to be with him now. They were both tired after the long journey from the east by train and carriage, which had taken longer than expected, so that they had spent the night in a hotel in Oban as Mr. and Mrs. Stewart. While the sweet joy of those hours together lingered, she knew Dougal

255

felt even more pressed to get out to the lighthouse rock. Arriving on Caransay less than an hour earlier, he had learned that his crew had taken visitors out to Sgeir Caran already that day.

"I want to go out to the rock with you," she said.

Norrie huffed. "I am thinking everyone wants to go out to the hard place today. A steamer came to Mull yesterday," he continued, "with a group of men dressed all in black, with tall hats. A bunch of ravens, they looked, ready to feast on your lighthouse, is my thought."

"You might be right," Dougal said.

"They sailed out to the rock this morning. The one who owns Guga was with them, the one who calls himself your cousin, Margaret."

"Sir Roderick is my cousin through Strathlin. You know that, *Seanair*."

"Aye, but I do not like that he is your kinsman. He and the others were going out to inspect the rock and the stonework there. A good thing I was still on the island, so I could take you over to the hard place quicklike."

"A very good thing," Dougal said.

"So, we are together, are we? I am thinking you are good friends now, is it?" Norrie asked mildly, hand on the rudder, eyes twinkling.

"More than good friends, sir," Dougal said. "And she's not going out to the rock."

"I am," Meg said.

"Well, you will want to fetch wee Sean back, so we may as well all go there and back."

Meg gasped. "Sean is out there?"

"What in the devil—why?" Dougal asked in a growl.

"Is there aught wrong with it? He asked Sir Roderick, who said he could, and the lad was in the boat before we knew it. Your grandmother told me to fetch him back, and then you came in, and so we will all do that."

"In that case, I am definitely going out to the rock," Meg said, looking grim at Dougal.

"But straight home with Norrie—and Sean," Dougal replied, frowning.

Hearing Norrie's amused grunt, Meg realized that even if he did not like Roderick, he did not suspect the man might scheme to harm the child.

But she knew better. Reaching for Dougal's hand again, she felt the strength in his answering grip. They sailed on in silence as the waves splashed the sides of the boat and Norrie shifted the rudder to speed them with the current and the wind.

Ahead loomed the long, distinctive shape of Sgeir Caran. Norrie guided the boat carefully through the treacherous path between toothy rocks as they approached Sgeir Caran, his focus intent as the sea sluiced and swirled through the maze of partly submerged rocks.

Then the black bulk of the rock soared above as the boat drew up inside its shadow. As the boat rose and fell with the slop-slop of the waves, two men came down the crudely cut stone steps to assist them.

"HULLO!" ALAN CLARKE said heartily as he helped them disembark on the stone quay. "It's good to see you, Miss MacNeill!" He turned to Dougal. "You're back just in time, sir."

"Aye," Dougal said as they climbed the stone steps toward the upper rock, Norrie with them, intending to fetch Sean. "I hear we have visitors."

"Och, they came to see our progress," Alan said. "They may contribute to the lighthouse funding and perhaps some future projects, so it is a good thing, it seems. Though inconvenient to have them here at such a time."

"Are you still working on repairs following the gale?" Dougal asked.

"We cleared a good bit of damage and repaired what we could. And we retrieved all but one of the stones that were swept into the water. And that one is roped and ready to bring up. But there could be a problem with the rock beneath the water, sir," Alan added. "Evan Mackenzie went doon the deep to check on the repairs as we brought up the fallen stones. He found a crack in the foundation stone."

"How large?" Dougal asked quickly.

"A sizeable fissure. Evan will be glad to see you're back. He has been anxious to go back down to measure it for shoring up. He will be glad of a partner—risky when we have but one diver. And I hope you recovered some funding while you were away. We will need it. Evan says we may have to build a sea wall."

Dougal swore low and paused to ask Alan more questions. Standing on the topmost surface of the rock, Meg felt the heavy push of the wind across the plateau, whipping her cloak and skirt. She looked around, anxious to find Sean, Roderick, and the others.

Hearing Evan Mackenzie call out, she waved as he came toward them. Dougal hurried to speak with him, while Norrie turned to answer Alan's questions about the ever-important subject of the weather, for the wind was rising and the rushing waves were tipped with white.

Then, across the width of the rock, she saw a group of men in dark suits and hats, some with canes, each one looking out of place. Roderick stood tall and broad in the midst of the visitors. With relief, Meg saw Sean, his hand caught in Roderick's gloved fingers. Safe enough for the moment, but she only wanted her son safe with her—and his father.

"Sean!" She hurried forward, skirts billowing. Seeing her, he broke free and ran toward her. Stooping to catch him in her arms, she knelt to embrace him, knees in a cold puddle, but she hardly cared. Straightening, she looked up at the man who approached.

"Roderick," she said coolly.

"Why, Lady Strathlin! What a fetching picture, mother and

child. I am surprised to see you here. Have you ever come out to see the lighthouse construction?"

"I have. Why are you here? And why did you bring my son with you?"

"I came out with members of the Lighthouse Commission. Some of us are considering donating funds, but we were very interested to see the place, and see the progress. The boy wanted to come. No one objected. His mother was not here to care for him," he chided.

"Sir," she said pointedly, "I wonder that you have any funds to contribute. According to my secretary, you have been borrowing from me for the last three years. Yet now you are making promises to the lighthouse fund. Do you have another source of wealth?"

"To be honest, madam, I expect to be married very soon to a very wealthy baroness. I hope you have not reconsidered your promise, madam. That would be unpleasant." He smiled and reached out to touch Sean's golden head.

She pulled the boy away and stepped in front him, hiding her child behind her full skirt and petticoats. "But I have changed my mind," she said. "I cannot marry you, Roderick. It is in fact quite impossible."

He glowered down at her. "Impossible! I doubt that."

"Good day, Mr. Matheson," Dougal said, striding toward them. He tipped his hat. "I believe you are misinformed. The lady is already married."

"She's married!" Roderick barked out. "Preposterous. What would you know about it?"

"I am her husband," Dougal said, offering his arm to Meg, who slipped her hand in the crook of his elbow, natural, familiar, solid, and safe.

"It is true," she said, looking up at Matheson. "We are married."

"That cannot be," he muttered. "I saw you only days ago. You scarcely know each other."

"Truth is—we were married years ago," she said.

"Aye." Dougal glanced down at her. "We had a simple ceremony, but we—became estranged. But we have reconciled and resolved our differences."

"And you expect me to believe that? A clumsy lie to rescue the lady from embarrassment that she has earned, sir. She had a child out of wedlock, with no father, no husband in sight. I have it on the best authority."

"Her kin know exactly whose child that is," Norrie said, walking up to them just then. "Come here, lad," he told Sean. "Your Cousin Fergus is over there looking for you. Run see what he wants." Sean took off.

"Walk!" Meg called after him. "Do not run on the wet rock!"

"That wee lad," Norrie said, looking hard at Roderick, "is the son of my granddaughter and her husband, this fine fellow, Mr. Stewart. He came to our island years ago. They were wed, just as they told you, and that fine son came of it. They were apart for a few years. Youth," he said, shaking his head. "They do not see love and happiness even when it sits on their shoulders like a bird, hey? But they have come to their senses." He grinned at Meg and Dougal, then turned to Roderick. "All the residents of Caransay know about it. No one is asking for your approval!"

Roderick sputtered. "This—is unbelievable."

"But true," Norrie said. "Eh?"

Dougal smiled in answer, knowing and sure, and rested a hand on Meg's shoulder.

She felt tears rise in her eyes—not the salt wind, but love and gratitude and relief. "Aye, everyone will swear to it."

"Though we want a ceremony to renew those vows," Norrie said, scowling almost playfully at Meg and Dougal.

"We will make sure of it," Dougal said.

"Preposterous," Roderick repeated.

"I have known Dougal Stewart for a long time. Even before Lord Strathlin died, though he never knew about our—secret marriage."

"Marriage!" Evan said, coming up to them, overhearing. "Congratulations! And I understand that you can be called Lady Strathlin now," he added.

"It is true," she said. "I—did not mention it before."

"Humble as well as beautiful," Evan said, grinning. "Dougal, you have done well. And my lady, your husband is a fine man, and a lucky one too."

"Thank you," she said.

"Lady Strathlin?" Alan Clarke said as he joined them. "I just heard. You kept it secret!"

"I did. I am sorry. I should have told—my husband's friends."

"Whenever you were ready, that was the time to tell us." Evan smiled and turned to Dougal. "Sir, I am honestly delighted. And add to that, a child, I hear. This news will thrill anyone who hears it. People love a romantic story and a happy ending. Isn't that so, Sir Roderick?" Evan fixed Matheson with a stare.

Roderick Matheson mumbled something under his breath, then turned on his heel and stalked off to join the other gentlemen in his traveling party.

Evan turned to Dougal. "Are you ready, sir, before the weather changes?"

"Aye," Dougal said. He turned to Meg. "We need to go down to look at the flaw in the rock."

"Now? But the waves are picking up."

"Just briefly," Dougal said. "We need to decide what is to be done about it. We will be right back up, love. The gear limits how long we can safely stay down. If you wait, rather than go back with Norrie, Sean might find the diving venture quite interesting. Bring him along to see it."

"I will." As she watched him walk away with Evan, she felt a dread spin heavily in her gut.

Roderick was with his fellows, his back turned to her. Certainly his objections and arguments had been laid to rest—he had no weapon now to threaten her or Dougal.

There was nothing to worry about, she told herself. Just a

quick dive, and they would all sail back to the island before the storm hit.

Standing in the whipping wind, she watched the sea. The water was choppy and opaque; far to the west, the sky was leaden gray. She could not shake her unease.

SLIDING HIS GAUNTLETED hands along the curving slope of the rock, Dougal followed its contours. The water was not as clear or still as he liked for the task, but he could see well enough to judge the dimension of the flaw. Beside him, Evan pointed to another area, and Dougal made his way there. His steps were like clumsy, slow dance to the clicking cadence of the air going in and out of his helmet valves. Nearby, two diving platforms banged randomly against the side of the submerged rock. Overhead, suspended on thick ropes, the large dressed stone that had tumbled into the sea in the earlier storm was trussed and ready to be cranked back to the surface.

All that, and the clean seabed beneath his feet, reminded him how much work his crew had done and would continue to do to ensure that the lighthouse went up and the rock stayed safe. Appreciating that effort, for a moment he felt so grateful that the work would continue, thanks to Meg, Lady Strathlin—life and love to him now—who waited on the surface for him to return.

Following Evan's gestures, Dougal saw the long fissure in the dark rock face; the split began above his head and ran downward, narrowing to disappear midway. Breathing rhythmically, he half climbed the incline for a closer look. Above, the massive rock thrust upward through the water, and he could see the underside of Norrie's boat rocking on waves driven by wind.

The storm was coming in fast. They could not stay down here much longer.

With a measuring tape pulled from the canvas bag at his belt, he estimated the length and width of the crevice as the tug of underwater currents pushed at his heavily weighted suit. Reaching his gauntlet into the fissure, he found the crack to be fairly deep. A few small fish drifted out of the crevice and he batted them away.

Moving toward Evan, who was measuring another part of the rock, he waved to catch his attention and signaled they should return to the surface. He had seen what he needed to see; the split in the rock was large enough to be of concern, considering the weight of the lighthouse to be erected on its surface.

"Dougal." Alan Clarke's voice came crackling through the speaking tube.

"All is well down here. Up there?"

"Storm brewing. It will not reach us yet, but wind and waves are strong. Come up! We need to return to Caransay."

"Aye. We're coming up."

He and Mackenzie moved toward the two wooden platforms hovering nearby, suspended on ropes. Stepping onto one wooden deck, Dougal tugged three times on a rope to indicate his readiness. Evan did the same. Hanging on, Dougal saw Evan's platform move upward first. Soon, he felt his own platform shift as it was drawn up through the water. Grasping the ropes, he looked up to see the underside of Evan's deck moving ahead.

Sudden and strong, a wave washed through like a train, smashing Dougal's wooden platform against the side of the great rock, knocking so hard that he was nearly thrown free. He hung on, bending his knees to keep his balance. With one booted foot, he shoved the planking away from the rock, felt it come free and begin to rise again.

Once more his deck paused, Evan's too, just above. Halting their ascent was necessary for safety. Holding the ropes, Dougal took long, slow breaths to give his lungs a chance to adapt. With a lurch, the platform moved again.

Another wave cracked the planking against the rock. This time, the impact spun him outward, and his feet slid off the wooden deck. Scrabbling back to the shifting deck, he snatched the rope of the platform, which tilted precariously against the steep rocky incline. Looking up, he saw Evan's platform swaying above him, coming closer to the surface.

Another hard wave slammed through and a wealth of water swept around the platform, so that it bucked like a horse, knocking into the rock again. Dougal felt one heavy boot slide over the edge, and he hung on, tugging on the rope, asking to be pulled up.

Moments later, he felt and heard a rumbling vibration, then a loud, horrid sound like a roar as the undersea world shuddered all around him. Glancing up, he saw the trussed granite block break loose from its moorings, crash into the rocky slope, and begin to tumble and slide down the incline. Dougal swung his weight to shift the platform out of the way as the stone grazed past him, just missing him—and catching on one of the platform ropes, ripping it free at a corner.

The deck tilted as the immense granite block skittered downward. Silt and debris clouded the water, turning it to midnight darkness. Reaching out, he felt the wall of dressed stone just in front of him. It had missed him by inches. Breathing out in shaky relief, he stepped back from the edge of the sharply tilted platform.

But he could not move. The thick toe ridge of his lead boot was caught just under the block.

CHAPTER TWENTY-THREE

A STRONG WIND blew Meg's cape backward, nearly tearing away her beribboned bonnet. Not so far off now, the western sky thickened into a dark, boiling mass.

"They need to hurry," she told Norrie beside her. "They have to come up now!"

"They do. That storm is blowing fast this way," Norrie said.

"Oh, thank God, the crew is bringing them up now!" Seeing the commotion at the rock's cliffside, where the diving platforms were raised and lowered, she exhaled in relief, ran toward the iron railing embedded in the edge, and looked down.

A diver burst out of the water, clinging to the platform ropes as crewmen hauled him upward. The man gestured insistently as Alan and others unscrewed the bolts that secured his helmet to the wide brass collar that covered his shoulders. Evan Mackenzie emerged.

"Dougal," he gasped. "He's caught! The block broke loose, hit his platform. I saw it just as I came up"

Meg rushed forward. "Is he hurt?"

"I cannot say," Evan replied, shaking his head as one of the crew worked on his suit. "Leave it in case I have to go down again."

"You cannot go down there so quickly," Alan Clarke replied. He grabbed the speaking tube and set the funnel to his mouth. "Dougal! Are you there!"

Silence. Meg pressed a hand to her mouth. Nearby, Norrie and others tensed, waiting.

"Dougal!" Alan listened through the earpiece, then nodded. "Wait!" he called into the hose. "Wait, we will tell you what to do."

"Is he hurt?" Meg asked.

"His boot is caught," Alan said. "He says he is trapped."

"What of his air hose?" Evan snapped.

Alan repeated the question. "Open and fine so far," he reported to the others.

Evan Mackenzie grabbed his helmet. "I'm going back down there."

"Do that, man, and risk your own life," Alan said. "Your lungs cannot take the up and down of the pressures. Someone else must go down."

"Who else is here to do that?" Evan growled. "No one else is trained to use this equipment but Dougal and me."

"I can do it," Alan said. "I have not, but I know the equipment."

"But that takes time, and I am already suited up." Evan set the helmet over his head, gesturing for the nearest crewman to screw it in place. Moments later he stood and stepped onto the platform.

"God be with," Alan muttered, gesturing for the platform to be lowered again. He turned to call out order to the men on the air pumps and hose cranks. "Give Dougal as much slack as you can, and keep the airflow steady for both of them," he reminded them. "Aye, that's it."

"Evan is coming down," he told Dougal through the funnel, and listened for the reply. "He is swearing. You do not want to hear it, lady," he told Meg.

"I do, I want to know everything!"

Meg paced, watching, listening, hoping as Evan's platform sank into the heaving waves. She whirled, skirts billowing, to come face-to-face with Roderick Matheson. He grabbed her elbow.

"Margaret!" he said. "Come away from the edge!"

"Let me go!" she snapped.

"It isn't safe! Let me help," he said. "What can I do?"

She could hardly believe the offer, but shrugged. "Just stay back and let the men do this."

"I am not as heartless as you think," he said. "I was wrong. I was desperate, loving you. I acted poorly—"

"Poorly?" She laughed, bitter, distracted as she watched the waves.

"I do not like Stewart, but he's in difficulty and I would help if I could."

She stared at him, frowning, wondering if he had some other motivation. Then Norrie joined them, standing beside her to stare at Roderick.

"If you have had a change of heart, sir," Norrie said, "go help with the cranks and pulleys."

Roderick turned away at that, taking off his coat and offering to take hold of the crank arm on one of the giant spools that held the hoses. Norrie turned away, too, running to help guide the ropes that spilled over the edge of the rock into the water.

Alan was speaking to Dougal again through the funnel and hose. Meg ran to him. "Please, let me talk to him," she said. Alan handed her the funnel.

She held the metal cone to her mouth. "Dougal!" She moved the cup to her ear for the reply.

"Meg?" His voice through the funnel was small, tinny, yet achingly familiar.

"Dougal! Are you hurt?"

"I am fine. My boot is caught. Evan is just here. We will work it free."

"My love," she said. "Come up quickly. Hang on!"

Alan took the speaking tube again, and Meg stood by as he explained to Dougal that they would send down a steel crane to haul the stone away and free him. She saw the men wheeling the great thing into place.

"Hanging on," Dougal said, his voice faint.

The wind tore over the rock, whipping at her skirts and cape. Meg set a hand on her bonnet and braced her arm over her chest, watching the sky roil, gray and foreboding. Far out, breakers rose frothy white, rushing toward the reef. Rain spattered over her in cold droplets.

Suddenly, vividly, she remembered standing on this very rock in another lashing storm. Dougal had appeared in its midst, his presence, his courage, his body shielding her.

Alan directed the crew working furiously on the machinery, ropes, and hoses. "We need more hands on the ropes to help Evan haul that stone away!"

She saw Roderick and Norrie roll up their sleeves to pitch in while the bankers and visitors in black stood observing. Her cousin Fergus held Sean, picking him up to comfort him. Meg ran toward him, but her cousin waved her back, shaking his head to tell her he would keep Sean safe.

She turned to Alan. "Can they move that stone down there? Is it possible?"

"It is not easy," he said grimly. "It has to be trussed with ropes to lift it. But if it can be shifted just enough to free Dougal's boot, that is all we need right now."

"But it weighs tons," she said.

"Aye, on land. Down there, the weight seems lighter. It can be moved by two men." He stripped off his coat as he spoke, unbuttoning his vest. "I beg your pardon, Miss MacNeill—Lady Strathlin. I need to go down there to help." He pulled off his boots and tossed them aside. His ash-blond hair ruffled in the wind, and his linen shirt blew flat against his broad chest and arms.

"But Alan," she said, "you are needed up here."

"My friends are in danger. I need to help," he said. "Dougal is forty feet down, we think."

"But you have no gear," Meg said.

"A man can go down that far without gear, just holding his breath. But he canna stay down for long. I'll do what I can." He handed the funnel to Meg. "Talk to him. Let him hear your voice. And pray for us, lass. It is a grim thing, this, I will not lie."

Standing on the cliff edge, beaten by wind and dappled by rain, Alan dove cleanly over the side, cutting through the water.

"Dougal," she said into the funnel, "Alan is coming down."

"What the devil!" Dougal replied.

"He can help you push the stone," she told him. But there was silence. "Dougal?"

"Meg—air…"

"Dougal!"

More silence. Meg caught her breath, then looked down over the side. Bubbles rose where the various hoses and ropes entered the water, and she saw a few shadows moving below the agitated surface of the water.

"Dougal!" she called into the funnel. No answer.

She turned, saw Roderick and the other men busy on the cranks and pulleys and hoses, saw Fergus holding Sean tight, watching from a distance. Her grandfather hurried toward her.

"He's not answering," she said. Norrie took the funnel.

"Dougal Stewart!" he called, and repeated the name.

Meg looked down and down into the greenish, slopping surface of the water, roiling with peaks and waves. He had to live—he had to. She could not bear to stand on the rock and wait, listening, watching, hoping, while he was so far below, in danger. She could not endure life without him now.

She wanted to tear off her clothes and dive in, as Alan had done. Dougal had saved Sean and so many others. He had saved her on this rock from the first moment she had met him. He had saved her since, body and soul. Alan said a man could endure forty feet down. So could a woman.

Tearing off her bonnet, she set it aside. The wind took it and skittered it into the ocean. She unbuttoned her cape and bent to unfasten the loops and buttons on her ankle boots.

"What are you doing?" Norrie asked. He lifted the funnel again. "Dougal Stewart! Answer!"

Below, Alan burst out of the water, gasping, treading and rocking in the waves. "The hoses!" he called. "Dougal's hoses are caught! Toss me a lever!" Someone dropped a long iron rod; it fell into the sea, for Alan missed it in the wind and waves.

Reaching beneath her skirts, Meg undid her petticoat tapes. She wore no crinoline that day, but with four petticoats for fullness, she wished desperately that she had changed into the simple garments common to Isles women before coming out here. She dropped petticoat and skirts.

"What in blazes are you doing?" Roderick called. "Here, stop that, madam!"

She ignored him, standing in linen blouse, chemise, and knickers. "Get this thing off me," she said to Norrie, yanking at the laces of her stays under her blouse.

"Madam!" Roderick called again.

She turned as her grandfather—who wisely did not protest, seeing her determination—gave the corset cords a few yanks. "I am going down there," she told Norrie.

"So I see," he only said, helping draw the corset away, tossing it aside.

"The men are needed on the equipment. Alan needs help and there is no one else to spare. Make sure Sean stays with Fergus," she said.

She had to do this. She could not bear to watch this any longer, knowing that she could help as well as any of the men, and better than some, with her smaller frame and nimble hands and her ability to swim and dive. Not all the men could help, she knew. Fergus, for all his fishing skills, did not swim well.

"Lady Strathlin!" one of the commissioners in black called.

"I'm going in," she insisted, while the men stared at her in dumbfounded shock. She walked to the edge of the cliff. "Give me a lever! Now!"

One of the men, less stunned than the others, handed her

another iron bar.

"Dougal Stewart," Norrie called into the funnel, "your lass is coming down for you." He turned toward Meg. "Go find your kelpie, lass!"

"The kelpie, aye," she said. Taking a deep breath, feeling the cold bite of the wind through thin cotton and silk, she looked down at the water below and drew a long, deep breath, let it out, and drew another.

The iron bar took her down quickly, and she plunged feet first into the waves.

EERIE, MURKY, THE watery world around him was colder, dimmer. Dougal shivered as the deep cold entered his bones. The rubber suit, normally inflated with air to add buoyancy and warmth, had torn along the sleeve and water was seeping in, making the suit even heavier and exposing him to the water's cold brunt. The valves in his helmet clicked and whooshed with the reassuring sound of air, but it was thinner. He could not seem to fill his lungs properly.

He was tapping all of his strength to shove, with Evan pushing beside him. Alan Clarke had appeared a few moments earlier to lend his effort, setting his bullish shoulder to the block. They repeated the attempt, and this time he heard the scrape of the stone on the underwater hillside and felt his lead boot give way. He pulled it back, motioning sluggishly to show that it was free.

But he could not escape to the surface. Shifting the block from his foot had further trapped his hoses, compressing the flow of air into his helmet. The world was growing dimmer, fainter.

Alan surged up for air, returned, set his shoulder to the stone to push again.

Dougal pushed too, but a strange buzzing began in his ears. Sucking in a breath, he could feel the constriction in the airflow.

He was in real jeopardy now.

The stone shifted a little more, and a stream of air came through the hose. Dougal pulled it in, exhaled, glad to hear the *click-click* of the valves. The stone shifted a tiny bit, and the valves quieted ominously again.

He had to get free, or die here, at the base of the reef where his parents had died so long ago. He had faced risks, stared down danger too many times now. Sooner or later, the wheel of fortune would spin again, and he would lose.

But he had too much to live for now. The woman he adored held his heart in her keeping. She waited for him above the water with their son. He could not leave them. Not yet, and never.

Gasping for stale air, he gestured to the others—he was suffocating. He would have to detach the hoses and take his chances going up in a beast of a suit that could just drag him down to the bottom of the sea. There had to be a way—he could not die here like this.

He looked up at the fast-swirling water, the sea dusky green. His lungs were burning.

Alan burst away and surged upward again. Dougal pressed the last of his strength into the unyielding stone that compressed the hose. His head was in a fog. He clutched at the valves, ready to tear out the hoses, ready to tear at the bolts in the oppressive helmet.

Another tiny shift in the stone and a trickle of air came in, enough for another breath, enough to clear his head for a bit. Alan surged down again, lungs refreshed, and the three of them shoved once more at the granite block.

Dizzy, Dougal felt the airflow stop again. His head pounded.

Then he looked up to see a vision sinking down through the greenish water. Sliding down on a beam of eerie light, a pale, graceful sea fairy streamed toward him, veiled in white garments, golden hair streaming outward. She lowered beside him like an angel, reached out to hand a wand to Evan—a bar, an iron bar— and placed her hands on either side of his helmet to look at him.

Meg. God, how he loved her. He reached for her but she slipped away, turning, to help Alan and Evan work the bar under the lip of the stone. They pressed, pushed, pressed.

The stone gave way, long enough for Dougal to snatch the air hose free. He looped it around his shoulder, moving slow, as if in a dream.

Evan and Alan grabbed him by the arms and pulled him onto the platform, tugging at the ropes in a frantic signal. As the tilted deck began to rise, creaking with the load of two divers in gear, Alan let go of the ropes and took the sea fairy's hand. He pulled her upward with him as they rose toward the swirling surface.

Moments later, they burst through the surging water into air and freedom.

MEG STOOD SHIVERING, draped in a blanket Norrie had draped over her, while men worked frantically to free Dougal's helmet and Evan's as well. When Dougal's helm came away at last, she cried out in relief. His pale, ashen face was the most blessed sight she had ever seen.

She waited impatiently while the crew loosened his gauntlets, weighted belt, and boots, and as others worked to free Evan of his gear. Alan, draped in a blanket too, helped.

As Dougal met her gaze, she stifled a sob with a trembling hand. His slow, weary smile told her he was well, he was here. He reached out a hand and she stepped closer.

When the men finally lifted away his brass collar and heavy belt, she sank to her knees beside him. He lifted an arm to draw her closer, his suit of treated canvas stiff and wet, seawater dripping between them, and she slipped her arms around his neck. She did not care a whit who saw or what they thought as she pressed her cheek to his.

"My love," he said. "When I saw you down there, I

thought—my sea fairy has come back to me. I thought I was dreaming—or dying. I thought you were not real. My God, I am glad you are real." He kissed her wet hair.

"I am here. I am yours, love," she murmured as he held her close. Overhead, the wind gusted, carrying rain.

"We'd best get into the boats," Norrie said. "Or we must crowd into the caves on this rock to wait it out."

"Oh, not that," Meg said with a laugh.

"Alan, can you take a group in one of the boats?" Dougal asked. "Are you fit for rowing?"

"Very fit," Alan said, and ran toward the steps and ramp to hurry down to the boats.

Meg stood, waiting as Dougal was divested of his boots and the canvas suit. She tossed a blanket over his shoulders.

"Where's Sean?" he asked.

"With Fergus—oh!"

She heard a shout at the same time as she saw Fergus running across the plateau of the rock. Seeing why, she screamed in protest and ran there as well.

Sean stood at the edge of the rock, looking down into the water. Meg hurried to him, stockinged feet slapping on wet rock as the wind shoved at her.

"Sean! Come away from there!" The wind tore her words away, and rain began to pour. Waves sloshed and slammed against the rock, each higher than the last.

"I want to see the kelpie!" Sean called. "I want to see him!"

"Come here, please, come here," she told him as calmly as she could.

He sighed and turned, and she grabbed him into her arms. Dougal appeared at her side, clad in the damp long-limbed woolen underthings, a blanket around his shoulders. He crouched beside them, wrapped his arms around both of them.

"Sean, lad," he said. "Aye, now you're safe. Come with your mother away from the edge."

A blast of wind knocked at them, and Meg closed her eyes for a moment, feeling Sean in her arms, and Dougal's arms around both of them. The wind tore wildly at them, at clothes and hair, but she felt their spirits snug and warm together.

"Let's go," Dougal said, standing, bending to pick Sean up. But the boy stepped away.

"I found a wee rock! I forgot it," he said, and ran back to the cliff edge, stooping in the wind, which pummeled him as Sean stretched a hand to grab a loose rock.

Meg gasped and Dougal whirled, strode forward. But in that moment, Roderick pushed past them to snatch the child up in his arms, standing at the very edge of the rough precipice. Wild spray from the heavy waves spattered over them, receded.

Meg cried out, running with Dougal, fear filling her throat, her heart.

Roderic turned, wind shoving at him, and walked toward them. He handed Sean to Dougal.

"Your son, sir. Madam," he said, and moved past them.

"Roderick!" she called, as Dougal held Sean in one arm and gathered her close under the other. "Roderick, thank you," she said in a hoarse voice.

He turned to stared at them, and nodded. "Of course. Sir," he said to Dougal. "What I saw today was incredible bravery—from all of you. Margaret, you as well. Incredible devotion. I will not forget it. You need not fear anything from me. I give you my word." He frowned at them for a moment, then nodded again, turned, and walked away, down the steps toward the boats.

With a little sob, Meg put her arms around Dougal's waist, sensing his exhaustion, propping him up even as he held her, little Sean snug between them. Dougal smoothed a hand over the boy's golden hair, then kissed Meg's head.

"We must go," he said.

She nodded, but no longer felt the sting of the rain and cold wind. She only felt Dougal's strength, his love, with their child tucked safely between them. She tipped her head for the warmth of Dougal's kiss and returned it with relief, with love, with fervor.

She felt full of love. Nothing, no storm or threat, could weaken that.

"Come on!" Norrie called from the rough-cut steps. Meg called a reply as she walked with Dougal, arms about each other, Sean safe between them.

In that moment, the wind lessened, the rain lightened, and the waves quieted a bit. A pale green, eldritch light cut through the gray clouds to touch the rock where they walked.

"The gift of the kelpie," she said. "He calms the storm to give us a chance to get home."

"Where is the kelpie?" Sean asked, looking around.

"Right here, lad," Dougal said, laughing. "He has always been here. Let's go home, my lady," he added. "We all need some rest."

"Rest, and dreams. Wonderful new dreams," she said.

He smiled. "They do seem to come true. Coming, Norrie MacNeill!" he called, ushering his family down the steps to the waiting boat.

EPILOGUE

"A LL THE WAY up?" Sean asked as he and his parents stepped into the shadows in the high, narrow stairwell.

"Straight to the top," Dougal agreed, as he shut the door to the lighthouse behind them. Turning, he smiled at Meg and Sean. "The lighthouse keepers and the commissioners will be here soon, but I wanted to take you two up before the ceremony begins."

"I want to go first!" Sean scrambled up the steps.

Dougal held out a hand. "My love, are you sure you want to do this?"

"Of course, but go ahead. You and Sean move faster than I do these days. I will be careful, I promise," Meg assured him, for he hesitated. She patted her expanding abdomen, hidden under the tented shape of her dark-blue woolen half cape. That casual gesture made his heart, his spirit, swell with love.

"Come on!" Sean yelled from above, hopping impatiently.

"Wait for us, lad, and do not jump about. It makes your mother anxious." Dougal bounded up the steps two at a time to meet Sean on the first landing of the long climb. He paused to look back, wanting to be certain Meg had no difficulty climbing.

She was so beautiful, he mused, watching her. So graceful, every bit a baroness today in an outfit designed by that English fellow in the Paris shop, a jacket and skirt in dark-blue velvet with a bonnet of indigo blue perched on her golden hair, now twisted in a silvery net. Her rounded shape and full bosom, her slow steps as she ascended, deepened his love, his desire, and his respect.

To be sure, he liked best to see her hair gloriously loose and her clothing plain, her laugh free as she ran on a beach or on the machair. Today, she was elegant Lady Strathlin. He was equally proud of her, equally in love with her, in any guise.

He and Sean were dressed nicely today too; he wore the same black suit he had worn to their small wedding last year, and Sean wore a new outfit of brown velvet, even though the lad had protested when Mrs. Berry produced the thing. But Meg had explained that he had grown and needed a new suit.

"And besides, we must all look our best today," she had told her son. "Guests will soon arrive to celebrate Papa's new lighthouse on the Caran Reef. And we will christen the lantern."

"And there will be music and dancing on the island later!" Sean had added proudly, allowing Berry to button his snug and fancy jacket.

Now, smiling up at Dougal, Meg waved him ahead. He nodded, knowing she was strong and healthy, but he would always keep watch. He knew how busy she was when at Strathlin Castle and the Edinburgh townhouse, though when she was at Caransay, she eased into a slower pace and took on the important work of islanders—fishing, weaving, caring for others, and continuing her beautifully illustrated journals.

Today, she was here as Lady Strathlin, about to christen the Caran Light.

In the past year, Dougal had learned to negotiate the changing rhythms of life as husband, father, engineer, whether on the mainland or on the island. For him, the constants were always Meg and Sean. Love did not change with outer responsibilities, and family was paramount.

Though some thought he took on much in marrying a wealthy young baroness, a radical change in his life, he knew it would be smooth and joyful, and so it was. His work increased, designing and consulting on lighthouse construction, and rather than involve himself in his wife's business and wealth matters, as a husband might do, he knew Meg was capable and left it to her and her trusted advisors. Dougal gave his opinion when asked and helped as needed. But most of his focus, and hers, resided in their marriage, their life together, their love.

His other heartfelt focus was as Sean's father, making up for what they had both missed, and being with his wife and children. Only days before, he had turned down an offer to build a lighthouse on a wild northern sea rock. Not yet for long, lonely weeks doing dangerous and exciting work; other opportunities, other light towers would come along. He needed to be with his family now.

"I will open the door!" Sean said, running ahead of Dougal up the stairs to the top.

Laughing, Dougal stood back while the boy turned the gleaming brass knob in the oak door to the lantern room. So far, they had paused at each level so Sean could open doors to peek at the kitchen, sitting room, sleeping quarters, and storage rooms.

Soon Meg joined them at the top, the faint flush in her cheeks brightening her pretty aqua eyes, shining like the sea in sunlight. "It's not so high," she said. "The exercise is good for me."

"Here we are. After you, my dear," Dougal said, as she preceded him into the lantern house.

The walls of the compact, circular room were glassed all around above the wainscoting, giving an expansive view of sea and sky. The room was dominated by a huge, complex arrangement of glittering prismatic lenses in amber and clear glass.

Meg gasped. "What a beautiful lantern! I have not seen it this close yet."

Taking Sean's hand, she walked with him around the perimeter of the huge light. It gleamed like a diamond: hundreds of polished-glass surfaces cut like prisms, arranged in slightly angled rows to provide a powerful illumination. The brass fittings added more brightness and beauty.

Sean stood on his toes to see, and Dougal picked him up to

hold him high.

"Go ahead, touch it," he told Sean, who reached out. "The lamps are not burning yet. Oil lamps will be used to light the lens," he explained. "They will be lit at dusk to burn until dawn."

"So this is what they call a Fresnel lens?" Meg asked.

"Aye, a Fresnel of the first order—there are seven levels of size and power. It was rather expensive to acquire a lantern as powerful as this one, but well worth it. Our investors will be pleased, I think. This lighthouse will endure, and protect this part of the coast for hundreds of years, with luck." Dougal smoothed his hand over one of the glazed surfaces.

Meg went to the window to gaze out over the sea and sky. "How far can the light be seen?"

"About eighteen miles on a clear night. In deep fog, the light may not cast as far, but there are bells in the roof cupola above. One of the lighthouse keepers will ring out patterns to warn passing ships that there is a reef and a lighthouse nearby."

Meg nodded. "Fergus and Norrie will be quite busy."

"Aye, our first lighthouse keepers! They are suited perfectly to keep the Caran Light. The Lighthouse Commission prefers local men as the lightkeepers, particularly seafarers, since they know the sea and the changing weather best in their own region."

"Grandmother Thora is pleased, too—she worried about Norrie going out each day for the fishing, now that he's older. And with two men tending the light, Norrie still has time to fetch the mail, which he insists on doing. He will not give that up."

Dougal set Sean down, and they joined Meg at the window. In the pale, vast sky, gray clouds moved fast over the horizon. Far below the high tower, down at the base of the immense dark rock, the sea was choppy and greenish in the rising wind.

"There! I see a boat!" Sean cried, pointing.

"Very observant, lad," Dougal said, peering toward the south. "You'll be a help to your grandfather and your Cousin Fergus when we come to Caransay." He ruffled the boy's golden curls. He knew that Sean enjoyed the weeks and months they spent on the mainland, but loved the island best. Caransay would always be his true home.

Before the wedding, he and Meg had gently explained to Sean the truth about his parentage, as much as a child of six and some could understand. Sean had readily accepted the news, delighted to have a father, especially one he already loved and admired. Deeply grateful, Dougal realized that Sean's happy, trusting heart had been shaped by the generous love he had learned within Meg's islander family. He, too, had learned that from them.

Life had eased tremendously in the past year—and the roots of the change had begun in a great storm on this very rock.

"Norrie is bringing several guests over the water," Meg said, looking out the great windows at the boat crossing from the island to the rock.

"Aye. My dear, I should tell you that Sir Roderick is among them. One of the commissioners said he might join them."

"I see him. He is welcome." She touched Sean's head as she spoke. "We will always be in his debt for grabbing Sean from the edge that day."

"I still have the rocks I got that day!" Sean said, listening.

"You might be a geologist someday, you and your rocks," Meg said, laughing. "Dougal—I meant to tell you that I asked my solicitors to inform Roderick that his monetary debt to the Strathlin estate is forgiven. It seemed best, once I learned of his arrangement with the bank."

"Your generous and forgiving nature," he murmured, "is just part of what I love about you."

"Oh, I learned something about generosity and forgiveness from a certain engineer," she said, wrinkling her nose. "Even though I thought he was odious at first."

He chuckled, setting his arm around her, watching the boat sail closer. "One of the men coming in today is an experienced lightkeeper."

"Aye, the Commission sent him over to train Norrie and Fergus," she agreed.

"Three keepers are best for a light such as this. Two can be on duty while the third rests. Perhaps he will like it here and stay."

"Who would not like it here?" Meg smiled. "I am thinking," she said, her speech falling easily into the pattern of the islanders, "that I was wrong, and that the odious engineer was right."

"What do you mean?"

"He wanted it to go up when I wanted it to come down. Yet now I see that this light is truly a beautiful monument, a lantern that honors the lives of those lost in these waters—while it also shines on the future."

"And now," he murmured, "we can hope that no more lives will be lost on this reef. That makes the future even brighter, my love." He pulled her closer, dipping his head to kiss her cheek under the tilted brim of her bonnet. For a moment, his throat tightened and he could not speak.

"I wish," he added, "my parents could have known you. They would have loved you and Sean, and the new little one, and our life here."

She smiled up at him, tears glazing her eyes.

"They are here!" Sean said, jumping up and down, hands pressed to the window glass.

"Good!" Dougal said. "But the winds are picking up. We'll have a storm before long."

"We need to finish this ceremony before it sweeps in," Meg said. "Though I would not mind being stranded with you again on this rock, Mr. Stewart." She smiled up at him so fetchingly that he felt desire spin inside of him.

"I would not mind it either," he said. "Someday, we could try that again."

"Not now!" Setting one hand on her son's head and the other high on her abdomen, she laughed in delight. "Though today I do not relish the thought of spending the day in the company of lighthouse commissioners."

"They will probably try to solicit more funds from Lady Strathlin, who has been so generous. Be strong, lass." He grinned.

"The ceremony will be quick. We will go back down to cut a ribbon at the door, smash a bottle of whisky, and share a dram from another bottle."

"No whisky for Sean and me! Berry sent a fruit brose for us to drink."

"Look!" Sean said, pointing. "Do you see them? There! There!"

"See who, dear?" Meg asked, turning with Dougal.

"The water horses! On the water, see! The *eich-uisge,* many of them, coming this way!"

"What?" Meg gazed in the direction where her son pointed.

"What do you see out there, lad?" Dougal asked.

"White horses in the water!"

Narrowing his eyes, he watched the moving sea. "Wave curls," he said. "The white foam on high waves can look like horses."

"Dougal, look again," Meg said. "The kelpies are here."

He saw them then, the prancing shapes of a legion of white horses, hooves pounding, manes spilling down as they moved forward, rising and dipping with the waves, heads proud, bodies racing. He watched, entranced.

"I do see it," he said. "Just where the light comes through the cresting waves."

"Kelpies!" Sean laughed with delight as Dougal scooped him up to give him a better view.

"They are giving their blessing to the lighthouse," Meg said. "Sean saw them first. He has the magic of seeing the water horses. And so he should!" She smiled up at Dougal. "He is the son of the most wonderful *each-uisge* of them all."

"I am what?" Sean asked, looking up.

"Son of a kelpie, and do not forget it," Dougal said, laughing. He drew them close, his son and his wife and the small one she carried, tucked them in his arms, and closed his eyes in silent thanks. Waves of love poured through him, magical, powerful, so real.

Meg tilted up her head and he kissed her lips tenderly.

"Stop kissing," Sean said, wrinkling his nose.

"We should go downstairs now, my dear baroness, my lovely lad," he said. "It is time to welcome our guests to the new Caran Light."

Author's Note

In this beautiful new edition of this story—previously published by Penguin as *Taming the Heiress*—I have lightly revised for clarity and pacing without changing the story. If you read it at some point years back, I hope you enjoyed this refreshed and updated version.

Scottish legends often tell of kelpies, the water creatures that inhabit rivers, lochs, and oceans. River and freshwater kelpies that took the form of dark horses or great bulls were common— unpleasant beasties that could drag a human to a drowning death. Sea kelpies are even more ancient, appearing in the oldest Celtic tales, supernatural water creatures apparently inspired by high, foaming waves thundering to the shores of Ireland and Scotland.

The *each-uisge,* or water horse (*eich-uisge* is the plural in Scottish Gaelic) was said to appear either as a white horse dancing and racing in the strongest waves—or as a strong and handsome man, often with green eyes, walking out of the sea. In the guise of a man, the kelpie would seek a maiden to bear him a child; later he would return for his offspring and take them with him under the waves, never to be seen again. Tradition claimed that if a maiden gazed upon the kelpie in dawn's light, she would be haunted by her love for him forever.

I have always been fascinated by Scottish lore and legends, and so I often weave a touch or more of that content in my books, whether the setting is medieval, Regency, or Victorian. With this novel, I wanted to write a romantic tale that would blend Celtic myth with the "modern" setting of Victorian Scotland, when the dynamic tension between tradition and improvement was high. The integrity of the Gaelic culture had been compromised over centuries by English rule, scientific and societal advancement, and the devastating Highland clearances further diminished Scottish history and culture. Dedicated Scotsmen and Scotswomen worked to protect and preserve the ancient and beautiful Gaelic culture—language, legends, music, crafts, traditions—to keep them from being lost in a British stew of elements and traditions.

Throughout the Regency and Victorian eras, engineering feats from roads to trains and lighthouses transformed Scotland and opened the remote, beautiful Highlands to the world. In Queen Victoria's day, rising national pride, the queen's love of the Highlands, and the Victorian appetite for adventure fueled the growing tourist industry and Scotland's destination popularity.

In researching this story, I was intrigued by the history of Scottish lighthouses—the need for light towers, the elegance and practicality of their designs, and work involved in building them. For instance, deep diving with cumbersome equipment was used routinely by bridge and lighthouse engineers. The great novelist Robert Louis Stevenson was an engineer like many of his kinsmen, and wrote about his diving experiences when he examined the submerged foundation of a lighthouse. Today, the magnificent lighthouses that ring Scotland owe much of their existence to several generations of the Stevenson family. I am especially indebted to Bella Bathurst's brilliant study of those men and their work, *The Lighthouse Stevensons* (HarperCollins, New York, 1999).

I hope you loved Meg and Dougal's story. Please look for Books 2 and 3 in my Victorian Scottish trilogy, featuring some of Dougal's friends; Aedan MacBride goes on a quest to break an ancient curse that prevents him from ever knowing true love; and engineer Evan Mackenzie, the newly inherited Earl of Kildonan, returns to the Highland mountains of his childhood to face a private demon and meet a Highland angel.

You can find me at www.susanfraserking.com or on the blog I share with a few good friends and well-known authors at www.wordwenches.com. Please look for my other books when you have the chance. Thank you!

Sláinte mhaith (good health) and happy reading!

About the Author

Susan King is the bestselling, award-winning author of (so far) 28 historical novels and novellas, a hefty nonfiction history, and dozens of magazine and web articles on education and the craft of writing. Her books, including mainstream historicals Lady Macbeth: A Novel and Queen Hereafter: A Novel of Margaret of Scotland, have been published by Penguin, Random House, HarperCollins, Kensington, ePublishingWorks, and Dragonblade. Praised for historical accuracy, lyrical writing, and storytelling quality, she is a USA Today bestselling author with numerous awards, nominations, and career achievement awards as well as starred reviews from Publisher's Weekly, Booklist, and Library Journal. Most of her books are set in Scotland ranging from the 11th to the 19th centuries.

Susan is a former university lecturer in art history, a private school teacher, and a founding member of one of the longest-running author blogs, "Word Wenches" (wordwenches.com). She holds a Bachelor's in studio art and English literature, a Master's in art history, and completed most of her Ph.D./ABD in medieval art history. Raised in Upstate New York, she lives in Maryland with her husband and three sons in an ever-growing family.

Website – www.susanfraserking.com

www.ingramcontent.com/pod-product-compliance
Lightning Source LLC
Chambersburg PA
CBHW071538030726

47598CB00001B/147